MINUTES TO KILL

A SCARLET FALLS NOVEL

MELINDA LEIGH

Montlake
Romance

Text copyright © 2015 Melinda Leigh
All rights reserved.

Published by Montlake Romance, Seattle

www.apub.com

Amazon, the Amazon logo, and Montlake Romance are trademarks of Amazon.com, Inc., or its affiliates.

ISBN-13: 9781477829752
ISBN-10: 147782975X

Cover design by Marc J. Cohen

Library of Congress Control Number: 2014921970

Printed in the United States of America

To Gramps
for everything

Chapter One

He's gonna kill me.

Standing on the closed lid of the toilet, Jewel looked through the dirty glass on to the dark parking lot of an industrial park. She dug at the dried paint with her fingernail, then tried the lock again. It gave. Gripping the sash, she tugged at the window. It moved a millimeter, the creak of old wood reverberating in the tiny motel bathroom. *No!* He'd hear. Sweat broke out under her arms. She reached down, flushed the toilet, then leaned over to the sink and turned on the faucet, hoping the running water would cover the sound of her escape.

She turned her attention back to the window. How long does it take the average person to wash her hands? A minute? That's how much time she had left before he came looking for her. She shoved up the sash, flinching at the volume of the resulting groan. Did he hear that over the sound of the water?

The client knocked on the door. "What are you doing in there?"

He heard.

"Be out in a sec," she called. She put her arms through the opening. No time to be quiet now. Just get out. She wiggled her shoulders past the sill. Once she was past her chest, she'd slide out like a newborn baby. Banging echoed in the small room. The doorknob rattled.

"Open the door. Now." Mick.

Shit. Fear jolted her heart. If he got his hands on her, she was dead. Or worse.

Her pulse scurried, and her breaths accelerated until tiny points of light dotted her vision. If he caught her, there'd be no going back to undo what she'd done. Some people thought dying was the worst thing that could happen to a person, but Jewel knew better.

Mick had taught her that being alive could hurt enough to make a girl pray for death.

Wood splintered. The door burst open. His brown eyes shrank to a mean, angry glare.

"You little bitch." Mick lunged for her, his big hands closing around her ankle. Halfway out the window, she flailed, fingers grabbing at the window jamb, her free foot kicking out. Determination and desperation were no match for brute strength. Pain shot through her hand as a nail ripped to the bed. Panic scrambled for a hold in her belly.

He dragged her back down into the bathroom and dropped her. Jewel's head struck the toilet tank lid, rattling the porcelain. Mick raised a hand across his body. The backhand sent her reeling sideways. She fell into the tub, and the shower curtain tangled around her body. He bore down on her, the need to inflict punishment clear on his lean face.

She kicked with both feet. The sole of her left shoe struck him under the chin. He fell back onto his butt, and Jewel scrambled out of the tub. She climbed onto the toilet lid and dove out the window, shimmying her hips. Sliding through, she landed on her hands on the pavement.

"You're dead," Mick shouted through the window. But there was no way his big body would fit through the small opening. He ducked back inside. She heard him arguing with the client as she straightened her shaking legs and ordered them to get moving. He'd be after her.

Jewel got her feet under her body and sprinted across the blacktop. She ducked into the shadow of a Dumpster, her lungs heaving in loud and ragged gasps. She put her back to the rusted metal and covered her mouth with her hand. Her body shook in uncoordinated waves. Quiet. She had to be quiet. He was going to hear her. He was going to find her.

He was going to hurt her.

She peered around the edge of the receptacle. The motel edged an industrial area and shared a parking lot with the surrounding businesses. Most appeared closed, their windows dark, the spots in front of their doors vacant. On the other side of a field of blacktop, rows and rows of cars lined up in front of a lighted warehouse-type building. An overhead billboard adorned with colorful Latin dancers announced "Carnival: Las Vegas's Premier Dance Club." There would be people there at all hours.

Jewel felt a presence. Lola, another one of Mick's girls, came around the corner of the building. Squinting and bending low, she came closer. Jewel pressed against the rusted metal at her back. The other girl's dark eyes went wide. Jewel mouthed, *Come with me.* Boots pounded on the blacktop.

Mick.

"Have you seen her?" he shouted.

Lola pointed at the Dumpster—at her.

Jewel paused, stunned by the other girl's betrayal for a split second. They weren't exactly friends, but Jewel had expected Lola to sympathize or at least share Jewel's desire to escape. Big mistake.

Fear and survival instinct kicked in. Jewel sprinted on fear-loose legs toward the club. She couldn't let Mick catch her.

A vivid memory clawed its way into her mind. Things he'd done to her when he first snatched her off the street in Toledo. She pushed it away before terror paralyzed her.

But a dozen strides later, she heard boots on the pavement behind her. She glanced over her shoulder. Barely thirty feet away, Mick bore down on her. Her leg muscles burned. Her throat and lungs cried. She felt her steps slowing, no matter how much she wanted them to move faster. The pills Mick supplied his girls helped her get through the days, but they hadn't made her more fit. She raced across the asphalt. The footsteps behind her quickened. She tried to scream, but her throat squeezed tightly on to her voice, silencing her.

The first row of cars was just ahead, but there were no people in sight. She veered right, toward the entrance to the club, hidden in the shadow of an awning.

Behind her, Mick's shoes scraped on loose sand. Closer. Closer. Her breath locked in her chest as he closed in.

Chapter Two

Fifteen more minutes and she'd be free.

The glass enclosure of the private skybox muffled the din from the club below, but the floor vibrated with bass. Hannah's gaze swept over the *Viva Las Vegas* glitter of Carnival, an enormous club off the Strip themed after the Brazilian celebration. The box was outfitted in chrome, disco balls, and leather. Though it was only early November, topiaries in each corner glowed with white Christmas lights. At one end of the room, long tables held an array of appetizers and desserts. A bar flowing with top-end liquor spanned the opposite wall. Waitresses in glittery showgirl costumes served more drinks from shiny silver trays. The firm's client, club owner Herb Fletcher, knew how to throw a party Vegas-style.

"Ms. Barrett, what do you think of Herb's club?" British investor Timothy Stark swirled an olive in his martini glass. While the rest of the men had dressed casually for the event in open-collared shirts and sport jackets, Timothy was never less than perfectly presented. At fifty, his fit and trim frame was attired in a custom-tailored charcoal suit, and no amount of desert heat could wilt his French cuffs. "I still can't believe he owns this establishment."

He said *establishment* as if he'd just gotten a whiff of raw sewage.

She bit back a laugh. Timothy was afflicted with a chronic case of tight-ass-itis. Carnival was clearly not his scene.

It wasn't Hannah's either. She gazed through the glass over the main floor, fifty thousand square feet of crowded floor space designed to look like a Brazilian street. Lights and music pulsed across glistening skin. Girls danced on stages and in Plexiglas boxes on risers. Jugglers performed on stilts. At midnight, a parade would wind its way through the crowd. Afterward, a nightly samba competition tempted inebriated guests onto the stage. The club touted itself as wilder than the festival in Rio.

A waitress in a rhinestone-and-sequin costume in peacock colors approached and offered them a selection of hors d'oeuvres. Her headdress, a fan of blue speckled tail feathers, waved as she moved.

Hannah took a napkin and selected a piece of grilled meat on a stick. "Herb turned Carnival from a warehouse into a very successful club."

Though the noise and flash wasn't Hannah's style, she appreciated the detail in the design. Every inch of the space pulsed with lights and color. Even the ceiling had been transformed into a starry night sky.

That afternoon, Herb Fletcher and a half dozen foreign investors had signed on a thousand dotted lines, committing to the purchase and refurbishment of the High Roller Casino. The tired casino hotel would be gutted and given a complete renovation to turn it into an exclusive luxury accommodation with another of Herb's famous themed nightclubs. All parties involved hoped the endeavor would be as successful as Carnival and the other two hotels Herb had refurbished. Everything Herb touched seemed to turn into giant piles of money.

Hannah watched a side stage closest to the box. A drunken woman in a Snookie-tight skirt and sequined halter top climbed onto the platform, bent at the waist, and writhed. *Oooh kaaay.*

"What *is* she doing?" Timothy asked.

"I believe that's twerking." Hannah's lips twitched as she suppressed a laugh.

"Tacky. Like everything else about this place." Timothy plucked the toothpick out of his empty glass and ate the jumbo olive.

"It's harmless fun. People seem to be enjoying themselves." A lot. Part of her envied the crowd's ability to let loose. Tomorrow's hangovers aside, they were having a grand time. While other people relaxed as they imbibed, Hannah hated the artificial lack of control that came with alcohol consumption. It made her feel blunt instead of sharp, as if she were trying to cut a ripe tomato with a plastic knife. Hannah's control was her security blanket.

Timothy huffed. "Speaking of tacky, here comes Herb. I know the man can afford a decent suit. Why does he dress like a thug?" His backhanded snootiness irritated her. His willingness to use the other man's talent with money and simultaneously insult him felt traitorous.

With a manicured hand, Timothy set his glass on a nearby tray.

Hannah glanced over her shoulder to see Herb walking toward them. She couldn't picture him getting a manicure or standing for a custom suit fitting. She turned back to Timothy.

He checked the time on his watch. "Oh, look at the time. I'd better go. You've put in your obligatory time. You should feel free to leave, too. Honestly, I can't believe you showed up. You are far too classy for a place like this."

"I'm glad I had the chance to see the famous Carnival." Plus, invitations from important clients were obligatory. She smiled, but the muscles of her face felt tight. Timothy made her sound as snobbish and uptight as him. Was she? She hadn't come from his upper-crust background. She was a military brat. She wore expensive clothes, but only because that was what was expected in her profession. A corporate attorney had to look successful to attract clients. The first thing she did when she went home was change into her oldest jeans. She couldn't do anything about the tension in her posture. That was both inborn and ingrained. Being raised by a decorated army ranger and colonel left its mark.

"Hello, beautiful," a voice said over her shoulder.

Hannah turned. Herb Fletcher, CEO of Fletcher Properties, grinned over a glass of whiskey. Despite his unassuming attire, or maybe because of it, the sixty-year-old pulled off gray hair and blue eyes with Paul Newman appeal. "Staying for the samba competition, Tim?"

"No, I'm sorry. I was just leaving," Timothy said. "Perhaps we'll see each other on another deal."

"I'm sure we will." Herb sipped his drink. His eyes went cold. He knew exactly where he stood with the British investor: good enough for his money but not his social circle.

Timothy turned to Hannah. "Royce said you're going to London next?"

"After a short vacation, yes," she said. Though her firm was based in New York City, Hannah spent very little time there. She traveled from one deal to another in a seemingly endless tour of international cities. After she was made a full-equity partner, her salary would justify the expense of a Manhattan apartment. "I expect to be there for three to four weeks."

Timothy nodded. "I have another deal under consideration. E-mail me when you get in so we can discuss it."

"I'll do that," Hannah said. She scanned the room. The crowd was starting to thin.

"It was a pleasure working with you." Timothy held out a hand. She shook it. "Thank you. Likewise."

With a bow, he headed for the door, stopping to say good-bye to a few other guests on the way out.

"Tim made a quick exit." Wickedness glinted in Herb's clear blue eyes. "Why were you wasting your time with him when you could have any *man* in this room?"

Hannah wasn't going anywhere near that loaded question. They were both her clients. "The party is fabulous, Herb, and your club is spectacular."

"You should enjoy some of it." He leaned in and dropped his voice. "I've been watching you. Any of these men would run to you at the snap of your fingers, but here you are, all alone."

Herb didn't spend much time alone. He usually had one of his very young dancers hanging off his arm. But then alpha males didn't play by the same rules as the rest of humanity. They'd followed their own code since they'd emerged from their caves. Sometimes it seemed like that happened yesterday. Raised with three brothers by the Colonel, Hannah knew all about dominant men. Though when compared to the men in her family, Herb's moral bar hung much lower.

"I don't like to mix business with pleasure," Hannah said.

"That's no fun, because I suspect you work most of the time. You're young. You need to enjoy life." His hand swept through the air. "Look at all those people down there, blowing off steam."

"They do appear to be having a good time." The wistfulness in her tone embarrassed her.

"Other people like to have fun. You should try it sometime." He lifted a flute of champagne from the tray of a passing waitress and handed the glass to her. As the girl passed, Herb gave her butt a quick squeeze. She shot him a flirty smile over her shoulder. "You should drink a bottle of champagne and samba all night."

Herb had never acted inappropriately with Hannah, and she couldn't help but appreciate his brass and style. At the same time, the way he treated his female employees made her uncomfortable. Hannah twirled her glass by the stem without drinking, exhaustion sliding over her body in a sudden wave. The whole obligatory corporate party thing felt old. Hannah could never let down her guard for fear that someone like Herb would get the wrong idea. Being a successful woman required above-reproach behavior 24/7.

He raised a laughing brow over his tumbler. "You seem distracted tonight."

Hannah checked her watch. "I have a red-eye to catch."

"More work?" Herb frowned. "Already? Surely, even you will take a few days off after a project of this duration."

"No work. Vacation. I'm going home to see my family." She didn't mention that her *vacation* would include checking in with the prosecutor who was preparing for the murder trial of her brother and sister-in-law's killer. Lee and Kate had been dead for eight months. Some days she forgot they were gone. She wondered if her brothers had those moments, when work was humming along and they suddenly *remembered*. Guilt weighted her shoulders. How could she forget, even for a second, that Lee was dead? Grief clutched her heart, its sharp nails digging in with determination.

How appropriate that this deal had been concluded in Vegas. Under the bright lights, revelry, and glitter, a thick layer of darkness spread, like the sadness that lurked under her success. Would making equity partner make her happy? Because since Lee's death, all her professional successes felt hollow in a way she couldn't explain. Her brother was gone, and his absence was a wound that would never heal. There was a giant hole inside her, and trying to fill it was like pouring sand through a sieve.

"Hannah?" Herb's brow wrinkled. "Are you OK?"

She smoothed her expression, but her smile felt empty, too. "I'm fine."

"Great party, Herb." Her boss, Royce Black, one of the three founding cousins of Black Associates, appeared at her side.

"Thanks, Royce. They all worked hard and deserve some playtime." Herb waved a hand over a group of sloppy drunks heading for the door to the main floor. His hand stopped, the fingers pointing at Hannah. "Even your hardest-working staff."

"Well, we certainly appreciate your generosity." Royce signaled the waitress and ordered a Glenlivet. "But I can't allow you to monopolize my star junior partner." He wrapped an arm around Hannah's shoulders and gave her a friendly squeeze.

Hannah stiffened. The impromptu hug was not Royce's style. He was acting strangely. Was it the liquor? Normally, he was a conservative drinker. She scanned his face. He didn't appear intoxicated. Trouble with his new girlfriend maybe.

Her evening bag vibrated, the alarm signaling it was time for her to leave for the airport. She slid out from under Royce's arm. "I have a flight to catch. I'd better go."

"Thanks for making an appearance." He followed her to the door of the box. "Call me when you get to London."

"Of course," Hannah said.

He scuffed a foot on the floor. He looked like he wanted to say something else, but didn't.

"Is something wrong, Royce?"

"No. It's just been a long couple of weeks." He nodded. "Have a nice visit with your family. Safe trip home."

"Thanks. Talk to you next week." Just thinking she had to be in London in ten days sent another wave of fatigue through Hannah. She would have rather taken a nap than gone to this party. The door closed with a firm click. Hannah sighed. The corridor was blissfully quiet. She could still feel the beat thumping through the soles of her shoes. But she was free.

Her luggage was in the trunk of her rental car out in the lot. In a couple of hours, she'd be in the sky on her way home. Her heels were silent on the carpet as she made her way down the corridor toward the elevator bank. She pressed the down button. While she waited, she fished her phone from her purse and checked her e-mail and the status of her flight. *On time.*

She opened a message from her brother Grant. Why was he up? It was three a.m. on the East Coast. An extreme close-up of her niece, Faith, popped onto the screen. The accompanying message read: you're coming to my party, right? Faith's first birthday was Saturday.

Hannah smiled at the photo and typed: wouldn't miss it. leaving for the airport now. is Faith having a tough night?

Grant messaged: she's cutting molars. text me when you're close.

K, she typed.

Luv u.

With a hollow ache in her chest, she typed u2 and pressed send. Part of her wanted to see them with a frightening intensity. The other was terrified of the hold she felt on her heart every time she went home. If Hannah closed her eyes, she could smell baby shampoo. She'd only have a long weekend with them this trip. Four days seemed simultaneously like too much and not nearly enough time. Grant, who'd left the military to raise Lee's kids, was taking them to Disney World, and Hannah had promised to dog- and house-sit. It was the least she could do. Grant let her use his house as her permanent address.

Would she run into Brody while she was in Scarlet Falls? Detective Brody McNamara had investigated Lee's murder. Hannah had seen him on previous visits, when he'd been tying up his loose ends of the investigation. But the case was in the prosecutor's hands now. Hannah had no reason to see Brody on this trip.

So, why was she disappointed?

Brody had stuck by the Barrett family when Lee's killer had filed assault charges against Grant. To Hannah, Brody's proven loyalty was more attractive than Royce's shallow good looks. Not that Brody wasn't hot, because he was, but the cop had something special: integrity. After spending twelve hours a day mired in the moral flexibility of Herb Fletcher and Las Vegas, integrity was damned appealing.

She opened her photos app and flipped through the images Grant had sent her. Six-year-old Carson in his lime-green soccer uniform, his smile showing the gaps of two missing teeth. When had he lost those? Faith in her high chair, face, hands, and tray smeared with something red. Spaghetti sauce?

Hannah clutched the phone to the center of her chest. Since Lee's death, being away from the kids ripped her up inside.

She rode the elevator to the ground floor and headed for the lobby, where she passed two bouncers and a short line of patrons waiting to pay their entrance fees.

"Could you hurry up?" one woman complained. "The parade's about to start."

Hannah exited onto the concrete apron and took a solid breath of cool night air. Vegas spread out flat and open in front of her. The club was located in an industrial neighborhood. An express tire and lube sat dark across the street. The building next door housed a hotel uniform distributor. Except for the motel on the other side of the parking lot, the surrounding businesses were closed. Lights glared from a billboard advertising Carnival.

Two couples hurried past her and went inside. The parking lot was oddly empty considering the packed space inside. But then, the main show was about to start. She supposed no one who paid a seventy-five-dollar cover charge was going to leave before the big event.

She made her way to the rear of the large lot, where she'd parked the rental car. As she walked, she opened the voice memo app on her phone. "Contact Timothy in London." She slid the phone into her purse.

By the time she crossed the fourth row, she was shivering and regretting the sleeveless sheath dress and strappy Jimmy Choos she'd selected for the party. She spotted the sedan fifty feet away and quickened her pace. Her jacket and flats awaited.

Shoes scuffled on pavement. Quick footsteps and labored breathing sounded like someone running.

"Fucking bitch," an angry male voice said.

What the—?

A body collided with Hannah, knocking her over. They both went sprawling across the pavement. Pain shot up Hannah's spine as her tailbone hit asphalt. A body landed on her and rolled off. A young girl of about fourteen looked up at her. Slim and small, she was dressed in crotch-skimming spandex hot shorts and a tube top. Tears slid from terror-rounded eyes.

"Come back here!" Footsteps on pavement.

The girl grabbed Hannah's shoulder. "Please help me. If he catches me, I'm dead."

"Who?" Alarmed, Hannah scanned the lot.

"He'sgonnakillme." Panic blurred the girl's voice. Hannah could barely understand the words.

A man emerged from between a minivan and an SUV. He was a lean six two or three, with black hair and a goatee. His gaze swept the scene and locked on Hannah. He paused, hard eyes considering her.

Hannah untangled her legs and scrambled to her feet.

He focused on the girl. "Let's go."

Breathless and whimpering, the girl cringed on the pavement. The man moved toward her. "I said—"

Hannah scooped her purse off the ground and stepped between them. "I don't think she wants to go with you."

"I don't give a fuck what she wants." His dark eyes narrowed to mean slits. "You're gonna want to mind your own business." He leaned sideways to peer around Hannah and held his hand out toward the girl. His fingers curled in a *Come here* gesture. "Let's go."

"No." The girl's voice trembled.

His head tilted, as if he couldn't believe she'd defy him. He shoved Hannah out of the way and grabbed the girl by the arm, dragging her upright.

Options raced through Hannah's mind. Precious few of them. She wanted to run back to the club, but she couldn't make her feet turn around. The pair would be long gone before she could return with club security or the police. Wanting more agility, she slid out of her heels.

The girl's eyes pleaded. Her lips moved. *Help me.* The man started dragging her away. But she threw her butt backward and sank her weight low, fighting in earnest now.

Hannah sucked in a deep breath and screamed, "Help!"

"Fucking *move*," the man shouted at the girl. He slapped her hard across the face. But she continued to resist.

Hannah dug her phone from her purse, her thumb already dialing 911. *Come on. Come on.* The dispatcher answered.

"Assault in the parking lot of Carnival. Send police." She could hear the dispatcher asking questions. The man shifted his grip on the teen from her arm to her long ponytail and stalked toward Hannah, dragging the girl in his wake.

"Hurry," Hannah said into the phone.

The opportunity to run had passed. Her options whittled down to one. In the split second he spent covering the pavement between them, she analyzed body targets. She had a single chance. A man of his size could easily incapacitate her with one blow. At five-ten, Hannah was tall for a woman, but he had several inches and a fair weight advantage. His fists looked well used.

She lowered the phone. If she could just get him to drop the girl. The teen could run while Hannah distracted him. At minimum, Hannah needed to keep them here, in this public space, where chances were better that eventually someone would hear or see the commotion. A patron was bound to come out of the club any second. If he got away with the girl, who knew what he'd do to her.

She had to stall him however she could until the police arrived.

He neared, his eyes shifting from angry to wary as if he was confused by her decision to hold her ground. Hannah took advantage of his hesitation. She sent up a silent prayer and lunged. Clutching the cell in her fist, she swung her arm in an upward arc as if pitching a softball into his groin. Her blow caught him square. He doubled over, swearing.

Hannah's shoulder bounced off his torso. She stumbled, catching the movement of his arm in her peripheral vision as it arced toward her face. She turned away, but the back of his fist impacted with the side of her head and spun her around. She slammed against a minivan. Something popped. Sound muted. Hannah staggered to her feet. Her cell phone clattered to the blacktop. Her purse strap slid off, her bag falling to the pavement.

The man was on his knees, but his head was up, and he was staring at Hannah. He wouldn't be incapacitated for long.

"Come on." Hannah crawled to the teen and prodded her. They clambered to their feet. She grabbed the girl by the arm and pushed her toward the rental car just a few vehicles away. Hannah snatched her phone and purse from the ground and dug in her bag for the car keys. Her fingers closed over them, and she yanked them out. The club was too far. They'd never make it on foot. She clicked the fob and unlocked the car doors. "Get in!"

Sobbing, the girl jumped into the passenger seat. Hannah slid behind the wheel. The sound of the doors locking filled her with relief. *We're going to make it.* Hannah started the engine and put the vehicle into reverse. She looked over the seat and pressed the gas pedal with her foot.

A weight smacked against the vehicle and rocked the car. The girl screamed from the passenger seat. Hannah startled, her pulse shooting through her veins. The man glared through the windshield. His upper body lay across the hood.

"Get out of the fucking car, now!" He slapped both palms into the glass. "Or you're dead." He pointed at the girl.

"It's going to be OK," Hannah said. Heart careening, she stomped on the gas pedal. The car lurched backward. He slid off the hood. Turning the wheel, she shifted into drive and accelerated, all her thoughts on the bouncers in the lobby of the club. Damn rental was sluggish. *One minute.* They'd be there in one minute. She glanced in the rearview mirror. He was standing in the center of the aisle, arms crossed over his chest.

As if he was waiting.

Hannah paused, apprehension sliding over her like a damp cloak. *"He'sgonnakillme he'sgonnakillme he'sgonnakillme."* The girl rocked back and forth, zombie-like, in her seat.

"You're OK." Hannah focused out the windshield. The main aisle was just ahead. "What's your name?"

"Jewel." The girl sobbed again and grabbed the armrest.

"It's going to be all right, Jewel."

A mammoth black SUV shot toward them. *No!* She applied the brakes and spun the wheel, trying to avoid the collision. *Too close.*

Crash!

The SUV hit the front of the rental car, pushing it sideways. The driver's side fender smashed into the concrete block base of the overhead light. Metal crunched. Glass shattered. With no seat belt, Hannah hurtled forward, hitting the steering wheel hard, the impact knocking the air from her lungs. Head spinning, she wheezed.

The young girl's panicked screams filled the car. As Hannah's lungs seized, lights danced in her vision. She watched, detached, as another figure appeared in the passenger window, a metal bar in his hand. *Tire iron?* He was shorter and darker than the first man. She caught a glimpse of a square face and mean black eyes. He raised the iron over his shoulder and baseball-batted the glass, shattering it. Small bits of glass rained into the vehicle. Jewel's screams melted to sobs. He reached through the opening and pressed the unlock button with his knuckle. He wrenched open the car door. Jewel went feral, arms and legs flailing. But her kicks and wild fists had no effect on the big body that leaned into the car.

A second shadow slanted across the windshield. "Get that blond bitch. She saw me. And hurry up. She called the cops," the first man said.

The driver's door handle rattled. "You'll have to pull her out that side. The door's stuck."

"Fuck it. Just go. We need to get out of here." They dragged Jewel from the vehicle. One of them reached back into the vehicle and took Hannah's purse and phone from the floorboard.

Minutes later, men shouted. Footsteps approached. Hannah's vision blurred as her eyes teared.

"Miss, are you all right?" Someone was at the car window. "Hold on. The police are pulling into the lot."

Too late. Sirens blared, and voices shouted. The emergency crew arrived, pried the door open, and lifted her out of the vehicle. A single idea dominated her thoughts: in the span of five minutes, she'd failed, and that poor girl was gone.

Chapter Three

Mother. Fucker.

What to do?

Smoothing his goatee, Mick glanced over the seat at the girl lying prone on the floor of the SUV. "You just fucking don't get it, do you?"

Her only response was a whole-body flinch. The two girls who shared the second row of seats in the big SUV had drawn their legs up onto the seats. Three more girls crowded the third row. None would so much as look at Jewel, as if the sight of her was enough to earn them a pounding.

Maybe it would.

Mick had learned early on in this business there was nothing like a good beating to make a girl behave.

"What are you going to do with her?" His little brother, Sam, glanced at him from the driver's seat. A cigarette dangled from the corner of his mouth. One hand dangled over the top of the SUV steering wheel. His white wifebeater showed off full sleeves of multicolored tats covering wiry arms and shoulders.

"I want to kill her."

"That would be fun." At twenty-three, his skinny brother was a Chihuahua, small but always eager to attack. Regret filled Sam's words. "The boss would be pissed."

They both went quiet for a second, remembering their last meeting with the boss, when Mr. K had personally castrated one of his other lieutenants before slitting the man's throat. Bad management skills weren't tolerated.

"You're right," Mick said.

Sam was the only person on earth that Mick trusted.

His little bro could kill effectively with any weapon, explosives, or his bare hands. The US Army had trained him well, then kicked him out when his love for violence became too apparent over in Iraq. Sam had never been the same after he'd come back. Instead of PTSD, Sam had acquired a bloodlust that he couldn't legally satisfy back in the States. Killing was as natural to him as swimming to a dog.

"She'll pay." Sam flicked his cigarette out the window. "Just in another way."

Curled on the floor of the SUV, the girl cringed. Mick craned his head over the seat. "I've told you this a hundred times: We own you. If you try to run, we will hurt you. What is it about that statement you don't get?"

Sam steered the SUV off the main highway and drove into a residential area. Small, cracked houses squatted on small, cracked lots of dried earth. He turned right and passed two vacant properties before pulling into a stained concrete driveway. A small whimper sounded from the backseat as he shifted the car into park.

"You gonna kill the blond?" Sam asked. "She saw us."

Mick scratched his goatee. "Maybe."

"It'd be fun." The gleam in Sam's eyes caught the moonlight. "No restrictions on her. I'll do it for you if you want to keep your hands clean."

It wouldn't be the first time Sam had killed for him. At the age of twelve, he'd taken out the neighborhood bully with a hammer to the head to defend his brother. That kind of loyalty couldn't be bought. Not that Mick had needed the help, but he'd wanted to consider all his options. He had a tendency to overthink a situation. They hadn't been caught, and Mick had learned to trust his little brother's killer instincts.

Jewel groaned.

Mick leaned over the seat. "Hear that, Jewel? Whatever happens to that bitch is on your hands. You involved her in this." He got out and opened the back door. "Let's go."

Five girls made a hasty exit, but Jewel, with her hands tied behind her back, was wedged in tight. He pulled the knife out of his pocket and unfolded the blade. Her eyes widened as he leaned over her. His hand trembled. He wanted to do it. But she didn't belong to him. She belonged to Mr. K.

The boss had hammered the math into Mick's head. An ounce of cocaine or a hit of crack can only be sold once. A girl can be sold hundreds of times.

"Get the fuck out of the car." He reached in, sliced the plastic ties, and grabbed a handful of her hair. "I said *now*."

Jewel stumbled across the curb. She went down on her hands and knees on the hard-baked earth of the front yard. Mick closed the vehicle door. Anger flowed into his chest. Hot and thick, it fueled his body almost as well as coke. He kicked her in the ribs, sending her sprawling. He reeled in his excitement. *You break it, you buy it* was the boss's motto.

"Get up." He stalked toward her.

She rose onto her feet, swaying like a drunk. Mick grabbed her by the arm. "Inside." He opened the door and threw her across the threshold. She fell to her knees on the stained carpet, balled up like an armadillo, and stayed there.

The living room was empty except for Lisa, Sam's girlfriend. The other girls, smart little bitches, had scurried for their holes like rats. Leaning over the glass table with a rolled dollar bill up one nostril, Lisa was halfway through a short line. Stringy white-blond hair hung over her pasty face. Sound effects—bells—from the game show on the TV clanged through the room. She snorted the last of the powder in one quick sniff, then swiped her hand under her runny nose. "What happened?"

"Bitch tried to run." Mick crossed to the glass table. "You'd better not have done all my coke."

Lisa shrank onto the couch cushion. "You said I could have one line. That's all I did. I swear."

Still eyeballing her, he stepped up, opened the square tin, and checked his supply. The glimmer of fear in her eyes pacified him. He nodded, and she exhaled.

That's what he wanted to see: obedience and appreciation. He was in control. It didn't matter that Lisa was Sam's girlfriend. Mick could have her any time he liked. But he was done with whores. The finer things in life were trickling into his grasp, one by satisfying one. He'd come up in the world, and he wasn't letting anything shove him back down again.

"What are you gonna do with her?" Lisa gave Jewel—curled, shaking, and smelling like fear—a glare. Lisa wasn't going to let that little bitch ruin what she had going. If one girl escaped, what would stop the others from thinking they could do the same? Mr. K demanded a high level of efficiency, and no one who could testify against Mick would ever walk out of this house alive.

"I don't know. I have to think."

He turned to Jewel. Her eyes were squeezed shut, as if she didn't want to see what was coming.

Smart thinking on her part.

Anger flared fresh in his veins. Tonight's act of rebellion could ruin everything. This gig was good, but he was tired of worrying about Mr. K's rules.

He grabbed her by the hair and dragged her toward the back door. She got her feet under her body and stumbled behind him. The yard was a twenty-by-twenty rectangle of concrete and dirt, walled in by a heavy wooden fence that sagged in places. His big pit bull slunk out from behind the garage to greet him.

"Sit." Cringing, Butch obeyed. If only the girls learned as quick as the dog.

A small metal shed squatted in the rear corner. Jewel stumbled as Mick shoved her into the darkness. She fell onto her knees then curled up into a miserable ball. He handcuffed her to a pipe sticking out of the dirt. Then he walked out, shutting the door and fastening the padlock. Dumb bitch acted like Mick was new at this. He wasn't. He'd practiced taking a girl to the edge of death and holding her there. Some girls held on a long, long time.

He went back into the living room. His brother was kicked back on the sofa, his posture deceiving. No matter how relaxed Sam appeared, violence flowed just under his skin. His eyes were coke-bright. Mick snorted a spoonful and poured himself a glass of vodka. The numbness slid over him like crushed ice flowing through his veins. Five minutes later, he felt reenergized, as if anything was possible.

Jewel was off-limits, but there was no reason he couldn't kill the blond. Mick went out to the car and got her purse. Back inside, he flopped in a chair and pulled out her wallet. It was a fancy job with two zippered compartments. He rubbed a hand across the deep gray leather. Felt expensive. He slid a thick stack of bills from the billfold.

Sam whistled. "She's loaded."

Mick split the cash with Sam.

"Thanks, bro." Sam peeled off two bills and tucked them between Lisa's enormous boobs.

Mick nodded and opened the second zippered compartment. He pulled a driver's license from the clear pouch. Hannah Barrett lived in Scarlet Falls, New York. He stared at the thumbnail-size picture of the blond bitch. Not the most beautiful woman in the world, but even in the crappy digital photo, there was something about her that made a man look twice. Confident and intelligent, she was the kind of woman who hung from rich dudes' arms.

A stack of business cards bulged from an outside slot. He took one out and read it aloud. "Hannah Barrett, Attorney-at-Law, Black Associates." Office and cell phone numbers were listed, as well as her e-mail address.

Mick contemplated his options. He glanced at the license and business card. He knew where she lived. Finding her wouldn't take any longer than plugging her address into Google Maps.

On the sofa, Lisa climbed onto Sam's lap and ground down on him, her giant tits right in his brother's face.

Watching them, Mick got hard, but he wanted new and shiny. The blond was cool, aloof, untouchable. She was exactly what he deserved.

He opened his laptop and accessed the map function. Taking turns driving, he and Sam could drive straight through to New York in thirty-nine hours. But first things first.

Mick took his phone and computer into the kitchen for privacy. He called Mr. K's well-paid contact in the Vegas PD. While he waited for a callback, he accessed his spreadsheet and entered his income totals for the week. Emptying his pockets, he counted the total cash income, took his cut, and stuffed the rest in an envelope. He saved his file and e-mailed it to the boss's accountant. Then he made the call requesting the recycling of one of his assets. Jewel would be gone by Tuesday.

Thirty minutes later, his contact called him back with the information. Hannah Barrett had given the police a decent description of him, but Mick had successfully avoided surveillance cameras. She was expected to sign her statement and head back to New York ASAP. The detectives would call her if they needed her to ID a suspect.

Like Mick was going to let that happen. If the police managed to finger Mick, Hannah Barrett's eyewitness testimony would be the key piece of evidence in their case.

Mick closed the computer and went back into the living room. "Hey, Sam. How do you feel about a road trip? We'll make the drop and take off right afterward."

Sam's eyes brightened. "I'll get my stuff." He pushed Lisa aside and disappeared down the hallway.

Mick turned to Lisa. "You'll have to handle business for a few days."

"Sure." Her nod was quick and eager. It wouldn't be the first time he'd left her in charge. Mr. K required girls to be recruited out-of-state.

He opened his tin and took out a bag. "There's enough in there for you to have a little party when you get home each night."

She reached for the coke.

Mick lifted it out of her grasp. "If you don't make the totals each night, I'll be taking the money out of your hide when I get back. If you do a good job, you'll be rewarded. Understand?"

She nodded, eyes locked on the baggie.

He dropped it into her open palm. Her greedy fingers closed around it slowly, as if she couldn't believe it was all hers.

"Follow my rules, do your job, and there'll be more when I get back." He reached out and lifted her chin until her gaze lifted to meet his. "If you don't, I'll know."

Her eyes widened. Fear rimmed her irises with white. "OK, Mick." Her voice shook.

"Jewel is being picked up Tuesday night. Make her clean up, and keep her alive until they come for her," he instructed. "But just barely. I don't want her to be too energetic."

"OK."

"I'm going to pack." He went into his bedroom and pulled out a duffel bag. Everything he owned fit inside. He grabbed his jacket from the back of the closet. New York would be cold. On top of his clothes, he tossed the kidnapping kit: zip ties and duct tape. He grabbed an extra box of bullets and a flashlight from the top shelf of the closet. He patted his pockets. Gun, knife, check.

He paused, looking back at the bed. Just in case . . . He slid his hand under the mattress and withdrew a bundle of cash. He'd been saving his cut for months, plus skimming a little off the top each week. He tucked it in his bag.

Sam was waiting in the living room, a small duffel bag in one hand, his usual backpack in the other. "Ready."

"What's that?" Mick nodded toward the duffel.

"Just a few toys." God—or maybe the devil—only knew what Sam had in that bag.

Mick reached for it, but Sam pulled it behind his back. "It's a surprise."

"OK." Mick backed off. His brother had always been short-tempered, but after Iraq . . . Mick had learned it was better to let some things go. Once Sam went apeshit, there was no calming him down until his rage ran out of steam. Mick swiped the manila envelope of cash from the coffee table. "Let's go."

Sam followed him out to the garage. Mick unlocked the door and raised it. His hand trailed along the shiny black fender.

Sam whistled softly. "Badass car."

Mick unlocked a wooden storage bin in the rear of the garage. He took out two assault rifles and a box of ammo Sam had bought off one of his ex-military pals. He put the firepower in the trunk and covered it with a tarp. Then he slid behind the wheel and settled into the black leather seat with a satisfied groan. The engine started with the satisfying rumble of a V-8. He grinned at his brother through the open window.

Mick backed out of the garage. Sam opened the back gate, closing and locking it with the chain and padlock after the Charger passed through. He got into the passenger seat.

"No smoking in the car." Mick stroked the steering wheel and inhaled the new-car smell.

Sam sighed. "OK, Mick. Gonna be a long drive, though."

"I've barely driven her. She isn't even broken in yet." Mick thought about the cool blond waiting for him in New York. He couldn't wait to break her. "Tell you what. When I'm done with the blond, I'll let you have a crack at her before I kill her."

"Promise?"

"You bet. We're family, right?"

"Right." Sam's eyes lit up as if he were eight, and Mick had promised him a new bike.

He checked his phone. A text message showed on the screen. Every week the drop was in a different place, which wasn't revealed until thirty minutes prior to his drop time. He opened the message. The address wasn't familiar. Mr. K never used the same location twice.

"Plug this into your phone." He read the address to Sam.

"It's in an industrial park. Turn right at the light."

Mick cruised through the residential streets, more slum than neighborhood. He followed Sam's directions, and fifteen minutes later, he pulled up in front of a vacant warehouse. Litter piled up against the bottom of a Dumpster. There were no people in sight, but Mick knew they were being watched. A member of Mr. K's inner circle was nearby, waiting to pick up the cash. He drove around the building. In the far corner of the lot, in the middle of a flat, open space with absolutely no cover, huddled a blue Goodwill donation bin. Mick pulled the car up to the receptacle. Leaving the engine running, he stepped out of the car. A cool night breeze swept across the flat and empty space.

Goose bumps rose on his arms, and the hairs on his nape lifted. Eyes were definitely on him. And maybe the crosshairs of a sniper scope.

His bowels clenched as he walked to the blue bin and dropped the envelope in the chute. The drop landed with a dull echo. As always, he pictured a little red dot between his shoulder blades and half expected a bullet to strike his back. But nothing happened. He turned and walked the four strides back to the car.

Back in the driver's seat, he slowly turned the vehicle around and headed for the exit.

"Those drops are freaky," Sam said.

"Mr. K doesn't screw around." Mick turned onto the access road and made his way back to the highway. His sweat-dampened shirt clung to his back. Every week when he made his drop, his balls wanted to crawl up inside his body. "You know what? I'm sick of this shit. What would you think about not coming back?"

Sam scratched his belly. "Rules are getting old."

"I'm tired of giving away eighty percent of our money." Mick punched the gas pedal. "You leave anything important back at the house?"

Sam shook his head. "What about Mr. K?"

The brothers had been recruited after they'd robbed a convenience store, and Sam had beaten the clerk to death with his bare hands. The cops hadn't solved the case, but Mr. K's men had come calling with a job offer. There hadn't been an exit clause, but Mick and Sam were very good at disappearing.

"Won't miss us until the drop is due next week. By that time, we'll be on the East Coast." Mick changed lanes. "We can grab a few girls and start our own business."

"No rules."

"No rules," Mick agreed.

A memory of the blond formed in his mind. Long-legged, polished hair and nails, expensive clothes. Everything about Hannah Barrett screamed class and money. He deserved her. But without exceeding the legal speed limit, he'd be parking outside Hannah Barrett's house Saturday night, planning her abduction and his revenge.

Chapter Four

The hospital hallway bustled with activity. From the bed nearest the door, Hannah held an ice pack to her face. The ache in her temple echoed all the way down to her tailbone. She was glad the second bed had been empty all night.

"I called your brother." Royce frowned down at her.

Hannah turned her head to listen out of her uninjured ear. "You shouldn't have done that."

Royce shot her a *Seriously?* look. "You were assaulted, and you've spent the night in the hospital."

"Only because you made me," she scoffed. "I need to call Grant and tell him I'm fine." Grant would worry, and his anxiety had been elevated since they'd lost Lee.

Hannah sat up. The small pains radiating through her body foretold of up-and-coming bruises. But her injuries were minor. She was lucky, unlike the girl who'd been abducted.

"He's already on his way." He glanced at his watch. "In fact, he should be here soon. His plane lands at ten forty-five."

Hannah adjusted the hard pillow. "He's going to miss Faith's birthday tomorrow."

"I've booked you two first-class seats into Albany leaving this afternoon. I'm going to New York to get up to speed on the Tate contract."

Hannah's brain absorbed the breadth of his statement. He was taking her client away. "Why? I worked my butt off preparing for that deal."

Royce sighed. "Did you not listen to the doctor?"

"I heard him."

"In case he wasn't clear," Royce said, "you have a ruptured eardrum and a concussion, but thankfully, there's no bleeding in your thick head. You are taking some time off whether you like it or not. There'll be other deals. Besides, I've been in car accidents. I know every part of your body must hurt right now."

She tried to summon a glare, but scrunching up her eyes hurt. "The doctor said the concussion was mild and my eardrum will heal on its own. I'll be fine by the time my vacation is over."

"You will not return to work until *my* neurologist clears you." Royce's voice softened. "Your job is not in jeopardy, Hannah. It will be waiting for you no matter how long it takes for you to get better." He stepped closer. His fingers closed around hers. "You know I care about you."

The way he touched her hand set off warning bells. If her head didn't feel like it was stuffed with dynamite, she would have been shocked by his admission.

"You're my boss. Our relationship is entirely professional." Hannah slid her hand away. Her reputation would be shredded if anyone heard Royce's comment. She would not be that woman who slept her way to success. She'd advanced her career through hard work. Even without professional restrictions, he wasn't her type.

Though good-looking, Royce was too polished. The man used more hair products than she did.

A knock sounded on the door frame, and a man in a suit walked in. A badge on his belt identified him as part of the Las Vegas Metropolitan PD. A folder was tucked under his arm. Hannah had given a statement to another policeman hours earlier in the parking lot of Carnival.

"Ms. Barrett." He narrowed critical eyes at her. "I'm Detective Douglas. Are you up to answering more questions?"

"Yes."

Douglas nodded toward Royce and the door, obviously suggesting her boss exit.

"I'm Ms. Barrett's attorney." Royce stepped back, but he didn't leave the room.

The cop sighed, ignored Royce, and focused on Hannah. "I have some pictures I'd like you to look at." The cop opened his folder. "Based on the description you gave me, I pulled the mug shots of some of our known local offenders."

"All right." Hannah found the handrail controls and raised the head of the bed until she was sitting upright.

He set a stack of photos in her hand. "See if any of these men look familiar."

Hannah flipped through a few dozen photos and handed them back. "I don't see either one of them here."

"Are you sure?" he asked.

"I had a good view of the first man. I only had a quick glimpse of the second."

"I guess that would have been too easy." The cop frowned. "See if any of these girls look like the one you saw." He handed her a different set of pictures.

Hannah looked at each one, sadness pinging in her chest as she flipped through school pictures and family snapshots of dark-haired teenage girls. "My God, they're all so young. Are they all missing?"

"Yes, ma'am." The officer clasped his hands behind his back and stood square.

Hannah shuffled the last picture to the back of the stack. "I'm sorry. She's not here."

"I started in southern Nevada, but I'll expand my query to the surrounding states." The cop stuffed his photos back into their envelope. "I'll call you if I have more pictures for you to view."

All those girls were from this region. How could so many innocents go missing? The sheer number was dizzying. Hannah clenched her hands in the sheet at her waist as if her grip on the fabric would hold her distress at bay. "Were you able to trace the GPS on my phone?"

"No, ma'am. We assume he removed the battery or destroyed the phone," the cop said.

"Have you found anything else?" Hannah couldn't get the girl's desperate eyes out of her head. *Help me.*

The cop tapped his pen on his notebook. "The club has surveillance cameras in the lot, but they don't have a hundred percent coverage, and the section of the lot you were attacked in technically belongs to the motel. No camera coverage there, so we don't have an image of your assailants. Surveillance cameras caught the black SUV on its way out of the parking lot, but the license plate was obscured, probably intentionally. We questioned the Carnival staff and did a sweep of the area. But the club borders on an industrial park. Most of the surrounding businesses are closed at night, and there isn't much foot traffic." He flipped the page. "The clerk at the motel denied that anyone fitting those descriptions checked in today. We did find another motel guest who thinks he saw a few other underage girls going into rooms, but he wasn't close enough to be sure." The cop closed his notebook. "Our fingerprint tech managed to lift several prints off the inside of the rental car."

"But hundreds of people have been in that car. It's a rental."

"The prints are likely recent. Fingerprints evaporate, especially in this desert environment. I'd like to send our tech over to take your prints for comparison."

"Of course," Hannah said. "But I valet parked several times yesterday, with clients in the car."

"It's still our best lead." He stacked the envelope of pictures with his notebook. "I have your cell number and address in New York. If we get a match on the fingerprints or I have more pictures for you to view, I'll call you."

"But you're not hopeful?" she asked.

The cop was quiet for a few seconds. "My team specializes in investigating possible cases of human sex trafficking. From the scenario you described and what we've discovered at the hotel, we suspect she was being trafficked. One of the men with her could have been her pimp or her boyfriend."

"She's a child." Even as she protested, Hannah saw the truth in his assessment. Outrage and sickness welled in her throat.

"Yes, ma'am," he said. "Our best bet is the fingerprints. If we've arrested either one of them previously, we'll have their prints in the database. If the prints we lifted from the car aren't theirs, then we might be out of luck. We'll be watching the motel, but her pimp will probably move to a different location after tonight."

Hannah's mind spun. She moved her foot. An ache shot up her ankle. No doubt she'd discover more bruises tomorrow, but she didn't care. Somewhere in the city, a young girl was being victimized, maybe killed, and the authorities were powerless.

"We appreciate your efforts, ma'am," Douglas said. Despite his words, his eyes told Hannah he didn't expect to find either the man or the girl.

"Isn't there anything else you can do?" she asked. There must be something.

"I'll check with the National Center for Missing and Exploited Children and the FBI's National Crime Information Center for missing females who fit the basic description you provided. We'll keep looking. The odds are against us, but sometimes we get lucky."

"I understand," Hannah said. "Please don't hesitate to call me if you need anything."

"Thank you. And take care, ma'am. Keep in mind that he stole your purse and phone. He has personal information about you. Have you canceled your credit cards?"

"Yes. I did that while I was in the ER." She'd been carrying a small evening bag containing just the bare essentials, but her wallet had been inside.

"Be on the lookout for identity theft."

Hannah nodded. The cop left, leaving her empty and hopeless.

"I'm sorry." Royce moved to the bedside. He reached for her hand, then stopped with a frown. "I know you wanted to help that girl."

"He was going to hurt her. Really hurt her. I could see it in his face." The images were permanently branded into Hannah's mind. The cold anger in the man's eyes. The girl's fear. Was she still alive?

"I'm sorry." Royce shifted, glancing toward the door as if willing Grant to appear.

Grant . . .

Last night's incident would disturb him. "Look, my brother doesn't need to know all the details."

Grant had suffered post-traumatic stress. He was doing better since he'd left the military, but crimes against kids were Grant's weak spot. She didn't want anything to disrupt the peace he'd found or impede his progress. Why should they both suffer?

Someone knocked on the door frame. Tears burned the corners of her eyes as Grant walked into the room. The safety and comfort his presence offered flooded her with relief.

Grant's gaze swept over Hannah, his blue eyes assessing her with military precision. She suspected he'd never truly be able to shake the soldier inside of him. "What happened?"

She offered a weak smile. "I got in between a big guy and his girl-friend."

Grant's eyes hardened.

"What can I say?" She picked at the blanket weave. "You know me. All leap, no look."

Royce cleared his throat.

"I'm sorry." Hannah introduced them. "Royce Black. My brother, Major Grant Barrett."

"It's just Grant now. I've dropped the major, remember?" Grant shook Royce's hand. "Thanks for calling me."

Royce summed up her condition in a few sentences. Grant nodded and asked Royce a few questions about her follow-up care.

"Hello, I'm right here." Hannah waggled her fingers.

"Thank God." With an indulgent expression he usually reserved for the children, Grant leaned over and kissed her cheek. He turned back to Royce. "You're sure she's supposed to be released today? She looks terrible."

Hannah would have rolled her eyes if movement of her eyeballs didn't hurt. "You're still talking about me as if I'm not here."

Both men ignored her.

Royce said, "Yes, discharge papers are on the way. She tried to refuse admittance."

The men exchanged an *Of course she did* look.

"I just want to go home, Grant," she said, embarrassed at the piti-ful tone of her voice. "My injuries are minor." Really, she was achy and bruised, but Royce's worries seemed overboard. The doctor hadn't seemed nearly as concerned.

He squeezed her hand. "OK."

Royce turned to Hannah. "I'll call you in a couple of days."

After a long flight and drive, Hannah's sore muscles and bruises had stiffened. Grant led her inside the fixer-upper he and his surely soon-to-be fiancée, Ellie, had bought over the summer. Hannah limped into the house. Baby gates blocked off the dining and living rooms on either side of the foyer. Though Halloween had passed more than a week ago, three paper bats hung from the foyer light fixture.

Barking, AnnaBelle the golden retriever barreled down the hall. Grant stopped the dog with one hand. "Whoa."

"She's fine." Hannah scratched behind the silky ears. "Good girl."

Hannah vaguely registered a gated-off room full of building and painting supplies.

"Aunt Hannah!" Carson ran down the stairs in race-car pajamas. He threw his arms around her waist and buried his face in her sweater. "I missed you."

Her bruised tailbone protested as she stooped to hug him. She held him close, the contact with his small body—and giant affection—softening her like butter left in the sun. "I missed you, too. It's so late. What are you doing up?"

"I heard AnnaBelle bark, and I knew you were here." He rubbed his sleepy eyes.

An earsplitting scream rattled the walls.

"And the baby who never sleeps wants her hug." Ellie appeared at the end of the hall. In her robe and slippers, she looked ragged. "You might want to change first."

"How long has she been up?" Grant asked.

"Half hour," Ellie said. "I gave her some Tylenol."

Stretching her grubby hands toward Hannah, Faith tottered down the hall.

"Oh, my God. She's walking." With one arm around Carson, Hannah reached for the baby. "What is that on her hands?"

Carson eased away. "Ew."

"Looks like dog food." Ellie sighed. "I thought the bowl was empty. AnnaBelle must have filled up on macaroni and cheese. I swear more of Faith's food ends up on the floor than in her mouth. She's the Tasmanian Devil baby."

Faith reached Hannah, squealed, and grabbed her aunt's slacks with two disgusting fists. Hannah scooped her up. Definitely dog food. "Girlfriend, let's wash those hands."

The baby babbled as Hannah carried her into the kitchen. Propping Faith on her hip, she turned on the faucet, tested the water temperature, and leaned the baby toward the stream. She soaped up one chubby hand.

"Watch out!" Ellie said.

Faith grabbed the pull-out nozzle and pointed it at Hannah's face. Water soaked her sweater and dripped off her face.

Laughing, Grant shut off the water. "Sorry about that. She discovered the pull-out feature last week."

"You are a little pistol." Hannah kissed the baby on the top of the head. Sniffing her baby shampoo–scented hair, she felt the tension inside her loosen further. The love that crowded her heart when she was with the kids filled her with equal parts joy—and terror.

Faith kicked her feet and twisted.

"Can I let her down?" Hannah scanned the room. Everything appeared to be barricaded except the kitchen and hall.

"Sure. The kitchen is babyproof." Grant picked up the dog's bowl and set it on the counter. "Are you hungry?"

"No, just tired." Hannah mopped at her drenched sweater with a dish towel.

"Let's get you settled, then." Upstairs, he led her into a guest room that smelled faintly of fresh paint. A white iron bed faced the window. White curtains framed a view of the dark woods behind the house. The soft green walls and white linens looked serene. "I'll bring your luggage up. Ellie took your clothes from the trunks in Lee's attic and put them in the closet and drawers." Grant headed for the door.

She ran a finger across the glossy white window trim. "What?"

After she and her brothers had moved their father to a nursing home, Lee had convinced her to keep her few belongings, mostly off-season clothes, at his house. *The cost of living in New York City is outrageous. Save your money, and you'll be able to purchase a unit with less debt later*, he'd said. At the time, she hadn't known his anti-debt spiel was coming from personal experience, but he'd been right. She had a nice down payment in her brokerage account. After Lee's death, Grant offered her his new place as her official address. But she'd never asked for a room of her own.

Her protest had to wait for him to return with her luggage. A few minutes later he lined her bags up in front of the closet.

"Ellie didn't have to go to all that trouble," Hannah said. Having her personal belongings in the dresser and closet felt . . . permanent. Her brother was playing hardball. He knew how much she feared attachment, and he was forcing her hand.

"You don't have that much stuff. This is your room. You might not be here very often, but it's yours whenever you want to be here." Grant dug into his front pocket and pulled out a key. "I had a house key made for you, too." He put it on the dresser. Pointing to a doorway, he said, "You have your own bathroom, too."

"Really? How did you get all this done since I was here last?"

"Two months is a long time, and we want you to feel at home."

The address on her license was a formality. She'd never intended to actually live in Scarlet Falls again. She floated from city to city, with no permanent ties to any particular place. In the beginning, she'd liked the feeling of freedom. But Lee's death had changed everything. Hannah's world was tilted. Instead of free, she now felt lost. As soon as her promotion came through, she'd start looking for an apartment. It would be in the city, not her hometown, but she couldn't hurt Grant's feelings. "Thank you."

"I'm going to help Ellie get the kids back to bed. You should try to sleep, too." Grant left the room.

Had it really been two months since she'd visited? How could she let that happen? She stared up at the freshly painted ceiling for a minute, then got up and went into the new bathroom. Grant and Ellie had kept the vintage feel of the house with a modern pedestal sink and a mosaic tile floor in the same pale green and white they'd used in the bedroom. A deep, modern freestanding tub invited her for a soak, and the shower had more jets than an airport. Had this been a bedroom or a closet before her brother had reallocated the space for her? Guilt lay in a thick layer on her skin. She needed to visit more, no matter how painful it was to leave.

As much as she resisted, Grant's house felt like home. It felt too good. Almost good enough to blot out the image of a frightened teenager Hannah had left behind in Vegas. Almost.

Suddenly, she needed to wash the trip from her skin. She took a hot shower. The clothes in her suitcase were dirty, but she found her battered Syracuse University sweatshirt in one of the dresser drawers. She tugged it on with a pair of yoga pants and thick socks. After the warmth of the desert, the damp of autumn in New York State chilled her to the marrow.

Tired but restless, she fluffed up the pillows and settled in bed with her laptop. Her e-mail account was full, as usual. There were several messages from concerned coworkers and clients who'd heard about the attack in Vegas. She sent quick thank-you notes back.

Her mouse hovered over an e-mail from theking@hmi.com. The subject line read *Jewel*. Hannah's hands froze. A wave of cold swept over her skin. Only the police and Royce had been present when Hannah had given her statement. No one else would know the girl's name—except the girl and the men who took her.

Hannah clicked on the e-mail. The message was short: *Help. The end comes Tuesday.*

Chapter Five

"You sure this is the right address?" Brody shifted his unmarked police car into park at the curb in front of a narrow two-story home. A dozen blocks from the town center, the houses crowded together on small lots. White with black shutters, the place was plain but neat. No trash littered the tiny chain-linked yard. A maple tree had turned to crimson in the center of the small front yard, and its fallen leaves had been raked recently.

In the passenger seat, Chet Thatcher, the only other detective on the small Scarlet Falls PD, checked his paperwork against the brass numbers affixed next to the front door. "This is Jordan Brown's last known address. Maybe he moved."

Brody pointed to the small script letters that spelled *Brown* on the side of the black metal mailbox.

Chet tapped a forefinger on his report. "His parents' house."

"What do we know about him?" Brody asked. Chet had been working this case for the last month, but he'd asked for Brody to ride backup today.

"Jordan is twenty. He's been arrested for burglary and once for narcotics possession. He got out of rehab six months ago." Chet flipped a page on his clipboard. "A house was burglarized two blocks from here last night. The resident came home to find her window smashed, jewelry and two hundred dollars in cash missing. In her words, *Must be that no-good piece-of-shit Brown kid who lives on Tyler Street.*"

"Anybody actually see Jordan in the act?" Brody asked.

"No. I don't have enough probable cause for a warrant, but the theft follows his established pattern of behavior. We arrested him two years ago for breaking into neighbors' cars to fund his habit." Chet showed him the kid's mug shot. "There have been three similar break-ins in this neighborhood over the past six weeks."

"Let's go see if he's home." Chet got out of the car.

Brody stepped out into the street. "No car in the driveway."

"Maybe Mom and Dad are at work." Fifty-six years old and balding, Chet had a skinny frame and moved with a jerky, bow-legged stride as if he'd spent his life on horseback. The closest he'd been to a horse was the stands at Saratoga on race day.

Brody knocked on the front door, but the house remained quiet. Chet stepped into the flower bed, cupped his hands over his eyes, and peered in the living room window.

"See anything?" Brody asked.

Chet shook his head. "Maybe no one's home."

Behind the door, something slammed. The house rattled. Brody and Chet ran around the side of the house. A thin man in jeans and a black T-shirt raced across the small back lawn and vaulted over the three-foot fence, landing next to three grade-schoolers playing in a sandbox. He paused on the other side and glanced over his shoulder. Brody recognized Jordan Brown from his photo.

"Stop! Police!" Brody yelled.

The kid bolted, and Brody followed, tossing the car keys at Chet. Brody chased the kid through a neighbor's side yard into the next street. Jordan ducked around a group of kids playing baseball and sprinted into another yard. He passed a shed and turned into a grass alley that ran between two fenced lots. Brody skidded through the sharp left, his dress shoes sliding on the muddy ground. He almost collided with Jordan. The kid had stopped short. A Dumpster blocked the exit. On both sides, six-foot-high wooden fencing blocked Jordan's escape. He'd never get over an obstacle that high before Brody could get his hands on him.

Gotcha.

Jordan bulldozed Brody. The kid's shoulder rammed Brody's solar plexus. They went down to the ground. The kid rolled off Brody and bounded to his feet. He took one running step before Brody grabbed his ankle and sent him sprawling. But Jordan recovered with the speed of youth, getting his feet back under his body.

Where was Chet?

Brody kept his ears tuned for the sound of the unmarked police car as he lurched to his feet and grabbed Jordan by the collar. The kid spun around. His hand went into his pocket. Sunlight gleamed on a knife. Jordan lunged. Brody turned his body to dodge the blade. He grabbed the knife hand and twisted the kid's wrist until the weapon dropped to the ground. Converting the wristlock into an arm bar, he forced Jordan facedown on the ground and pinned him to the weeds with one knee in his lower back. "You are under arrest."

"Get the fuck off me." Jordan squirmed.

"Hold still." Brody leaned harder. Anger sent another shot of adrenaline into his bloodstream. Scarlet Falls used to be a nice, safe town. He didn't appreciate scumbags like this one ruining it. Decent people were trying to live here.

His heart rammed against his breastbone, and a drop of sweat ran into his eyes. He wiped a forearm over his brow and pushed aside a vivid memory: another drug addict, another criminal—another near miss. A car door slammed, and Brody shut the mental door on his unwelcome vision with equal force.

Chet ran up the alley, gun drawn. Pale faced and wheezing, he pointed his weapon at Jordan. His gaze fell to the knife. "Shit. Guess I'm a little late."

"It's OK. I got him." Brody reached for the cuffs on his belt.

Frowning, Chet returned his unneeded weapon to its holster. "You all right? He didn't cut you, did he?"

"I'm fine." Brody handcuffed Jordan's hands behind his back and patted down his pockets. "Why did you run, Jordan?"

"I'm not talking to anyone except a lawyer," Jordan said to the grass.

Brody pulled a small baggie of white powder from Jordan's jeans pocket. He scanned the kid's arms. Jordan sported more tracks than Penn Station.

"Is that heroin, Jordan?" Chet asked. "You just got out of rehab."

Jordan didn't respond.

"Did you call for backup?" Brody asked Chet.

Chet nodded. "Patrol car should be here any minute."

Brody hauled Jordan to his feet. Chet holstered his gun. They walked Jordan to the end of the alley. A Scarlet Falls PD cruiser pulled up, and Brody put the kid in the back. Then he took a minute to catch his breath. He inhaled a lungful of crisp November air, cooling his blood.

"Book him on assaulting an officer with a weapon, to start," Chet said to the officer. The patrol car pulled away to transport Jordan to the police station.

Chet's phone rang. He stepped aside to answer it and returned a minute later. "I'm working on a search warrant. Your suit is destroyed," Chet said as they walked back to the unmarked car. "I'm sorry I couldn't keep up on foot."

Brody brushed at the mud on his trousers. Spotting a tear in the fabric, he gave up. Good thing he didn't buy expensive suits.

"I guess it's not a bad thing that I have to retire soon. These knees don't have any more foot chases in them." Chet had six more months before the mandatory retirement age kicked him off the force.

But they both knew it wasn't Chet's knees or age that had ruined his health.

"I'm fine." Brody's finger lingered on a slice in the fabric of his jacket. That had been a close call. If he'd been an inch or two closer to Jordan, Brody would have been gutted.

"You almost got stabbed because I wasn't there."

"I almost got stabbed because that kid pulled a knife on me. I'm fine, Chet. Let it go."

Chet didn't look convinced.

None of this was Chet's fault, any more than Brody's old partner in Boston was to blame for that disaster. Brody changed the subject. "If you're going to retire, you need a hobby."

Chet snorted. "Can you see me playing fucking golf?"

"Retired bankers play golf. Retired cops get boats," Brody clarified with a grin.

"I hate fishing, too."

"Woodworking?"

Chet snorted. Brody slid behind the wheel and drove back to the Brown house. Brody's phone played the *Hawaii Five-O* theme. He glanced at the display but didn't recognize the number. "Detective McNamara."

The caller said, "This is Hannah Barrett."

"Hannah." He wouldn't have been more surprised if the president was on the line. "I thought you were out West."

"I was. I'm in town for Faith's birthday party tonight."

And she'd called him?

Don't get excited. She probably needs to discuss her brother's case.

Brody tried not to get personally involved with the people in his cases, but every once in a while, a case came along that he couldn't shake. The murders of Lee and Kate Barrett had been the most intense of Brody's career, and he'd kept in touch with the family.

He'd seen Hannah a few times since he'd arrested her brother's killer. She'd arrive in town wearing a conservative, high-style suit, and change into jeans as if she changed her identity upon her return to Scarlet Falls, like Superman ducking into a phone booth. But when he imagined her, which was more often than he liked, her polished corporate attorney mode wasn't what he pictured. No, he saw her barefoot and mud-streaked, having just chased a potential kidnapper away from her nephew. Hero tendencies seemed to be hardwired into the Barretts. Hannah was fierce and fearless like a primitive protective female, and no fancy clothes or law degree could fully hide her don't-mess-with-mine attitude. It was hard to resist a woman like that. Damned hard.

Thinking about her warmed him again in a way no deep breathing was going to cool.

She hesitated. "I need your help."

Brody straightened, his interest piqued. "What can I do for you?"

She didn't answer right away, and he pictured her face turning serious. He pictured other things about her, too. Her long, lean body was constantly in motion. Short blond hair framed an angular no-nonsense face. Those bright blue eyes snapped to attention when she focused on a problem. And most of all, Brody pictured the few brief moments of vulnerability that seeped through her competence when she was with her niece and nephew.

"It's a long story," she said. "Do you have time to meet?"

"Are you at Grant's house?"

"I am."

"Why don't I drop by later? I have some news for you and Grant anyway. Not good news, I'm afraid."

Chet tapped Brody's sleeve.

"I'm sorry, Hannah," Brody said. "I have to go. I'll see you in a few hours." He ended the call and turned to his partner.

Chet stuffed his phone in his chest pocket. "Judge Marks is meeting us at the courthouse to sign the warrant."

Brody pulled away from the curb. Ideally, they'd have a patrol car babysit the Brown house while they picked up the warrant, but Scarlet Falls didn't have the manpower for such luxuries. There were times they operated on a cross-their-fingers budget.

"Who was that Hannah woman who called you?" Chet asked.

"Hannah Barrett. Her brother was murdered last spring."

"That's the case you caught while I was on vacation?"

"Yes."

"So why is she calling you?"

"I don't know."

"What's she look like?" Chet waggled an eyebrow.

Scorching hot. Instead, Brody said, "I'm sure this is a professional matter."

"You're going to see her later?"

"When we're done."

"I can get someone else to help me," Chet offered.

"Because everybody is dying to spend their Saturday afternoon searching a junkie's room for stolen goods?"

"Because I don't remember the last time I saw you distracted by a woman." Chet lowered his sunglasses. "Besides, I've been a cop on this force for more than three decades. Plenty of people owe me favors."

"Good to be the Godfather."

"I wish I was seeing a pretty woman later," Chet said wistfully. His wife had suffered a heart attack and died years before. On the rare occasion he talked about his family, he said his wife's heart had broken the day their teenage daughter, Teresa, had run away and gone missing.

"I expect she's calling me about her brother's case." Brody would have to give her the bad news he'd learned from the prosecutor this week.

Chet shook his head. "The prosecutor would be able to handle questions about the trial."

"We'll see."

The first time Brody had met Hannah, he'd thought her cold and aloof, but he'd soon realized she was the exact opposite. Her cool demeanor concealed a vivid intensity. Whenever he was in the same room with her, everything looked brighter, as if she cranked up the saturation of his color palette.

"Do you like her?" Chet asked.

"I do."

"Then go for it."

"She isn't in town very often. I doubt she'd be interested in starting something."

"What do you have to lose? For a bachelor, your life is pretty lame."

"Good point." Brody laughed. What did he have to lose? He'd dated on and off over the years, had a few relationships that hadn't gone anywhere. When they were over, he'd shrugged them off. But his instincts told him that a relationship with Hannah wouldn't be as easy to forget.

Chapter Six

Brody parked his car in front of the Barrett farmhouse. Paint gleamed fresh white in the setting sun. A gust of wind stirred dead leaves in the flower bed. He brushed at the grass stains on his trouser knees. He should have gone home and changed, but the search had taken longer than he'd expected. And he was stupidly anxious to see Hannah. He had taken the time to stop at Walmart and pick up a toy for the baby. Priorities.

Shifting the pink-wrapped package in his hand, Brody rang the bell.

Grant opened the door. Surprise lifted his eyebrows. "Brody?"

"Hey, Grant. How are you?"

Grant's gaze dropped to the brightly wrapped package.

"It's for Faith."

"How did you know it was her birthday?" Grant moved back.

"Hannah mentioned it when I talked to her earlier." Brody stepped into the warm house.

"You talked to Hannah?"

"I did." Brody took off his jacket and hung it on a coat tree by the door. "I have some news for you."

Grant scanned his face. "Something I'm not going to like?"

"Yes. Sorry."

"Brody, I didn't know you were coming," Ellie said from the end of the hall.

Grant lowered his voice. "Will the news keep 'til after the party?"

"It's not pressing." Brody nodded, following Grant toward Ellie.

"The house is really coming along," Brody said. The exterior of the home might be finished, but inside, the place was clearly a work in progress.

"Thanks." Grant moved back to let him into the foyer. "Got those windows replaced just in time. Looks like a cold snap's coming next week."

Quiet conversation buzzed from the back of the house. They walked past the formal living room, currently housing construction supplies, and a dining room begging to be renovated, into the newly remodeled kitchen. Wood floors, honey-colored cabinets, and bronze granite made a warm space. A picture window looked out on an expanse of grass. A shallow stream separated the rear yard from the woods that backed the property. A tire hung from a massive old oak tree. The Barretts were making a home here. They deserved it. They'd been through hell.

He set his gift down on the center island.

"You didn't have to bring a present, Brody." Ellie smiled. She looked to Grant. "How did you know it was Faith's birthday?"

"He talked to Hannah earlier," Grant said.

Ellie blinked. She put a hand on Grant's arm, no doubt assuming the call was about the case.

The thought of Lee and Kate's murders brought Brody's molars together hard enough to send a spike of pain through his temple. He loosened his jaw. The Barretts were moving forward. He needed to do the same, but the Barrett case had tainted Scarlet Falls with extreme selfishness and violence.

"Where's the birthday girl?" Brody asked.

"You might want to keep your distance. Faith is heavily into textures these days." Ellie nodded toward a high chair pulled up to the long farmhouse table. An orange substance coated the baby's face and hands. Carrots, he decided. With a happy squeal, she fished in the bowl suction-cupped to her tray, grabbed a chubby fistful, and squeezed. Mushed carrots oozed through her fingers. The dog circled the chair, licking bits of food from the wooden floor.

He laughed, the sight of the happy, goo-covered baby easing some of his tension. "Did she get any of it into her mouth?"

"Not much," Ellie said. "Sit down. Let me get you something to eat."

Faith squealed again and banged her fists on her plastic tray. A scattering of Cheerios danced like Mexican jumping beans. Grant dropped into the chair next to her and gently hushed her. Odd. Usually, he let her squeal to her heart's content.

Brody greeted the rest of the family. Grant's six-year-old nephew, Carson, responded with a subdued "Hey." Ellie's grandmother, Nan, stood to give him a quick hug, and her teenage daughter, Julia, waved hello from across the table. The whole family was strangely quiet. Eight months after facing a terrible tragedy, Brody had thought the family was slowly healing, but today everyone seemed subdued and wary. Faith flung a handful of mushed carrot. It hit the floor with a splat. The baby was the only one acting normal.

Brody took the chair next to Grant and leaned toward him. "Is something wrong?"

Grant frowned. He opened his mouth then abruptly closed it, his gaze shifting to the doorway. Brody tracked his line of sight to see Hannah gingerly walking into the room. Yoga pants and a fitted, long-sleeve top hugged her lithe frame. Brody blinked in shock as she walked closer. The one word he'd never thought he'd use to describe her was frail. But that's what came to mind. Normally, Hannah was tall and long-limbed in a kick-ass, athletic way. Her blue eyes, usually barbed-wire sharp, were clouded with pain and something else. Anxiety.

What the hell?

She met his questioning gaze and gave him a quick shake of her head. Whatever she wanted to say to him would wait until they were alone.

"Aunt Hannah." Carson bolted from his seat. "You took a longer nap than Faith."

Grant caught him around the middle. "Easy, sport. Aunt Hannah had an accident, remember?"

Carson slid to a stop, but Hannah smiled at him. "I'm fine, Grant, just a little stiff, and I could really use a hug."

She eased into the only vacant seat, next to Brody.

"Yeah, that's better." She wrapped her arms around her nephew. Her muscles appeared to loosen as she rested her head against the child's. "Hugs always make me feel better."

"You should come see us more." In three seconds, Carson squirmed out of her embrace.

"You're right." She brushed his sun-whitened bangs off his face.

"Uncle Grant," the boy said. "Can we have cake now?"

"Soon," Grant said with a smile.

Hannah turned to the baby. "Girlfriend, we need to talk about personal hygiene."

Faith shrieked and reached both sticky hands for her aunt.

"Let me clean her up," Grant said. "Ellie, could you toss me a dish towel?"

"I don't mind sticky." Hannah half stood and gave the baby a smacking kiss on her orange-smeared nose. Faith clapped her aunt's cheeks with both hands. Hannah winced, but covered it with a smile.

Brody looked closer. At the edge of her hairline, a bruise extended from her ear to her temple. The puffy, darkening patch was the size of a fist. Brody's jaw muscles went taut again.

"You all right?" Grant asked. Ellie brought her a wet towel.

"Fine." Hannah wiped orange handprints off her face.

"You should ice that egg on your head." Grant got up and went to the freezer.

She pulled a foot up onto the chair and hugged her knee. Her pant leg rode up. A ring of bruises surrounded her slender ankle. Like fingerprints. Fury rode hot up the back of Brody's neck. Accident his ass. He'd find out who hurt her and . . .

He stopped himself. He sounded like Grant. There could be a perfectly reasonable explanation for her bruises.

Catching her gaze, Brody whispered, "What happened?"

Hannah stared back. "I fell."

"I thought you were in an accident," he shot back under his breath.

"Well, I can assure you what happened wasn't intentional." Her voice sharpened, which made him feel better. The clop on the head clearly hadn't affected her keen brain or quick tongue.

She smiled as her brother handed her an ice pack. Letting the subject go for now, Brody sat back and enjoyed the company. But he wasn't leaving until Hannah told him everything.

The rest of the party went smoothly. Ellie's grandmother was a hell of a cook, and Brody was happy to dive into a plateful of roast chicken and macaroni and cheese. Cake, candles, and the birthday song followed. When was the last time Brody had celebrated a traditional milestone? He took Chet out for a burger on his last birthday. Maybe that's why he and Chet were so close. Neither of them had a personal life.

When Faith tired of smearing icing and cake over her face and head, she screamed for her freedom in a pitch that could scatter dogs.

"Shh." Hannah lifted her from the high chair.

The baby snagged a handful of her aunt's sweatshirt with an icing-laden fist. Hannah gently pried the stubby fist from her clothes. "I think a bath is in order, birthday girl."

"I'll hose her down, Hannah." Ellie took the baby and left the room.

"Thanks for dinner." Brody caught Grant's eye. "Can I talk to you for a minute?"

"Sure." Grant stood. "Let's go into my office."

He speared Hannah with a gaze. "I'd like to talk to you, too."

She paused. Their eyes locked for one long breath before she blinked away. Brody could have studied her all day. She wasn't the most beautiful woman he'd ever seen, but she was by far the most compelling.

"I'll be right there." She went to the sink, wet a paper towel, and wiped at the icing stain on her shirt.

Grant led him to a small room in the front of the house. Not yet renovated, the office was covered with wood paneling and blue carpet that called to the 1980s. He closed the door behind them and sat on the edge of the desk, the same chipped old desk and chairs that used to sit in his dead brother's study. "What's up?"

"It's about the trial, but we might as well wait for Hannah. She didn't fall, did she?" Brody asked.

Grant crossed his arms over his thick chest. "No, she didn't, but she didn't want to upset Carson."

"Understandable, but she looks like she's in rough shape. What happened?" Brody asked.

"Why don't you ask her?"

"Because she scares the crap out of me." To be specific, it was the powerful interest for her stirring in his chest that intimidated him.

Grant laughed. "Hannah's not scary unless she's armed."

Brody gave him a pointed look.

"OK. Maybe she's a little *fierce*, but not scary," Grant admitted as he studied Brody. Did Grant suspect he had a thing for his sister? "Try softening her up with Dunkin' Donuts. Boston Kreme is her kryptonite. Mushroom pizza is also a favorite."

Brody made a mental note. "You're going to be away next week. She'll be alone out here."

"I wouldn't be going if I wasn't sure she was all right," Grant said. "And Mac is scheduled to be home on Thursday."

In Brody's opinion, the youngest Barrett, a wildlife biologist, was highly unreliable. "Where is Mac?"

"Brazil."

"So about Hannah . . ."

"She was assaulted in a parking lot in Las Vegas Thursday night," Grant continued.

"What?" Brody snapped to attention. He'd become immune to many things in his twelve-year career in law enforcement, but violence aimed at women and children hit a perpetually raw nerve.

Grant nodded, grim faced. "She walked into some guy beating on a girl."

"Let me guess. She intervened." From past experience, Brody knew Hannah would never be able to turn her back on some girl in trouble. She seemed to foster the same hero complex as Grant, except she wasn't a former army officer.

"Yeah. He popped her in the head." Grant tapped his temple. Fury flared in his eyes. Clearly, he was working hard to keep his temper in check.

Knowing some criminal had put his hands on her sent Brody's blood into a silent boil. Call him old-fashioned, but there was no excuse for a man to ever raise his hand to a woman.

Grant agreed with a grim nod. "Hannah rallied, but after she got the girl into her car, he rammed them with his SUV."

Footsteps in the hall silenced them. The door opened, and Hannah walked in. Grant gave her his chair. She eased into it as if her entire body hurt. But when she turned to face Brody, her gaze was as sharp as usual. "Grant said you have some news."

Brody hesitated. Why couldn't he ever bring her good news? "The defense attorney for Lee and Kate's killer has filed for another postponement."

She leaned back and crossed her legs. "What's their claim this time?"

The trial had already seen delays due to a mental health evaluation for the defendant, assault charges filed against Grant by the defendant, and a psychological examination of Carson, who the defense attorney insisted testify though the prosecutor said it shouldn't be necessary.

"They want to move the trial, claiming that publicity has tainted the potential jury pool."

"I'm not surprised. I should have predicted it." Hannah's expression turned stormy.

"The prosecutor will be in touch later this week. I just wanted to give you a heads-up."

She lifted her eyes. "I know notifying families isn't your job, so thank you."

"I didn't want to see you blindsided." Brody wished he could make it all go away. She and her family deserved peace.

"I appreciate it. Grant will be away, but I'll meet with the prosecutor this week." Hannah hugged her waist. Despite her confident tone and words, she looked vulnerable, and when Brody imagined a man hurting her, he wanted to break something. Like a head.

Through the door, Ellie called Grant's name.

"Excuse me for a minute." Grant went into the hall, leaving the door open.

"Now you want to tell me what really happened in Vegas?" Brody asked. "Unless you fell into a fist, you've been bullshitting me with that accident story."

Hannah got up and closed the door. Turning, she gave him her opposing-counsel scrutiny. "Grant told you, didn't he?"

Brody leaned forward, hands clasped, forearms resting on his thighs. "He said you intervened between a man and his girlfriend."

"That's not exactly what happened." She shivered. "I didn't tell Grant everything. The man got away—with the girl."

"Oh." Brody sat back. Shock and alarm filled him as she told him her story.

"And yesterday I got an e-mail that appears to have come from that girl."

"And you're just telling me now?"

Hannah glanced away. "I reported it to the Las Vegas police. I was waiting to hear back from them. I didn't think I was in any immediate danger."

"He took your purse?"

"My phone, too." Hannah nodded. "He has my e-mail and cell number as well, though I had my provider disconnect service and remotely wipe the contents of that phone."

"Does he have this address?"

"Yes. He has my driver's license, et cetera. But he's thousands of miles away. The Vegas cop was more concerned with identity theft."

Thousands of miles didn't feel like enough distance to Brody. "What did the e-mail say?"

"'Help. The end comes Tuesday.'" Hannah's voice broke. "That's it. The subject line was the girl's name. The detective in Vegas said it was untraceable. It was sent from an anonymous e-mail account called Hide My Identity, and the IP address of the computer was shielded with a virtual private network. He suggested I let my local police know about the incident." She smiled weakly. "So I called you."

Because he was the only cop she knew? Part of Brody wanted the reason to be more, but Hannah Barrett was a complicated woman. She stirred up too many unknowns in his gut. It was easier to date women who didn't keep him up at night, not that he dated much. The shooting in Boston and his subsequent divorce had driven him to Scarlet Falls in search of a fresh start. The events had also left him wary of intense experiences, and Hannah Barrett's intensity meter was stuck on high.

"I don't want to unnecessarily alarm Grant," she said. "He knows the man took my purse and has this address."

"Your brother installed a very high-end security system. Your assailant is probably thousands of miles away, but you should keep the alarm on at all times. If you forward me the e-mail, I'll have a look at it." Brody rubbed his jaw. "I don't know what this means, but I don't like it. Please call me if anything seems odd. Anything."

"All right," she said. "I don't know what 'the end' is, but it doesn't sound good, and Tuesday is only a few days away."

"Try not to think about it. You notified the Las Vegas police. There's nothing else you can do." But Brody wasn't going to be able to put it out of his mind. "And do not respond. This could be a trick to get more information from you, like your current whereabouts. Anyone who is good enough to conceal his own current location has enough skill to trace yours."

Tormenting a woman could also be some sick bastard's idea of fun—or revenge.

ω

Mick pulled up to the pump. Colored light from a gas station sign gleamed off the hood of the car. The V-8 engine was powerful, and the tank emptied like there was a siphon attached. But they were in

Scarlet Falls on Saturday night, just as he'd planned. With pit stops, the trip had taken a little longer than he'd anticipated. He stretched his back. Considering how many hours they'd spent in the car, he didn't feel too bad. Alternating sleeping and driving had helped, so had the coke.

"I'll go pay." He got out of the car and zipped his jacket. The upstate New York cold was a smack after living in the desert. He went inside to pay for their gas in cash, and the attendant turned on the pump. Enjoying the heat in the store, Mick watched through the window as Sam slid the nozzle into the tank. An old Camry pulled up behind the Charger. A young woman got out and swiped her credit card at the pump. Her long brown ponytail swayed as she inserted the nozzle in her tank. While the gas pumped, she came into the small store and asked for a pack of cigarettes. She handed the clerk some cash, then pocketed the receipt and her change.

Mick walked back to the car. His brother's eyes were bright in the reflection of the sign. Too bright. Damn it. He shouldn't have let him snort that coke. The pump shut off, and Sam removed the nozzle. Taking his sweet time, he hung it up and screwed on the gas cap.

He got into the driver's seat, his eyes straying to the rearview mirror.

"Don't even think about it," Mick said. Looking back, he watched the woman return the nozzle to its place, close her gas cap, and get into her car.

Sam grinned. "Why not? No rules, remember?"

"We have to keep a low profile."

His brother started the car. He waited until the little sedan pulled out ahead of them. "We can do that and have some fun."

"Better to scope out the town first and find somewhere to crash, and I want to see the blond tonight."

But Sam was on the highway behind the woman. "Tomorrow's soon enough, isn't it? Like you said, we need to find a place to stay."

Mick knew, before they even approached the stop sign, what Sam was going to do. "Don't do it. Not in my car—"

The sedan stopped. Sam tapped her bumper. "Relax. The car is fine. It was just a kiss."

Both vehicles pulled to the shoulder. Sam was out of the car. Mick hunched in the front seat, fuming. His car better not have a fucking scratch in the paint. But he didn't intervene. There was no stopping his brother once he was in motion.

Sam approached the front of the Charger, his posture apologetic. The woman got out of the Camry, and they both bent to examine her bumper. Sam pointed to the car. In the same movement, he punched her in the face. She hit the ground like a cinder block. Sam went to the open driver's door. The trunk popped up. He ran back to the woman, scooped her up, and heaved her into the trunk. Slamming the lid, he jumped into the car and drove off. Mick followed. Where were they going?

He followed the Camry four miles until it turned off the country road into a dark lane. They parked in front of a mobile home with some sort of big building in the background. Mick got out of the car. A couple of dogs barked in the dark.

Sam got out of the Camry.

"Where are we?" Mick asked.

"Her place." His brother had a purse in one hand. "I checked the phone listing. No man listed on the house or business. Let's see if she lives alone."

They went up to the front door. Sam used the key to open the door. He flipped the light switch. It was a mobile home, but a large one. They'd certainly lived in worse.

"Not bad." Sam walked through the rooms. In the kitchen, he picked up an electric bill from the table. Only one name on the label: Joleen Walken.

Mick went into the bedroom. He checked the closet and drawers. "No men's clothes."

"Second bedroom is an office." Sam closed another door. "Just girl stuff in the bathroom."

Maybe this would work out. "Nice job, Sam."

Sam grinned. "Gotta have faith. I know what I'm doing."

He'd certainly had enough practice.

He went back to the car to get the girl. Mick held the door. Her body looked limp when he picked her up, but by the time his brother got her to the front step, she was awake and kicking.

Mick shut and locked the door. Sam dropped the girl on the floor. Her body hit the thin carpet with a breath-expelling thud. She crabbed backward. Her chest heaved, and her eyes searched for an escape route.

There wasn't one.

Not with Sam.

"You want to go first, Mick?" Sam's voice was tight with restraint. Edgy from being cooped up in the car, he needed to vent.

"No, that's OK. I'll pass on this one."

"You sure? She looks like your type."

"I appreciate the offer, but I'm tired. I'm going to take a nap."

"OK." Sam moved in.

Mick went into the bedroom and closed the door. It was best to let Sam work out his rage. Mick could wait. Soon he'd have the blond all to himself.

Chapter Seven

"I'm fine. Really." Hannah studied her brother's profile across the center console of his pickup. Physically, Grant hadn't changed much over the months since he'd left the army to raise their murdered brother's children. His frame was naturally large, and physical labor kept him heavily muscled. It was his eyes that were different. For the first time ever, he seemed content.

"Are you sure?" he asked. "I can cancel our trip." Grant and the family were scheduled to leave the next morning.

"That's ridiculous," Hannah said. "You've been planning this vacation for months. Carson wants to see Mickey Mouse. After all he's been through, he deserves a visit to Disney World. So do Ellie, Julia, and Nan. There's no reason to let them all down. Besides, AnnaBelle and I aren't going to do anything except take leisurely walks, watch movies, and eat pizza while you're gone."

He gave her a doubtful look. "Yesterday you told Brody you'd talk to the prosecutor."

"That'll take an hour, at best. Look, I'm still tired, but the aches and stiffness are better every day." She wasn't a hundred percent, but two days of rest had helped.

"You'll keep the alarm set?"

Hannah raised her right hand. "I promise, and I know where the gun safe is."

"All right." Grant nodded. "Brody said he'll be around all week."

There was something about Brody McNamara. Something she couldn't quite define, but when they were in the same room, she was acutely *aware* of him in an irritating and consistent way that made her simultaneously want to avoid—and seek—his company. So what? She was attracted to him. She could fight that off. She'd been battling her feelings her whole life, though lately, her hold on them seemed tenuous.

Her gaze drifted to the rural highway stretching out in front of the truck.

She wasn't staying in Scarlet Falls. She'd get that clearance from the neurologist. Next week she was off to London. Royce wouldn't need to handle the Tate deal. She'd worked for it, and she was going to make sure it was hers.

The sound of Grant shifting into park startled her. She looked through the windshield at the familiar one-story brick building of the nursing home where their father lived. Sunday afternoons were prime visiting hours, and the parking lot was full.

They went through the lobby and signed in at the reception desk. Hannah's heart slid into overdrive. Under her silk sweater, sweat broke out at the base of her spine. The hospital smell made her queasy.

At the nurses' station, a woman in lavender scrubs greeted them with a smile. "Good morning, Mr. Barrett."

"Morning, Maria." Grant introduced Hannah. "How is he today?"

Her smile turned sad. "About the same."

"Thanks." With his hand on her elbow, Grant steered Hannah down a long hall covered in flat-napped gray carpet. A tiny woman hunched over a walker shuffled toward them.

"Good morning, Mrs. Henry," Grant said.

"Morning, handsome." She flashed him a perfect set of dentures. "Did you come to break me out of this place?"

"Name the day." He grinned back at her.

Hannah laughed, the humor easing her nerves. They turned left into the acute-care wing. If the Colonel had been ambulatory, his dementia would have put him in the secure Alzheimer's ward. But his physical limitations ensured he couldn't wander.

Twenty feet from his open doorway, she stopped and took a deep breath. "Any advice?"

"First of all, relax. It'll be all right." Grant reached out and rubbed her bicep.

"The last time I was here, the visit didn't go well. He got really angry." Shame flooded her. She hadn't known what to do when the Colonel's temper had exploded.

"I know," he said. "I don't want you to be shocked at his appearance. He's fading. Honestly, I think it's a blessing. A man like him shouldn't have to live like this. If he wasn't the toughest, most stubborn man on the planet, he wouldn't still be here."

Hannah swallowed. The hallway smelled like death. Most of the residents of this wing were here to die, the Colonel included. No amount of disinfectant or air freshener could sugarcoat that hard fact. "How often do you see him?"

"I try to get here at least twice a week."

"I didn't come in September. I should have, but . . ."

"It's OK." Grant shrugged. "He doesn't know. His short-term memory is nonexistent. He doesn't remember me. He has no idea I was here last Thursday. Every time I visit, he thinks I'm someone else."

"How do you deal with that?" Staring at the Colonel's open doorway, horror and fear curled inside her, waiting to unfurl. The hospital bed, the IV, the air of hopelessness, all brought back the memory of sitting at her mother's side with the sole goal of minimizing her pain while she died over the course of several months.

"Coming here is for his benefit, not mine. My only goal is to give him a pleasant hour or two in the middle of what have become endless days of mental and physical misery. I let go of expecting him to know me. He doesn't remember anything that happened over the last twenty-five years, but sometimes he surprises me with clear recollections of our childhood or his. When I bring the kids to see him, he thinks Carson is one of us boys and Faith is you."

"You bring the kids here?" Sure, now a six-year-old could handle what Hannah couldn't bear.

"Only if Ellie can come with me. So if the Colonel's in a bad way, she can take the kids home. But he seems to have his best days when they're here. Their presence perks him up. He doesn't know specifically who they are, but he always senses they're family."

"So what should I do?"

"Play it by ear," Grant said. "The hardest thing for me is remembering not to call him Dad. It confuses him, and he gets upset when he knows he should be remembering something and the information isn't there. I always address him as Colonel or sir. That appears to take the pressure off. Then I just go with the flow."

"You make it sound easy."

"We both know it isn't." Grant gestured toward the door. "Let's see how he is today."

Hannah's insides trembled as she stepped toward her father's room. Grant put his hand on her elbow, and she tried to absorb some of his confidence.

The Colonel was asleep. Hannah couldn't suck back the quick and quiet gasp as she registered his deterioration. His face was gaunt, his hands skeletal. His skin had tightened, as smooth as plastic, over his bones. Under the white linens, his body had shrunken. She had few memories of the Colonel before the explosion, bits of images and impressions that littered her mind like confetti. But even confined to a wheelchair, he'd been a formidable presence. Now his body was barely a shell.

A clip from her childhood played in her mind. The Colonel zooming through the forest on his specially rigged ATV. He'd been paralyzed in Desert Storm, but back then, he'd been determined to stay active. His descent into madness over the past few years had been the ultimate kick in the face for a man who'd confronted trial after trial with a warrior's courage. It was as if Fate just wasn't happy until she'd broken him.

Anger and hurt welled up in Hannah's chest at the overwhelming unfairness.

Grant squeezed her arm. She ripped her eyes off her father's shrunken figure and stared at her brother. Grant had inherited the Colonel's size and natural leadership. The stubborn gene had been passed to all the Barretts. But their father was a soldier through and through. He'd shown his love for his children by pushing them as hard as new recruits. There was enough of Mom in Grant to soften his hard edges. He bonded with Carson and Faith in a way that had been impossible for the Colonel. Grant would never leave Faith behind, and he'd never exclude her, even unintentionally, and he wouldn't put those two kids through drills that could break twenty-year-old men.

Grant walked to the bedside and inspected the bags hanging off an IV stand.

Hannah shuffled to her father's side. Within a few seconds, lack of movement allowed anxiety to build in her bloodstream like a toxin.

"Colonel?" Grant touched Dad's hand.

The Colonel opened his eyes, confusion and suffering clouding the once-sharp blue of his irises. "Gary?"

Hannah bit back a tear. The Colonel's younger brother had been dead for fifteen years.

Grant didn't miss a beat. "I brought you a visitor."

The Colonel's head moved on the pillow. His eyes blinked on Hannah. Recognition, then affection dimmed his pain, and relief flooded Hannah. He knew her.

All his joy came forth in one word. "Hope."

The sound of her mother's name from his lips nearly took out Hannah's knees.

"Don't just stand there, Gary," the Colonel barked in a raspy, weak voice. "Get Hope a chair." He coughed, the effort of issuing orders clearly taxing his lungs.

Grant rounded the bed and set a visitor chair behind Hannah. His hand on her shoulder steadied her legs.

This visit is for the Colonel, not for me.

She willed her disappointment away. It slunk to the wings and sulked, waiting. She knew it would be back.

Her father turned his hand over. His fingers curled in a *Come here* gesture. Hannah closed her hand over his, leaned over, and kissed his cheek. The strength of his grip around her fingers surprised her. She eased onto the plastic seat.

"Beat it, Gary," the Colonel said with a slight jerk of his head. "I want to be alone with my girl."

Wiping tears from her cheeks, Hannah laughed. Even impending death couldn't break the Colonel's fighting spirit.

With a sad smile, Grant bowed out, but Hannah knew he'd be lingering in the hallway, within earshot, in case she needed him.

"I'll walk again. I promise," the Colonel said.

He thought it was 1991, and he was just returning from Iraq. How often did he have to relive that awful time?

He squeezed her hand. "Don't cry. Everything's going to be all right."

And, oddly, it was. Hannah wiped her cheeks. He was too weak for much conversation, but he seemed to be content to sit in silence and hold her hand. When he fell asleep, his face was relaxed and peaceful. She waited until his breathing leveled out before slipping from the room.

"He thought it was just after the explosion." Hannah stopped at the nurses' station to pluck a tissue from the box on the counter.

"That happens. Are you all right?" Grant wrapped an arm around her shoulders and steered her down the hallway toward the exit.

"The best visit I've had with him in years, and he thought I was someone else."

"He can't help it. I know you're hurting, Hannah. But *he* had a really good hour, and you gave it to him."

"I know," she sighed. Outside of her hometown, she fared better, but here in Scarlet Falls, painful memories overwhelmed her. She was instantly reduced to a nine-year-old girl left behind while her father took her brothers on an outing in the woods. He usually let her go if she asked, but he'd never been happy about it. And the fact that she always had to justify her inclusion spoke volumes of their relationship.

Her therapist had not been surprised she had trouble forming attachments.

Grant pushed the door open, and they walked out into the daylight. The breeze swept cool over her face, but the sun rallied for warmth on her skin. Her brother started toward the truck. "Do you want to talk about it?"

"Not really," Hannah said.

"I'm here for you when you're ready."

"When did you get so touchy-feely?" She regretted the snipe as soon as it left her lips. "I'm sorry. That was bitchy."

"I won't let you push me away, Hannah." He stopped in the middle of the parking lot. "Mom's death was devastating. For me, it was a hell of a lot easier to fly in for two weeks a year and let Lee handle the family. We drifted apart over the years, but Lee's death taught me that was a mistake. We all let him down. I won't let that happen again. We need each other. "

Hannah thought the opposite. To her, Lee's death reinforced how much it hurt to lose someone she loved.

"After Mom died, I didn't want to be here either, but now, raising Faith and Carson, being with Ellie . . ." Grant paused, as if the intensity of his feelings for his new family was too much to explain. "In a way, it was easier to sever all those connections and let my career take over. Getting shot at overseas was less scary than taking on the responsibility for Lee's kids. But I didn't know what I was missing."

"Are you this determined to rein Mac back into the fold?" she asked in an attempt to divert the conversation to their youngest brother, who was the wildest of them all.

"Don't worry. Mac is next on my list. *After* you." Grant had their father's piercing blue eyes, and the sharpness of his gaze pinned her in place. Hannah looked away, her lungs tightening until little dots appeared in her vision.

Her new phone rang. Royce.

"Hold on. It's work." She stepped away from a frowning Grant and answered the call as if she were in the middle of the ocean and Royce was tossing her a life ring. "Hello."

"How are you?" Royce asked.

"Better," Hannah lied. After the visit with her father, she felt empty, every drop of emotion wrung out of her body. This is why she stayed out of Scarlet Falls. Visits home drained her.

"I'm glad to hear it." He sounded doubtful.

"Did you get my e-mail?" She could hear the sounds of traffic over the line.

"I did."

"Well?"

"I'm not sending you anything," Royce said.

"What?"

"You are supposed to be recuperating, not working."

"I can do both."

"Not this time." Royce's voice softened. "I'll never forget how pale you were when I saw you in that parking lot. I thought you were dead, Hannah." He paused. "I told you in Vegas. Your job will be here when you're fully recovered, but I won't allow your ambition to get in the way of your recovery."

"But—"

"No buts." Impatience sharpened Royce's tone. "I care too much about you to let anything happen to you." His voice deepened. "But I will say that I miss your company."

Hannah had no words. When she went back to work, she and Royce were going to have a long conversation. She liked him in a professional, friendly way. That was it. She wouldn't allow him to destroy her reputation.

"Feel better, Hannah. Maybe if you rest, you'll be well enough to join me in Madrid." Royce hung up, leaving her listening to an empty line.

She walked back to the car. Grant was in the driver's seat. She climbed in, and he started the engine.

"Everything OK?" He backed out of the parking space and shifted into drive.

"Yes." The lie came out of her mouth automatically.

Instead of driving off, he studied Hannah's face. The car trembled, waiting for the brake to be released. Grant's face tightened. "You don't have to pretend with me."

"Then no." Hannah rubbed the ache in her temple. "I don't know."

"If there's one thing I understand, it's total confusion." Grant nodded as if her change of answer pleased him. He moved his foot, and the truck eased forward. "You're going to get through this. Everything's going to be all right."

"That's exactly what Dad said."

"Lee used to say it, too."

"I don't know how they could both be such perpetual optimists," Hannah said. "Dad was paralyzed, and he just plowed ahead, pretending everything would turn out fine, and we both know Lee had his share of problems."

"He made the best of a bad situation." Grant pulled out of the parking lot. "When you're going into combat, you plan extensively for worst-case scenarios, but you can't focus on them. To do the job, you have to believe you're going home in one piece." Grant released his grip on the steering wheel and shook his hand as if he'd been clenching it tight enough to stiffen his knuckles. Maybe he wasn't as recovered as he seemed.

Hannah turned to his profile. "You don't have to pretend with me either. How are you, really?"

"I'm all right. The VA hooked me up with a PTSD support group. But I miss Lee, and I worry about the kids." A smile loosened his face. "Having Ellie helps. I'm going to ask her to marry me at Christmas."

"That's great." Hannah patted his shoulder. She approved of Ellie one hundred percent. She was loyal, kind, and totally in love with Grant. How many women would be willing to take on a man with PTSD, a willful infant, and a traumatized little boy? "I'm so happy for you. How is living with her daughter and grandmother?"

"Chaotic but good." Grant stopped at an intersection and turned right. "We're getting into a rhythm. Everybody pitches in."

"You all seem happy and busy."

"The kids don't leave me much time for reflection. Faith won't remember any of this, but I worry about Carson. His parents were murdered. Something like that is bound to leave a scar."

"You're doing great with him."

"He'd like it if you visited more."

"I'll try," Hannah said.

"Where are you going next?"

"London." She hoped. Sort of.

"Don't be a stranger, Hannah," Grant said. "I never understood how important family is to my sanity. Dad had Mom. That's how he got through his days after the injury. After she was gone, he just couldn't hold it together anymore. She was his lifeline. Today, you gave him his memory of the happiness he had with her, even if it was just for a little while. That's priceless."

Hannah nodded. It hadn't been priceless. It had cost her. But Grant was right. She needed to put her own expectations and needs aside.

"You'll visit him while I'm away?"

"Yes." How would she get through *that* by herself?

"I know you spent most of your life trying to please him, but that's in the past. You can't hold on to it. Let it go. You'll feel better."

"He wasn't interested in having a daughter." There. She'd said it. It sounded pathetic and selfish coming out of her mouth. The man was paralyzed and dying, and she couldn't let go of her childhood daddy issues. Sad. Just sad.

"He didn't mean to slight you. He just didn't know what to do with a girl. He grew up with four brothers and went to military boarding school. He honestly thought you'd be happier doing girl stuff with Mom. He was always so surprised when you wanted to go camping or hunting with us."

"If I didn't do all the wilderness excursions, I wouldn't have spent any time with him at all." Even with tagging along, she'd always felt like an afterthought. And on that note, time to change the subject. "What time is your flight tomorrow?"

Grant's glance told her he wasn't finished with the conversation, but he'd let her off for now. "Disgustingly early."

"Need any help getting the kids packed?"

"No. We're about done. Carson is so excited, I doubt he'll sleep at all, and Faith is up half the night anyway." Grant steered the truck through a bend. "If you need anything, Brody will be around. He might stop in."

"Why?"

Her brother lifted a big shoulder in a faux shrug. He wasn't fooling her.

"I don't need a babysitter."

"Didn't say you did."

"Are you trying to fix me up with the cop?"

"Of course not." He gave her a quizzical look. "Where did that idea come from?"

Where *did* that idea come from?

"Because you can keep your bromance with Brody to yourself." Hannah lowered the window an inch and welcomed a stream of country air into the cab. "How did you end up so tight with him?"

"We're not tight." Grant laughed. "But he's ex-military, too. Takes one to know one, I guess."

"Brody was in the military?" She wouldn't have guessed. While Grant was all barely contained aggression, Brody always seemed to be completely in control. Usually, his Mr. Cool act annoyed her. During Lee's murder investigation, Hannah had barely held on to her emotions, but the cop's never faltered.

"He did four years in the navy to pay for college, then worked with the Boston PD before moving here."

"Why would anyone come to Scarlet Falls?"

"That's a question you'll have to ask him."

No, thank you. She had no intention of getting to know Brody that well. Though the fact that Grant obviously knew Brody's background but wasn't talking piqued her curiosity. *No piquing.* She needed to stay focused. "I'm only here for a week. I doubt the topic will come up."

But she was sure she'd be seeing Brody soon. She'd sent him the e-mail, not that there was much he could do.

As soon as they arrived back at the house, Hannah booted her computer and checked her inbox. Scanning her messages, she froze at a subject line: *Jewel.*

Chapter Eight

When a body was dumped in the great outdoors, insects were the first responders. The faint drone of insect wings buzzed in the background as Brody got out of his unmarked police car. He skirted the rusted skeleton of a child's bike. The old rail yard was a grave site for more than unused freight cars. The enclosed area was a dumping ground for everything from abandoned vehicles to rotting mattresses. It was an excellent place to acquire tetanus—or dispose of a body.

He walked past an SFPD cruiser. Two teenagers, a boy and a girl, stood next to the vehicle's bumper. The boy shoved his hands in the kangaroo pocket of his hoodie. The girl, dressed in leggings and boots, wrapped a knee-length sweater tightly around her body as if she was freezing. Brody bypassed the kids. He'd interview them after he saw the body.

Twenty feet of wet weeds separated the dirt road from a patch of waist-high scrubby plants. Treading carefully, Brody skirted a used condom and ducked under a strip of crime scene tape. Near the center of the space, a body sprawled next to a tractor tire. The wind shifted, and a fresh meat scent hit his nostrils.

The sole female in the small SFPD, Officer Stella Dane stood on the periphery writing on a clipboard. She turned serious blue eyes on him. "The medical examiner should be here any minute."

Brody's gaze shifted to the body. The victim lay on her back, her arms flung out. His gaze fell on her face. Disgust segued into anger. The victim's features were pulp, and her skull partially smashed. She was dressed in a gray "I Love NY" sweatshirt and a light jacket. The bottom half of her body was naked, but dead pine needles, leaves, and loose dirt partially covered her. She didn't seem to be positioned in any particular way. Her body looked truly dumped.

He allowed himself one brief *Who could do this to another human being?* before settling back to work. He couldn't bring her back to life, but he could catch the guilty bastard and make sure he never hurt another woman.

"Those kids found her?" Brody asked.

"Yes," Stella said.

"Did they say why they were here?"

"They were taking a drive," Stella deadpanned. Kids came to the rail yard to engage in one or more of the teenage triple threat: booze, drugs, and sex. "The boy said he walked out here to relieve himself and nearly stepped on the remains. I didn't press them or search their vehicle. They could have hightailed it out of here, but they chose to do the right thing and report the find. Besides, they've been traumatized enough today."

"Agreed," Brody said.

His gaze swept over the ground, still spongy from a rainstorm the previous day. Two empty water bottles and a Styrofoam fast food container had blown up against the knobby tire. Dirt and scratches covered all three items, as if they'd been here a while. Except the random litter, nothing appeared out of the ordinary—other than the presence of a corpse. He spied a cigarette butt. "Is the county CSI team on the way?"

"Yes." Stella checked her watch. "They should be here any time."

With limited resources and a small police force, Scarlet Falls relied on Randolph County and the state police for assistance.

The afternoon had been warm and sunny, and blowflies had found the body. Ignoring a swarm of insects, Brody leaned in for a closer look at the victim. He looked past her ruined face. He saw no obvious or visible knife or bullet wounds on the body, as if the trauma to the head wasn't enough. Under splatters of mud, a rusty stain discolored the front of her shirt. Blood. Pine needles and a dead oak leaf matted her long dark hair. She was slender and small to average in size. Bruises mottled her legs. A small heart tattoo adorned her right hip. Though her face was battered beyond recognition, her body seemed young.

Young, slender, long dark hair. *No. It couldn't be.* Brody couldn't stop the sharp intake of foul air. He straightened. "Do you know where Chet is today?"

"No, sir." Stella's pencil paused. She lifted her gaze to meet Brody's. Her mouth went grim. "You don't think this could be Teresa, do you?"

"I doubt it. Last time Chet got close to her, she was in New York City, but that was last winter. She hasn't been seen around here for years." Brody stared at the famous New York City heart logo on the victim's sweatshirt. A mental image of a troubled teen with long dark hair appeared in his mind. His gaze moved back to the ruined face, and his stomach soured. He couldn't match the brutalized body in front of him to his memories of Chet's daughter. "It's probably not her." His instincts were telling him this wasn't Teresa, or maybe Brody simply didn't want to think this savagely beaten young woman was his friend's daughter. "But the general physical description fits. So let's keep Chet away from the scene."

"Good luck with that."

Brody sighed. Once Chet found out they'd found a body that roughly matched his missing daughter's description, keeping him away from the case would require a tranquilizer dart dosed for a black bear.

A door slammed, and Brody looked toward the road. A car parked on the shoulder. The medical examiner got out and opened his trunk to don coveralls and boots. As animated as one of his subjects, Dr. Frank Jenkins was not known for small talk. He approached the clearing and pulled the zipper of his tan coveralls from his stomach to the base of his neck.

"Afternoon, Frank," Brody said.

Frank acknowledged him with a nod as he set his kit on the ground and gloved up. He scanned the body and surrounding scene. His face tightened as he leaned over the corpse, and he murmured under his breath, "Someone beat the shit out of her."

After an initial external examination, he lifted the victim's sweatshirt and examined the torso. Brody could see the darkened skin along the victim's left side. Upon death, blood pooled in the lowest part of the body. Lividity became fixed within six to eight hours. The victim was now positioned on her back, indicating she was killed elsewhere and dumped.

The sounds of car doors and voices drifted over the clearing. A three-member team of the Randolph County Crime Scene Investigator unit approached, their hands full of cameras and plastic containers that resembled tackle boxes. They waited in silence for the ME to finish his initial assessment. No one wanted to irritate Frank. After he waved them into the scene, they began by circling the corpse, measuring distances, and snapping pictures. They started at the outside of the clearing and spiraled inward. Frank issued orders while they worked.

"What can you tell me, Frank?" Brody asked.

"You know I hate to guess, Brody."

"And you know how important these first few hours are to my investigation, Frank. I won't hold you to anything. Just give me somewhere to start." Brody lowered his voice. "For Chet."

Frank frowned at the body. "Do you have any specific reason to believe it's his daughter?"

Brody glanced around. He didn't want any false statements getting back to Chet or to the media. "Nothing beyond basic description. I'd like to ease his mind if possible."

Frank met his eye. "My preliminary observations. Victim is female. Caucasian. Body is slender. Hard to age her with the amount of damage to her face, but skin and muscle tone indicates she is likely young. Facial trauma will make identification by appearance impossible. From the bruising patterns on her forearms I'd say she tried to block the blows, maybe even fought back a little."

"Maybe we'll get some DNA under her nails," Brody said.

"We can hope." Frank scratched his bald head.

"Time of death?"

Frank's lips pursed. Hands on hips, he stared back at the body. "Twelve to twenty-four hours. I'll narrow that window when I get her on the table."

"When do you think you'll get to the autopsy?"

"First thing tomorrow morning. I'd do it tonight, but I don't have the staff available. I won't half-ass it, though. I'll get the body fingerprinted ASAP."

"Thanks, Frank," Brody said.

"I hope it's not her." The ME turned back to the clearing. Brody watched him slip paper bags over the victim's hands to protect any tissue that might be lodged under her fingernails.

Don't we all. Brody walked through the scene with the lead crime scene investigator. They agreed on the search perimeter and discussed evidence to be bagged. Brody pointed out the used condom by the lane. "Plus, the usual soil and bug samples."

"Hey, Brody." A tech brought him a slip of paper. "We found a receipt in her jacket pocket."

Brody brightened with thoughts of store surveillance tapes and an easy visual ID. "A receipt?"

"Unfortunately, it's a generic register tape. No store name." The tech showed him a small plastic baggie containing the paper. "I'll get you a copy of this."

"Thanks." *Why is it never that easy?* Brody squinted at the paper. She'd purchased cigarettes yesterday at eight in the evening. Today was Sunday. She'd been killed between four p.m. Saturday and four a.m. Sunday. This receipt just narrowed the likely window. She was probably alive at eight p.m.

Brody headed toward the teenagers. Stella broke into a jog to catch up. In the street, she introduced him to the seventeen-year-olds, who confirmed the accidental finding of the body. Stella had already taken their statements, driver's license numbers, and contact information, so Brody let the kids go home, despite the faint scent of marijuana wafting from them. Like Stella, Brody was willing to give them a break for doing the right thing. They climbed into an aging Honda and drove off. A van from the medical examiner's office parked in the Honda's place. Two attendants jumped down from the cab, opened the back, and wheeled out the gurney.

"Oh, no." Stella tapped his arm and pointed down the road. A dark blue sedan pulled onto the shoulder near the gate. Chet got out and walked toward them.

"What do you have?" Chet braced his hands on his hips. His suit jacket and white shirt bagged on his frame. He'd given up eating real food when his wife died.

Brody tried to act casual. "Road crew found the body of a dead woman. The ME's crew is collecting her now. Scene is being processed by county."

Chet turned and took a step toward the woods.

Heart bleeding for his friend, Brody planted a hand in the center of Chet's chest. "Don't go back there."

"I heard she's young and has long dark hair." Chet knew everyone in law enforcement and emergency response, from the clerk's office to animal control. Someone had called him.

"It's probably not her," Brody said quietly. "But you don't need to see. Don't torture yourself."

"Move your hand, Brody." Chet spoke through clenched teeth. "If there's any chance that woman is Teresa, I have to see her."

But Brody held fast. "Please. Don't do this." Once Chet saw this woman, he would see her every time he closed his eyes.

Morgue attendants wheeled a stretcher through the grass toward the road. A black body bag was strapped to the gurney. Chet held up a hand to stop their movement.

Frank, walking next to the body, stepped up. "Are you sure? We have no proof it's her."

Chet nodded. "I need to see."

"Brace yourself. Once this is in your head, you won't be able to get it out." Frank waited for Chet's tight nod before he unzipped the bag. The crew had wrapped the body in a white sheet to preserve evidence. Frank peeled the sheet off the upper part of the body, leaving the unclothed lower half covered.

Chet flinched. His face went gray, and his lips mashed together until every drop of blood was forced out of them. His gaze fell to the "I Love NY" logo on the victim's T-shirt, and the light in his eyes dimmed faster than taillights on a car speeding away in the darkness.

No one spoke. Just as Chet knew all the municipal employees, the entire town knew his story as well. Three years before, his fifteen-year-old, mentally ill daughter had run away. Chet had been unable to track her down for a year. He'd caught sight of her last winter, in New York City, but she'd evaded him. He'd stopped actively searching since her eighteenth birthday this past spring, when Chet had taken his vacation and spent two weeks trying to drown himself in Johnnie Walker.

Frank straightened the sheet, zipped the bag, and motioned for the attendants to roll onward. He paused and spoke in a low voice to Chet, "We'll take care of her."

Discomfort at the ME's unusual display of emotion spread through the group in a wave of bodies shifting position.

"I'll have her dental records sent over to your office," Chet said.

The morgue crew loaded the body into the van and drove away.

"I'm going home. You'll fill me in later?" Chet spoke to the grass at his feet.

"I will," Brody answered. "I can stop by your place when I'm done here." He didn't want Chet to be alone while he waited for news.

"No need. I'll be fine." Chet's jaw tightened. "I have work to do." He turned away, then paused, his face nearly as gray as the corpse's skin. "This isn't the first time I've seen a body that could be hers."

But it might be the last.

"Let me remind you that you can't base an identification solely on very basic physical characteristics," Brody said.

With slow steps, Chet walked back to his car. He drove off slowly, as if even his vehicle were weighted with despair.

Brody watched the sedan disappear, frustration and sadness filling him. Then he went to his car and brought up Teresa's file on his laptop. The photo was several years old.

Stella leaned into his vehicle through the open driver's door. "It's possible, but I wouldn't put money on it."

"Hard to tell. I haven't seen her for a long time." If that body was Teresa, how would Chet survive? He'd given up actively searching for her, but there was still hope that someday she'd come home. And even if she didn't, he knew she was out there somewhere, alive. What would he do if he learned she was gone for good?

"When will we know for sure?" Stella asked.

"Chet's been through the identification process before. He doesn't have Teresa's fingerprints on file, so dental records will be compared when Frank x-rays the body in the morning. Hopefully, the X-rays won't match, and Chet will have his answer before lunch."

In the meantime, Brody was going to do everything in his power to identify the dead woman and prove she wasn't Teresa.

Stella went back to her duties. Brody checked his cell for messages. The sun sank over the trees, and the forensics team broke out overhead lights and turned them to high noon. The next twelve hours were going to be the longest in history. Chet was going to have a very bad night.

Chapter Nine

Jewel opened her clenched fist and stared at the business card she'd snatched off the floor of the woman's car. Hannah Barrett, whoever she was, had tried to help her. But look what she'd gotten for her good deed. Mick had cracked her good. She'd gone down hard. Had Mick and Sam gone back for her after they'd dragged Jewel from the car? Maybe Mick killed her. Maybe Mick was going to kill Jewel.

Maybe that would be best.

The last six months had made her feel less than human. Most people treated their dogs better, except Mick. He starved and beat Butch, too. Asshole.

Sunbeams slanted through the dust-encrusted window high on the opposite wall. She licked her cracked lips. She'd been freezing all night, but the temperature in the shed had been rising all day. Sweat soaked her skirt and top. Dirt stuck to her damp skin. She straightened her leg to ease a cramp. Pain wracked her torso, her ribs screaming with every breath.

What day was it? Sunday?

Death couldn't be too far away. She couldn't last another day without water. The desert climate wasn't natural to her. She never thought she'd say it, but she missed Toledo. At this point, she'd be happy to go back to her mom's house and deal with the new boyfriend. Lenny's abuse seemed like nothing after the hundreds of men since she'd been grabbed off the street and brought here.

Mick was a master at causing pain. He wasn't going to forgive her this time, and if he ever learned what else she'd done . . .

Stupid is exactly what she was. All that risk for nothing. She'd thought she was smarter than him? That she could take him down? She shuddered. This beating was bad, but Mick could do much worse. But the worst thing was, despite her current misery, she could still envision escape. She didn't *want* to die.

The cuffs dug into her wrists. She rubbed them in the dirt to move them to a fresh quarter inch of skin. The dog whined at the back of the shed. Jewel inched to the wall and stuck her hand in a two-inch gap between the dirt and the side of the shed. A wet nose sniffed her fingers. As the dog licked her hand, Jewel's eyes filled. Too bad Butch couldn't dig her out.

Footsteps outside the shed filled her with hope and dread. She wanted out of this shed, but Mick was pissed. Would it be better to die slowly of dehydration? If Mick did it, he'd make sure it hurt.

The door opened. Jewel tried to slide backward, to get as far away from her visitor as possible.

Lisa stood in the opening, a bucket in her hand, a plastic bag in the other. Behind her, Jewel could see Butch chewing on a large hunk of red and raw meat.

Walking through, Lisa closed the door. Jewel squinted up at her. Silhouetted against the sunshine, Lisa looked as pale as a cloud. The skin of her shoulders and arms were nearly glowing white. The sunshine rarely touched her skin.

"Stupid bitch. I don't care if Mick kills you. How dare you fuck up my life?" Lisa squatted in front of Jewel, grabbed her hair, and lifted her head off the ground a few inches. "Last thing I want to do is go back to working. Did you actually think you could get away?"

With her head craned backward, Jewel's throat was too stretched and dry for a response.

"Mick wants you clean, but if I was you, I'd drink this water first or you're gonna be dead by tomorrow morning. Not that I care, but I don't need Mick any madder than he already is. He wants you alive."

Pain seared through Jewel's scalp. Lisa opened her fist, and Jewel's head smacked into the dirt. Lisa put the bucket within reach. Jewel got her knees under her body, lifted her shoulders, and stuck her trembling hands into the bucket. She lifted a palmful of water to her cracked lips. The cool moisture slid down her throat. It tasted of rusty pipes, but she didn't care.

"Is Mick here?" Her voice creaked.

Lisa shook her head. "I ain't never seen a girl piss him off as much as you, but this time, girl, you fucked up big-time."

Lisa dug a bar of soap from her pocket and tossed it into the dirt. "Get washed. Put those stinking clothes by the door."

For an ex-whore, Lisa had an OCD thing about being clean. She showered three times a day, as if she couldn't get the scent of men and sex from her skin, even though she hadn't worked in the whole time Jewel had been here. Sam made her do nasty things, but at least he was only one man.

Lisa took a key from the pocket of her ripped shorts. She unlocked the handcuffs on Jewel's wrists. "You make one wrong move, and I'll hurt you. After what you done to me, I'd like nothing better."

Jewel rubbed her wrists, cupped another handful of water, and drank. She wiped her mouth with the back of her hand. "Why do you do what they say?"

"Because I have no interest in being dead, and this is the best I've ever had it. Unlike you, I appreciate three meals most days and a place to sleep at night. Now that you pulled this stunt, guess who has to do your hours?"

Well, that explained Lisa's anger. Mick was making her work. Jewel wasn't going to get any help from her.

Not wanting to be sitting in mud, she dragged the bucket a few feet away from her corner and began to wash. She stripped off her filthy clothes. The water cooled her skin. As she lathered her body, she took stock. She couldn't see her face, but her lip didn't feel too bad now that she'd had some water. Just a bit swollen and sore on one side. The big bruise on her ribs was the only mark Mick had left on her. How had he made her hurt so much over her entire body without leaving much evidence?

Practice.

She shivered, goose bumps rising on her thighs. Best not to think about that. She used her cupped hands to rinse, making sure to keep both soap and dirt out of the remaining water in the bucket.

Lisa kicked the dirty clothes to the door. "Back to the corner."

Jewel contemplated rushing her. Could she overpower the other woman in her weakened condition?

"Don't even think about it." Lisa reached into her pocket and pulled out a knife. She unfolded the blade with one quick, practiced flick of her wrist. The desire to hurt Jewel shone from her eyes.

Jewel went back to the corner. She was still hot and hungry, but she no longer felt like she was going to die at any moment. The bucket of water was still half full. She could save it for later.

Lisa reached into the plastic bag and took out a Styrofoam container and a change of clothes. She handed the items to Jewel. The water had nearly evaporated from her skin already. She tugged on the shorts and T-shirt, then opened the container. Half an order of fries. They were cold and nasty, and obviously someone else's leftovers, but she ate them. Couldn't afford to be too particular about her calories. The salt tasted spicy on her swollen lips.

"That's all you get." Lisa collected the dirty clothes and shoved them in a black trash bag.

"Thanks," Jewel said.

Lisa flushed, her eyes turned angry. "Don't thank me. You ruined everything. We lost a night's income and a good location, plus Mick has to lie low. He's pissed. And I sure as hell don't want to go back to hoing. So don't look to me for favors."

And with that tender statement, Lisa kicked over the bucket. The remaining water poured into the dirt. A tiny rivulet wound its way to Jewel's knees. No water for later.

Lisa gestured with the blade. "Put the cuffs on."

Her chance for escape, as slim as it had been, was gone. With a sinking sensation in her belly, Jewel squatted and fastened the handcuffs around her wrists.

Lisa left the shed. The padlock closed with a metallic snap.

There couldn't be more than a few hours of daylight left. She'd had enough water to keep her alive until tomorrow. But then what? What did Mick have planned?

Chapter Ten

Hannah blinked the airbag dust from her eyes. The dashboard light cast menacing shadows on the man's lean face as he leaned into the car and dragged out the screaming girl.

"He's gonna kill me," she sobbed.

Terror rounded her eyes as she scrambled for a hold on the car seat. She reached for Hannah, panic stiffening her fingers into desperate claws. Hannah struggled to move, but her body was held fast by the seat belt. The latch refused to release her. The space between them grew as if being stretched.

"No!" Hannah's fingers worked at the jammed belt release.

Jewel's face blurred and shifted until it was little Carson being carried away, his small body kicking and fighting for freedom, his eyes pleading with Hannah to save him.

Fear squeezed her lungs in a vise grip. Her breaths locked down.

Hannah jolted. Her body jackknifed to a sitting position. Light-headed and confused, she drew in a lungful of painful air. She put a hand on her chest. Under her sweat-soaked T-shirt, her heart rapped against her ribs like insistent knuckles. She'd been well and truly immersed in her nightmare. Despite her disorientation, she knew the dream hadn't woken her.

What had?

Pushing away the confusing jumble of images, she focused on her surroundings. Moonlight slanted through the blinds onto the duvet, and a dull headache throbbed in her temple. Accustomed to waking in a different hotel every few weeks, she found the change of scenery no surprise, but the intimacy of the homey decor unsettled her.

A storm of barking erupted downstairs. Again? She checked the clock. Four a.m. Grant and the family had left in a flurry of excitement, and Hannah had gone back to bed only an hour before. But she was glad to have been woken. She didn't need to experience the terror of that dream. She had enough anxiety. Today was Monday. Whatever end was going to come to Jewel would happen tomorrow, and the Las Vegas police were no closer to finding her. As if failing Jewel hadn't been enough, her imagination had reconstructed the events of last spring until Carson hadn't been saved either. Eight months later, the memory of the week little Carson had been targeted by Lee's killer still haunted Hannah's sleep.

She swung her legs out of bed. Out from under the heavy comforter, the chill settled on her damp skin. She snatched a sweatshirt from the foot of the bed and tugged it over her head. Barefoot, she crept out of the room and down the steps. Dog tags jiggled, and she turned her head to locate the sound. Her hearing was almost back to normal. More barking told her AnnaBelle was in the rear of the house. Hannah walked down the dark corridor into the kitchen. Light flooded the backyard. The hair on Hannah's nape quivered. Something or someone had tripped the motion sensors. Her gaze swept the lawn. The grassy area was clear. She squinted into the dark beyond the light's reach. Something moved near the creek. The dog growled, and fresh sweat broke out between Hannah's shoulder blades.

"Shh." She reached down and placed a hand on her head to silence her.

A gust of wind rattled the windows and rustled the branches of the giant oak in the center of the yard. Hannah moved to the pantry, opened the door, and examined the alarm panel mounted on the inside wall. Round lights blinked in a steady and reassuring green line. The security system was armed; all zones were quiet. She closed the pantry door and glanced out into the darkness again. An intruder would trip the alarm, but out in the country, help wasn't around the corner. It could take the police twenty minutes or more to respond to a call.

A lot could happen in twenty minutes, and the Colonel hadn't raised a damsel in distress. He'd raised a damsel who caused distress.

Hannah retraced her steps. In the upstairs hall, she went into the master bedroom. In the walk-in closet, she located Grant's gun safe and spun the combination. The heavy door opened to reveal a hefty collection of weapons. Three rifles, a shotgun, a few handguns, her father's combat knife. Her Glock was in the bottom drawer. She grabbed her holster and a full magazine before closing and locking the safe. In her room, she dressed in jeans and a sweater. With her gun in hand, she went back downstairs. The dog was still growling at the sliding glass door.

Wind gusted again. Carson's tire swing swayed. Beyond, in the darkness, movement caught Hannah's eye. A large body bounded in the shadows. The deer flashed past, the light catching red in its eyes as it sprang through an open area and disappeared into the woods.

Hannah looked down at the dog. "Really?"

The dog pricked its ears forward and focused on the door. She emitted another low growl. Maybe it hadn't been the deer. AnnaBelle whined.

"Oh, no. We are not going for a walk at dark o'clock."

The dog kept watch for another ten minutes, then she yawned, stretched, and trotted across the room to curl up in her dog bed.

"At least one of us can sleep."

Several hours remained until dawn. Too keyed up to go back to bed, Hannah returned to the door and stared out into the darkness. The lights had gone out. Whatever had been moving around in the backyard was gone. She went to the couch and sat down, setting her gun and holster on the coffee table. If the kids were home, she'd have secured her weapon. But this morning, she was very much alone.

ᛟ

The motion lights went out, leaving the yard dark again. The big farmhouse blotted out a chunk of night sky. From the cover of the woods, Mick raised the binoculars to his face and focused on the back door.

Hannah Barrett. Long and lean, with her fresh face and just-out-of-bed hair, standing in her designer-perfect kitchen, symbolized every woman who would never be his. She was staring at the spot where he'd been standing just minutes ago. It felt as if she could see him. As if their eyes were meeting. As if she knew what was coming. Despite the cold night, excitement warmed his blood.

Mick backed farther into the woods. A branch swiped his head. Cursing, he swatted at it. He'd forgotten how much he hated the outdoors.

She moved away from the window. He needed to go. Couldn't be caught out here in the daylight. He skirted the property, staying just inside the trees, until he reached the road. He'd parked the car behind a clump of evergreens on the other side of the road. But watching from a distance hadn't been enough.

He'd gotten too close, close enough for the dog to sense him and wake her. The motion lights had been a surprise. A security system was a possibility. He needed to case the place in daylight, but this wasn't a neighborhood. People did not walk past houses in the middle of nowhere. Getting Hannah Barrett wouldn't be easy like all the other women he'd grabbed. She was no dumb runaway.

Sunday had been a wasted day. He and Sam had dumped the body before dawn, then gone back to the house. The dogs in the kennel had been barking nonstop, so he'd tossed them some food and then crashed. He hadn't woken up until night. But then, being up all night was normal for him, and the time difference between here and Vegas had screwed up his hours further. At home, it was one in the morning, and he wouldn't be going to sleep for hours yet. It had all worked out for the best, though. He'd gotten here in time to see the family leave an hour earlier, everyone except the blond.

She was in there, and she was alone.

Patience was a virtue, but Mick wasn't a virtuous man. He didn't want to wait until the opportunity to grab her presented itself. He wanted her now. His fingers curled into a fist and punched his thigh.

If only he had something—or someone—to relieve his frustration.

Chapter Eleven

At seven o'clock Monday morning, Brody parked his sedan in front of Jim's News Agency. He went inside. The scent of tobacco hit his nose. Not cigarettes. He walked through the store. Rows of displays filled the long, narrow shop. Books and magazines occupied two aisles. The third was filled with tins of pipe tobacco. Brody picked up a red tin. Cherry-flavored. A whiff of the tin brought back memories of his grandfather. He carried it to the register.

An elderly clerk sat on a wooden stool behind the counter. Three people lined up to pay for their items. Brody waited while the clerk rang up their newspapers, coffees, and packs of cigarettes. Brody put the tin of tobacco on the counter and paid in cash. The clerk gave him his change and a receipt.

"Is the ink always red?" Brody asked.

"I've been working here five years. Been red that whole time." The clerk's dentures clacked.

Not the store where Jane Doe bought her cigarettes.

"Thanks." Brody left the shop. He tossed the tin on the passenger seat of his car. Why had he bought tobacco? He didn't smoke. He hadn't thought about his grandfather in a long time, but today, he missed him.

He was midway down his list of local cigarette vendors where Jane Doe might have purchased her pack of smokes. He'd spent most of yesterday evening generating a list of newsstands, liquor stores, convenience stores, and gas stations that sold cigarettes within ten miles of Scarlet Falls. Following the receipt was a long shot, but for the moment, it was the only clue Brody had at his disposal.

He'd pared his initial list down to a dozen of the most likely possibilities. He crossed any large chain stores off his list. A large franchise would have its name at the top of the receipt. He'd already visited two independent gas stations and a convenience store. No matches.

He started his car and drove four blocks to park in front of Smith's Food Mart. He stepped through the door and walked toward the register. The familiar smell of coffee and newsprint brought the vision hurtling through Brody's imagination. He was transported back to another convenience store, when a simple stop for coffee changed Brody's life forever, the day he learned a few important life lessons: Even a veteran cop can freeze like a rookie when confronted unexpectedly with an armed robber pointing a gun at a hostage's head. Just because your partner has twenty-five years of experience in law enforcement doesn't mean he'd ever drawn his gun in the line of duty. When wearing body armor, a bullet to the chest felt like being struck by a baseball bat. PTSD sucked, and having your spouse walk away while you're dealing with the ugly fallout sucked more. Finally, killing a man, even in a justified shooting necessary to defend innocent lives, leaves a permanent stain on a man's conscience.

"Excuse me, are you in line?"

Brody startled. His heart was sprinting, and the back of his shirt was damp with sweat under his jacket. A woman with a quart of milk in her hand stood next to him.

"No, you go ahead." He grabbed a copy of today's *New York Times*, tucked it under his arm, and stepped into line behind her.

He hadn't thought actively about the Boston shooting in a long time. Between the close shave with Jordan Brown and the badly beaten corpse, it was no wonder his brain was revisiting the violence from his past.

At the register, he tossed a few dollars on the counter and picked up his change and small white register receipt. Black ink. Narrow tape. Could he have gotten lucky?

He went back to the car, pulled out his copy of Jane Doe's receipt, and compared the two. The fonts and spacing were definitely different. He grabbed his list and marked off the two stores. This was pointless. He didn't even know if the dead woman was a local. She could have bought those cigarettes fifty miles from Scarlet Falls. But what else was he going to do? He tossed the newspaper onto the passenger seat of his car.

The interior of the vehicle smelled like cherry tobacco, and the scent brought back bittersweet memories. His grandparents had been married for fifty-three years. In that time, they'd buried their only child and raised Brody. Despite their grief and the added pressure of unexpectedly being saddled with a young child, he'd never seen anything but love between them. Sure, they argued, but always with respect. They'd handled life's traumas and dramas by supporting each other. In their eighties, they'd still held hands. Though Brody's marriage hadn't withstood the test, he knew what was possible. If he ever did it again, he wouldn't settle for less.

Looking up, he stared at a Dunkin' Donuts three doors down. Hannah Barrett and her supposed weakness popped into his head. She'd be alone today. After the incident in Vegas and that distressing e-mail, he should stop in and check on her. His desire to see her had nothing to do with the hollow space the Jane Doe case had left in his gut or the fact that he was suddenly, inexplicably thinking about his grandparents, his ex-wife, and the fact that he had no one on this earth to call family. But he knew instinctively that seeing Hannah would clear his mind of the violent reruns. So, what did that mean? Brody had spent most of the last eight years alone, but this was the first time he'd felt lonely.

ᴡ

Barking startled Hannah. She jerked to a sitting position. The remote hit the hardwood, and two AA batteries popped out and rolled under the sofa. AnnaBelle raced into the room, thrust her nose in Hannah's face, and returned to the door. On the turn, her paws sent a throw rug sliding into the wall.

"What now?" Hannah blinked. The morning sun poured through the windows, nuclear-bright. "A squirrel on the porch?"

The ringing of the doorbell was punctuated by the dog going bonkers again.

This was domestic bliss? But even with the craziness, the thought of an impersonal room in a five-star London hotel, complete with a feather bed, blackout shades, and room service, held no appeal.

Hannah stood and stretched, her back aching. She must have dozed off after the deer incident. She went to the door and peered through the peephole. Brody stood on the porch. As if he knew she was looking, he raised a white box in his hands. Hannah's gaze darted from the pink-and-orange logo to his face. Lean and weathered, he wasn't classically handsome or polished like Royce, but if she was keeping score, Brody took all of the points for masculinity. Royce used far too many personal grooming products to be a manly man. But then, she'd been raised with military men. Bug-out packs had room for spare ammunition and MREs, not wrinkle cream or hair gel.

Brody grinned, and the tanned skin around his eyes crinkled. Her heart did a quick shimmy. She ran her tongue over her teeth. No time to run upstairs to freshen up. *Wait.* She did not preen for men. But she wanted to. She pressed a palm to her forehead.

Not feverish.

Scarlet Falls was a whirlpool, and Hannah was circling the drain. She needed to get the hell out of town before she was sucked under. Every moment she spent here, her job held less and less attraction. Maybe she was caught in a *Doctor Who* episode about parallel dimensions.

Resigned, she retreated to the kitchen to turn off the alarm, then opened the door. "Dunkin' Donuts? That's cheating."

"Boston Kreme." His smile faded as he scanned her face. "You look terrible."

"Thanks."

His gaze raked her from her slept-in jeans and sweater to her likely bed head. "Did I wake you?"

"No. Yes. It doesn't matter." Hannah pressed her fingertips to one closed eye. "What brings you here, Brody?"

His eyes flickered to his brown loafers. "I was passing by."

Hannah snorted. "This house isn't on the way to anywhere."

Brody lifted a palm, feigning innocence. The sincerity in his warm brown eyes could almost convince her.

"I'm sorry. I'm a bitch before I've had my coffee. You're welcome to come in if you like."

"Thanks, I'd love to come in for a cup of coffee and a donut." He stepped over the threshold, forcing Hannah backward.

With a sigh, she turned around and headed for the kitchen. "All right, but be warned. I need a shower, some sugar, and a vat of caffeine before I can hold a conversation without snapping off a head."

"Fair enough." He followed her back to the kitchen. She fed the dog and started a pot of coffee. Surveying the room, he set the bakery box on the counter. His sharp eyes paused on the gun and holster on the coffee table in the adjoining family room. Putting the gun away would have been a good idea. AnnaBelle scarfed her food and padded to the back door. Hannah snatched the leash from its hook.

"Grant and Ellie just let her outside by herself," Brody said.

Hannah stomped into a pair of her brother's boots standing by the back door. "I am not taking a chance of losing Carson's dog while the kid's in Disney World. I have *one* job while I'm here, and that kid has already lost too much. Yesterday I couldn't get her to come in, and last night she went nuts over a deer in the yard. I don't need her running off after the wildlife." She contemplated a row of jackets hanging on wall hooks. "Is it cold out?"

"Yes." Brody got up and walked over to her. He smelled like cedar and spices. His navy-blue sport coat and gray slacks looked good on his rangy body. The jacket bulged around the weapon in his shoulder holster. Her tongue found her teeth again. Not cool. Neither was the way his quiet masculinity affected her.

Smiling, he took the leash from her hand and gently shouldered her away from the door. "Go get your shower. I'll walk the dog."

"Thank you." Hannah kicked off her brother's boots and took her coffee upstairs. Her short hair stood straight up on the top of her head like a rooster's comb. *Ugh.* After a two-minute shower, she brushed her teeth and gave her short locks a quick finger comb. Not that any of this mattered. Brody had already seen the real her. But at least now she didn't look—or smell—like she'd been on a three-day wilderness survival trek.

Back downstairs, she settled at the island and concentrated on caffeine consumption. The door opened, and a wave of cold air swept into the kitchen with Brody and the dog. Hannah double-handed and drained her mug.

Brody shed his jacket and took the stool next to her. He peered into her cup. "Is it safe to talk now?"

"Almost." Hannah suppressed a grin and refilled her mug. She lifted the pot in his direction. "Coffee?"

"Please."

"Cream or sugar?"

He shook his head, settled back, and waited for her to sit down. Then he opened the box of donuts and nudged it toward her. His eyes were full of questions, but she couldn't be bribed. He was behaving for now, but she knew from past experience, the cop had a subtle way of nosing for information. He was a natural at getting people to talk without thinking. He'd make a clever lawyer. But as a cop, he probably didn't like attorneys.

She'd thought he didn't like her. But it seemed she'd been wrong.

Hannah bit into a donut. The explosion of vanilla cream and chocolate icing set off a major foodgasm. Maybe she *could* be bribed.

"You look troubled this morning." He studied her face. "You worried about the upcoming trial or the e-mail?"

"Both." She licked a bit of chocolate icing from her lips and caught him watching. "There's nothing I can do about the change-of-venue request, but the thought of Carson having to testify breaks my heart, and the assault case against Grant worries me."

"The assault case doesn't have much heft," Brody said. "But you should talk to the prosecutor."

Hannah smiled. "It's so hard to get a straight answer out of a lawyer."

Brody laughed. "It certainly can be."

Grant had beaten the hell out of the man who'd killed their brother. Over the past eight months, Hannah had used her lawyerly powers to keep the charge against her brother at bay.

"The circumstances were extraordinary. Regardless of the letter of the law, your brother is a soldier with post-traumatic stress. Considering his exemplary military service, I have trouble believing any jury would hold his actions against him. The scumbag he beat up murdered his brother and sister-in-law and tried to kill the rest of his family. Grant was protecting them, and he lost control. If the assault wasn't tied to a high-profile murder case, it wouldn't be an issue."

The criminal defense attorney she'd consulted agreed, but she'd put him on retainer in the event the case against Grant went to trial.

Hannah nodded. "Opposing counsel is simply doing his job. He's pulling every thread he can find in hopes that he can unravel the case. That's how the system is supposed to work." Even though, at the moment, she hated every legal right given to Lee and Kate's killer.

"Isn't that what you would do if it was your case?" Disapproval hardened his eyes.

"I don't think I could be a defense attorney, not after Lee's murder," she said.

"I guess not. But none of this tells me why you're sleeping with your gun handy." And there it was. Patient as always, he'd cleverly circled around to the question he'd undoubtedly wanted to ask since he'd seen her weapon on the table.

Hannah bristled. The cop hadn't liked her handgun back in March. Obviously his opinion hadn't changed since then. "I have a permit, and if I'd had my gun in Vegas, the situation would have had an entirely different outcome."

"I wasn't commenting on the legality of your weapon." Brody's gaze bore into hers. "I want to know why you think you need it in Scarlet Falls."

Hannah flushed and blinked away. "The dog wouldn't stop barking last night. Turned out to be a deer in the yard."

Brody's head tilted, as if her statement didn't compute. "It's not like you to be easily spooked."

"I wasn't spooked. I was being careful. There's a difference."

"So the dog barked, and you armed yourself and went out to investigate?" His voice rose.

Irritation warmed her. "What are you talking about? Why on earth would I go outside if I thought there was a possible threat out there? I would never leave a secure location to chase an unknown danger in the dark. That would be stupid. Do you think I'm an idiot?"

"Um. No." He leaned back, confusion creasing his features. "I'm sorry. I misunderstood."

"No, you assumed," Hannah shot back.

"You're right. I did. But I learned from experience that you Barretts have a habit of taking matters into your own hands. Like that night in Vegas."

"Only when absolutely necessary." It was Hannah's turn to look away. "What was I supposed to do, ignore her? I called for the police. There wasn't any help handy."

"I know. I'm sorry." Empathy softened his eyes. "Now tell me why you slept with your gun." He covered her hand with his. For a few seconds, the contact was good, solid, and grounding. Royce's similar touch had spurred her to snatch her hand away, but this she welcomed. Brody's touch felt right and tempted her to return the intimate gesture. Then the weight of his hand grew heavier and heavier until she felt trapped. Brody was a good man, but she was not staying in Scarlet Falls.

She pulled her hand out from under his, got up, and moved across the floor to refill her mug. Distance. She needed a larger personal boundary. Ten feet of kitchen wasn't enough. Brody waited, his features steady with patient determination.

"I received another e-mail."

Brody's body went rigid. "When?"

"Late yesterday. Same message."

"And you're just telling me now?"

"I forwarded it to the detective in Vegas. Untraceable, just like the first one." Hannah's control slipped. "I can't get that girl's face out of my head. She needed help, and I failed her."

Brody was on his feet and in front of her in two strides. He took her by the arms. "You can't take responsibility. You tried to help her, at great risk to your own safety. Most people would have run the other way."

"Maybe if I'd have run away, I could have gotten help."

"No." He gave her a light shake. "You can't go back and second-guess your decision. At the time, you made the call based on the information you had in front of you. That's all anyone can be expected to do. It's too easy to question your actions with the benefit of hindsight." His face went grim. Clearly, Brody had his own demons. "Besides, you just said it two minutes ago. You had no options. You couldn't toss her to her assailant and run for it."

"I didn't have time to think. I just reacted." Hannah met his eyes. "The end result is the same. He dragged that poor girl away, and I couldn't do a damned thing about it."

"Hannah, you did your best."

"It wasn't good enough." Hannah pulled out of his grip and turned away. She went to the window and stared out into the yard. Two robins hopped across the back lawn. One shoved its beak into the damp grass and ripped a worm from the turf. Its body flailed until the bird ate it in two gulps. A shudder rippled from Hannah's torso to her bare feet. The pretty scene faded, and she pictured Jewel being yanked from the rental car, her arms pinwheeling, small fists landing useless blows on her attacker's shoulders, the girl's terror palpable even to a stunned Hannah.

She rubbed her arms. "Do you think those e-mails are really from her? That she's reaching out for help?" If she was, her time was running out.

"Why would she contact you and not the police?"

"I don't know. It doesn't make any sense." Hannah covered her mouth with a fist. "But it feels like I'm letting her down all over again."

"Do you do this all the time?"

"Do what?" She glanced over her shoulder.

Brody's arms were crossed over his chest, and his gaze had sharpened. "Not allow yourself to be human. Try to shoulder the weight of things that aren't your fault."

She turned back to the yard. The robin moved on, its hunger not sated by one slender earthworm. Predators never stopped hunting.

"Some things are out of your control." The harsh edge to Brody's voice made her want to ask him what terrible event from his past had been out of his control. Who or what had put the pain in his eyes?

"I know that. Doesn't mean I have to like it." There would be more girls at risk, Hannah knew, all because she hadn't seen that SUV coming.

"I'm glad you're all right."

"You're not going to lecture me on putting myself at risk?"

"Maybe later." Brody smiled. "You are what you are. Sometimes all that ferocity is a little scary. But I wouldn't change anything about you."

A different kind of spark heated Hannah from the inside as she registered the respect—and interest—in Brody's eyes.

"But you could dial down the impulsiveness just a little. Your family doesn't deserve to bury another member." A grim frown dimmed his expression.

"True." A sad sigh slipped from Hannah's lips. "But I wish I could have helped her."

"I know," he said. "Would you like me to call the Las Vegas police and see if they've made any progress on the case?"

Hannah hesitated. "What's the point?"

"They might tell me more than they'd tell you."

"Maybe." She considered his offer. *What could it hurt?* "OK. Thank you." She opened her phone and read the detective's name and number from her contacts list.

Brody checked his watch. "I have to go. Please, if something freaks out the dog—or you—call me."

"Thanks, Brody."

"I'll stop back tonight and let you know what I find out."

"You don't need to go to any trouble."

"It's no trouble. I'll bring dinner."

She walked him to the door. "I don't need—"

"Stop. I didn't say you *needed* me to bring you dinner, but I'd *like* to." Brody put a finger under her chin and studied her face.

"Thank you." Hannah's pulse scurried. He wasn't going to kiss her. Was he?

Before she could contemplate how she felt about that idea, he lowered his hand and backed away. "Get some rest, Hannah. You look tired." He went out the door into the chilly morning air.

That's it?

Hannah stared after him for a minute. Nudging the dog out of the way, she closed the door. "What do *you* think about Brody?"

AnnaBelle wagged her tail.

"You like everybody." Hannah patted the dog's golden head. "I have to admit, Brody's different. Obviously, the man has never heard of flattery."

But somehow, Brody's concern had more of an effect on her than all the empty compliments she'd been given by other men trying to slip past her professional defenses and into her bed. He was honest. He didn't just *look* at her; he *saw* her.

And she liked it. Most of the time.

"I don't want to deal with this right now," she said to the dog. "I have nothing to do today. I'm going back to bed. No barking."

The dog wagged its tail but made no promises.

"Maybe if I get some sleep, Brody won't tell me I look awful when he comes back tonight." Hannah's steps quickened. He was coming back.

"Don't get excited," she said to the dog. "Nothing is going to happen with him. I'm not staying in Scarlet Falls."

Chapter Twelve

The medical examiner's office was located in a concrete building in the county municipal complex. In the antechamber to the autopsy suite, Brody suited up in a gown, booties, and cap. He pulled the clear plastic shield over his face and went inside. The smell of disinfectant didn't come close to masking the odor of a decomposing corpse.

Frank peeled off his gloves.

"You started early." As much as Brody felt the need to attend the autopsies of his cases, he was relieved to have missed this one.

"I have a full plate today. But I didn't want her to wait, in case . . ." Aw. Frank did have a heart. Nice to know. "So far nothing's come back on the fingerprints. Too bad Chet doesn't have a set for his daughter. That would have made it easy to rule her out. Waiting must be tough." Frank paused. "Anyway, I'll send the DNA in for analysis. The lab promised to expedite the testing. Results should be back in two to three days at the latest."

"Did you compare her dental records?" Brody asked.

"I did. I can't comment. Her teeth and jaw are too damaged, and some of her teeth are missing." Frank shook his head. "I requested a consultation with the state police forensic odontologist." The New York State Police made forensic dental specialists available through the Medicolegal Investigation Unit. "He's at a conference and won't be available until Thursday."

"Blood type?"

"The corpse is O positive. So is Teresa Thatcher and about one-third of the general population."

But it was one more factor that weighed in favor of the remains being Teresa. *Damn it.* Poor Chet.

Brody looked back at the body. An autopsy tech was sewing up the Y-incision with huge black stitches that railroad-tracked up the corpse's abdomen. "What can you tell me? I'd like to clear this up for Chet faster than three days."

Frank lifted the clear shield over his face, grabbed a paper towel from a wall dispenser, and mopped the sweat from his head. "The victim is female, Caucasian, approximately seventeen to twenty-five years old, brunette, brown eyes, five foot six inches tall, one hundred ten pounds. Internal organs show no evidence of drug or alcohol abuse, to be confirmed by toxicology reports."

"Scars?"

"None. She wasn't wearing any jewelry. Nothing in her pockets except the cigarette receipt we discussed at the scene. We found fibers in the wounds on her face and numerous hairs on her body and clothing," Frank continued. "Facial trauma was inflicted both pre- and post-mortem, with fists and a blunt instrument, possibly a baseball bat. No tissue under her fingernails. She was raped, but we didn't find any semen. So he likely used a condom. Cause of death was asphyxia by manual strangulation."

Frank moved to the table and positioned both of his hands over the base of the victim's bruise-ringed throat, just below her ruined face. Hovering two inches above the body, his thumbs lined up with two dark purple circles at the base of her neck. "The hyoid bone was fractured. The bruising pattern suggests she was strangled from the front."

Frank stepped back. He moved to a nearby sink and turned on the water with a foot pedal. "This was a very violent death, but the greatest injuries to her face were inflicted post-mortem."

"He beat her up, raped her, strangled her, then beat her again?"

"Yes." Frank lowered the clipboard.

Rage. Pure rage, thought Brody. "Can you tell me anything about the killer?"

"The deepest bruise on her neck is from his right thumb. He was likely right-handed. The span of his hands indicates an average to large adult male."

Not much help. Ninety percent of humans were right-handed.

"I'll let you know as soon as the rest of the lab tests come back."

"Thanks." On his way out of the suite, Brody glanced back at the corpse. A visual played in his head: a man sitting on top of this woman, punching her, wrapping his hands around her throat until she stopped breathing, then getting up and pounding her face with a bat. His gaze strayed to the photos fixed to a board next to the body, close-ups of her injuries, X-rays of her throat. Manual strangulation was a very intimate means of murder.

Did he know you?

Most murders were committed by someone who knew the victim. In this case, Brody hoped that was true. An intimate killing might be a one-time thing. If not, Scarlet Falls had a very violent and unpredictable killer on the loose.

Brody left the medical examiner and walked across the parking lot of the municipal complex to the neighboring building that housed the crime scene investigator's offices. He paused to sniff the crisp air and clear his nose, mostly, of the foul stench that had accumulated in his nostrils in the autopsy suite. But the scent of death clung with stubborn determination. Two minutes in the morgue, and Brody swore his hair and clothes stank of decay.

The CSI unit occupied a suite of rooms on the first floor. Brody found Darcy Stevens, latent fingerprint examiner, at her desk.

He knocked on the door frame.

Darcy looked up. Though he knew her to be almost fifty, Darcy's coffee-colored complexion was wrinkle free. She wore her hair pulled back in a painfully tight bun. Her suit and blouse were solid black to defy the dark powders intrinsic to her job. Sipping from an extra-large paper cup of coffee at her elbow, she waved him in.

"Hi, Brody." Her voice was deep, the 900-number richness of it countered by her severe dress and hairstyle, no doubt as she intended.

Brody smiled at the picture of a wrinkled newborn tucked into the corner of her blotter. "Morning, Darcy. How's the new grandbaby?"

Handing the photo over, she beamed. "He is eight pounds and four ounces of adorable perfection."

"Wow, that's a lot of hair." Brody gave it back. "How does it feel to be a grandma?"

"Wonderful. I get to cuddle with him all I want, then go home and get a full night's sleep."

"Sounds perfect."

"It is." She slipped the picture into place. "I bet you're here about the Jane Doe that came in yesterday?"

"I am. Have you had any luck?"

"Not yet. I scanned her prints into our regional fingerprint database, but none of the matches the computer generated were true."

"You mean the computer isn't going to spit her ID out as fast as on an episode of *Law & Order*?"

"I wish we could solve all our cases in forty-three minutes. Heck, I wish we could solve all our cases in forty-three *days*." Darcy rolled her eyes. "When the regional AFIS was a bust, I moved on to the state of New York." She stood and rounded her desk. "Let me see if the query came back with any hits."

"You've been busy this morning."

"I came in early. Frank called me last night. You know we'll do whatever we can to determine if this woman is Chet's daughter. Besides, whoever killed that woman needs to be locked up before he hurts someone else."

Darcy would have taken the fingerprints herself, so she'd seen the body. With determined strides, she crossed the gray tiled floor to a row of computers on a long table pushed against the wall. Sliding into the seat, she moved the mouse. The blank screen came alive. She moved the blinking cursor to a row in a table. "We have eleven possible hits so far, and the query is still running." She glanced up at him. "The visual comparisons will take some time. Depending on how many results that computer cranks out, I might be here all day. Want me to call you when I'm done?"

Unlike television crime dramas, where a mug shot of the suspect or a photo of the victim popped onto the screen in seconds, in real life, the ridge lines of each possible match had to be manually compared by a certified latent fingerprint examiner. The matching software erred on the side of caution and generated as many matches as possible, leaving the examiners to sift through the possibilities.

"I'd appreciate it," he said.

"If none of these match up, I'll try the neighboring states and the FBI."

"Thanks, Darcy."

"How's Chet holding up?"

"As good as can be expected." Brody started toward the door.

"I can't imagine how he deals with it."

"Me either." *Because he doesn't.*

Brody exited the building. A gray and cloudy sky hovered over the parking lot, and the wind that whipped around his neck contained the first real bite of damp New York winter. Autumn had been unusually warm, a brief but welcome stay of pleasant temperatures, but now it seemed like Mother Nature was making up for lost time.

His cell rang. Brody answered with the hands-free device on his steering wheel.

"Hi, Brody, Stella here. Have you seen Chet?"

"No, isn't he at the station?"

"He stopped in, then said he was going to interview a witness for the drug bust you two shared last week." Stella dropped her voice. "But that was an hour ago, and he's not answering the radio or his cell. The chief has been looking for him. I just thought you might like to know."

"Thanks. The interview might be taking a long time." But these follow-up interviews consisted mostly of quick clarifying questions. None of them should take over an hour, and Chet should have checked in with the station in between stops.

He slid behind the wheel of his sedan and turned toward the station. On the way, he cruised past Chet's place. The former cop still lived in the same house in which he and his wife had raised their only daughter. Brody pulled into the narrow driveway in front of the small Cape Cod in the center of town. He walked up to the stoop and rang the bell. Chet didn't answer. Brody listened but the house was silent. He cupped a hand over his eyes and peered through the sidelight. The house was dark. Worried, Brody circled to the back of the house.

Where could he be at ten in the morning? He didn't have any hobbies. Back in his car, Brody called Chet's home number and cell phone. No answer on either line. He left a message on Chet's voice mail saying that he didn't have any new information and was just checking in.

He drove to the station, his thoughts consumed by the dead woman, Chet's absence, and Hannah's predicament.

There was nothing he could do about Chet except work the case. But maybe he might be able to help Hannah. He left a message for the cop in Vegas. He did a new search in ViCAP, the FBI's violent crimes database, with the information provided by the medical examiner. While he was searching for similar crimes and missing women, he'd check the National Crime Information Center to see if there were any missing persons reports in Nevada for a teenage girl named Jewel.

But Brody couldn't get the violence of the attack on Jane Doe out of his head. Darcy had put it best: the assailant had to be found before he unleashed his rage on another innocent woman.

Chapter Thirteen

Brody pulled into the driveway of the Barrett house. Pizza box in hand, he exited the vehicle. A Honda Accord parked next to his sedan, and a redheaded woman got out.

"Thanks for doing this, Kailee," he said. "I owe you."

"No, you don't. I'm glad to help." Her long red ponytail flipped as she pivoted and walked toward the front porch. Brody rang the bell, and a dog exploded into barking.

A few minutes later, the door opened. Hannah stood in the foyer, blinking at the light as if she'd just woken up.

Brody ushered Kailee into the house. "Hannah, this is Kailee. She's a police sketch artist. She's not here in an official capacity, but as a favor to me."

Hannah brushed a hand through her hair, but instead of settling into place neatly, it remained stubbornly disheveled as if she'd been sleeping on it. Disheveled looked good on her, he decided. Real rather than perfect and polished. Sexy. Not many women could pull off the just-out-of-bed look.

She held out a hand to Kailee. "You worked with Carson, didn't you?"

Kailee smiled. "Yes."

"He talked about how nice you were." Hannah gestured toward the kitchen. "Please come in."

Brody set the pizza box on the island and opened the lid. "I told you I'd bring dinner."

Hannah sniffed. "Mushrooms?"

"Of course," Brody said.

"You seem to know all my favorite foods." Suspicion laced Hannah's voice.

"Must be a coincidence," Brody lied.

She cast him a quick not-buying-it glance before opening the fridge. "I have Coke, beer, wine, and iced tea. Or I could make coffee."

Kailee slid a sketch pad and thick pencil out of her bag. "I'd love a Coke."

"Me, too," Brody said.

Hannah poured three drinks and pulled plates from the kitchen cabinet. Brody opened the box, took out a slice, and folded it. He didn't bother with the plate. Hannah ate two slices, then broke off a piece of crust for the dog.

Kailee stopped at one, then wiped her hands on a napkin. She lifted her pencil. "Why don't we get started?"

Brody got up. "I'll walk the dog while you work."

Kailee did her best work if the witness was relaxed and open, two words that did not describe Hannah. The fewer people in the room the better.

He headed for the edge of the woods. They skirted the forest at a leisurely pace. The scent of wood smoke tinged the air, and Brody wondered if Grant's fireplace was usable. The dog sniffed and snuffled along the ground. Brody was in no rush. Kailee would need some time, and maybe if he gave the dog a long walk, AnnaBelle wouldn't wake Hannah in the middle of the night.

They looped the property twice and started back. A twig snapped. The dog's head shot up, and her tail went rigid. She lunged into her collar. Brody two-handed the leash as the retriever went from docile to defensive in a heartbeat.

"Easy." He pulled her back to his side, but the fur on her back was up, and a growl sounded low in her throat. AnnaBelle didn't growl often. Something was out there. Something only the dog could sense.

And Hannah hadn't reset the alarm when Brody went outside.

Keeping the retriever close, Brody hurried back to the house. Through the kitchen window, he could see Kailee and Hannah working together. Kailee was smiling, talking, and sketching. Hannah's body was tense, and her brows were furrowed in concentration. The young artist had her hands full getting Hannah to relax.

Brody led the dog inside. He unsnapped the leash and locked the door.

Kailee set down her pencil and turned the pad around. "We did two drawings. Hannah has a good eye for detail." Kailee turned the sketch pad toward him.

The first sketch was of a scroungy-looking man in his late twenties. Goatee. Thin. Mean eyes. The second sketch made Brody suck wind. Beyond the physical characteristics—young, dark hair and eyes—Kailee had captured the terror and hopelessness on the young girl's face. Brody didn't have to ask to know Hannah was seeing that face every time she closed her eyes. No wonder she was exhausted.

"Are you satisfied with the pictures?" he asked Hannah.

"Yes." She nodded. "Both of these look accurate. I'm not as comfortable with my memory of the second man to attempt a sketch." She turned to the artist. "Thank you so much, Kailee."

"I'm glad I could help." Kailee tore the sketches from her pad. "I need to go. I have a date."

Brody walked her to the door. Then, considering the dog's behavior in the woods, he escorted her all the way to her car and watched the young woman drive away. When he went back into the kitchen, Hannah was still sitting at the island, staring at the drawings. Maybe this hadn't been a good idea.

"You should reset the alarm."

"What did you see?" Hannah asked.

"Nothing. But the dog was agitated."

Hannah went into the pantry, and Brody heard a few digitized beeps.

"Are you all right?" he asked. Reliving the attack had obviously been stressful, but Brody knew better than to let her suppress the images. Denial didn't work in the long run.

She nodded. "I can't get her out of my head. Why didn't the Vegas detective have me do a composite image?"

He looked over her shoulder. "I talked to him this afternoon. Because of budget cuts, they're using a computer program instead of artists. The new software is giving them problems. Composites are a crapshoot, but Kailee is unusually good." Brody paused. "You have to take these drawings with the knowledge that your mind could be conjuring up details all on its own. It wouldn't be your fault. It just happens. If Kailee worked with a dozen witnesses, she'd get twelve slightly different images of the same suspect. Everyone sees things from their own perspective."

"So you're saying these drawings might not be accurate?"

"It's hard to say. It's been a few days since the attack. Memory fades fast."

"Then why did you bring Kailee here?"

"Because it's worth a try, and sooner is better than later." Brody also thought taking action might help Hannah. "The Vegas PD hasn't had any luck matching the fingerprints they lifted from the rental car, but if they do, it can't hurt to get these drawings before your memory fades further. Having both fingerprints *and* an eyewitness will strengthen any case." Brody tapped on the picture of the girl. "I'll run off a copy of this. I'm trying to identify a dead woman who also had long dark hair." In fact, Hannah's victim and the woman in the morgue had a few things in common. "I'll be checking missing persons cases. You never know. I could get lucky." His gaze shifted to the sketch of Hannah's assailant. The girl's eyes were full of terror, but this man was freezer cold.

Hannah's gaze was full of the same terrible knowledge. "He's going to hurt her. If he didn't kill her already."

"You don't know that."

"It was in his eyes," she whispered. "And there was nothing I could do about it."

Brody nodded. "I get it. Even if I identify this woman and find her killer, I can't really help her or her family. I can't bring her back to life, and that's all they really want."

"You can't change the past, but you can give them closure." Her eyes softened. She knew what it was like to have a family member murdered. "It helps to know that the person responsible for Lee's death was caught. It doesn't take away the pain, but it's far better than having his killer on the loose."

"I'm glad," he said. What if the dead woman *was* Teresa? Brody would have to take that news to Chet. And even if the dead woman was someone else, he couldn't bring Chet's daughter back—she'd been lost to Chet for years—and Brody would have to tell some other family their loved one had been murdered.

"That girl in Vegas *was* very much alive. I have to live with the fact that she might be dead now because of me."

"You did everything you could. You can't blame yourself because a man chose to commit an act of violence. You were injured trying to help. Most people would have run the other way." Brody understood. Most people sense danger and run the other way. Cops and soldiers run toward trouble. Hannah had the same spirit. It was the very quality that drew him to her.

She was silent. She wasn't going to give herself a break. He glanced around the quiet house. Moping around these empty rooms all day couldn't be good for her. Hannah needed action.

"What have you been doing all day?"

Her brow crinkled. "Replaced my wallet and license. I took the dog for a walk."

"That's it?"

She shrugged. "We napped afterward. The dog was tired."

Not good enough, and he doubted it was the dog that was tired. She was surely still sore from the assault and accident. "Tomorrow, I'd like to take you out to dinner."

"You mean like a date?" Surprise lifted her voice.

"Yeah. Exactly like a date."

Indecision crossed her face.

"It's just dinner, Hannah. No big deal."

"Feels like a big deal," she said.

"We'll keep it casual." But it did, indeed, feel like a real BFD. When was the last time he was this nervous about asking a woman out? Dating seemed like a lot of effort, and he rarely connected with anyone. Until Hannah.

"I don't know, Brody. I'm only in town for another week. Then I'm off to London for who knows how long. I'm not looking for anything permanent."

"I'm aware of that." Too aware. "Just dinner. Say yes. Take a risk. Unless you're afraid," he dared.

Her chin lifted, a spark of challenge brightening her eyes. "You're on. But no funny stuff. Just dinner."

"Deal."

"It'll have to be late, though. I have a follow-up with a neurologist tomorrow." An irritated frown tugged at her mouth.

"What's wrong?"

"Nothing."

"Feel all right?"

"Yes. I'm still a little achy, and my ear isn't a hundred percent, but otherwise, I feel fine." She sighed. "I only made the appointment because my boss won't let me come back to work without official clearance."

Good for him. "So if you pass, you can get back sooner?"

She nodded. "Yes."

"Then why don't you want to go?"

"I didn't say I didn't want to go."

He said, "You looked irritated."

But not as irritated as she looked now. Unfortunately—and perversely—he found the annoyed purse of her lips sexy.

She folded her arms across her waist. "Commuting to New York for a doctor's appointment is inconvenient."

"You couldn't find a doctor closer?"

"My boss is picky. He insisted I see this particular doctor, which is ridiculous and unnecessary."

Brody almost called bullshit and was instantly thankful that she had a boss who was concerned enough to look out for her. "Why don't I take you? Three hours is a long drive if you're not a hundred percent."

"Not necessary. I wasn't planning on driving. I can take the train into the city."

"I didn't say it was necessary. I'll take you to New York. We can have dinner afterward."

"Don't you have to work?"

"I'll take the day off." He was spinning his wheels on his case anyway, and the chief had been on him to take some of his unused vacation. Tomorrow would likely be another day of waiting, and even if the chief wasn't happy, Brody didn't like the idea of Hannah making that long trip alone. Either the victim or the perpetrator of the Vegas kidnapping had e-mailed her—twice. Two thousand miles could be covered in five hours by plane. As a bonus, he'd get to spend the whole day with Hannah. The longer they were together, the more he liked her. And the less he cared about her transient nature or their complicated relationship.

Brody collected his keys from the counter. "What time is your appointment?"

"One o'clock."

"I'll pick you up at nine. If we don't get held up by traffic, we'll have lunch before your appointment."

"All right. Though we both know that won't happen. Traffic in and out of New York is a given." Hannah walked him to the foyer, flipped on the porch light, and opened the door. "Thank you for helping me."

"You're welcome." Brody turned to face her. Tired, her face looked soft. His gaze dropped to her lips. Would it be inappropriate to kiss her now? Because he really wanted to do it. But this wasn't the time, just as it hadn't felt right early this morning. Some things couldn't be rushed, he decided. When he kissed Hannah for the first time, he wanted her completely on board, not upset or confused. It was inevitable, though. He would kiss her. Soon.

"Good night, Hannah."

"See you tomorrow, Brody."

The door closed firmly behind him. He glanced over his shoulder as he stepped off the porch. She was watching him through the sidelight, and he instantly regretted not kissing her when he had the chance.

Chapter Fourteen

Frustration churned in Mick's blood, making him edgy. He lowered the binoculars. Who was the guy walking the dog? His shape was obscure in the dark. Mick could see just enough of the figure to know it was male.

Mick had been staked out in the woods behind the blond's house since darkness fell. His plan had been to snatch her while she was out back with the dog. He wasn't worried about the mutt. Golden retrievers weren't threatening, and Mick was good with dogs.

But that man had stolen Mick's opportunity. He eased back into the woods, taking his time. Dead leaves formed a damp and quiet carpet under his boots as he sneaked away from the house. He crossed the street and ran back to his car, concealed behind some trees.

In the vehicle, he cranked up the heat. The temperature had dropped thirty degrees since they'd left Vegas. Maybe he and Sam should head south after they took care of business here. Forget the frigid Northeast. Everything about this trip had sucked.

He drove back to the house. The dogs were barking so he went out back and tossed them some more food. Sam had wanted to shoot them all, but Mick talked him out of it. The dogs hadn't done any-thing wrong. Inside, Sam was sitting on the couch, his feet up on the coffee table, remote in his hand, eyes fixed on the TV.

"No one's come looking for our host?" Mick asked.

"Nope. Phone hasn't even rung."

"We can't stay here long. Someone will come looking for her eventually." Mick jerked his thumb toward the back wall. "And the owners of those mutts will start showing up."

"Closest neighbor is a half mile away, but you're right. We should leave before we wear out our welcome." Sam looked up. He took one look at his brother's face, pointed the remote at the TV, and turned it off. "Let's go out."

"Where?" Mick went to the table and scooped a spoonful of coke. His supply was getting low. He hated this town. He hated the whole fucking state of New York.

"I don't know. Must be a bar around here somewhere." Sam stubbed his cigarette out in the ashtray. "We need some noise. The quiet is creeping me out."

Mick drove to the highway and cruised a couple of miles. They passed one restaurant. "Is that it? A fucking Applebee's? This sucks."

"Keep going. I'm not in the mood for screaming unless it's female."

Mick was feeling itchy, too. He'd been pumped to take care of the blond tonight. A couple of drinks would smooth him out. His stomach growled for a meal that didn't come in a white paper sack.

"I see something." Sam pointed.

Mick steered the Charger off the next exit. They spiraled the ramp and emerged at an intersection. Andy G's Sports Bar occu-pied the near corner. A hundred yards up the road, a Hampton Inn glowed. A strip mall sat dark on the other. It was only ten, and the grocery store was closed. Small towns fucking sucked. Vegas started to roll at midnight.

"Doesn't really look like our kind of place, does it?" Sam commented.

Mick didn't feel like driving for another hour. He backed the Charger into a spot in the rear of the lot. Not that there were many other cars, but he didn't want some asshole to ding his door. "It'll do."

They got out of the car. The wind blew straight down the back of Mick's neck. He flipped up his hood. Fucking A, he hated the Northeast.

Locking the car, they crossed the asphalt to the entrance. The skinny white bitch who greeted them had a dozen eyebrow rings and ear gauges the size of quarters. A talent show played on a flatscreen mounted on the wall. Across the bar, another TV played a UFC fight.

"I wanna watch the fight," Mick said.

"'Kay." She deposited them at a table with a direct view.

Mick pulled out a chair and sat, still edgy.

Sam tapped his fingers on the table. "Where the fuck is the waitress?"

Only two tables were occupied. A family of four sat in a booth near the door, and a single businesswoman read an electronic tablet over a plate of pasta. The two white-blond rug rats yammered. The nonstop whining tempted Mick to pull out his knife and slit both their pasty little throats. "Place is dead. Probably isn't one. Go on up to the bar and get drinks and a menu."

On his way back, Sam eyed the lone woman as he passed her table. He set two menus and a double shot of vodka in front of Mick. He jerked his head toward her. "I'd be interested in some of *that*."

"*That's* not on the menu tonight." Mick unfolded the laminated cardboard.

"It could be." Sam's pupils were big as manhole covers. No wonder the coke supply was low.

The woman glanced around as if she could sense his scrutiny. The family gathered up their belongings and headed for the door. The two young boys shoved each other.

"Knock it off." The father separated them. A pleasant quiet fell over the bar as they left.

Mick sipped his vodka. "Kids are fucking annoying. Why do people want them?"

But Sam didn't answer. His eyes were fixed on the woman. Mick glanced at her. Wearing a black suit jacket and pants paired with a white shirt, she was in her mid to late twenties. Her brown hair fell in shiny waves just past her shoulders. With little makeup, she was normal-pretty. Wedding ring on her left hand. She was the sort of woman Mick wanted. Sam usually went for T and A. This woman didn't have much of either. Course, that hadn't stopped him with Joleen Walken.

Mick studied his brother. "Not your usual type."

"I know." Sam's eyes gleamed with malice. They should have brought some weed to mellow him out. Coke brought out Sam's mean streak, honed his nasty edge 'til it was switchblade-sharp. "Women like that don't want anything to do with the likes of us. You got to *make* her do what you want. Woman like that might put up a good fight, too."

"We don't want to attract any attention." Mick set the menu down. "I'm getting a burger."

"Sounds good." But Sam's eyes remained on the brunette.

"Cool it." Mick went to the bar and ordered two hamburgers and another round of drinks, hoping the vodka and food blunted Sam's mood. Ten minutes later, the bartender brought their order to the table. Mick settled the bill with cash. They ate in silence. Sam didn't mention the brunette again, and Mick hoped he'd let it go.

He tossed back the rest of his drink and stood. "This place isn't helping. Let's go."

"I'll meet you at the car." Sam veered toward the men's room.

Mick hunched his shoulders against the night air. Vegas might be hell on earth in the summer, but he didn't miss the East Coast damp. He walked across the lot and slid behind the wheel. The leather froze his ass. He'd go back to the house and sleep. Tomorrow, he'd face the blond rested and fresh. She was going to challenge him, and he had payback to administer. His balls ached at the memory of her well-placed strike. She'd pay for that. The thought of extracting his vengeance from her perfect skin sent his pulse on a trip.

Anger and ideas of how to get even churned in his head. He'd never sleep if he was this excited. He opened his wallet and took out the blond's license. Staring at her picture, he imagined her bound, gagged, and naked.

Tomorrow. *You're mine.*

He turned the key in the ignition. A faint cry from behind the car caught his attention. He glanced in the rearview mirror. The brunette slumped against Sam. His brother opened the back door and laid her on the seat. The girl stirred.

"Where did you get her?"

"She was walking toward the motel. No one saw. I had a stun gun in my bag."

What else did his brother have in his duffel?

"Go." Sam slid into the backseat.

Mick leaned across to the glove box. He pulled out a few zip ties and a roll of duct tape. He tossed the items over the seat to his brother. While Mick drove, Sam trussed the woman like a Thanksgiving turkey. She started getting lively, and he zapped her again. When they reached the house, Sam pulled her out and threw her across his shoulder. The dogs barked as they walked up to the mobile home and let themselves in with the key.

The woman let out a scream, the volume muffled by the duct tape across her mouth.

"Shut it." Sam slapped her on the ass. "Or I'll cut your tongue out." She went quiet, her voice dialing down to sobs.

Sam carried her to the bedroom. Tossing her on the mattress, he secured her bound wrists to the headboard. The brunette flopped.

"Why her? Why tonight?" Mick's head spun with the possible complications. "We can't keep snatching women. This isn't Vegas. It's a small town. People will notice."

"I got her for you." Sam sounded hurt. "And I told you no one saw."

Above the gray rectangle, her eyes were round and bright with fear, but she was still struggling.

Women like that don't want anything to do with the likes of us.

The thought of being with men like him or Sam was the end-of-the-world scenario to her. Rage rose in Mick's chest. He deserved a woman like this. Clean. Classy. But they all thought they were so superior. There was only one way he'd ever get one. As usual, Mick would have to take what he wanted. It didn't matter how much money he made, a woman like this brunette or the blond bitch could see through his new car and clothes to his dirty origins. He and Sam were garbage at the curb.

"We can't keep her," Mick said. "She's too old."

A woman like this would be useless to them. Men paid extra for young bodies. The demand was highest for underage girls, and the younger ones were easier to intimidate. Didn't take much to control a teenager. Show them who's boss, feed them some pills, and most of them were compliant. If they weren't, there were profitable ways to dispose of them. This woman had to be near thirty, and she was anything but compliant.

"I wasn't planning on keeping her for long." Sam sat down on the chair by the bed to wait his turn.

Mick turned his attention to the woman. She twisted like a fish on a hook. High-pitched screams sounded behind the duct tape gag. *God damn, she's loud.* "No dead bodies in my trunk."

"Don't worry. I'll figure something out." Sam lit a cigarette. He leaned forward and rested his forearms on his spread thighs. His posture was relaxed, but excitement danced in his dark eyes. "Want me to tie her feet down?"

"No. I'm in the mood for a fight."

Chapter Fifteen

"Could you hurry up, please?" Hannah zipped her jacket to her chin to block the night air. Drizzle fell in a heavy mist and beaded on her nylon jacket.

AnnaBelle sniffed the grass. The dog pulled toward the rear of the property. Hannah let her sniff until they were twenty feet shy of the creek that separated the grassy yard from the woods beyond. Moonlight glistened on the shallow water tumbling across the rocky streambed. The musical trickle would have been soothing, if the temperature had been above freezing.

Hannah stomped her feet to move her blood. Inside her boots, her toes stung from the cold.

The retriever pulled toward the narrow wooden bridge spanning the shallow water. A trail led into the trees.

"Oh, no." Hannah resisted. "We're not going on a hike in the dark. Nighttime walks are backyard only. You should have done all your business when Brody walked you."

The wind gusted, sending leaves cartwheeling across the grass. She glanced back at the house. Lights glowed in the kitchen windows.

"It's warm in there," she said to the dog.

AnnaBelle looked toward the darkness of the trees and whined.

"Oh, sure. You're wearing your fur coat." Hannah hunched against the chill. The temperature seemed to be dropping by the minute. "You have five more minutes. If you have any business to do, you'd better get on with it. I'm freezing."

A scratching sound emanated from the forest. The dog's ears pricked forward, and her body went taut.

Not again.

Hannah tugged on the leash, but moving the large, stubborn canine proved impossible. She lifted her jacket and slid her weapon from the holster at the small of her back. The dog growled and lunged.

She wrapped the leash around her wrist. "No. Come."

What was up with this dog? Normally, except for some barking, AnnaBelle was well behaved and would follow her humans anywhere.

AnnaBelle whined. The dog turned and backed away from Hannah.

No.

Hannah saw the disaster unfolding and was helpless to stop it. AnnaBelle ducked her head, slipped out of the collar, and bolted for the woods. The retriever splashed across the creek and disappeared down the dark trail. *No. No. No!*

She raced after the dog. Entering the woods, she switched on the flashlight and played the beam on the ground in front of her. A carpet of dead leaves covered most of the ground. Tracks would be difficult to find. Within minutes, the futility of her task filled her with panic. She had a vision of Carson crying as Grant told him his dog had run away. She had to find AnnaBelle. That little boy had lost both his parents. He was not going to lose his dog, too.

She needed a bribe and help.

Securing the weapon in her holster, she jogged for the house.

She unlocked the door and disabled the alarm. Brody's lecture about keeping the system armed at all times echoed in her head.

Brody.

She grabbed a flashlight from the kitchen drawer and a package of hot dogs from the fridge. She reset the alarm and went back outside. With the door locked securely behind her, she set off for the woods again. She jogged across the grass and across the bridge, dialing Brody's number as she ran.

ᚥ

Rain pattered on the window of Brody's home office. Sitting behind his desk, he flipped through the search results from the query he'd run in ViCAP. Unfortunately baseball bats and strangulation were popular methods of committing violence, and Brody had far too many possibilities to sift through. The amount of rage directed at the victim pointed toward a significant other or a seriously disturbed killer.

A raspy meow sounded at his feet. He reached down to gently scoop his ancient tomcat, Danno, into his lap. The old cat kneaded his thighs, claws digging in. Wincing, Brody rubbed the orange tabby's head. "Am I keeping you up?"

Danno butted Brody's hand with his head.

"All right. All right." Brody scratched the side of the old cat's face. The purrs that sputtered from the bony body sounded as rough as a lawnmower engine that needed a tune-up. "I get it. It's late and we should be in bed."

The cat jumped to the floor, the sound of his paws hitting the wood surprisingly loud considering he weighed all of nine pounds. He trotted, loose-limbed, to the doorway and cast a *Well?* glance back at Brody.

"I'm coming." He closed his file. The cat was right. Time for bed. His eyes were starting to cross, but he was taking tomorrow off and wanted to make sure he hadn't overlooked a clue. He hadn't.

His cell phone buzzed on the desk. He picked it up and glanced at the display.

Hannah.

His eyes went to the clock. Midnight. Alarm woke him faster than a triple espresso.

"What's wrong?" he answered.

"I lost her." Hannah's voice was breathless, as if she'd been running.

"Who?"

"AnnaBelle. I lost Carson's dog. She took off into the woods."

"Where are you?"

"I'm looking for her."

Unease pulled Brody to his feet. "You're in the woods?"

"That's where the dog went."

Striding down the hall and into the kitchen, Brody tucked the phone between his face and his shoulder and reached for his jacket and keys. "Get back in the house and lock the door. I'll be right there."

"I'm not going back inside until I find this dog," she said.

"Hannah, it isn't safe to be running around in the woods alone in the middle of the night."

"I assure you, I'm fine." The sound of wind and fabric rustling came through the phone. She was out there moving through the dark. Alone. Vulnerable. Maybe *vulnerable* wasn't the best word to describe Hannah. But she was alone, and that was enough to make Brody sweat.

"I'm on my way. I will help you find her. All right?"

"Yes." Her voice hitched. Was she crying?

Hannah had taken on a thug to help a young girl, but the thought of losing her nephew's dog undid her.

"I'll be right there. Will you please go back into the house and wait for me?"

"How long will it take you to get here?" Her refusal to answer told him she wouldn't.

"Fifteen minutes."

"I'll meet you in the backyard." The line went dead.

Swearing, Brody shrugged into his jacket. On his way out the door, he secured his weapon in the holster at his hip. The drive out to the Barrett place seemed longer than usual, even as he pushed the car over the speed limit. Parking in the driveway, he grabbed a flashlight from the glove compartment and jogged around the house. *Where is she?* Spotlights illuminated the rear yard. The wind blew light rain into his face, and silvery shadows played under the big oak tree. Beyond the creek at the rear of the property, the trees loomed black as tar. Brody headed for the woods.

He cupped a hand around his mouth. "Hannah."

"I'm here." She emerged from the darkness. Her pale face shone in the light. Rain darkened her blond hair, and drops of water raced down her temples.

Relief flooded his system with adrenaline. His boots clomped on the bridge as he closed the gap between them.

"She went this way." Hannah turned and walked into the forest.

Brody fell into step behind her. "You shouldn't be out here."

"I have to find Carson's dog. I can't let him lose anything else."

"It's dangerous."

Hannah stopped and called for the dog. They listened for an answering bark. Nothing. Wind rustled in the trees and knocked droplets of water from the foliage overhead. Brody wiped a rivulet of rain from his forehead.

"I waited for you," she said, continuing her path on the trail.

"I appreciate that." Brody's voice went dry.

"Brody, I've been running in the wilderness since I was born. My father was big on survival training. I can build a shelter, rig a snare for small game, find clean water, and start a fire without matches. Plus, I'm armed." She patted her hip.

"I know all that, but I was worried about you," he admitted.

Her sure steps faltered. She halted, her face turning toward him. "You were?"

"I was." He couldn't read her expression in the dark, but her body language was unsure.

The rustle of wet leaves punctuated a few seconds of silence before Hannah resumed her stride. "I'm sorry."

"I know you're concerned about the dog, but Carson would be much more upset if anything happened to you." *And so would I.*

"I hadn't thought of that."

How could that be? "Well, you should have. Do you really think Carson loves his dog more than you?"

"No," she said. "I just never thought about it at all."

"You are important to your family. You have a responsibility to them." He reached across the darkness and took her hand. "No more impulsive risks, all right?"

"I'll try." The sadness in her voice broke his heart.

"Try not. Do," Brody said in his best Yoda voice.

With a short burst of laughter, she gave his fingers a quick squeeze. "Thank you."

"For what?"

"For being here, and for giving me perspective."

Brody tightened his hold on her hand. Did her step lighten, just a little?

"But I'm still going to find this dog."

"I never doubted it for a second." He sniffed. Over the smell of trees and rain, he smelled . . . meat? "What's that smell?"

Hannah pulled a package from her pocket. Brody shone the beam of his flashlight on it.

"Ball Park Franks?"

"AnnaBelle's crack." She opened the top and waved the package in the air. "Retrievers are hunting dogs. Theoretically, she should be able to smell the hot dogs if she's nearby." She stuffed the bag into her pocket and funneled her hands around her mouth. "AnnaBelle! Here, girl."

They paused and listened. Nothing. Hannah strode off again. She moved through the forest with more confidence than Brody. Clearly, her childhood lessons had stuck.

They plowed through a thick layer of wet, dead leaves. He looked behind them. Dark, dark, and more dark. How far had they walked? "Shouldn't we mark the trail so we don't get lost?"

"We're not far from the house." Hannah stopped at a fork in the trail. Crouching, she played her beam on the ground and examined a paw print in the dirt.

Brody leaned over her shoulder. "That doesn't look like a dog print."

"That's because it's a possum track." She stood and pointed her light at one trail and then the other. "You want left or right?"

Oh, no. He was not letting her out of his sight. "We stay together."

She propped a hand on her hip. "Doesn't that defeat the purpose of calling you?"

"We stay together."

"All right," she sighed.

"You realize she'll probably return to the house on her own."

"Maybe. But I can't just sit there and wait."

No, Hannah needed to take action. They tromped around the woods for another hour, until the wet cold seeped through the sleeves of Brody's jacket and froze his fingers.

He shoved his hands into his jacket pockets. "It's getting late. Let's go back and check the house. She's probably sitting on the back deck."

Hannah turned around. Even in the dark, he could read the distress on her features. "I hope so."

How she knew her way around in the dark boggled his mind, but twenty minutes later, they emerged from the forest to stare at Grant's backyard. They crossed the bridge, Hannah's pace increasing to a jog across the lawn.

She drew up at the deck steps. "She's not here."

Brody wrapped an arm around her shoulders and pulled her to his chest. He didn't realize she'd been crying until he saw the tears glistening on her face. Hannah rested her forehead against his chest for a solid minute. Then she pulled away and wiped her cheeks with her fingertips.

"I'm sorry."

"Don't be."

"I don't know what to do. I have to find that dog." She sniffed. "I know what you're going to say. I'm more important than any dog, but it's not a contest. Carson shouldn't have to lose either of us."

He sure as hell shouldn't, Brody thought. "You're right. I'll ask whoever's on patrol tonight to keep an eye out for her. If she doesn't come back by morning, we'll call animal shelters and veterinarians."

A faint bark drifted through the trees. Brody lifted a hand. "Wait. Did you hear that?"

Her head tilted. She shook her head.

Brody strained to listen. The barking grew stronger. "There's a dog coming this way."

"I hear it now." Hannah's voice brightened. "Which direction?"

He pointed toward the woods. They hurried back onto the trail. They picked up the pace, excitement fueling their legs. A squeal and a high-pitched whine echoed. Hannah broke into a run. Brody kept pace. Mud splashed under his boots. A hundred yards down the trail, they entered a clearing. AnnaBelle stood in the center, head down and whimpering. The dog swiped a paw at her face.

"Here, girl." Hannah approached the retriever. "Oh, you poor dog."

"What is it?" Brody directed the beam of his light on the dog's face. Dozens of quills poked out from her muzzle. "Ugh. Looks like she tangled with a porcupine."

Hannah fastened her collar around her neck. "Let's get her back to the house."

Luckily, the dog had been nearly home when she'd been quilled. They tracked mud and water through the back door into the laundry room. In the bright light of the kitchen, Brody and Hannah examined the dog's face.

"That's a lot of quills, and some are in her mouth." Hannah stroked the dog's head. "She needs a vet."

Brody whipped his cell phone from his jacket pocket. "I'll call mine."

"I doubt they'll be open." Hannah glanced at the clock. "It's two in the morning. Is there a twenty-four-hour veterinary clinic nearby?"

"Dr. Albert will pick up," Brody said. The vet's groggy voice answered the call on the third ring. Brody explained the situation and disconnected in less than a minute. "He'll open his office for us. Let's get her in the car."

They wrapped the dog in a beach towel and put her in the backseat of Brody's vehicle. Hannah sat with the dog to keep her from pawing at the quills. "I know it hurts. It'll be OK."

Brody drove into town. Rain glittered on the blacktop. He kept one eye on the rearview mirror and listened to Hannah croon to the dog. The tough hotshot lawyer turned into a marshmallow when kids and animals were in need.

Ten minutes later, Brody turned into the parking area. The vet's office was in a small building next to his house. Light glowed in the clinic windows.

Dr. Albert opened the door. He'd pulled his lab coat on over flannel pajamas and boots. His white hair tufted out from the sides of his head. "Bring her in here." He gestured toward a lighted exam room. A tray of instruments, including a set of pliers, was laid out on the counter.

Brody introduced Hannah to the old vet as he picked up the big dog and hefted her onto the stainless steel table.

The vet set a pair of black-rimmed glasses on his nose and frowned. "I'm going to give her some anesthesia." He patted the dog on the side, shaved a patch of fur on one foreleg, and set up a butterfly catheter. With a syringe, he pushed some medication into the line. The dog's breathing eased, and her body went quiet on the table. For the next thirty minutes, the vet pulled quills out of the dog's muzzle with pliers.

"Does anyone see any more?" He moved the overhead light and lifted AnnaBelle's lips to inspect her mouth.

"I don't," Brody said.

Hannah shook her head.

"Then I'm going to give her a shot of antibiotics." He filled a syringe and injected the retriever's flank.

The dog stirred. Minutes later, her eyes opened, and she gave them a feeble wag.

"You can take her home. She'll probably be tired tomorrow, and you might need to give her soft food for a day or two, but she should be fine. Don't worry. She's not my first patient who thought chasing a porcupine looked like fun."

"Thank you." Hannah reached into the slim purse that hung from her shoulder.

The vet waved her off. "I'll send you a bill."

Brody carried the dog back outside. The rain had picked up, falling from the sky in a curtain.

"Good night." With a wave, the vet jogged across the gravel parking area and disappeared into his one-story house.

Rain hit Brody's head, and the cold was a slap to his still-damp body. He shuddered hard, a wave of exhaustion sliding over him.

Hannah opened the SUV door so he could put the dog inside. Rubbing her biceps, she huddled on the leather seat.

"You know your vet well enough to call him in the middle of the night?" Her voice quivered. A shiver shook her body.

Brody cranked up the heat in the car and directed the vents at Hannah. "My cat is a hundred years old."

She raised a brow and tilted her head. "You're a cat person? I thought men preferred dogs."

"The cat came with the house. I'm not home enough to have a dog, but I like them both." Brody turned the car toward Grant's house. "You're pretty good in the woods at night for a lawyer."

"I told you. My childhood wasn't typical."

"Because your father was disabled?"

"That was part of it." Hannah glanced in the back. Seemingly satisfied that the dog was fine, she settled down and raised her hands to the heat vents. "Even after he became a colonel, my father was an army ranger in his heart. After the explosion, he decided that if he couldn't be a ranger anymore, it was his job to pass along all his skills to his sons."

"Just his sons?"

"I had to beg to go along on all the survival training weekends." Her face turned toward the passenger window.

"Survival training?" Brody prodded. "That sounds serious."

"The Colonel didn't do anything halfway. I remember one particularly bad trip when we lost Lee."

Chapter Sixteen

Hannah dropped her backpack in the foyer. "I'm ready."

The Colonel gave her a quizzical look. "Are you sure you want to come?"

"Yes." Hannah dropped to one knee to lace her hiking boot.

Her father spun his wheelchair to face her. "This is not going to be a leisurely camping trip."

She wasn't slouching, but the Colonel's scrutiny made her feel as if she were.

"I know." She stretched her head toward the ceiling. In school, she didn't advertise her height. At twelve, being taller than most of the boys in your class wasn't an asset, but the Colonel valued size, strength, and intelligence.

"Wouldn't you rather stay home and bake with your mother?" the Colonel asked. "She really enjoys doing that with you."

Hannah flinched. "No."

The Colonel didn't understand why his daughter would want to traipse around the woods with the boys. The Colonel didn't understand her.

"*The boys aren't going to slow down for you,*" *he said, maneuvering to inspect her pack.* "*And the weather isn't on your side. It's going to be cold and rainy.*"

"*Yes, sir.*" *Hannah lifted her chin.*

"*Women don't belong in the field.*" *The Colonel had never been shy about voicing his opinion on women in combat.* "*You know I don't believe in all that politically correct bullshit.*"

"*I do,*" *Hannah said. And so did everyone else. She had to fight for inclusion. Every. Single. Time.*

He sighed and shook his head. "*You can go.*"

Why did he not see that she consistently kept pace with his sons, and in some areas, outperformed them? Because he didn't want to admit his beliefs were outdated and maybe even wrong. The Colonel was old-school military.

Even though Grant was physically superior in every way, Hannah was the marksman. Mac never got lost. He had a wolf's sense of direction. Sometimes she swore he smelled his way through the forest. Lee was the one the other three would have to carry for the next forty-eight hours, and they all knew it. They didn't mind, though. It wasn't his fault.

"*Hannah won't hold us up.*" *The oldest of the Barrett siblings, Grant, stepped up next to her. Six-three, well-muscled, and still growing, he shifted until he was shoulder to shoulder with Hannah. His sheer bulk filled her with confidence and simultaneously intimidated her. On one hand, she knew Grant would see them safely through the weekend. He always did. On the other, how could she ever compete with the likes of him? He was perfect in the Colonel's eyes. Top of his class at the military academy and athletic, he was the boy his classmates turned to for leadership. Even at the age of seventeen, Grant was clearly senior officer material. But then, he'd been raised to continue the Colonel's military tradition.*

The Colonel turned away from her. "*Grant, I'm counting on you to ensure nothing happens to my girl.*"

"Yes, sir," Grant said. No one argued with the Colonel, but the four Barrett siblings all knew it wouldn't be Hannah who needed help.

With a shrug, the Colonel addressed his second son. "Lee, are you ready?"

"Yes, sir." Lee pushed his glasses up the bridge of his nose. At fifteen, he was still waiting on a growth spurt, but it was already evident he wouldn't attain Grant's size or strength. Lee would rather hole up with a book than spend the weekend training in outdoor survival drills.

"Lee, I know you don't enjoy these weekends, but every man needs to know how to protect himself and his family," the Colonel said. "Someday you'll thank me."

"Yes, sir," Lee answered automatically, but he didn't sound convinced.

"Do you mind if your sister goes along?"

"No, sir," Lee said. "She's better in the woods than I am."

The Colonel ignored Lee's statement, but Hannah's heart warmed at her brother's praise. Grant spent most of the year away at boarding school, and Mac favored the forest over human companionship. Lee and Hannah shared a love for learning. Secretly, Hannah preferred books over hiking and camping, too, but she'd never admit that. Not to the Colonel. Today, with light rain beading on the windows, staying home for the weekend sounded tempting. But bowing out might get her labeled a fair-weather soldier. She could be excluded from future weekends. Most of the time the Colonel spent with his children was focused on survival training, shooting, and self-defense, as he sought to pass along all the skills he'd accumulated as an army ranger. It was as if, after that roadside bomb in Operation Desert Storm robbed him of the use of his legs, he was living through his sons, particularly Grant.

"Mac!" The Colonel shouted into the hall.

"Coming." The youngest of the Barretts, ten-year-old McClellan, skidded into the foyer. His half-empty backpack hit the floor at his feet with the metallic clunk of a loose canteen. Whippet-thin, Mac was wiry, quick, and much stronger than he appeared. The Colonel didn't bother

to inspect his youngest son's pack. Mac was part wild thing and could likely exist for years in the forest with nothing more than his instincts.

Their father wheeled himself through the front door and into the dawn.

"Ready?" Grant asked her.

"You bet." Hannah feigned confidence. Honestly, the weekend was going to suck. Two days of trudging through mud and a night of camping on the wet ground didn't appeal, but this was what it took to be a Barrett, and Hannah wasn't going to be left out because she hadn't been born with a penis.

Grant led the way into the light rain. The three younger siblings fell in behind him. Hannah hoisted her pack over one shoulder and headed for the specially adapted SUV their father drove. They piled into the vehicle, and the Colonel headed west into the mountains. Hours later, he stopped the vehicle, and the four children stepped out into a clearing. Hannah zipped her jacket and fished a cap and gloves from her pack. Early autumn had an icy bite. They lined up for last-minute instructions.

The Colonel stayed in the vehicle. Though he was fully capable of getting out of the SUV and into his chair solo, the process wasn't quick, and the mud would be an issue. Depression dimmed the blue of his eyes. The Colonel did his best to ignore his paralysis, but he would have loved nothing more than spending the next two days playing Rambo.

He issued orders through the open window. "Grant, you're in charge." The Colonel held up a walkie-talkie. They all had matching units on their belts. "Stay together. You have the coordinates for the rendezvous?"

"Yes, sir." Grant answered.

"Be safe. See you tomorrow." The Colonel's gesture was more salute than wave. The SUV turned around and drove away, leaving the four children alone in the dripping forest.

Grant unfolded his map. Lee, Mac, and Hannah gathered around. The Colonel was old-school. No fancy GPS equipment was allowed.

Grant tapped a forefinger on a red dot drawn on the map. "Here's where we are, and here's our extraction point." He pointed to another location.

Mac took one glance at the two dots and set off down the trail with a long and contented stride. "Water's not going to be a problem."

Trusting his internal compass, the rest of them followed in single file.

"Ready?" Grant asked Hannah.

"Always," she answered his challenge.

Lee hunched his shoulders against the drizzle. "If we keep up a good pace, is there any chance we can finish this today?"

"No." Grant studied the folded map as he walked. "It's too far, most of it uphill, and we lost daylight to the drive."

"Half the distance today and half tomorrow. We can do that by lunch." As much as he hated these weekends, Lee's optimism impressed her. "Suck it up" should have been their family motto.

The rain intensified until even Mac's shoulders started to droop. Water found its way into the neck of Hannah's jacket. She shivered as a rivulet snaked down her chest. She lowered her chin. Grant picked up the pace, anxious to cover ground. The incline steepened until she strained to keep up. Talking ceased as they saved their breath for the climb. Hannah was grateful the rush of rain on her nylon hood drowned out the sounds of her labored breathing. She stayed tight on her brother's heels. Visibility worsened as rain became downpour. She slipped in the mud, going down on one knee.

Grant stopped to grab her elbow. He shouted over the rain, "Are you all right? Need to stop for a while?"

She shook her head. There was no way she was going to be the one to suggest they rest. No way. Not even if her feet were numb. She'd walk until her legs dropped off before she'd cry uncle.

"Suit yourself." He turned and strode off.

Hannah scrambled to catch up. Rain washed into her eyes, and her legs trembled. Her jacket and boots were waterproof, but below the jacket's hem, rain had soaked the thighs of her pants. The underlying muscles cramped in the cold. She tugged the brim of her hood down lower on her forehead. She could keep up with Grant. Pushing forward, she focused her gaze and her will on the back of his navy-blue jacket. Stopping would be the worst thing. Unless they found shelter and could start a fire, being still would only make her colder.

The rain slowed back to a fine drizzle.

Mac doubled back. Bareheaded, his blond hair was soaked, but he didn't even look cold. "Hey, where's Lee?"

"He was behind me." Shivering harder, Hannah scanned the trail behind them. When had she seen him last?

"Shit." Grant turned and hurried back down the path, Hannah and Mac close behind. "Where is he?"

The trail was empty.

Fear blasted Hannah with a surge of energy. Jogging next to Grant, she cupped her hands around her mouth and called, "Lee!"

"He was behind you. Didn't you notice that he disappeared?" Grant asked.

"I couldn't hear anything over the rain." But it was her fault. She should have been watching out for him. But she'd been so obsessed with keeping up with Grant, she'd forgotten about Lee. "Damn it."

Twenty minutes later, Mac came to a sudden stop. He pointed down the trail. "I see him."

In a shallow trailside ditch, Lee's bright blue jacket stood out among the brown autumn colors.

The path dropped off sharply for a few feet. Lee sat in a six-inch puddle of muddy runoff. Grant jumped down to land next to his brother with a splash. Hannah and Mac scrambled down the embankment.

"What happened?" Grant squatted next to Lee.

"I slipped. T-twisted my ankle." Lee's teeth chattered. His lips were blue. He'd been sitting in a cold puddle of water for at least forty minutes.

"Let's get you out of the water." Grant lifted him from the ditch.

Lee groaned, and his face went paper-white.

Grant set him on the ground. "We need a fire."

"I'll find some dry wood." Mac scampered off into the woods.

"I'm going to take off your boot." Grant loosened the laces. "Ready?"

Lee nodded, his eyes shining with moisture.

"One, two, three." Grant slid the boot off. A moan escaped from Lee's lips.

Hannah stared. Lee's ankle was more than twisted. It was bent at a sharp angle—sideways.

"Shit." Grant stood and rocked back on his heels.

"I'm sorry," Lee said.

"Not your fault," Hannah said. It was hers.

Mac came back with an armload of dry shrubbery. Hannah cleared a place for him to build a fire.

"We're going to splint your ankle and call Dad." Grant opened his pack and pulled out his first-aid kit. "Hannah, I need a straight stick about six inches long."

"On it." Hannah rooted through Mac's pile of twigs and found one with the right diameter. She pulled the folded knife from her cargo pocket and sawed the stick to the correct length, then passed it over.

Grant handed Mac the map. "Find the closest possible pickup location."

Hannah took over fire building, layering the dried brush over the bark scrapings he'd likely taken from the underside of a fallen tree. There was always dry timber somewhere if a body knew where to find it. She dug her waterproof matches out from inside her pack. In a few minutes, she was coaxing a tiny flame to life.

"Thanks." Lee leaned closer to the small heat source.

"This is going to hurt," Grant said.

The sky was darkening.

Squatting like a monkey, Mac tapped on the map. "This is the closest logging road. The terrain looks fairly flat. How are we going to get him there?"

"Going to be a hell of a hike, but I can carry him." Grant glanced at Lee. "Good thing you're skinny."

Lee nodded, pain pushing him past where laughter was possible.

Hannah rooted through Lee's pack for extra layers of clothing. She helped him take off his jacket and tug a fleece crewneck over his head. Then she zipped him back into his waterproof jacket in case the rain started again.

"Can you eat something?" She held a candy bar toward him. "The calories will help with body temperature."

He shook his head. "I can't."

"OK." She repacked her bag.

"We have a plan." Grant unhooked the walkie-talkie from the side of his belt. They all stared at it for a solid minute, dread transmitting between them as if on a sibling frequency, before Grant radioed their father and broke the news. Concern—and disappointment—came across loud and clear in his voice as they discussed the pickup point.

"Are you ready?" Grant asked.

Lee nodded. The color had returned to his lips, but his body was trembling.

"Can you get on my back?" Grant asked. "It's the easiest way to carry you."

"I guess so." Lee's voice shook. Hannah helped.

They trudged through the mud. It took them a full hour to travel the single mile to the logging road. The Colonel waited in the SUV for Grant to load Lee into the passenger seat, then he checked the splint. "Nice job, Grant. What the hell happened?"

"I slipped." Lee rested his head on the window.

The rest of the kids piled their packs in the cargo area and climbed into the backseat. Sitting down never felt so good to Hannah. Her leg muscles went lax.

"I should have canceled the trip. The weather turned out much worse than predicted," the Colonel said in a rare moment of self-doubt.

"But you all reacted well. I'm proud of the way you handled yourselves out there. You worked as a team, and you used your heads to get out of a bad situation." His eyes caught Hannah's in the rearview mirror. "But maybe now you see why women don't belong in combat. If Grant hadn't been there, you couldn't have carried Lee out."

Mac couldn't have done it either, *Hannah thought, but she kept her mouth closed.*

"Hannah would have figured something out," Grant said.

But their father didn't respond. There was no arguing with the Colonel.

"You could have called for help. A rescue team would have come and gotten you." Anger colored Brody's statement.

Hannah shrugged. "None of us even thought about it. We were taught to take action, and we did. We handled it fine. Dad trained us to operate as a team. I guess he did a good job of it."

"No offense, but your father sounds a little psycho," Brody said.

"No offense taken." The memory used to make her angry, but now that Lee was gone, it just depressed her. "I pushed him to include me on all those survival training weekends. But that was the only time he spent with any of us, teaching us to be good little rangers. He was supposed to be a general. He wasn't cut out to be a father. Looking back on it now, I realize how crazy it all was."

"What about your mother?"

"She was the one who held the family together. A strong woman, but very traditional. She stayed home while we played in the woods. I don't think she had any idea what the trips were actually like." Pain wrapped around Hannah's heart. "She was diagnosed with stage four cancer during my freshman year of college. She faded quickly. I took the second semester off to nurse her through hospice. She was gone before summer."

"I'm sorry." Brody's voice grated with empathy.

"The four of us kids were close, growing up. We stuck together like a troop. But after Mom died, the Colonel fell apart. Her death fractured our family. Grant's career was advancing. I went back to school. Mac ran with a bad crowd. Lee did his best to be the family touchstone, but the rest of us wouldn't cooperate." Guilt sandbagged Hannah. She and Grant and Mac could have tried harder. "What about your family? Grant said you were in the military?"

"Just four years to pay for college. I appreciated the training, but the army wasn't for me," Brody said. "I came home, joined the Boston PD, got married."

Hold on. "You were married?"

"Not for very long." His fingers opened and closed on the steering wheel, as if he'd been holding it too tightly. "A few years into my career in Boston, I was involved in a shooting at a convenience store. It was all clean and justified, but I had some . . . issues relating to the incident."

"Post-traumatic stress?"

Brody hesitated. "That, and my partner froze, putting me in a very bad situation."

"No."

"Unfortunately, yes." He nodded. "I was shot in the chest. I was wearing a vest, so I wasn't hurt, but it's hard to walk into dangerous situations with no confidence in your partner."

"Did you report it?"

"No. But he retired shortly after that. I think shame drove him off the force." The windshield fogged, and Brody turned on the defroster. "I eventually went for help, and it got better."

Hannah could hear the *but* coming. "I hope you got a new, better partner."

"I did. Unfortunately, while I'd been wallowing around in depression, my wife was having an affair with her coworker."

"What a bitch!" Hannah covered her mouth. "I'm sorry. That just slipped out." She hadn't had many relationships in her life, because she took commitment seriously. Hearts should not be traded lightly. And the thought that Brody's ex had trod on his made her angry and sad. "I can't imagine turning your back on the one person you're supposed to support."

"No. You wouldn't." Brody laughed. "Long story short, we got a divorce, and I moved out here for a fresh start."

"I was trying to figure out why anyone would move *to* Scarlet Falls."

"I like it here." Brody pulled into Grant's driveway. "Doesn't traveling all the time get old?"

Yes. But sadly, Hannah doubted she was settle-down material.

He carried the dog inside. Hannah was tempted to ask him to stay the rest of the night, but that wouldn't be fair. She wasn't here to stay. She wouldn't treat him with the same disregard as his ex. A good man like Brody deserved total honesty.

Instead, she set the alarm and slept on the couch next to the dog. Again. As she closed her eyes, all she could think of was that it was three a.m.—well past midnight. Tuesday had arrived. Whatever end was coming to Jewel would happen today.

Chapter Seventeen

Perched on the edge of the exam table, Hannah shifted her position at the knock on the door. Paper crinkled under her jeans-clad butt. She checked her watch. This was taking forever.

Dr. Martin's white lab coat topped a pair of tailored gray slacks. She scanned papers stacked on a clipboard. "I have your test results."

"And?"

She tucked a strand of long brown hair behind her ear. "The computer program generates instant feedback."

"Well? How did I do?"

The doctor sat down on the swivel stool. She flipped through several sheets, then lifted her gaze to meet Hannah's. Her brown eyes were serious. "For a successful attorney, you have terrible short-term memory, slow cognitive function, and your balance is off. You said you feel perfectly normal, but that's obviously not true. Now why don't you tell me how you really feel?"

Hannah blinked. "Excuse me?"

The doctor set her clipboard down. She pulled her frameless glasses off her face and set them on top of the clipboard. "The test results don't lie, Hannah, and exhibiting symptoms less than a week following a concussion is perfectly normal. No one suffers a brain trauma and is *fine* a few days later. I can't help you unless you're honest with me."

"My hearing is still a little fuzzy on one side, but other than that, I am fine." Hannah craned her neck to see the paperwork. "Those results can't be right."

"How about sleeping? More or less than usual."

"Maybe a little more," Hannah admitted. But she had been working long hours for the last month. Being tired wasn't unusual after she'd finished a major deal.

"Dizziness?"

"None."

Dr. Martin lifted a skeptical brow. "What about reading?"

"No problems," Hannah said. "When can I get back to work?"

"Every individual is different. Some people heal quickly. Others might take a few months."

"Months? I don't have months." Hannah's head had felt fine before, but now pain spiked through her temple.

"Relax." The doctor's tone sharpened. "Getting upset will only make it worse. This is going to take some time, and there's nothing you can do about it."

And watch my career go down the drain. "But I feel fine, and I can't take months off from work. I'm supposed to be in London next week. Isn't there a medication that would speed things up?"

The doctor sighed. "No. If you don't take care of yourself now, you will pay in the long run."

"I really need to get back to work."

"That isn't going to happen," Dr. Martin said. "I want you to come back in four weeks for a reevaluation."

Four weeks . . . How would she cope with four weeks of inactivity? Royce said her job wasn't in jeopardy, but other associates were there to jump in and handle cases while Hannah was sidelined.

Hannah turned on her voice memo app and recorded the doctor's instructions. Then she zoned out while the doctor expounded on the long-term consequences from repeated blows to the head. Hannah was focused on the here and now.

Four weeks was a long time. Hannah needed to be busy. The more time she had to rest, the more time she could contemplate Jewel's fate and relive the terrors of last spring. The absolute last thing she wanted was more time on her hands.

ω

Sitting in the neurologist's waiting room, Brody checked his e-mail for the fourth time, then leafed through a six-month-old issue of *Time* magazine. *What was taking so long?* Hannah had been called into the exam room over an hour before.

The door opened. Her face was pinched and strained, her eyes clouded with pain—and disappointment.

She pulled her mouth into a tight smile. "I'm sorry that took so long."

"Are you done?" He glanced back at the sliding glass window that separated the reception station from the waiting room.

Nodding, Hannah crossed to the coat tree.

Brody reached over her shoulder and lifted her jacket off the hook. He held it open so she could slide her arms into the sleeves. After a slight hesitation, she did.

"Everything all right?" he asked.

"Yes." She adjusted her collar and headed for the door. "Can I tell you about it later? I have a splitting headache."

"Sure. I thought doctors were supposed to make you feel better." Brody opened the door.

"That makes two of us."

They took the elevator to the ground floor. "Do you want to wait here while I get the car?"

They'd left his sedan in a garage two blocks over.

"No. I'd love some fresh air."

"We're in Manhattan. Good luck finding any of that."

Hannah's short laugh eased the heaviness in Brody's chest. Outside, the sidewalks were crowded. They maneuvered around the line for a hot dog cart, Hannah threading through pedestrian traffic with the confidence of a person who spent a lot of time in cities. Her long legs had no trouble keeping up with his. A guy stepped out of a doorway directly in front of Hannah. Without breaking stride, Brody angled his body and shouldered the jerk out of the way. The man stumbled, then righted himself with a self-righteous shout of "Asshole!"

Hannah glanced over at him. Over the pain in her eyes, humor glinted.

Brody lifted a casual shoulder. "He should have been watching where he was going. He could have knocked you over."

"I can handle myself, but thank you," she said.

"I know you *can* handle yourself, but you shouldn't *have* to."

"I'm not disagreeing. The guy was rude. Grant would have *accidentally* put an elbow into his face."

"Your brother's temper is legendary in the department."

The cool air, exhaust-scented as it was, seemed to perk her up. They took the elevator to the fifth floor of the parking deck and crossed the stained concrete to Brody's SUV. He opened the passenger door. Hannah flashed him an inquisitive half smile as she took her seat. He rounded the car and slid behind the wheel.

"Something wrong?"

"No. I'm just not accustomed to having my coat held and doors opened," she said. "Not that I don't like it. It's charming."

"What can I say? I was raised by my grandparents." Brody steered the car down the spiraling ramp.

"Where did you grow up?"

He lowered his window and punched out with his credit card. "Boston. My parents died in a small-plane crash when I was little."

"I'm sorry." Hannah reclined her seat a few inches.

"I was only three. I don't remember them."

"Do your grandparents still live in Boston?"

"No. Gran had a stroke nine years ago. Granddad didn't last six months without her."

"That's sad and sweet at the same time."

Brody drove out of town. Listening to the traffic report, he exited the city via the Lincoln Tunnel, threaded his way through North Jersey to I-87. Once they were on the interstate, the highway opened up. "I don't miss city traffic."

Hannah didn't respond. Brody glanced over. Her eyes were closed, but even sleeping, she looked stressed. He bet the news from the doctor wasn't what she had wanted to hear.

He turned on the radio but kept the volume low as he tuned his satellite radio to a classic rock station. Three hours later, at six o'clock, darkness had fallen, and Hannah was still asleep, her head lolling against the seat rest. The trip into New York had taken its toll. He couldn't imagine the toll a six-hour round-trip train commute would have had on her.

He passed the green sign for Scarlet Falls and eased onto the exit. The car bounced over seams in the blacktop. Hannah jerked awake.

"We're almost home," Brody said.

She blinked and swept a hand through her short blond locks. It settled back into place as if it knew to obey orders. "God, I'm sorry. I slept through the whole drive."

"You were tired. I'm glad you slept. That was the whole point of me driving you."

But Hannah frowned. Obviously, she wasn't used to letting anyone take care of her.

"Are you going to tell me what the doctor actually said?"

Hannah stretched. "I need coffee."

"You need food. We skipped lunch."

She pressed the pads of her fingers to her closed eyelids. "I'm not hungry."

"Headache?"

"No. The nap cleared that up."

"What then?"

"I need coffee."

"Seriously. How are you? You looked a little rough coming out of the doctor's office."

"You are persistent."

He smiled.

Hannah sighed. "I failed the cognitive test, and my balance is off, but considering it's only been a few days since I was knocked down, the doctor says I'm recovering as she'd expect."

"But?"

"Regardless of what her tests said, I feel fine, and she still won't clear me for work."

"Oh."

"She won't even retest me for another month. I was supposed to be in London next week working with one of the firm's largest clients," she said.

"Were you looking forward to that?" Brody wasn't sure how he felt about her, but the thought of her leaving Scarlet Falls depressed him. Hannah was the first woman to interest him in a long, long time. Every time he thought he had her figured out, she threw him a curveball. The first time he'd met her, he'd thought her arrogant, aloof, and cold. But he couldn't have been more wrong. She'd grieved her brother and stood by her family, proving to be smart and loyal, stubborn to a fault. In a heartbeat, she could shift from sharp corporate attorney to affectionate aunt. When a man had attempted to snatch her little nephew, Hannah had chased the scumbag. Barefoot. With snow on the ground. Her foot had been bleeding, and she hadn't even noticed.

Complex was the only word for Hannah. She was a puzzle he wanted to solve but not in any rush. He wanted to take his time and get to know all her layers. The strength of that desire surprised him. His ex-wife only had two layers. At the first challenge, her pretty veneer had peeled back faster than steamed wallpaper.

For a long minute, Hannah simply stared out the window. "I thought so, but now I'm not so sure. I couldn't wait to get out of Vegas."

Brody brightened. "You won't lose your job?"

"No." She shook her head. "Royce won't fire me. I'm not worried about that."

"Then what's the problem? Take some time off. Make sure you're completely recovered. You don't want to go back at less than one hundred percent, right? Poor performance wouldn't help your career, and it's not worth risking your health."

"It doesn't look like I have an option." She glanced at him. Her brow lowered. "I don't back away from anything easily. The Colonel raised me to identify my objectives and devote my efforts to achieving them, to work around, over, or through obstacles. All my life I've had to scratch and fight for what I wanted. Now I'm not sure what I want, but the instinct to do battle is still there. Without a goal, I feel lost." She flushed and blinked away, as if embarrassed by her revelation.

"How about if I give you a task?" He eased the car around a curve. "Decide what you want for dinner."

"Coffee." She arched a challenging brow.

"I'll stop for coffee if you tell me what you want to eat."

She shot him a dirty look. "You suck."

He laughed at the childish retort. He liked this less-formal, more-familiar Hannah. "If you're tired, let's pick up food, and I'll cook something."

"Can you manage steak?"

That wasn't what he'd expected her to choose. "Yes, but most women ask for salad."

"Salad isn't a meal." Hannah's face scrunched. "I could really go for a steak, rare, and potatoes any way you can make them. You'll have to cook at Grant's house, though. The dog has been alone all day."

"I can do that."

They stopped at a grocery store a few miles outside town.

"Coffee," Hannah whimpered, making a beeline for the beverage counter.

Brody selected two hefty sirloins and a bag of potatoes. Hannah appeared at his elbow, bliss on her face as she took a long sip. She licked her lips. Distracting.

"How about a vegetable?" he asked.

Hannah gave him a sour-lemon face. "Not for me."

He grabbed a bag of string beans. "They won't kill you."

"I have no proof of that."

He paid for the groceries, and they went back to the car. Brody's step was lighter at the prospect of an evening with a smart woman, a quiet dinner, and some entertaining conversation. A man couldn't ask for much more.

His phone buzzed halfway home. Unfortunately, he recognized the number. The Pub. *Chet.* So much for balancing on the edge of the wagon.

Brody glanced over at Hannah. "I'm sorry. I have to answer this."

"Work?"

"Not entirely." It felt very personal, but there was no protecting anyone's privacy tonight. If Brody didn't answer the call, the Pub's bartender would have to call police dispatch. Pushing a button on his steering wheel, he answered the call.

"Detective McNamara?"

"Yeah."

"This is Todd down at The Pub. We have a situation," Todd said.

"What is it?" Brody's appetite dissipated. If Todd was calling Brody directly, Chet was involved.

"Chet. He's getting into it with another customer. They're both acting like assholes. So far it's just posturing and insults, but Chet's in a foul mood tonight, and I'm too damned old to break up a fight."

"I'm on my way."

The sound of indecipherable shouting came over the line.

"If shit gets physical, I'm calling the police," Todd warned.

"Be there in five." Brody made a U-turn and headed into town. He pressed the pedal to the floor. The SUV shot forward. The Pub was a quiet neighborhood bar. Most of the clientele would be regulars stopping for a few beers after work or popping in to catch the hockey game.

Hannah grabbed for the armrest. "Is something wrong?"

"Sorry." Brody straightened the wheel. "Yes. Do you mind if we make a stop? I should have asked you before I agreed."

"It's fine. I'm not in a rush to get anywhere."

"But you're exhausted, and I promised to feed you."

"I just slept for three hours and finished a large coffee. I feel better than I have all day. Can you tell me what happened?"

"It's complicated." Brody stopped at a red light. "I'll tell you the long story later. For now, my friend Chet is in trouble. He's an alcoholic and waiting on some bad news. He's been in AA and mostly sober for a couple of years, but this week was more than he could take. According to The Pub's bartender, Chet is looking for trouble and so are the guys he found."

The Pub sat on the outskirts of Scarlet Falls. The bar had a long history. Like every other old building in New England, The Pub professed that George Washington had slept, eaten pot roast, or changed his socks under its roof. After all, no one could prove he hadn't. Brody parked in the gravel lot and went inside. Hannah followed him. The halls were lined with historical photos and pictures of the owner with local celebrities. A row of beer mugs etched with the names of regulars hung over the bar.

Behind the polished wooden bar, Todd rubbed a beer glass with a dish towel. His ruddy Scottish complexion had gone red, and anger lent vigor to his strokes. He inclined his head toward a doorway. In the next room, Chet paced back and forth in front of the pool table, his movements too quick, jerky, and uneven.

Holding a tumbler of Johnnie Walker, he was gesturing at a big guy dressed like a biker in torn jeans, boots, and a dirty bandana over an equally dirty gray ponytail. Two more biker types occupied the table with Mr. Big.

"What's the fight about?" Brody asked. Hannah stepped up next to him. She pressed her arms against his.

Todd shelved the glass and flipped the towel over his broad shoulder. "The big dude recognized him and started in on him with the usual cop-themed insults. And Brody . . ." Todd waved him closer.

When Brody leaned over the bar, Todd said in a low voice, "Chet was in here the other day. He was on duty. He only had a couple of drinks, but I thought you should know."

"Thanks." Brody turned to Hannah. "Please go back to the car."

She eased backward toward the door.

Brody crossed the scarred pine floor and assessed the scene in the billiard room, a long, narrow, and dark space. Three pool tables were strung out end-to-end. Brody scanned the room. Shadows darkened the corners, but the room appeared to be empty except for Chet and the three bikers.

Should he call for backup? He didn't want the incident to get back to the chief. If he could defuse the situation, he wouldn't need assistance.

Mandatory retirement loomed in Chet's near future, but he was all cop, from his ugly shoes to his calculating brown eyes. Sober, he could ignore insults to the badge. But alcohol sharpened his temper and thinned his tolerance.

Standing in front of the three bikers, Chet raised the tumbler of amber liquid and used it to gesture at the bikers. "You think you're so tough?"

"Tougher than any cop." Mr. Big stood. He looked familiar in a been-arrested kind of way.

Chet tossed back his drink. "I don't think so."

Brody entered the room. "Hey, Chet."

Chet's chin jerked around. Bleary eyes blinked at Brody. "What are you doing here?"

"Picking up your sorry butt." Brody nodded at Mr. Big. "Excuse me, gentlemen."

"We're in the middle of something," Mr. Big said.

"Tell you what, guys. My friend had a few too many. I'm going to take him home. Why don't you guys sit back, relax, and have a drink on me?" Brody waved at the bartender through the doorway. "Hey, Todd, bring these boys a round of whatever they're drinking."

Brody was carrying his off-duty gun, but he'd prefer a quiet resolution. Besides, pulling his weapon would generate an excruciating amount of paperwork.

But Mr. Big wasn't sober or smart enough to take the bone Brody was waving under his nose. "I ain't done with him yet. I'll bet you're a cop, too."

"Then you would be right." Brody slowly reached into his pocket and pulled out his wallet. He flipped it open, showed his badge, and stowed it back in his jacket. He had no doubt the big dude saw his off-duty weapon on his hip. "But there's no need for this to go any further. I'm taking my friend out of here. You can enjoy the rest of your evening."

"But Brody, he said cops were pussies." Chet pressed forward.

Brody stopped him with a hand on his chest. "Everyone is entitled to his opinion."

"See? Cops are pussies." Mr. Big reached out. He shoved Chet's shoulder. "Pussy."

Chet threw the first punch. Stepping between them, Brody blocked it with his shoulder. He put his back to Chet and faced the biker. This was getting out of hand fast. He sent a silent prayer of thanks that he'd sent Hannah outside.

Without taking his eyes off the three bikers, Brody shouted, "Todd, call for backup."

"Already done," Todd yelled back.

Mr. Big puffed out a stream of angry air and sent a fist the size of a bowling ball straight at Brody's head.

Chapter Eighteen

Jewel woke to darkness. Somewhere outside, an engine rumbled. Disoriented, she lifted her head from the dirt floor. She'd lost track of time. How many days had passed? Mick hadn't made another appearance. Lisa had brought a small amount of water and food twice a day. Jewel had been hungry and desperate enough to devour leftover fries, lettuce and tomatoes picked off burgers, and pizza crusts with chew marks. It wasn't the first time in her life she'd been hungry enough to eat another person's scraps. If she was going to escape, *if* being the important word, she couldn't afford to be picky.

Her chances weren't promising. She sat up, the movement sending her brain into a spin. The heat and Mick's beating were taking their toll.

The engine sound grew louder. Deliveries weren't normal for this neighborhood. No one around here had the money to order stuff online. Brakes squealed. The engine idled. A door creaked open and slammed shut.

The truck had stopped.

Sweat broke out on Jewel's arms. For the next few minutes, she listened to the sound of her heartbeat echoing in her ears. Shoes scraped in the dirt outside the shed. The door opened, and cool evening air swept into the space, chilling Jewel's damp skin. The beam of a bright flashlight seared her eyes. She raised a hand to block the light, but the man set it down on the floor just inside the shed, pointing it toward the ceiling.

Grinning, he moved toward her. He was short and stocky, in baggy jeans and an oversize T-shirt. There was another man standing behind him. The uplight illuminated his face with devilish shadows. Jewel cringed, shrinking against the wall. Rough concrete scraped the skin of her back.

He unlocked the cuffs, grabbed her arm, and pulled her to her feet.

"What's happening?" Jewel hated the tremble in her voice, but panic sliced through her control.

He said something in Spanish.

"Where are you taking me?" she asked, trying, unsuccessfully, to keep her voice calm.

"Don't bother." Lisa stood by the door, arms crossed over her chest. "They don't speak English."

Outside, twilight had fallen, but the early evening wasn't completely dark yet. They switched off the flashlight, walked her out of the shed, and steered her toward the gate that led to the front of the house. There was no point in screaming. No one would respond. She'd tested that fact out a few times over the last few days. This was not the kind of neighborhood where people looked out for one another. Jewel walked through the opening. A U-Haul-size truck was parked at the curb. Once she was inside of it, there was no chance of her getting out. She knew it. Beyond it, the empty street stretched out in front of her. Freedom.

Jewel jerked her arm free. She sprinted toward the blacktop, but days in the shed with little food left her weak. A whimper left her mouth as footsteps pounded the pavement behind her. A hand grabbed her hair. She skidded to a stop, her scalp screaming. Or maybe that was her voice.

Tears streamed down her face as the man led her back to the truck by the hair. The second man was rolling the rear door up.

The driver said something in Spanish. Jewel didn't understand the words, but the shove to the middle of her back got the message across. Resigned, she turned to the open back of the truck, reached for the bumper, and hauled herself up. The cargo area was dark, but moonlight slanted inside. Jewel squinted. Figures lined the sides of the truck. She counted four thin, dirty, and shivering girls.

The driver climbed up beside her. He gripped her arm and led her to the side of the truck. He handcuffed her to a metal pole affixed to the floor of the truck. Horror slid over her like a layer of greasy sweat. Jewel put her back to the wall and slid to the floor. The metal was cold against her bare skin. Dressed in only a tank top and short shorts, she shivered. She hugged her knees. Sobs bubbled into her throat.

The interior was dark, but whenever they passed under a light, a small amount of light filtered through vents high on the truck's walls. She swallowed and hitched her breath. She turned to the girl next to her. Black eyes, hopeless and sunken, stared out of a gaunt face. The girl was about the same age as Jewel. Dark hair fell in a tangled mess to her chin.

"Do you know where we're going?" Jewel asked.

The girl shook her head and lifted a bony shoulder. "Does it matter?"

Jewel thought that it did, but she kept her mouth shut. The truck lurched over a bump and made a turn. Jewel braced herself by grabbing the pipe behind her. The vehicle sped up. The ride smoothed out, and she guessed they had hit the interstate.

The girl next to her stared at the floor. In her eyes, Jewel saw no trace of the terror that filled her own body to the point of bursting. She scanned the rest of the girls. They slumped, bodies limp. Two slept, awkwardly hunched against their neighbors. No fight left in any of them. No will to live. Nothing. They were empty. The girl across from her stroked a very pregnant belly and hummed softly.

This will be me if I don't get away.

But with every mile of highway that passed under the wheels of the truck, her chances at freedom ebbed away. For the first time Jewel thought that maybe it would have been better if Mick had killed her. Dying of thirst in the shed might have been a better end than what awaited her at the end of this journey. She thought of all the things she'd been forced to do over the last six months. Could she do this for years and years? Or was she better off dead?

Chapter Nineteen

Moving in, Brody caught the punch early, wrapped both hands around the thick wrist, and twisted the biker's hand into a wristlock. Applying pressure, he forced Mr. Big onto his knees. Then Brody angled his body to keep the biker's two friends in his line of sight.

"Help me out, assholes," Mr. Big called. His buddies lunged toward Brody.

He swung around to use Big's body as a barrier. The friends split up, circling around to attack Brody from either flank. *Shit. Shit. Shit.* The one on the left reached into his back pocket. The overhead light gleamed off a knife blade.

Brody dropped Big's wrist and backed up to gain distance. He reached for his gun. Before the barrel cleared the holster, something moved in Brody's peripheral vision. A cue stick arced through the air. *Crack!* The end struck the biker's knife hand. The weapon hit the floor and slid across the wide planks.

Hannah stepped out of the shadow. She held the cue stick in a wide grip with both hands. The biker lunged at her. Twisting the staff, she caught him across the temple with the tip. His knees buckled, and he face-planted on the floor. Man number two moved toward her.

No! Brody's vision tunneled.

"Watch out!" Brody cleared his gun from the holster, but the only man he had a clear line on was Mr. Big, who was climbing to his feet. The huge biker stood between Brody and the man threatening Hannah. "Freeze! Police!"

Mr. Big raised both hands in the air. *Not helping.*

"Get on the floor!" Brody circled around. Fear gripped his insides. Why didn't she stay outside? She was going to get hurt.

Her gaze was focused as she spun to face the new threat. She turned the stick ninety degrees to vertical and whipped the butt end upward right between the second man's legs. Shock saucered his eyes. He dropped to his knees, clutching his groin with both hands, and went over like a pine tree.

Stunned, Mr. Big froze halfway to the floor. "That was hot."

"Holy crap," Todd said from the doorway.

Sirens wailed. The door opened, and two uniforms came in. Brody holstered his gun and circled his finger in the air around the three bikers. "Handcuffs all round."

Officer Lance Kruger cuffed Mr. Big and took the arrest information from Brody.

"I'll write up a report in the morning," Brody said.

"We've got this, Brody." Lance heaved one of the bikers to his feet. "Just take care of Chet."

"Thanks." Brody watched the biker limp away.

He turned back to Chet. His friend hadn't moved. He was staring at Hannah with respect. Clutched in his fingers was the broken base of the tumbler. Light glinted off the shiny points of glass, and blood dripped from Chet's hand to the floor. Blood pooled in fat drops at Chet's feet.

"Looks like you cut yourself." Brody started toward him.

Chet lifted his hand and drew his brows together. "I didn't even feel that."

Brody didn't like the confused cast to Chet's eyes. "You must have crushed the glass in your hand. Maybe you should lay off the steroids."

But Chet wasn't listening. He turned his hand over and stared at the palm.

"You're bleeding all over the floor. How about you put down that glass before you make a bigger mess?" Brody asked.

Chet took the glass in his uninjured hand and poised the sharp tip over his opposite wrist. "Two inches north and I wouldn't have to worry about any of this shit anymore." A wistful look passed over his face.

Brody swallowed. His throat went dry as a sandbox. He'd been sweating from his altercation with the bikers, but his skin went clammy at Chet's suicidal reference. "Don't talk like that."

"It's her this time. You know that, right?" Chet's lack of inflection was equally alarming. He was losing it.

Brody shook his head. "No. I won't know anything until Thursday. I know the waiting feels impossible, but I need you to hold it together just a little longer."

In truth, Chet could never be whole again. He was already as broken as the glass in his hand. His daughter's disappearance and wife's death had shattered him until all that was left was a ruined shell. How much longer could he hang on? How much grief could a person handle?

Chet shook the tumbler at Brody. "I saw her hair. Her clothes. It's her."

"So you're basing the identification of a woman on the fact that she's brunette and is wearing a New York T-shirt in the state of New York?" There were other similarities as well, but Brody wasn't going to bring any of them up. Logically, the chance that the body was

Teresa was small, but if a doctor says the odds a tumor is cancerous are five percent, no one focuses on the ninety-five. "You know the chances are far greater that it *isn't* her. She hasn't been near Scarlet Falls in years. All we have are a couple of coincidences. If you were working this case, you would never make assumptions on this little information."

"Cops don't believe in coincidences." His craggy face cracked. A tear slid into the wrinkles below one eye as grief drowned his temper.

Brody softened his voice. His heart broke for his friend. In the last few years, Chet had lost everything. "How about you put that glass down?"

"OK, Brody. You win. This time." Chet sighed, and his chest deflated like a tire with a puncture. He set the tumbler on the pool table. He turned his hand over as if seeing it for the first time. "Wow. That's a nasty cut."

"It is. Come on. We'll get that taken care of."

Chet frowned. He pressed a fist to the center of his chest and burped. "That's prolly a good idea."

"OK, you ready then?"

"Yup." Chet lurched forward. Brody caught him, looping an arm over his shoulders to steady the older man.

But Chet straightened suddenly. "Hey, blondie."

Leaning on the wall, Hannah rolled the pool cue between her palms. "I'm Hannah Barrett. It's a pleasure to meet you."

"Pleasure's all mine," Chet slurred. "She with you, Brody?" He waved his loose hand. Blood droplets flew through the air.

"She is," Brody said.

"Since when?" Chet's feet tangled, and his body sagged.

Brody hefted him higher. "Since none of your business."

With a glance at the glass on the green felt, Hannah set the long stick next to it. She grabbed a cloth napkin from a nearby table and wrapped it around Chet's bleeding hand.

Brody half carried the older cop through the bar. Hannah opened the rear door. She put a hand on the back of his head to keep him from striking the roof of the car. He half fell into the seat and curled on his side. His emotions had run out of steam. Hannah made a futile effort to buckle the seat belt, but Chet couldn't stay upright. She gave up.

"I'll have to get my car," Chet slurred. "Todd has the keys."

Hannah dangled keys from her fingers. "Already got them. I'll drive it to your house."

"Sorry for dragging you out, Brody." Chet burped.

"Not a problem." Brody drove away. Hannah followed him. They stopped at an urgent care center. Everyone in the hospital ER knew Chet and Brody and all the other SFPD cops. By morning, everyone in town would know about Chet's cannonball off the AA wagon. His mandatory retirement likely just fast-tracked. But he still deserved some privacy. His life was in shambles, and Brody would not parade him in public in his current condition.

Chet was cooperative as the doctor closed the wound with a half dozen stitches. Hannah helped Brody get Chet in and out of the car. Ten minutes later, Brody parked in the narrow drive at Chet's house. The front yard was dark. Chet must have gone to the bar long before the sun set. Most likely he'd skipped dinner, maybe even lunch.

"Would you mind getting the door?" Brody handed Hannah the keys. He helped Chet into the house. After settling him at the table, Brody flipped on the porch light and went back out to turn off the car. "Hungry?"

Chet shook his head. "I just wanna sleep."

"You should eat." Brody pointed to a cardboard pizza box on the counter. "How old is that pizza?"

"Dunno." Chet shrugged. "Going to bed."

He stood, swayed, then staggered down the hall. A door closed. Springs creaked. And that was that.

"I just want to check a few things, if you don't mind." Brody went to Chet's fridge. He removed three moldy containers of Chinese takeout and sniffed the milk. Old. Fetching a trash bag from under the sink, he cleaned out the refrigerator.

Hannah peered around his body. "Is he trying to commit suicide by food poisoning?"

"He just might be." He made a mental note to bring Chet groceries the next day. Then he opened the cabinets and found a bottle of Johnnie Walker under the sink. He poured the liquor down the drain and rinsed out the bottle.

"Is he going to be all right?"

"I don't know," Brody said. "Chet's a detective on the SFPD. His daughter has been missing for a few years, and she looks a little like that body that turned up on Sunday."

"Oh, no." Hannah pressed a hand over her heart. "That poor man."

"I'm doing everything possible to identify her, but the waiting is killing him."

"I'll bet. When will you know?"

"Thursday." He led the way out the front door and locked up the house.

"It's only Tuesday." Hannah paused. "That's a long time. Why can't he identify his own daughter?"

Brody didn't want to add to Hannah's nightmares. "The victim's identity can't be determined visually."

"Oh." Her chin dropped as she continued to the car.

Brody opened the passenger door for her before getting behind the wheel. He started the engine.

Hannah stared up at the house. "Will he be all right tonight alone?"

"He'll probably be out cold until morning. But I'll come back here and sleep on the sofa after I take you home. Sorry about dinner." He pulled out of the driveway. Her brother's house was fifteen

171

minutes from Chet's place. "It's almost ten o'clock, and you haven't eaten all day."

"Your friend needs you." She might have a few faults, but she didn't suffer from any lack of loyalty. Hannah stuck by those she loved. She reached across the console and grasped his hand. "You can cook for me another night."

Considering the disaster of the past few hours, her invitation sent a surprising jolt of joy through him.

He intertwined their fingers. "How did you get into the pool room?"

"Back door."

He felt her focus on his profile. At a stop sign, he turned to meet her gaze. Light from the streetlamp spilled through the windshield and highlighted the delicate bone structure of her face. "I asked you to stay outside. You could have been hurt. What if you'd been struck in the head?"

"First of all, if you hadn't noticed, I don't have a mark on me," she said. "Secondly, you had no backup. While I hoped you could defuse the situation verbally, those bikers were goading your friend. They were looking for a fight."

"You're right."

"Chet was easy for those men to engage. Does he usually carry his weapon off duty?"

"Yes. But he wouldn't take it to a bar." Or would he? Todd had said Chet was at the bar on duty. But as Brody answered, he realized the truth behind her words. Chet was unstable. He shouldn't be on duty, and he sure as hell shouldn't be walking around with a gun. He needed to be put on leave. Brody's heart sank as if it had been filled with concrete and dumped in the Hudson. Tomorrow morning was going to be the worst day he'd faced in the past eight years. "Thanks for looking out for me, but next time, please let me know you're there."

"I didn't want to advertise my presence. I was just watching your back." She lifted a shoulder as if it were no big deal.

He squeezed her hand. "Thanks for that."

To Brody, that was the biggest deal of all.

ω

Hannah took her keys from her purse as Brody pulled into the driveway. He followed her to the front porch. On the other side of the door, the dog barked.

"So along with survival skills, the Colonel taught you to fight?"

"Yes. We did all sorts of drills." She opened the front door. AnnaBelle was all wags and snuffles. Hannah rubbed her silky ears. "I have to visit him this week. I promised Grant."

"Will that be hard for you?"

"It will." Straightening, she hung her jacket on the newel post. "He doesn't remember us, and he gets agitated, but mostly, it's hard to see such a strong man so helpless and weak."

"I could go with you."

"You have enough on your plate." And Hannah could get too accustomed to leaning on him. "You don't need any more of my family drama."

"I don't mind. I don't have a family."

"You have Chet, and it seems he's a handful."

Brody sighed. "Thank you for saving my ass tonight."

She sure as hell wasn't going to sit outside in the car while Brody faced three bikers alone.

The dog whined.

"Poor thing. I'm sure she's hungry, and she needs to go out. We've been gone a long time." Hannah started toward the back of the house.

Brody was right behind her. "After the porcupine incident last night, she probably slept all day."

Halfway down the hallway, her foot went out from under her body. Brody grabbed her elbow.

"Guess she couldn't hold it that long." Hannah laughed. Stepping around the puddle, she took off her boots. "I'll just go wipe these down and grab the floor cleaner."

"Let me walk her before I go." Brody went back to the kitchen and snapped AnnaBelle's leash onto her collar. "I don't like you wandering around the woods in the dark."

Hannah paused in the laundry room doorway. "Thank you, but I can do it if you want to get back to Chet."

"It'll just take a minute." Warmth lit his eyes. Something was different about his expression. "I'll feel better if you're all secure here before I leave."

"I usually carry my gun if I'm outside alone at night," she said.

While he took the dog into the yard, she cleaned her boots, wiped up the hall floor, and filled the dog's dish. Hannah couldn't shake the feeling that a key element had changed in her relationship with Brody. The connection between them buzzed stronger.

She'd been glad to have his support this afternoon, and she was even more glad she was there when that biker pulled a knife on him. Her bones chilled. What if he'd been alone? He'd put himself between those three bikers and Chet. He'd displayed a courage she understood too well. In her life, she'd said good-bye to dozens of soldiers, friends of her father, men who served with Grant. She'd known the risk her father and brother had taken on every deployment. Brody could just as easily die in the line of duty.

The door opened. Cold air blasted into the room as Brody and the dog entered the kitchen. He unsnapped the leash and hung it on its peg. Shivering, Hannah filled the teakettle and lit the burner.

Brody crossed the room. "I'd better get back to Chet."

"Thanks for taking me today." She rubbed her arms.

"What's wrong?"

Needing contact with his warm, breathing body, she reached out and touched his face. "You could have been killed tonight."

"Thanks to you, I wasn't." He smiled down at her, but his eyes were serious.

Brody cupped her cheek in one broad hand, his thumb caressing the line of her jaw. His head dipped, and his mouth settled on her lips. The taste of him filled her with warmth. Heat settled into the parts of her that had gone cold.

Her hands splayed on his chest. He tilted his head and deepened the kiss. His tongue slid between her lips. Opening her mouth, she met his tongue with hers head-on. The awfulness of the day faded. Her disappointment with the doctor and the incident in the bar became less vivid. All she could feel was Brody's mouth on hers, the soft glide of his tongue over her lips. The taste of him wiped her slate clean and recharged her.

Her fingers curled in the lapel of his jacket, pulling him closer, as if she sensed he was about to leave. She didn't want to say good-bye to Brody. Not for the night. Not at all. The realization disconcerted her.

He eased back and lifted his head. He leaned a few inches away from her, and his hands dropped to his sides. Bewilderment flooded Hannah, while Brody's eyes were full of resignation. *What the hell?*

"Was that not good for you?" she asked, indignation creeping into her voice.

Brody closed in again. His hands went to her hips and pulled their bodies together. Their torsos aligned from thigh to chest, the planes and angles in a perfect fit. He closed his mouth over hers again. This time there was no asking. If their first kiss kindled her desire, the second lit a raging bonfire. His fingers gripped tighter in the soft flesh of her hips, pulling her tightly against his need.

The teakettle whistled. Brody's body tensed. When he lifted his head this time, his pupils were wide open with desire. "On the contrary. It was far too good."

"Oh." Fluency in three foreign languages, and *oh* was the best response she could manage?

He broke contact quickly, cleanly, as if it took every ounce of his extraordinary self-control to walk away from her. "Good night, Hannah. Don't forget to lock up and set the alarm."

She turned off the burner. No need to warm up with tea now. Every inch of her was hot. She locked up and set the alarm. Taking a glass from the cabinet, she filled it with ice water from the dispenser on the refrigerator.

The dog butted Hannah's hand with her head. She stroked the retriever's soft fur. "This visit isn't going the way I'd planned."

AnnaBelle padded to the back door, the fur on her neck lifting. Hannah turned to face the glass, but her own reflection faced her. She moved to the wall and flipped two switches. The interior light went out, and floodlights illuminated the yard.

"I don't see anything." Her fingertips touched the dog's head. AnnaBelle growled softly. "But I'll take your word for it."

She ran upstairs to get her gun out of the safe. Her New York State concealed carry permit wasn't valid in New York City, so she'd left the weapon at home. The Glock on her hip soothed her nerves better than a cup of tea. Perhaps it was a herd of deer or a porcupine ambling through the woods, but a girl couldn't be too careful.

Something was out there in the dark, and it was watching.

Chapter Twenty

Mick watched the man's car drive away from Hannah Barrett's house. Where had she been all day? He'd been waiting for her for hours. Tree bark was digging into his ass. He stood and rolled his neck to work out the kinks. Now the man had walked the dog. The blond would be locked up and secure all damned night.

He raised his binoculars and watched her move around the kitchen. She stopped at the back door and stared out into the woods. The kitchen light went out, and lights blazed in the yard. Did she sense his presence?

Uncertainty slid over him, and he drew farther into the woods. Dead leaves rustled around his boots. She couldn't know he was out here. He was too far away, and his dark jeans and black hoodie blended with the shadow of the trees. It was almost as if they were connected.

As if he were meant to have her.

But it wasn't going to happen tonight. He needed to catch her outside and unaware. She wasn't going to be an easy score. He considered his options. Using drugs or a Taser would make the process simple. But he didn't want simple. He wanted her awake and kick-ing. She had to be aware of every moment, to look in his eyes and know he was the one who defeated her. That incident in the Vegas parking lot had been a fluke.

No point in sitting out here any longer. Restless, he tucked his binoculars into his hoodie pocket and headed for the car. The coke was low. A bottle of vodka waited back at the house with Sam, but Mick was tired of sitting around that crappy little place. The country was too quiet, and the cable sucked.

At the edge of the trees, he checked for traffic. Nothing but empty road in either direction. Very few cars passed down this road. He shook a clingy red leaf from his pant leg. Jogging across the road, he ducked behind the evergreens and got into the car.

The engine started with a low rumble. Mick curbed the urge to stomp on the gas and roar down the quiet street. He scratched his shoulder. He was jonesing for something, and it wasn't booze or drugs.

He wanted the blond bitch. Instead of heading back to the house, he cruised down the two-lane rural highway toward town. What was open late at night? The lights glowed on a building on the roadside. Mick slowed. A sign above the door read "The Scarlet Lounge" in neon blue script. He pulled into the lot. Pickups and tractor trailers dominated the parking area.

A small sign warned of surveillance cameras. Mick circled the building once, contemplating spots and finding two cameras attached to light poles. The bar's attempt at security was pathetic. Half the lot had no coverage. He parked in a blank spot between a couple of pickup trucks and an eighteen-wheeler. He was just going in for a drink, but there was no reason for his car to appear on any-one's recording.

Dark and seedy and smelling of stale beer, The Scarlet Lounge was exactly the sort of crappy little bar he and Sam had been searching for the other night. People shouted over classic rock blasting through the dim space. Mick went up to the bar and ordered a double shot of decent vodka. He tossed it back, hoping the fiery liquid would eat away at his frustration. But it didn't. He eased away from the bar into a dark corner to sip at a second round, letting the noise of the crowd wash over him. But the nighttime activity did little to subdue the itch in his blood.

A young woman stumbled away from a man in his twenties, saying, "Asshole. Find your own ride home."

The man tossed his hands in the air. "Whatever, bitch."

The woman turned and ran for the door. Mick slid out into the cool night air behind her. She dug in her purse. Keys jingled as she tottered across the asphalt.

She dropped her keys. "Damn it."

Sobbing, she bent down to pick them up. Tight jeans and high heels showcased a bitching body. Long blond hair swung in a shiny curtain around her pretty face.

"Can I help you?" Mick smiled, the expression feeling alien to his facial muscles. But it wasn't as if he hadn't done this before.

She sniffed. "I'm OK. Just going home."

"You look like you've had a lot to drink."

Straightening, she sniffed and wiped at the mascara running down her cheeks. But she was young enough to still be pretty with puffy eyes. "I'm fine. He cheated on me. I just want to go home."

"Do you live far from here?" Mick asked.

She shook her head. "No."

"Why don't I take you home," he offered.

"No." Suspicion dawned in her eyes, as if she'd just realized she was in a dark parking lot alone with a total stranger. Her gaze darted toward the bar, but Mick blocked her return path.

He scanned the area. Lot was empty of people. No cameras pointing in his direction. Sweet. He knocked her out with a single punch to the jaw, then caught her as she collapsed. He tossed her and her purse into the back of the Charger. He drove a half mile and turned onto a dark side road. After securing her with zip ties and duct tape, he transferred her to the trunk. He could barely contain his excitement as he drove toward the house.

Sam got up from his spot on the couch as Mick carried her inside. "Another one? We're going to run out of places to put them all." But Sam's protest was mocking. His eyes lit with pleasure as his gaze swept over her.

Mick took her into the bedroom he'd claimed. "You can have her when I'm done, but first we'll have to go get her car. I don't want it found in the parking lot of the bar." He took her keys from her purse. The beep of the unlock button on the keychain should lead him to her vehicle.

Sam nodded. "She's out cold anyway. Not my idea of a party unless they're awake."

Mick tied her spread-eagle to the bedposts. No chance of her getting away while they took care of business. Thirty minutes later they returned. Sam hid the girl's car in the barn out back. She was awake when Mick walked into the bedroom. Her terrified eyes and muffled screams sent all his blood to his groin.

As he approached her, he held up a pair of scissors he'd taken from the kitchen. "I'd hold still if I were you."

She froze. Mick knelt next to her head and snipped her long blond strands. He was no hairstylist, but when he was finished, her hair was cropped short to frame her face. He collected the hair from the bed and flushed it down the toilet. Tonight, he wanted no reminders that this woman wasn't Hannah Barrett.

Chapter Twenty-One

At seven a.m., the police station was mostly empty when Brody knocked on the chief's office door. He'd purposefully come in early to get his task over with before the administrative staff started at eight. Patrol shift had just changed, and Stella, who'd been on duty overnight, sat at a computer typing a report before clocking out.

Brody had woken Chet and ordered him into the shower. Nursing the mother of all hangovers, Chet had been a cranky old bear. There had been no further conversation. Feeling like a traitor and a coward, Brody had sneaked out of the house before Chet emerged.

"Come in."

Brody took a breath and turned the knob. He took three steps and eased into a chair facing the chief's desk. As usual, Chief Dave Horner was perfectly presented without a wrinkle on his starched navy-blue uniform or a spot of stubble on his chin to mar his clean-cut image.

The chief's focus sharpened as he studied Brody's face. "I heard Chet was involved in an altercation at The Pub last night. Tell me what happened."

Of course he'd heard. Horner was more politician than cop. Police chief was an appointed position, and his job security depended on the continued reelection of the mayor who had hired him. Information was the key to Horner's political game.

"Chet was drinking . . ." Brody relayed the basics but kept the details to a minimum.

The chief scratched his cleanly shaved jaw. "I should have expected him to snap. The news about his daughter must be too much for him to handle."

"We have no evidence that those remains are Teresa. Chances are they are not. I'm still investigating."

"Of course. You're right." Irritation creased his mouth as Horner corrected himself. He smoothed it over. "But not knowing her fate must be a huge strain on him. We'll need a statement from the woman who was with you last night." Curiosity lit Horner's eyes.

Brody had planned to ask Hannah for a formal, signed statement last night. The kiss had distracted him.

"Brody?"

Just as the memory of their lip-lock was distracting him now.

"Of course, sir," he said. "I'll have it by the end of the day."

Brody sent a silent thank-you to Hannah. The paperwork required by last night's incident would have increased tenfold if Brody's gun had been fired.

"I appreciate what it took for you to come in here this morning." Horner leaned back and spread his palms on the surface of his desk. "I'll take care of it from here. Thank you."

Dismissed.

But Brody didn't move.

The chief sighed. "I'll be gentle."

Feeling low, Brody exited the office. A receptionist, an admin, and two patrol officers had come in while he'd been talking to Horner.

All eyes were on Brody as he crossed the thin carpet. Stella leaned on the desk, her hands gripping the laminate edge. "Brody, wait."

He stopped, preparing to be ostracized. Cops stuck by cops. They didn't volunteer information that led to disciplinary action.

"We all know what happened last night."

Small towns.

"What you just did must have killed you inside, and as much as we love Chet, you did what had to be done. No one blames you," she said.

Brody lifted his head and scanned the room. No one avoided eye contact. This was a tight-knit group, and he felt like a traitor for reporting Chet's drinking.

"You have our support, and Chet does, too." Stella pushed off the desk. "Chet has been a mentor to everyone on this force. We all owe him. But he has no business with a badge or a weapon in his current state of mind." But they all knew how much the job meant to Chet. It was all he had left.

Brody's throat constricted. He couldn't say anything but "Thanks."

With the support of the other cops, Brody only felt twenty shades of shitty instead of fifty as he headed for his unmarked sedan. He had reams of paperwork to process from last night, but fifteen minutes later, he found himself staring up at the Barrett house. It was barely eight o'clock. Hannah could still be sleeping. He shouldn't bother her. He reached for the gearshift to put the car in reverse. The front door opened, and Hannah stepped out onto the porch. She nudged the dog back into the house and closed the door behind her. She was dressed in blue plaid pajama pants and an oversize jersey that hung to mid-thigh. Her eyes were sleepy and her short hair tousled in a way that made Brody yearn to climb into bed beside her. Considering they'd only kissed once—as smoking as that one time had been—it was too early to take her to bed. He was not interested in anything meaningless, especially not with Hannah.

But the sight of her pulled Brody from his vehicle. He climbed the steps. "Did I wake you?"

"No one sneaks up to the house with AnnaBelle on duty."

"It's cold. You should be inside." He tried to steer her toward the entry.

But she couldn't be budged. She studied his face. Alarm pinched her features. "Something's wrong. Did something happen to Chet?"

"I'll tell you inside."

She went with him, but her brows lowered with irritation. In the kitchen, he hung his jacket on the back of a counter stool and sat down. Standing next to his stool, Hannah wound her arms around his shoulders and hugged him close. Though surprised by the immediate show of affection, he rested his temple on her shoulder. His taut muscles loosened. Her hand splayed on the back of his head, her fingers sliding through his hair. He took a minute to soak up her strength. She had it to spare. After all she'd been through this week, *she* was comforting *him*.

He lifted his head. "What was that for?"

"I won't know until you tell me, but you looked like you needed it." She leaned back and scanned his face. "Ready to talk?"

The thought exhausted him. "Could I have some coffee?"

"Rough morning?"

"Very." Brody rubbed the back of his neck. "Chet's couch needs to be a foot longer." Though it hadn't been the sofa that kept him awake. He'd been dreading the arrival of morning.

"How about some breakfast?" she asked.

"I was supposed to cook for you."

She opened the fridge and took out a carton of eggs. "We'll get to that."

A new revelation occurred to Brody: No matter how bad a day

could be, having someone to share it with helped. He'd never minded being alone before. But now . . .

He squashed the warm and fuzzy feeling that swamped him. Hannah was only here because she was hurt. She didn't *want* to be in Scarlet Falls. As soon as she was fully recovered, she'd be back to the jet-set life she loved. Thanks to the doctor yesterday, though, Brody would have her for the next month. Maybe he shouldn't get too attached—as if there were anything he could do to stop himself. Just watching her make him breakfast made him want to spend many more mornings with her.

"I had to report Chet's behavior from last night." He glanced at his watch. "He's probably in the chief's office right now."

Taking an egg from the carton, she paused. "I'm sorry. Will he lose his job?"

"I imagine he'll be *encouraged* to retire. His drinking has been a problem in the past. He was hanging from his last fingertip with the chief."

Hannah whipped eggs and milk and dumped the mixture into a frying pan. She inserted four slices of bread into the toaster. "What will he do now?"

Brody shook his head. "I don't know. He doesn't like to have a lot of leisure time."

"I can empathize." She divided eggs and toast onto two plates and slid one in front of him. She brought orange juice and butter to the island and took the seat next to him. "He needs a distraction."

Brody glanced sideways at her. She was toying with her eggs.

"How do you feel this morning?"

"Fine."

He gave her a skeptical head tilt.

"I really do feel fine." She buttered a slice of toast and ate it. "Just bored."

"You seem a lot more accepting about being out of work for a month this morning."

"Watching Chet gave me some perspective last night. You'd think Lee's death would have been enough to knock some sense into me. Work can't be everything." She drank coffee. "Maybe I need a hobby."

"Like knitting?"

She snorted. Wiping her mouth with a napkin, she said, "I don't think that would work."

"Macramé? Bead art? Pottery?" He'd had this same conversation with Chet, and it was just as humorous to envision Hannah in some sort of sedentary task. Neither of them was suited to leisure activities.

"There's nothing wrong with any of those hobbies," she said with a laugh.

"No, but I can't picture you doing any of them." He considered her. "What skills do you have?"

"Lately? Sleeping."

"You could be a mattress tester."

"Very funny." She rolled her eyes.

"What about catching up on TV?"

"I'm not much of a TV person. It's been so long since I've had any real free time. Ellie left me DVDs of *Downton Abbey*. I watched three episodes last night after you brought me home. I felt . . . guilty."

"Why guilty?"

"It seems frivolous to lie in bed and watch television."

"Maybe a month off will teach you how to relax." Brody looked down to realize he'd finished his breakfast.

"That's what I'm afraid of."

He laughed. "I doubt I can interest Chet in watching *Downton Abbey*."

"Probably not."

"What do you do on vacation?" He wanted to know more about her than he'd learned during her brother's murder investigation.

"I come here." She poured a second cup. "How about you?"

"Skiing in winter. Kayaking in summer. Nice thing about living in the country is the proximity to outdoor sports."

"I haven't used my skis in years. Maybe I'll drag them down from the attic this year."

So they had something in common.

"Are you still trying to find that girl?" he asked.

She nodded. "I'm waiting to hear about the fingerprints from the Vegas cop. He said it could take a while."

Brody nodded. "Different regions and states use different AFIS software. The FBI maintains a national database, but every print doesn't make it into the national system."

"Seems inefficient."

"Sometimes it is, but persistence can pay off," Brody said. "Maybe Chet can help you."

"Why would he want to help me?"

"He needs a distraction, and after spending the last three years searching for Teresa, he knows all about looking for lost teenagers."

"I guess he does." Hannah collected their dishes and moved them to the sink. "Are you sure this wouldn't be the worst thing for him? Seems too close to home, if you know what I mean."

"I know Chet. Not being involved with the case is killing him. He's a take-action sort of person." Not unlike Hannah, thought Brody.

"In that case, I'd appreciate his help."

Brody separated his car key from the rest. "Besides, I doubt he'll want to see me today. I just ratted on him and ended the career he loves more than life."

"It wasn't your fault." She pointed at him. Anger flared in her blue eyes. "You can't take the blame for his dangerous behavior. You're doing everything you can to help him."

"How long will it take you to get ready?"

"Give me ten minutes." She headed for the hallway. "Does he like dogs? I don't want to leave AnnaBelle alone all day again."

"Yeah. Chet likes animals. Bring her along. I'll need a statement from you about last night, too."

"All right." True to her word, she was ready in minutes.

Brody walked her to the truck. "Are you sure you don't mind?"

"You have to work, right?" Hannah opened the passenger door of her brother's pickup. The dog jumped up into the cab.

"I have to testify in court this afternoon." He had a robbery case to work, and the chief would likely assign him Chet's open cases as well.

"And you'd like me to keep an eye on Chet?"

"I would greatly appreciate it. But he'll get defensive if he suspects I asked you to babysit him." Brody walked to the door of his sedan, parked behind the truck. "You'll really need to act genuinely serious about finding Jewel."

"I *am* genuinely serious about finding her." Hannah's eyes softened. "According to those e-mails, whatever was going to happen to her is done, but I'd still like to keep trying."

He glanced at her profile, and the determined set of her brow. "Then we have no worries. Chet can sense sincerity, or the lack of it, as fast as a narc dog sniffs out dope."

As he climbed into the sedan, nerves raised the hairs on the back of his neck. Brody paused, one foot inside the vehicle, and scanned the surroundings. His gaze swept over trees, roadside grass, and meadow, but he saw nothing unusual.

So why did he feel like they were in imminent danger?

ᙡ

Mick drove past the house. Big and white, the house looked like something from a movie set, the picture of domestic bliss. A big pickup truck and sedan occupied the driveway.

The sedan was an unmarked cop car.

Fuck. He sped up and drove down the road. When he was sure he was out of sight, he turned around and doubled back, easing behind the patch of evergreens from the other side.

What he wouldn't give to be stalking this bitch in an urban neighborhood.

He rolled down the window and listened. Nothing.

Mick tapped a finger on the steering wheel. The house sat on a big rectangle of open ground, but woods surrounded the cleared area. With a cop in the house, he wouldn't risk going to his favorite observation post. Maybe she'd called the police. Had she sensed his presence outside the night before?

"What do you want to do?" Sam asked.

He took his binoculars from the glove box, got out of the car, and went to the edge of the foliage. Putting the binoculars to his eyes, he peered through the pine needles and scanned the front of the house.

Nothing.

The windows along the front of the house were dark, and he didn't see any movement behind the glass. But someone was inside, including a cop.

A few minutes later, the front door opened. The blond and a tall man in a suit and tie, obviously the cop, walked out onto the porch, their bodies close in an intimately acquainted way. Mick hadn't gotten a good look at the man who'd been at the house the night before, but he bet it was the same man. The blond held the golden retriever on a leash. Mick increased the magnification, focusing in on a bulge on the woman's hip. He expected the cop to carry a gun, but a lawyer? They got into the two separate vehicles.

Mick lowered the binoculars. Time to go. He'd have preferred to avoid the cop, but Mick would follow the woman. He wanted to know where she was at all times.

He slid behind the wheel. With the window lowered, he waited until he heard two vehicles pass before he started the engine. Then he nosed the car out from behind the trees. He could just see the taillights of two vehicles far down the road. He waited until they were nearly out of sight before pulling out onto the road. He had no intention of letting the cop spot him.

A cop will spot a tail on an empty road in a minute. Irritation buzzed over Mick's excitement. He used the binoculars to keep them in sight.

Mick wasn't taking chances. The cop could be her boyfriend. Hell, he could be her husband. The thought of stealing a cop's woman sent an extra thrill straight to his groin. She'd be one of his spoils of war.

He thought of the gun on her hip. Why would a lawyer who lives in the middle of fucking nowhere carry a gun? Bears? Mick snorted. Just who was Hannah Barrett?

He wasn't calling off his hunt just because there was a cop involved or because the blond had a piece. This went far beyond him wanting a woman. This was a matter of pride, of being a man, of getting what he deserved. No bitch hit him in the nuts and got away with it. Despite exorcising his demons on the pretty little blond girl last night, Mick had saved plenty for the lawyer.

He eased up on the gas. Far ahead, the sedan made a right turn. The pickup followed. Mick took his sweet time approaching the intersection. Giving the two vehicles in front of him plenty of room, he followed them to a quiet neighborhood close to the center of town. They parked in front of a small, tired house. Mick circled around the block and pulled to the curb a few lots down. A generous curve in the road gave him a straight view of the house. He took his binoculars from the console. The blinds were up in the front of the house, and he had a clear view within.

He slid down in the seat and watched the cop and the blond lead the dog up the front walk. The ease of last night's grab reinforced Mick's belief that opportunity would come to those who were patient. If he watched and waited, he would find Hannah Barrett's weakness.

Chapter Twenty-Two

Brody escorted Hannah and the dog up Chet's front walk.

Chet's car was in the driveway, but the house was dark and still. The lawn needed mowing, and the clear morning light highlighted dirt coating the windows. The place looked almost vacant, which was appropriate. Chet *existed* here, but he didn't *live*. Would he let Brody in? "I'm worried about him."

"Nothing will happen to him today." She leaned over and scratched AnnaBelle's head. "We'll see to that. Won't we, girl?"

"He might not remember you were here last night."

"In that case, we won't remind him." She smiled.

Brody's heart did a double tap. He knew without a doubt she would take care of Chet. A verbal promise from Hannah was as good as a signed and notarized contract. She wouldn't let him down, and he was really hoping that, with Hannah here as a buffer, Chet would actually open the door to the man who had destroyed his career.

Here goes.

They rang the bell. Footsteps approached. Chet's face appeared in the sidelight. He stared at them for a few seconds, his face contorted by the swirls in the safety glass. Brody held his breath. The dead bolt slid away, and Chet opened the door, dressed in jeans and a flannel shirt. Brody had seen corpses that looked more alive. Chet's skin was gray. His eyes had been bloodshot when Brody had woken him that morning, but now they were lifeless.

With a questioning glance at Hannah, he stepped back to let them into the foyer. He squinted at her. "You look familiar."

"Hannah was with me last night at The Pub," Brody said.

"Ah, shit." Chet scrubbed a hand across his scalp. "Can we talk for a minute?"

He's going to kick me out.

"Sure. Would you excuse us?" he asked Hannah.

"Certainly." She took the dog into the kitchen.

"I'm sorry, Chet," Brody said.

"What the hell are you sorry about? I'm the one who fucked up. I shouldn't have put you in that position." Chet pressed the heels of both hands over his closed eyelids. "I can't do anything right these days."

"Chet . . ."

"Don't make excuses for me." Bitterness sharpened Chet's tone. "I should have called my sponsor last night instead of driving down to The Pub. I'd been drinking the other day, too. I knew I was in trouble."

"What happened with the chief?"

"He called me into his office this morning and strongly suggested I retire. I left my gun and badge in his desk drawer."

"I'm sorry."

"Stop fucking apologizing." Chet paced a three-foot square. "This is entirely on me." He pivoted. "I don't know how much longer I can keep my shit together, Brody."

A rattling sigh rolled through Chet's skinny chest. He shook like a dog shedding water from its fur. "So, who's the hottie?"

Change of topic. Chet really needed a distraction.

"Hannah Barrett."

Chet's brow shot up. "Really?"

"Really."

"Can I ask why she's in my kitchen?"

"I thought you might be able to help her." Brody gave him the rundown on Hannah's assault and her search for the young girl in Vegas.

"I happen to have some free time." Chet shook his head. "But that's like trying to find a needle in a hundred acres of haystacks. No word on the fingerprints the Vegas PD lifted from the rental car?"

"Last I heard, they hadn't found any matches, but we don't even know for sure that those fingerprints belonged to either of the suspects or the victim. Could have been the parking valet or one of Hannah's clients."

"Do you have a copy of the sketches Kailee made?"

"Hannah brought them with her."

Chet scratched his head. "I'll see what I can do."

"I appreciate it."

"You really like her, don't you?"

Brody glanced down the hallway toward the kitchen. "Yeah."

"Go to work. Thanks to me being a drunken asshole, your case-load just doubled. My files will be on your desk by end of shift. The least I can do is look out for your girl."

His girl. He wished.

But for now, Hannah was looking out for Chet, and Chet was taking care of Hannah. Brody could get back to work without worrying about either one of them.

Genius.

Unless together they got into more trouble than either one of them would alone.

ʊ

"Nice dog."

"She is." Hannah and AnnaBelle followed Chet up a narrow staircase.

The second floor of the Cape Cod was a converted attic. Two windows, deeply recessed into dormers, provided scant light, leaving the space dark.

Chet walked into the dim room. A bare bulb hung from a string in the center of the room. "I haven't been in here for a while."

Hannah's boots clunked on raw wood. Dust tickled her nose, and she sneezed.

"Sorry about the dust." Chet yanked on the pull string. The swinging light arced, sending light careening around the room.

Hannah's head swam. Swaying, she closed her eyes.

"I'm sorry." Chet reached for the bulb. He stilled it with one hand and rolled a desk chair behind her. One hand on her elbow guided her into the seat. AnnaBelle stretched out on the floor at her feet.

She sat. "I wasn't expecting that."

"No dance clubs for you."

"That's not exactly a hardship." She opened her eyes. Her surroundings settled back into place.

"Not a clubber?" Chet crossed the room to a desk nestled between the dormers. He switched on a desk lamp.

"No." Hannah remembered the evening at Carnival. The lights and music had been irritating. But she'd never reacted with dizziness. Maybe that neurologist hadn't been entirely wrong. She sneezed again. Or it was allergies?

He grabbed a metal folding chair and opened it in front of a computer monitor. "That's something you and Brody have in common. I don't think I've ever seen him in a bar."

Random comment? Or not . . .

Hannah scanned the room, her belly cringing. Magnetic whiteboards held dozens of images of a teenage girl with long dark hair.

In some of the photos, she was looking away, her body projecting discomfort, as if she didn't want her picture taken. In other shots, she clearly didn't know she was being photographed. Handwritten notes accompanied each shot. There were pictures of other people as well, and Post-it notes or index cards full of scrawled annotations. A date in red ink headed each group of photos.

It was a timeline of Chet's daughter's disappearance, and the progress of his investigation.

Hannah brought her gaze back to Chet. "Can I ask you a question?"

"Sure." He leaned over and pressed the on button of the computer tower under the desk. The computer hummed to life. Behind them, a printer beeped.

"Why haven't you been up here?"

Chet dropped into the chair. His gaze followed the timeline. At the very end, he'd scrawled "Happy Birthday" in blue. "Last March was Teresa's eighteenth birthday."

"So you stopped looking for her?"

He stared at his timeline, his eyes moving from entry to entry, the scrawled notes becoming neater and more detailed as his investigation wore on. "Teresa hit puberty, and she changed. She was a pretty normal kid until then, maybe a little shy. But from the age of about twelve, she became increasingly unstable and erratic. Her mood swings went far beyond any normal range, even for a teenager. The doctors diagnosed her as bipolar. We managed her condition with medication for a couple of years, but the drugs had side effects, and it was hard to get the dosage just right, the way her hormones were all over the place. She was nauseous and lethargic and didn't want to take the meds. With the medication, she felt sick. Without them, she was uncontrollable. School was out of the question. My wife attempted to homeschool her, but really, her full-time job was keeping Teresa safe. Eventually, she ran away, from us, from the medications we were forcing her to take." He paused for a few breaths, his eyes roaming over the photos strung around the room.

"She's an adult now. She's no longer a missing child. I can't make her come home. Even if I got her here, I can't legally make her take medication. I can't make her do anything. An adult is free to do as she pleases, even if that means living on the street and eating out of Dumpsters. Unless a person is dangerous to herself or others, and that is damned hard to prove, this is a free country."

"I'm sorry."

Chet pulled a pair of reading glasses from his chest pocket and cleaned them on the hem of his shirt. "Last March, on Teresa's birthday, I closed the door on this room and promised myself I'd never open it again. I took two weeks of vacation and spent the time hammered on Johnnie Walker. I went to The Pub, turned into my alter ego, Drunken Asshole Man, and picked a fight with the biggest guy in the bar. Luckily for me, *he* wasn't a drunken jerk. The bartender called Brody to come and get me. It wasn't the first time, but I'd been sober for almost a year. My last bender had been right after my wife died. No one was arrested, but word got round, and the captain found out. He gave me my last warning. No drunks on his force. He warned me that I wouldn't get another break." He sighed, the exhalation sounding shaky and painful. His eyes met hers. "You don't have to look so glum. I was coming up on the mandatory retirement age anyway. This week's stint of stupidity just moved the date up six months."

Hannah frowned.

Chet held up a palm. "The chief's not a bad guy. He's running a police department, not a rehab center. I either need to act like an adult and deal with my shit in a responsible manner, or I have no fucking business being on the police force." He grimaced. "Please excuse the language."

"I've heard worse in multiple languages," Hannah said. "And how can you possibly move on after this week?"

"When the DNA results come back, I'll have to." Chet stopped rubbing his glasses. "Closing the door on this room didn't do anything except let me not deal with my problems. I haven't even answered the e-mail in the account I set up for the search for Teresa in six months. I didn't return calls from my contacts. That is denial, pure and simple."

"Brody doesn't think it's her."

Chet's shoulders slumped. "Brody is an optimist."

Hannah wanted to assure him that the dead woman wasn't his daughter, but who was she to say? Hope was a balancing act. Too little left a person unable to hang on. Too much made bad news unable to bear. She had a clear memory of her father telling her that her mother would be fine. That everything was going to be all right. She could beat the cancer. He believed it in every corner of his soul. In turn, Hannah had believed him, even though the doubt in the oncologist's eyes told her otherwise. "I wish I could tell you to have faith, but it feels like empty advice. I tend to expect the worst."

"Then *we* have something in common." Chet rubbed his eyes, put on his glasses, and turned to face the computer. The monitor had illuminated. Icons lined up in neat rows on an enlarged photo of his daughter at a much younger age, maybe five or six, with a smile that didn't indicate the devastating mental illness that was to come. "Now let's see if we can do something to help somebody. I'm starting to feel useless."

"Where do we start?" she asked.

"Did you bring the composite sketches?"

Hannah pulled the drawings from the manila envelope and handed them to Chet.

"Brody called the cop in Vegas and got him to send the fingerprints they lifted from the rental car." Chet opened an e-mail. "We have three sets of possible fingerprints, we have a name, which may or may not be the girl's real name, and a rough idea of what she looks like."

"That doesn't seem like much."

"It isn't, but what we do have is time. I happen to have scads of that to kill, so there's no harm in trying." Chet looked at her over the rims of his glasses. "You have anything better to do?"

"Unfortunately, no."

"Now we have two things in common." Chet pulled a stack of index cards from his drawer. "Let's start with a timeline." He dated the first card. "Tell me what happened."

Chapter Twenty-Three

Brody stepped out of the courtroom, pulled out his cell phone, and turned it on. He scrolled through his messages and paused on one from Vinnie Schooler, a forensic investigator with the CSI division. Nodding hello to a passing assistant prosecutor, he walked to the end of the corridor and returned Vinnie's call.

"Hey, Brody. I got something for you on your Jane Doe case."

"Something good?"

"I think so."

Brody pivoted and strode for the exit. "I'm just leaving the courthouse. I'll stop by in three minutes."

The majority of the county municipal buildings were located in a large complex. Brody drove a quarter mile down the road, passed the ME's office, and parked in front of the CSI unit. Vinnie was waiting for him. Olive complexioned, with black hair and eyes, he looked Sicilian enough to be confused with a Corleone. Vinnie sported a five o'clock shadow by noon.

"Thanks for calling." Brody followed him down to the forensics lab. "What do you have for me?"

"Hair. Some of these samples were found on the victim's clothing. Others came from the body." Vinnie crossed to the countertop. He opened a cardboard box and removed a slide. He held it between his fingertips. A single strand of long brown hair was coiled on the slide. "That's the victim's hair." Vinnie exchanged the slide for another. "This is a different person's hair."

The sample was short and blond. Brody stepped away from the counter. "Be nice if we had a suspect to match that to."

"That's your job." Vinnie removed another slide.

"Can you extract DNA?"

"Possibly. But that's not all I have for you."

Brody glanced down at a short black hair between the thin sheets of glass. "More hair?"

Vinnie shook his head. "Dog fur. We found fur from at least six different dogs. We haven't analyzed them for specific breed yet," Vinnie grinned. "But either she really loves dogs . . ."

"Or maybe she works with them." Ideas reeled through Brody's head. She could work for a dog groomer, vet, animal shelter, or she visited some place where she was exposed to numerous animals.

"That's all I have for now." Vinnie stepped away from the microscope. "But I'm still sorting through the trace evidence. I'll call you if I come up with anything else that's interesting."

"Thanks." Brody left the lab and went back to the police station. He knocked on the chief's door.

"Come in," the chief answered.

Brody pushed through.

Chief Horner leaned back and gave Brody his full attention as he succinctly explained what Vinnie had found.

"Let's get this done quickly," the chief said. "Pull a patrol officer to help you chase down this lead."

"Who would you like me to use?" Brody asked.

"Officer Dane came to mind first."

"Any specific reason?" Brody rested a fist on his hip.

"As the first officer on scene, she's the most familiar with the case." The chief nodded. "Do you think she's detective material?"

A small tinge of sadness eased through Brody. The chief was considering Chet's replacement. As much as he'd rather work alone, he had to be realistic. He needed help. Chet's career was over, and the second detective slot needed to be filled. Someone was getting promoted. "I do. Her attention to detail is excellent."

"She is very thorough." The chief picked up a packet of papers on his desk. "I have to clear my morning to read her reports."

Brody nodded. "Yes, but all those details are important when a case goes to trial two years after an arrest."

The chief sighed. "You're right. Lance is my other top candidate."

"Lance is also a solid cop. Thankfully, that'll be your decision. My job is to identify that body." Brody kept his distance from department politics.

He exited the chief's office. Stella had been on night shift this week. Officers rotated shifts on a biweekly basis. She'd probably be asleep. But he had no doubt the prospect of helping with an investigation would wake her up.

He called her on her cell phone and explained the situation. "Are you game?"

"Yes. Definitely." Her voice shifted from groggy to excited in an instant. "When do you want me to start?"

"How fast can you get here?"

She didn't hesitate. "Half hour."

In thirty minutes, she met him in the small conference room. She held a cardboard drink carrier in one hand and a bakery box in the other.

"With my thanks." She handed him a coffee.

"No need to thank me. But I'll take the coffee."

Stella opened the box. "Apple cider donut? They won't last five minutes once I put them out there." She jerked her thumb at the doorway.

"Can't say no to one of those." Brody took a donut.

"I already had two." Stella went out into the main room and set the box on the counter.

Brody ate the pastry in two bites.

"What are we doing?" Excitement shone from her eyes.

Brody handed her a sheet of paper. "There are thirty-seven vets, kennels, groomers, and dog trainers in Randolph County. We're calling them all to see if anyone is missing a young female employee. If we don't come up with anything, we'll expand our search to the surrounding counties."

"How far down the list have you gotten?"

"Just started."

Stella dropped into the chair and tucked an escaped strand of long black hair back into the severe knot at the base of her neck. "Give me the bottom half of the list."

By lunchtime, they had thirty-six negative responses and one line with no answer. "This is starting to seem pointless."

Brody stood and stretched. "Let's take a break. We'll grab a sandwich and stop at this kennel where no one answered the phone. Then we'll attack the next county this afternoon."

Brody unlocked his county sedan. "You want to eat first or run out to the kennel?" he asked over the roof.

"Let's do the kennel. I'm still full of donuts." Stella got into the passenger seat.

He started the car. "You ate six."

"And they were fantastic." She patted her belly. The soft chatter of the radio underscored their conversation.

Brody drove to the highway and eased into the right lane. Afternoon traffic was light. "How far is it?"

Stella consulted the address. "Two miles."

A minute later, Brody slowed at the sight of lights flashing ahead of them. An SFPD cruiser had pulled over a minivan.

"That's Lance," Stella said as they passed. "The turn is just ahead."

Brody eased his foot off the gas and turned onto a narrow one-lane country road. An empty field ran along the left side of the road. To the right, trees and underbrush grew close to the pavement.

"There it is." Stella pointed to a break in the foliage. A sign nailed to a tree read Scarlet Creek Kennels. The metal gate stood open. Brody turned onto the dirt lane. A tan mobile home perched on an incline. Shrubs surrounded the foundation. Behind the house, barking erupted from a brown one-story building resembling a barn. Dogs barked from a dozen long, narrow runs. A few run-down outbuildings dotted the property.

Brody parked in a gravel rectangle next to the kennel and used his radio to report their location. He and Stella crossed the gravel lot and went through the open door to the barnlike building. A large open space housed rows of dog runs. In the open space in front of the kennels, colored nylon leashes hung on wall pegs. Hallways led in both directions. A sign with a gold arrow directed them down a hallway to an office.

"Hello?" Brody called out.

The dogs that had been outside rushed in, leaving the heavy rubber dog doors flapping. Barking echoed in the space. Inside the runs, piles of feces dotted the concrete. He walked to the closest chain-link gate. A black lab whined and wagged on the other side. Two stainless steel bowls sat empty.

"Remind me never to board my dog here." Stella stuck her fingers through the chain links of a kennel gate. A wiggling spaniel on the other side licked her fingers.

"I don't like it. Something is wrong here." He scanned the runs. "No one has cleaned these kennels for at least a couple of days. Water bowls are low or empty."

The din in the kennel dimmed as some of the dogs settled.

"Let's see if anyone is in the office." Brody led the way out of the main kennel area. The door closed behind them, muffling the noise. Following the "Office" sign, they turned down the corridor. Brody glanced in open doorways as they walked. Storage rooms held dog food and grooming supplies. One room contained a washtub and a stainless steel grooming stand. The office door was open. He knocked on the jamb and poked his head inside. No one sat behind the metal desk.

They went outside. The same *being watched* feeling that had bugged Brody outside Hannah's this morning whispered across his nape. "I don't like it."

Stella shrugged. "Maybe no one's home."

"I think somebody's here." Brody could feel eyes on him. "Call for backup. Maybe they'll open the door for a uniform."

Dispatch reported back that a unit was en route.

"Probably Lance." Stella leaned on the car. "We'll need to get the SPCA officers out here to see to those dogs."

"As soon as we know the property is clear, we can make sure they all have water."

When Lance arrived, he got out of his patrol car, and Brody filled him in on the situation.

They went up to the door. Stella rang the bell, and Lance hung back, his gaze scanning the windows. No one answered. Brody thumped on the door with his fist.

"Police," he called.

A creak sounded from inside the house.

"We need to ask you a few questions," Brody yelled.

Craning his neck to peer into the front window, Lance moved sideways.

A gunshot cracked. Glass broke. Lance's body jerked and folded to the ground.

Stella shouted into the radio on her collar, "Officer down."

ꟺ

Hannah closed her eyes and retold the story. Her hand stroked the dog sitting at her side. Though she tried to stick to the facts, panic crawled around inside her as she detailed the last minute of the attack, Jewel being dragged out of the rental car. Sweat broke out on her back. Chet got up and went downstairs. Floorboards squeaked and water rushed. He came back a minute later with a glass of ice water in his hand.

He handed it to Hannah. "Sounds like you did everything you could."

Unsure if she could swallow in her tight throat, she took a very small sip. The icy liquid soothed. "It doesn't feel that way." Her mind rewound to last spring. She pictured Carson being chased and the fire at Lee's house. It hadn't felt like she'd done enough then either.

"Never does, after the fact." Chet squinted at her. Guilt puckered his brow. "I'm sorry I acted like an asshole last night. You got pulled into another dangerous situation because of me."

"Brody sent me outside. It was my choice to go back into the bar."

"I heard you took out two dudes with a cue stick."

She sighed. "I didn't see many options."

"Brody said it was because of you that he didn't have to shoot anyone. So thank you."

Heat flushed her neck. The three drunken bikers had been intimidating, but not frightening in the same bowel-cramping way as the threat to Jewel or Carson. It was one thing to risk her own life, but she felt an entirely different level of fear when young innocents were in danger.

"I would have felt responsible if Brody had killed somebody off-duty because I was a drunken jerk." Chet snorted. "Cops have enough threats to deal with when they're on shift."

Hannah drank more water. "Is his job normally dangerous?"

Chet folded his arms over his chest. "Scarlet Falls used to be a really quiet place. But as folks migrate out of the cities into the country, gangs and drugs and crime follow them. Also, some people just suck, and there isn't a damned thing anyone can do about that. Your brother's murder is a perfect example. I was on my bender when it happened, but I heard about it. I'm sorry for your loss."

"Thank you." Hannah stared at the ice bobbing in her glass. "Lee used to call me every weekend. Sometimes when my phone rings on a Sunday, I still expect it to be him."

Chet nodded. "And when it isn't him, it's like being kicked in the nuts all over again. Metaphorically speaking."

Hannah laughed. "Yes, I suppose that's a pretty good analogy."

"Well, thanks for watching Brody's back."

She thought back to Brody's convenience-store shooting. "I'm glad I was there. I wish someone had been there for him in Boston."

"He told you about the shooting?" Chet's eyebrow lifted. "That's not something he ever talks about, not with anyone."

"He didn't dwell on it," Hannah said. Neither her brother nor her father ever wanted to talk about their experiences in combat.

Chet clasped his hands, leaned forward, and rested his forearms on his thighs. "I bet he didn't mention the commendation he received?"

"No." But that didn't surprise her.

"Well, he did. He saved three people."

"But at a huge cost to himself."

"Yeah." Chet stared at his joined hands for a few seconds. "So thanks for helping him out. I'm really glad he didn't have to shoot anyone because I was an idiot." His change in tone suggested he knew how Brody felt, and that he was done talking about it. "Besides, you can't imagine how much paperwork a shooting requires."

"So how do we start looking for the girl in Vegas?" she asked.

Chet turned back to his desk. "Normally, when looking for a missing teen, the go-to source is the friends. We can't do that. We also don't have cell phone, ATM, or credit card records to check. The Vegas PD is trying to match the prints. They'll start local and expand their search as they go along. But I learned a couple of things from my own experience. Within forty-eight hours, someone is going to try to lure a runaway into prostitution. Once a pimp gets ahold of a kid, it's very hard for the kid to get away—dangerous even."

Had he tracked his daughter that far?

"I know you're wondering about Teresa. Yes, I believed she was being trafficked. She was likely also using drugs. While she didn't like the side effects of her prescribed medicine, she did try to escape her symptoms with recreational drugs and alcohol." His fingers curled into fists. "I guess I provided the perfect example."

"So where does that leave us?" Hannah put him back on track. There was no use beating himself up for a past he couldn't change.

"If your teen is being trafficked, she might not be from Nevada. She could be from any state. Did she have an accent? Is there a possibility that she's from another country? Traffickers bring girls from Mexico or other foreign countries. Sometimes the girl's parents pay these guys, thinking their daughters will get a better life in America. Then when the girls are brought over, the traffickers tell them they have a debt to work off. Families are threatened. Girls who are here illegally won't go to the police. They're forced into prostitution to pay off a never-ending debt. Girls are also shipped around from state to state. It's harder for families to track a girl if she's frequently moved."

Hannah searched her memory. "I didn't hear a foreign accent or any indication that English wasn't her primary language."

"OK, then we'll focus on states in the continental US."

"This sounds like a very organized activity."

"Sometimes yes, sometimes no." Chet scrolled to a website and paused on a phone number. "Girls get trafficked by their boyfriends, by kidnappers. Or they're already turning tricks to put a roof over their head or buy a meal, and a pimp gets his hooks into them. And some girls are sole proprietors. Maybe she's hungry or has kids to feed and no marketable skills. If she only has one thing to sell, and she's desperate enough . . ."

Hannah supposed hungry children were motivation to do just about anything to feed them.

"Now. We're going to play a game. I'm going to ask you a lot of questions. The cop in Vegas probably asked you most of them. Just do your best to answer." He put two sheets of paper in front of her. On the top of one he wrote *Sure*. The other paper he headed with the title *Maybe*. "If you're one hundred percent positive of your answer, write it here. Be quick. Let's see if your subconscious is holding any information hostage. If it's more of an impression, write it here. When we're done, I'll put it all together and start making calls."

"OK."

His questions came rapid-fire. "Did she have a regional accent? Exactly how did she phrase that?"

When Chet's interrogation was finished, Hannah looked down at the paper. She'd remembered a few more details, but her head ached from the strain.

"Go on downstairs and take a break while I put this all together and make a few calls."

Hannah went down to the kitchen for more water. She took a Tylenol from her purse and swallowed it. Needing a distraction to take her mind off the never-ending replay of Jewel's abduction, she switched on the television, turned the volume on low, and sat on the couch. A blue scroll on the television caught her attention.

"Breaking news: Shooting in progress, Scarlet Falls, NY."

She ran to the bottom of the stairs. "Chet!"

He appeared on the top landing. His face was drained of color.

"You heard about the shooting?" She glanced back at the TV. A commercial played. The blue banner was unchanged. No new information.

"What shooting?" He descended the stairs.

She pointed at the TV. The thought of Brody shot and killed took Hannah out at the knees. She wobbled. Chet grabbed her arm and eased her onto the couch. "I'll find out what happened." He reached for the phone.

Eyes locked on the TV, Hannah wrapped her arms around her body. Chet had been upset before she'd told him about the shooting. He ended his call. "He'll call me back as soon as he has details."

Who was shot?

He sat on the sofa next to her, eyes riveted on the TV.

"What happened before I called you?"

"I opened my e-mail. There are more than three hundred messages in there from the last six months."

"Are you going to open them?"

"I don't know," Chet said.

A blond female reporter in a newsroom appeared on the TV. She read from a teleprompter. "A report just in. A shooting is in progress at a kennel in Scarlet Falls. At least one police officer has been shot."

Chapter Twenty-Four

Brody dove for the ground. A bullet whizzed past his head. Weapon in hand, he crawled to the steps and took cover behind the thick concrete. The suspect was firing through the windows from inside the house. At that angle, he couldn't shoot Brody without coming outside.

But Brody was pinned. He couldn't see the shooter from his position.

Where was Stella?

Had she retreated to the car? She couldn't have left him and Lance. Disappointment swamped Brody as he scanned the area.

Wait. He saw her moving behind the unmarked car. Crouching, she ran to the trunk, opened it, and removed Brody's AR-15. Holding the rifle across her body, she moved toward him.

She hadn't run. She'd gone for a longer-range weapon. *Smart girl.* Relief flooded Brody.

Another shot came from inside the house, puffing the dirt in front of Stella. Brody looked up. Just the tip of the muzzle of a rifle protruded through a hole in the glass. Stella went flat, took aim, and fired a three-shot burst. The shooter went quiet.

Had she hit him? And was Lance still alive?

Twenty feet away from Brody, the downed officer's feet kicked on the ground. Not only was he still alive, he was trying to inch away from the house. But his body didn't budge. His injuries were too serious, and he appeared too weak to move. Blood stained the grass next to his leg. Too much blood for Lance to last very long without help. But to get to him, Brody was going to have to cover open ground. He'd be a clear target, like a metal duck in a shooting gallery.

To save Lance, Brody would have to trust Stella.

"Can you cover me?" he shouted.

She nodded and lifted the rifle. Sweat soaked Brody's shirt. She yelled something back, but Brody didn't hear it. His hearing was muffled, as if he were wearing the double layers of ear protection he used at the firing range.

Brody levered a knee under his body, launched to his feet, and ran for Lance. Stella fired at the window as Brody crossed the grass, grabbed Lance under the armpits, and dragged him toward the police cars. Lance's blue eyes were wide open and hazed with fear and pain.

A shot rang from the house. A bullet whizzed by Brody's head. He dropped, covering Lance with his own torso. Stella took aim and fired again. Then she straightened, waiting. Quiet descended again. Brody's hearing returned as suddenly as it had disappeared. He heard the wind and Lance's groans beneath him. The thin wail of an approaching siren floated in the air.

Brody pulled Lance behind the police vehicles. The cop's pale face was turned away. Was he alive? Brody kept one eye on the house and reached for his neck. A pulse thrummed weakly against his fingertips.

In his peripheral vision, he saw a red stain spreading in the dirt next to Lance's leg. The bullet had struck him in the thigh. Blood was turning the gravel muddy. He was bleeding out fast. Brody yanked off Lance's clip-on uniform tie, folded it in half, and pressed it to the wound. Then he yanked off his own tie, looped it around Lance's leg, and tied it snugly. The blood flow seemed to slow, or was that Brody's wishful thinking? "Hang on, Lance."

Lance's eyes darted in wild circles. "Where is he?"

"No worries. Stella's got us covered," Brody said.

A door slammed. The shooter ran out the side exit of the house, a rifle in one hand, two bags in the other.

"Stop. Police," Stella yelled.

The man whirled and fired a round at them. Stella answered with a burst from the AR-15. The shooter stumbled. She'd hit him. He recovered, though his pace was slower as he limped toward the barn. A few seconds later, a Camry roared out of the barn and over the field on the other side of the house. The vehicle fishtailed as it made a high-speed turn onto the road and sped away.

Sweat dripped into Brody's eye, blurring his vision. He wiped his forehead with his sleeve. "Did you get the plate number?"

"No. Too far." Moving toward him, Stella used the radio on her collar to update dispatch and give a basic description of the vehicle and suspect.

"How's Lance?" she asked without taking her eyes off the house.

"Hanging in," Brody said.

Lance's eyes were closed, but he was still breathing.

Brody's heartbeat ran in triple time. His lungs heaved, and sweat poured down his spine as he turned his attention back to Lance.

"I think the bleeding is slowing," Brody said, mostly for Lance's benefit. Stella returned to the car for a blanket. She covered Lance's shivering body.

"I'm dying," he wheezed.

"No, you're not." Stella took his hand.

"We got this," a voice said over Brody's shoulder. An EMT. Brody turned. A paramedic unit and two state troopers were parked next to his vehicle. When had they arrived?

Brody and Stella stepped back and let the EMTs take over. A sudden wave of weakness swept over Brody as his adrenaline plummeted. He leaned on his thighs and waited for his vision to clear. Stella stumbled to the side of the road and heaved into the weeds. When his head settled, he moved back to his vehicle and sat on the front bumper. Stella joined him a few minutes later.

"You OK?" he asked.

"Yes." Her voice lacked conviction. She stared at him. "You're bleeding."

Brody looked down. His hands were coated in blood. More red stained his clothes. "It's not mine."

"You have a cut on your forehead."

"I can't feel it." Brody's whole body was numb.

More police cars and an ambulance arrived. An EMT taped a piece of gauze over Brody's cut. Emergency personnel loaded Lance into the back of the ambulance and drove away. He heard the *whump-whump* of helicopter blades. He covered his eyes and squinted at the sky. A news helicopter hovered overhead.

"Think he's going to make it?" Stella asked.

"Lance?"

"Yeah."

"I don't know." Brody turned to look at her. "You did good."

"I never shot anyone before." Her eyes were huge in her pale face. She was thirty years old, with seven solid years on the SFPD, but her pallor and shock made her look impossibly young. Stella scuffed a toe of an ugly black shoe in the dirt. "Most cops go through their entire careers without shooting anyone. I had hoped to be one of them."

"Don't we all."

"You ever shoot anyone?"

"Yeah."

"Get over it?"

"Not really," Brody said. Except for that one surprising conversation with Hannah, he never talked about his one and only shooting. Why had he opened up to her? "If you need to talk to anyone, I'm around. Don't let it fester. The chief is going to put you on administrative leave or desk duty for a week or two. It doesn't mean anything. It's just policy. He's also going to send you in for a psych eval. Do yourself a favor. Talk to the doctor. It'll help."

"Did you?"

"Not at first. I thought I could handle it." He paused for a breath. The shooting in Boston had been completely justified. He'd had no legal issues. But no amount of training had prepared him to take a life. "I was wrong. It would have been easier if I'd have dealt with it right away."

ω

Hannah stared at the television. Her vision swam. Chet pushed her head between her knees. "Relax. Shooter situations are usually patrol. Brody doesn't work patrol."

The scene shifted to an aerial view of a field and outbuildings.

"Shit. That's his car."

Chet's phone buzzed, and he answered it. He exhaled, his chest deflating with relief. He covered the speaker with his finger. "He's OK."

Hannah breathed.

Chet ended his call. "Apparently, Brody and another officer went out to a kennel to ask some questions, and some guy started shooting at them." He scanned her face. "You all right now?"

"Yes." Mostly. But, obviously, Brody meant more to her than she'd realized. How did she feel about that? "Someone else was shot?"

"Yeah. Patrol officer. Good guy. He's at the hospital. Doesn't look good." Chet went quiet.

"I'm sorry. You knew him well?"

"It's a small force, and I've been on it a long time." He paused. "I *was* on it for a long time," he corrected, as if his retired status was hard for him to believe. "We all know each other well. Brody is on his way to the hospital. Apparently, he has a very minor injury. Every other available cop will be looking for the scumbag who did this."

Hannah needed to see him. She needed to put her hands on his body and assure herself that he was intact. "Want to ride over there?"

Chet paused. "I do."

"Then let's go." Hannah took the dog outside for a two-minute walk. "Do you mind if I leave the dog here? She's not destructive."

"Not at all." He lifted his keys from a rack on the wall.

In five minutes they were on the road headed for the local hospital. The fifteen-minute drive seemed much longer. One woman in uniform and Brody sat in the ER waiting room. Hannah's stride faltered as she took in the bloodstains on Brody's clothes. He'd taken off his jacket and rolled up the sleeves, but Hannah could still see that his cuffs were stained rusty brown. His gray suit pants were bloody at the knees. A square of gauze was taped to his forehead.

"Are you all right?" She touched his cheek.

He put his hand over hers. "I'm fine. It's barely a scratch. Two stitches."

"How is he?" Chet asked.

Brody didn't take his eyes off Hannah as he answered. "They're stabilizing him here and medevacing him to the trauma center in Albany."

"Lance is a fighter," Chet said.

Another man motioned to Chet, and he crossed the room to sit in a plastic chair next to him. The low murmur of muted conversation followed.

Hannah took Brody's hand and led him into the hallway. She stepped closer, until they were toe-to-toe, and ran her hands up his arms, over his shoulders, to his chest. His heart beat under her palm.

Sliding her arms around his waist, she pulled him close and leaned her head against his chest.

She reveled in the movement of his chest beneath her face. Every breath that passed in and out of his lungs reinforced the fact that he was alive.

People she cared about tended to end up dead.

Brody tried to back away. "I'm covered in blood."

She tightened the grip of her arms. She would have waded through a river of blood to touch him. "I thought you were dead."

His arms folded around her. "I'm sorry."

She shook her head. "Not your fault. You were doing your job. Do you have to go back to work?"

He shook his head. "Not right now. I'm going home to change and shower. Come with me?"

"I brought Chet here."

Chet waved her off. "I'll get a ride home. Go."

Hannah went out to the truck and followed Brody back into town. They stopped at Chet's and picked up the dog. Brody parked in front of a large three-story house on a quiet side street near the business district. By the time they arrived, rain was falling. She got out of the pickup. The sky opened up, soaking her to the skin in seconds. They ran up the walk onto the porch.

The porch light and the rain brightened the bloodstains on Brody's clothes. He had a dangerous job, and she couldn't bear to lose another person in her life. She hadn't recovered from Lee's death.

But was it too late to make the choice? What did she feel for Brody?

Chapter Twenty-Five

The truck rumbled to a stop. The engine shut off, protesting with a series of metallic knocks. Jewel straightened, fresh fear bracing her spine. Though they'd spent the night in the truck, she doubted they'd traveled far. They'd picked up two more girls, but much of the time, the vehicle hadn't been moving.

Other girls stirred around her. There was no chatter, no hushed conversations, just apprehension simmering in the stale air. Jewel pressed a hand to the center of her stomach, where an anxious ache replaced hunger.

The rear door rolled up. A man climbed into the truck and started unlocking handcuffs. One by one, they clattered to the metal floor. A male voice outside shouted, "Everybody up and out."

Jewel stood, rubbing her wrists. She led the way, shuffling to the edge. A man standing behind the truck took her hand and helped her down with a rough hold on her bicep. Cold concrete chilled her bare feet. He waved her forward and reached for the next girl. The truck had pulled into a warehouse. Two other men hung back, their gazes assessing the girls as they lined up. A fifth man stood with his back against the closed overhead door. He held some sort of rifle across his chest. Or was that a machine gun? Jewel's head swiveled. Her eyes stretched wide as she took in her surroundings. Another armed man stood on the other side of the receiving bay.

I'm never getting out of here.

The column of girls filed out. They went through a set of doors into a makeshift locker room. Shower heads lined the far wall. Water swirled into drains.

One of the men stepped to the front. "Drop your clothes into the garbage can. After you shower, you will be issued new clothing."

The air was hot, but the girls were shaking.

"Where are we?" Jewel asked.

The man stepped up to Jewel and slapped her across the face. She fell backward a step, then willed her skeleton to straighten. She lifted her chin and stared back at him. With a smile, he moved to the pregnant girl and, without taking his eyes off Jewel, slapped the girl hard across the face. She fell to her hands and knees, clutching her swollen belly.

Jewel got the message. She stripped off her tank, strode to the trash can, and dropped it in. Her shorts followed. Naked, she moved into the shower. Cool water sluiced over hot skin. The other girls followed Jewel.

How the hell did she end up being their leader?

Gallon-size containers of shampoo, conditioner, and antibacterial shower gel sat on the floor. Jewel made use of them. Sure, she'd been whored out to hundreds of men, but showering in front of these men still seemed like an invasion of her privacy. As much as she hated their intrusion on such an intimate act, she had to admit that being clean felt good. She shampooed her hair with angry energy. They were instructed to use conditioner. Safety razors were handed out. No hairy legs or armpits allowed.

Jewel emerged from the spray and grabbed a towel from a rack. She dried off and wrapped the damp towel around her body. They filed into the next room. Clean shorts and T-shirts were stacked on shelves and sorted by size. She found extra-smalls and dressed, then wrapped the towel around her dripping hair and waited for the rest of the girls to finish. Twenty minutes later, the girls were herded through another door. Shock stopped her feet, but a hand on her back propelled her forward.

The door opened into a long corridor. Doors lined both sides. They were marched down the hall. At the end, five rooms stood open.

"Two girls to a room," a man ordered. He pushed the pregnant girl through the first doorway and pointed at Jewel. "You, in there."

Shit.

Pressing a hand to the small of her back, the pregnant girl shuffled in. That was the one person Jewel did not want to get to know better.

As Jewel passed by, the man blocked her path and whispered in her ear, "I heard about you. You're the troublemaker. Just remember, every time you act up, I punish you both." He stepped away and closed the door, leaving Jewel alone with the pregnant girl.

"What's your name?" Supporting her belly, the girl lowered her butt onto one of the cots. "I'm—"

"Don't say it. I don't want to know." Jewel crossed to the opposite cot, sat on it, and closed her eyes. She'd counted six armed men and twenty doors. With two girls to a room, that meant forty women could be held in this warehouse. This was no pimp and a few hos. This was big business.

"Penny. My name is Penny. And that's my real name, not the ridiculous one they gave me."

Jewel opened her eyes. Across the tiny room, Penny folded her arms over her belly and shot Jewel a *Screw you* look.

"What's that?" Jewel regretted the question, but it was too late to pull it back into her mouth.

"Fantasy."

Jewel snorted. "That is ridiculous."

"What's your real name?" Penny asked.

"We're not doing this." Jewel remembered Lola's betrayal. She couldn't trust anyone. People did what was best for themselves, and she'd better learn to put her own needs first.

"Doing what?"

"Getting chummy. This is temporary. Some kind of processing center. We'll all be redistributed. Who knows where we'll end up? You worry about you, and I'll worry about me. Got it?"

"Yeah, I got it," Penny snapped back. She curled up on her side, one hand cradling her belly. Jewel turned toward the wall. That baby wasn't her problem, but she couldn't help wonder what would happen to it after it was born.

ᚹ

Brody grabbed towels from the closet. He handed one to Hannah and rubbed the other over the dog's fur.

Hannah's teeth chattered as she unsnapped AnnaBelle's leash. "Your house is beautiful."

"Thanks. It's big and requires a lot of work, but it's home."

The dog trotted down the hall. She found the cat's water bowl and drank it dry. Brody refilled it. "She won't chase the cat, will she?"

"I have no idea," Hannah said. "Let me grab her."

But the old cat sauntered in, fearless, and rubbed on the dog's side. AnnaBelle gave him a sniff and a wag.

"What's his name?" Hannah stooped to scratch behind a scraggly ear.

"Danno."

She laughed. "Good name for a cop's cat."

Brody went to the thermostat and turned up the temperature.

"The retrofitted air-conditioning system isn't the most efficient, but these old radiators can put out some heat."

"What year was this built?" She trailed a hand over the wainscoting that lined the foyer and hallway.

"1885." He led her down the wide-planked corridor to the kitchen. "Why don't I give you something dry to put on? I have to shower and change."

"Would you mind if I took a quick shower?" she asked. "I'm cold straight through."

"Not at all." The thought of her naked in his house sent a bolt of hunger straight through his blood.

The narrow staircase forced them into single file. He flipped on the light in the guest bath. When renovating, he'd followed the house's original decor as closely as possible. The bath was fitted with retro fixtures: a pedestal sink and a cast-iron claw-footed tub he'd bought at auction and had re-enameled. The floor was cream-and-black octagonal mosaic tile.

"This is lovely."

"There's soap in the shower and towels in the linen closet behind the door."

"Thanks." She went into the room, pausing with the door half closed. She blinked back at him, a shocking amount of emotion swirling in her pretty blue eyes. With the crisis over, she looked lost.

He wanted to kiss her, but she was shivering hard, and he was filthy. "Need anything else?"

"No. I think that's everything."

"I'll put some dry clothes outside the door."

With a nod, she disappeared. A minute later, he heard plumbing squeal, and water rushed through pipes somewhere else in the house. He rooted through his drawer for a pair of sweatpants, a tee, and a flannel shirt. He piled them outside the hall bath. In the master, Brody stripped, dropping his bloody clothes in a trash bag.

He stepped into the glassed-in shower. While he'd maintained the house's antique integrity in the rest of the rooms, he'd fully modernized the master bath. It was ten minutes before he was satisfied that no more blood remained on his body. He dried off and wrapped a towel around his hips.

"Brody?" Hannah called from the hall. "Can I put my wet stuff in your dryer?"

He opened the door. She was standing just outside his bedroom, the lapels of his flannel shirt clutched in one hand, a pile of wet clothes in the other. Her hair was damp but combed, the short locks framing a heart-shaped face flushed pink from the hot shower. Though she was only a head shorter than him, her frame was narrow. She'd rolled the waistband of his sweatpants over twice, but they rode low on her hips as if they could fall at any second, something he could easily picture happening. Right now. A tiny sliver of skin showed between the hem of the shirt and the waistband of the sagging pants. His eyes lingered on that half inch of bare skin. If those pants dropped an inch . . .

Yes, he'd seen her in a silk blouse and tailored power suit, but *this* . . . This was sexy. And made him want to tug her into a bed beside him.

After the horror of today, he needed . . . He paused. What *did* he need? Hannah.

Her eyes strayed from his face down his chest and paused on the towel.

She was checking him out. *Nice.*

"I'm sorry." Blushing, she turned away. "I'll wait downstairs."

"No need." Brody moved closer and took the wet clothes from her. He leaned closer and inhaled. She smelled of mint and soap, and he wanted a taste. His gaze drifted from her mouth to her eyes.

Her hand in the middle of his bare chest stopped him. She was studying him with suspicion, almost wariness. "What are we doing here, Brody?"

"I don't know. I'm making this up as I go along." But he *was* thinking ahead. Maybe ten minutes ahead. No more. He refused to think about the reports he'd file tomorrow or about today's shooting. Or where Hannah would be in a month. There was only here and now.

He saw her hand inching lower, sliding down his abs . . .

"Do we have to have a plan?" he asked, his voice rough.

"I like plans."

"How does this fit into your plan?" Brody caught the back of her neck with his free hand, gently pulled her in, and covered her mouth with his. Her elbow bent, trapping her hand between their bodies. He turned his head, slanting his lips to taste more of her, easing his tongue inside her mouth. He dropped the clothes to place his other hand on her hip and touched the exposed strip of smooth skin at her waist. His thumb stroked her hip bone. He felt the shiver course through her body.

"Cold?" He lifted his head. Her eyes were closed. They blinked open, the blue clouded with confusion—and desire.

"Um. No." She slid her trapped hand to settle it on his shoulder.

Brody's gaze caught the fading bruise at her hairline. "Maybe this isn't a good idea. You're still recovering."

"Chicken."

Had he heard her correctly? "What?"

"You heard me." Her expression went from wary to wicked. How did she know that humor was exactly what he needed? "You started this, and now you're chickening out." Her hand dropped to the towel. She tugged the end free and let it drop. "Mm. I don't see any second thoughts."

"I want you, but that doesn't mean I'm going to take advantage of you." The tension inside him eased with her teasing.

"You are the one who had a hellacious day. Am I taking advantage of you?" Hannah took a step back and unbuttoned the flannel shirt. Walking past him into the master bedroom, she tossed it over her shoulder. She slid her pants down her legs and stepped out of them. *Oh.* She'd been commando under his pants, something he should have known since her clothes had been wet through. Why did that thought zing straight to his balls?

The T-shirt hit the wall next to his head, and the sight of her naked body stunned him.

Challenge filled the glance she cast back at him. He'd always thought of blue as a cool color, but tonight her eyes blazed pure heat.

"Come on, Brody. What are you afraid of?"

You.

Somewhere inside Brody's head, under the raging *want* of her, an alarm went off. If he gave in to his desire tonight, nothing would ever be the same. One night with her would never be enough. He'd be giving her the power to hurt him. But tonight, he didn't care. He needed human contact.

He needed her.

She walked five paces and stopped next to the bed. She turned, giving him her body in profile. Long, long legs. Lean body. Small breasts in perfect proportion to the sleek length of her.

Deep in his chest, something gave, opened, unfurled. There was no choice to make. He had to have her.

Brody moved toward her. No risk. No reward.

Chapter Twenty-Six

Was he going to reject her?

Hannah paused in the doorway. The air in the room chilled her skin. Brody's bedroom was masculine, decorated in earth tones from pale gray to deep brown. An island-size sleigh bed dominated the space. Goose bumps rippled up her arms. Fear or cold?

Ten feet away from her, Brody wrestled with a decision. A thought bloomed in Hannah's mind. She needed to get to know this man better. There was more to him than he'd revealed. He'd kissed her, and his physical hunger for her was obvious. So why was he hesitating?

Brody kept his emotions bottled with a tight seal. From the desire in his kiss, she'd thought he needed comfort and distraction after today's turmoil. But she shouldn't have pressured him. Behind the want in his eyes, there was another emotion buried: pain. He'd downplayed his ex-wife's cheating, but clearly, her betrayal had left a scar. The sudden surge of anger shocked her. She couldn't bulldoze her way through Brody's walls. A kiss was not always an invitation to share one's bed. Sometimes a kiss was just a kiss.

Her gaze fell to the clothes she'd tossed on the floor. She stooped to gather them, shame bursting through her. "I'm sorry. The timing is all wrong. I didn't mean to—"

He crossed the gap between them in two long strides. His shadow fell over her. His hand grasped her shoulders, pulled her to her feet.

"Are you sure?" she asked.

He crushed his mouth to hers. His hands grasped her hips and pulled her body to his, every inch of him hard and lean. There was no bulkiness to his frame. He had the body of an endurance athlete. If the previous kiss had been warm, this one needed to be measured in degrees Kelvin.

One hand circled to her back, stroking up and down her bare skin. "I need you."

Desire crowded out Hannah's doubts. She pressed her body against his, skin sliding over skin, heat meeting heat.

He backed her toward the bed. Her legs hit the edge of the mattress. She fell backward, pulling Brody on top of her. They tumbled onto the duvet.

Brody's mouth cruised over her, his hands covering the skin his lips weren't touching, as if he couldn't get enough of her. He kissed her breasts. Heat blasted through her. Her hand closed around him then moved around to cup his balls. A masculine groan rumbled through his chest.

He lifted his head. One arm reached for the nightstand. He opened the drawer and pulled out a small package of condoms. Shock and horror crossed his face.

"What's wrong?"

"They're expired." He sighed. "It's been a while."

"Let me check my bag. We might get lucky." Hannah pushed off the bed. She went into the bathroom, where she'd left her purse. She unzipped the small compartments. Damn. Not there.

"Might?" He called from the bedroom.

"It's not like I use them by the dozen."

"Well, I'm glad to hear that."

Purse in hand, she went back into the bedroom and rooted in her handbag for her tiny cosmetic bag. She could feel his eyes on her. She looked back at him. He'd rolled onto his back, one arm over his head on the pillow, his body stretched out like a buffet. A sexy grin full of male appreciation spread across his face.

She paused. "What are you thinking?"

"That you should do everything naked."

The laugh eased her nerves. Kneeling, she pulled the nylon case out and opened the clasp. Her hand went to the small zippered compartments in the lining. She swept her fingers inside. "Bingo." Thankfully, her cosmetic case hadn't fit in the small evening bag that was stolen in Vegas.

Grasping the foil pouch, she moved back to the bed. "But I only have one."

"Then we'd better make the most of it." He reached for her.

Condom in hand, she crawled across the bed and straddled him. His hands encircled her waist, caressing the sensitive skin from her hips to her ribs. She opened the condom and sheathed him. Lowering her torso, she pressed their bodies together. Their lips met. His tongue was slick and hot as it slid between her lips. She could imagine it stroking other sensitive parts of her body.

The mad condom search had defused her. The heat built again, slower and steadier this time, marathon versus sprint. His hands were gentle, sure and clever, sliding, caressing.

A fingertip slipped inside her and sent her desire into a free fall. She lifted her head. "Brody . . ."

"Mm." The finger withdrew and circled.

"Any time now." She tried to sit up to grind against him, but a hand on her lower back held her in place.

"No way. I'm just getting started. We only have the one, remember?"

"I'll buy more." She pressed against his hand.

"Patience." His teeth grazed her throat.

"Oh." The exclamations slipped from her lips as control slipped from her grasp. Her hips rocked, the movements guided by pure physical sensation, by instinct. A primal groan vibrated in Hannah's chest. The sound that poured from her throat felt alien. He took her to the edge and held her there. Sweat broke out over her body. Pleasure built to an almost unbearable level, heat flowing from her core, through her thighs and radiating outward.

Hannah's breaths quickened. Her spine arched. Her head lifted. A helpless sound escaped. "Brody. Please."

He rolled her to her back. His gaze locked with hers as he slid inside her. He paused. There was more than sexual pleasure in the warm, brown depths of his eyes. He lowered his head and kissed her. Some unnamed emotions, raw and powerful, poured from him. He filled all the empty spaces inside her.

"More." She tilted her hips to take all of him. Her legs wrapped around his rib cage. He synced his rhythm to the movements of her body, driving her higher, until the air locked in Hannah's lungs and the arches of her feet cramped.

"Please." She didn't recognize the breathless plea as her own voice.

Brody surged, his thrusts shifting from controlled and deliberate to instinctive. Harder. Faster.

Watching him lose control pushed her higher. Hannah bowed back, her hips fusing to his as the tension inside her broke. She pulsed around him, still hard and thick inside her, drawing out her orgasm.

His body went rigid. He seated himself deep inside her and shuddered. He lowered his chest and buried his face in the side of her neck.

Hannah concentrated on breathing. Her lungs craved oxygen. The wave of emotions building in her chest tightened her breaths, a potent and heady mixture of fear and elation.

This was happening too fast, and yet there didn't seem to be any way to stop it. She needed time to process the day. The week. The year.

She poked him in the ribs. "I can't breathe."

"Sorry." He rolled to his side, his chest still heaving.

Sweat coated Hannah's skin. "I need another shower."

He grinned down at her. "We only had the one. I wanted to make it count."

Her heart swelled.

Brody threw his head back and laughed. "I'll buy a case tomorrow."

"Good idea." Happiness bloomed inside Hannah. The emotions felt strange, as if it had been a very long time since she'd experienced it. So long she barely recognized it. She held it close. In her life, joy was rare and elusive. Not that she was an inherently unhappy person, but Fate had a way of snatching happiness just before she had it in her grasp. She was more familiar with suffering, determination, and fortitude than joy. Barretts barreled over obstacles, and they didn't stop to appreciate their triumphs. Another impediment always lingered on the horizon, waiting to be overcome.

"How can you be so calm after all that happened today?"

"Maybe today made me realize I need to appreciate every moment of happiness. Life is uncertain. Bad things will happen, and that makes the good times all the more precious." And with that he kissed her, as if she were the most precious thing of all.

"I'll be right back." Brody got up and strode into the bathroom. Watching him, she drank in the sight of his naked body.

Hannah settled back on the pillows, determined to savor every second with Brody. It was only a matter of time before she would be back at work. The thought of leaving Scarlet Falls disturbed her instead of filling her with relief. The feelings that Brody elicited from her were simultaneously terrifying and beautiful. Most of the time, she didn't think about her personal life. Professional ambition directed her decisions. Like all things rare and precious, personal happiness was fleeting.

He sat down on the bed, and she curled against him. "I don't have much time."

He'd barely gotten the words out when his phone vibrated.

He picked up his phone. "Excuse me." He got up and walked toward the window. "Yes, sir. I was just getting cleaned up. I'll be right there."

"I'm sorry." He went back to the bathroom and picked up his toothbrush. "That was the chief. I have to go back to work."

"Right now?"

"Ten minutes ago." Brody sighed.

"It's all right." Hannah stood. "I have to meet with the prosecutor about Lee's case early in the morning. I should go home."

"I wish I could stay."

"Me, too." She glanced at the pile of wet clothes in the hallway. "Do you mind if I wear your clothes home?"

"Not at all." He went to the closet and started dressing while Hannah went downstairs and found the dog's leash on the kitchen table. AnnaBelle and Danno were curled up together on Brody's overstuffed sofa.

"Time to go, girl."

AnnaBelle looked disappointed. Hannah knew how the dog felt. For once, she was the one who was being left. She didn't like it. Not one bit.

ᴡ

Brody hunched against the cold. The door of the mobile home outside the kennel opened, and a crime scene tech entered, his hands full with a box of small envelopes and a roll of evidence labels. Outside, rain beat against the windows, and the temperature had dropped since Brody had been at the crime scene earlier. The front yard was filled with emergency vehicles and news vans. What he wouldn't give to be in a warm bed with Hannah right now.

"Our suspect is a cocaine addict." Officer Carl Ripton pointed at a laminate table littered with small packets of white powder. A crime scene photographer snapped a close-up of the drugs next to a yellow evidence marker.

With a gloved hand, Ripton lifted a driver's license. A pretty young brunette smiled at the camera. "The homeowner's name is Joleen Walken. Joleen leases the property. The kennel business was hers."

Brody followed Ripton out of the kitchen into a living room. A rectangular patch one shade lighter than the wall-to-wall indicated where an area rug once lay. A dark red stain marred the middle of the lighter area. Ripton pointed to the wall and ceiling. Lines of rusty red streaked the white paint. Brody envisioned the bat hitting her face, blood splattering the room on the killer's backswing. "He didn't even bother to clean up."

Brody's gut twisted. This guy had been living in a dead woman's house, presumably since Saturday night, surrounded by blood spatter. "Who is he?"

"We don't know. No sign of a boyfriend in the house." Ripton's lips compressed. "Her father showed up a half hour ago. He saw the house on the news. The mother died a few years ago."

Brody closed his eyes for a second, not allowing himself to imagine the father's reaction. "Where's the father?"

"At the station. The chief said he'd do their interview personally." Ripton's face remained impassive, but irritation flashed briefly in his eyes. "Before he was escorted to the station, the father said he'd been on a business trip for the past week. Just got home yesterday. He hadn't talked to Joleen, which wasn't unusual. They were both busy. He was supposed to see her on Monday for their standing weekly dinner. From their last dinner, he didn't think there was a current boyfriend. She was focused on building her business. I got the impression the father was helping her financially."

Framed snapshots lined a shelving unit in the living room. Brody stooped to look at a framed photo of two bikini-clad young women, a blond and a Joleen, standing on a beach. He focused on the brunette. Long hair. Early twenties. Slight frame. The tiny heart tattoo on her hip matched the one on Jane Doe's body. Brody's gaze flickered to her face. Her wide, happy smile sent a rift of anger through his chest. Her killer had obliterated her identity. The violence of her murder was staggering. He pointed to the tattoo. "That confirms it. Jane Doe is Joleen Walken."

Ripton nodded. "She worked in a bank two years ago. We'll contact her former employer and get her fingerprints sent over to the medical examiner for official corroboration." He led Brody down a short hallway. A closet door stood open. Inside, a baseball bat leaned in the corner, right below a floor mop. "We believe this is the bat he used to beat her face in." A valid conclusion, since he hadn't bothered to wipe off the wood. A yellow evidence marker stood on the floor of the closet next to the bat.

"Are you going to call Chet?" Ripton asked.

"I am." Brody stepped outside and dialed Chet's number. His friend picked up on the first ring. "It's not her. The body isn't Teresa."

"I know," Chet slurred. He was drinking. Damn it.

"How did you know?" Brody asked.

"I found an old e-mail. One of my contacts said she was seen in Vegas last month with a known pimp."

"I'm sorry, Chet." Brody could feel his friend's pain through the connection.

"Don't be sorry. At least she's still alive." Glass clinked in the background. Chet wasn't hopping back on the wagon tonight.

"Are you all right?" Brody asked. "I can come there when I'm done at the scene."

"I promise I'm not going anywhere." Chet hiccupped. "I hid my keys from myself."

"She's alive, Chet."

"She's being trafficked, Brody."

Shit! Brody curled his fingers and punched his thigh. "I'll come over when I've finished here."

"I know you're worried, but if you go anywhere tonight, go see Hannah. You need her. She needs you. Don't fuck that up." His voice slurred. The sound of liquid pouring into a glass came over the line. "I'll be out cold as soon as I finish this last drink."

Damn it. He should have known Chet had a stash of booze. Brody wanted to go to Chet's house and, once again, pour every ounce of liquor down the drain. As sad as it was, passing out for the night was likely Chet's safest option. Besides, Brody wasn't likely to have any time until morning. Maybe not even then. "Tomorrow we're calling your sponsor. Together."

Chet answered with a long sigh filled with resignation. "Fine."

"Detective McNamara?" Ripton prompted.

Brody nodded and held up one finger. "I have to go, Chet."

He ended the call. Officer Ripton pointed toward the back door to the trailer. "I want to show you something in the shed."

They walked across the yard. The rain had stopped, but the cold air blowing across the field was frosty. Brody buttoned his overcoat. It seemed unbelievable that a couple of hours ago, he'd been in a warm bed with a woman. They walked into a sagging shed. Two portable lamps brightened the space. A cheap oriental-style rug lay on the barn floor. The center was stained dark red. Hair and other matter clumped on the pile.

Brody shoved his hands into his coat pockets. "The missing rug."

Ripton's mouth went flat. "We found teeth, Brody. Six teeth."

The sound of a trunk popping echoed in the open space.

"Ripton, over here," another cop called.

Brody and Ripton walked to the rear of another car, a battered old Corolla. The trunk stood open. Inside, the nude body of a young woman lay on its side. Brody gasped, and his pulse stuttered a beat. For a second he'd thought it was Hannah. But a second glance told him that other than the short blond hair, there was little resemblance. This girl was younger. Her eyes were brown instead of blue. She was a head shorter and curvier. Plus, he'd just left Hannah alive and well.

The hair must be a coincidence, but the similarity left him with an uneasy feeling in the pit of his belly. He would not breathe easily until they caught Joleen's killer.

Chapter Twenty-Seven

Brody spent the early morning hours on Thursday walking through the rest of the scene with the lead crime scene tech. The shooting of a police officer and the sheer brutality of Joleen's killing eliminated the normal gallows humor of a death scene.

The second woman had been identified as Chrissi Tyler. A few phone calls determined that she'd had a fight with her boyfriend Tuesday night at The Scarlet Lounge. The security tapes showed a man following her out the door, a man who knew how to keep his face away from the surveillance cameras. Both Chrissi and the man had disappeared from the range of the parking lot cameras. Chrissi's hair had been long in the tape, and a few snipped strands had been found in the mobile home bedroom. The killer had given her a haircut that looked just like Hannah's. How the hell could that be a coincidence?

Brody drove toward the station but somehow ended up sitting in front of the Barrett farmhouse. Through the windshield, dawn brightened the tops of the trees. For a minute, he leaned on the headrest and closed his eyes. The things human beings did to one another never ceased to appall him. That was probably a good thing.

The day he could shrug off a man beating a woman to death with a baseball bat was the day he should hand in his badge.

He checked the time on his phone. Six thirty. Would Hannah be awake? Probably. She had an early morning meeting with the prosecutor. His morning, maybe his whole day, would be consumed with Joleen's murder case and assisting the task force formed to find her killer. Good luck to him in trying to make sense of a total cluster of a night. What he needed was twelve hours of solid sleep. But how would he get the image of that girl out of his head? Sure, there were plenty of women with short blond hair, and the other victim had been a brunette, but Brody was still uncomfortable.

He dialed Hannah's number.

"Brody." The sound of her voice smoothed his rough edges. It also highlighted the horrors he'd witnessed in the last few hours. "I assume you had an awful night."

"Good assumption. I didn't wake you, did I?"

"No. Where are you?" she asked.

"Outside."

She paused. "Well, come in."

The front door opened as he climbed the steps. She was in full lawyer mode. Tailored gray slacks and a charcoal blouse draped her slim body. A single strand of pearls encircled her neck. Her hair was polished rather than tousled. When was the last time he'd seen her wearing makeup? She was stunning, but seemed less touchable, less approachable, in her corporate attorney persona. He suppressed the urge to ruffle her hair.

"Do you want some coffee?" She led the way back to the kitchen. A mug of coffee cooled on the counter. Next to it, a plate held a slice of toast.

Brody followed her. "Sure."

"Are you hungry?" She pushed the plate of toast toward him then poured a mug from the thermal carafe.

"Not really." He wandered to the window and watched the tree-tops sway in the morning breeze. A squirrel raced across the grass and ran up the trunk of the big oak in the backyard.

Hannah's arms slid around his waist, and her body pressed against his. "Are you all right?"

"Yeah."

She rested her head on the back of his shoulder. In her heels she was only a couple of inches shorter than him.

"He'd been living in her house, sitting on her sofa, watching her TV, without even cleaning her bloodstains off the walls." Brody turned around. "I'm sorry. I shouldn't have told you all that. You don't need those images in your head."

Her eyes sharpened. "Don't ever think you can't be honest with me."

"Thankfully, I rarely see cases this bad."

"Still, if you need to unload, unload." She reached up and cupped his jaw. "I'm tough."

"You are." He leaned into her hand. "But I prefer to leave the violence at work."

"I understand that, too," she said.

"Be careful today." He told her about the second victim's haircut. "It's probably a coincidence, but . . ."

"I should be safe enough at the courthouse." She registered the information with a tight nod. "How is Chet? Relieved?"

"I think so, but his reaction wasn't as joyous as I expected." How would Chet have fared if his wife hadn't died? If he'd had someone to support him in his time of need? Brody had seen marriages torn apart by tragedy, and other couples brought closer. "He was drinking last night."

"I'm sorry."

"Thanks." Brody squeezed her hand.

She moved to the counter, picked up both mugs of coffee, and handed him one. When he perched on the edge of a stool, she nudged the toast toward him. "Want me to check on him on my way home?"

"I'll do it later. He might be in a state."

Hannah put two more slices of bread into the toaster. "I grew up with a disabled father, and I nursed my mother through hospice. Trust me. I've seen worse than a man with a hangover."

She hadn't had an easy life. Brody resolved they'd talk about her past, just not today. But when? It wasn't likely she'd be here much longer. She looked and seemed recovered. Even though the neurologist hadn't cleared her for work this week, it would have to be soon. Then she'd be on a plane. Brody wouldn't see her for weeks. Maybe digging into her emotions wasn't the best idea.

"Chet would be embarrassed if you found him like that," he said.

She nodded. "All right, but if you change your mind, call me."

"I will."

Her toast popped up. She buttered it and bit a corner. "Mac is supposed to be home today."

"Have you heard from him?"

Hannah snorted. "Of course not. It's Mac we're talking about."

"What is up with him?"

"He's Mac." She shrugged. "Of the four of us, Mac was the one who really needed a firm hand. Unfortunately, by the time he came along, there wasn't one available. Mom was overwhelmed, and the Colonel wrote off his wildness as boys-will-be-boys behavior."

"What do you think it was?"

"Escapism. Mac loved being in the woods because the forest wasn't filled with medical equipment and suffering. My father was paralyzed. He was also in constant pain. Therapists and nurses were in our house all the time. The Colonel was tough, but he was also obsessed and bitter. Our home wasn't always a pleasant place to be." Hannah crumbled the remaining corner of her breakfast. "Grant was away at the military academy at least part of the time. Lee and I had our books, and Mac had the woods."

Brody looked down at the plate. Empty. He'd eaten without thought, and the toast had soaked up the pool of acid sitting in the center of his gut. Or maybe talking to Hannah had eased the tension inside him.

"I have to go." He stood, fortified by more than the coffee and food.

"Will I see you later?" She set the mugs and plates in the sink and reached for the dog's leash. Wagging, AnnaBelle rushed to the door and waited.

"Want me to walk her?"

Hannah donned a short trench coat and snapped the leash onto the dog's collar. "No. She already had a long walk at five thirty. She can pee next to the deck."

Brody laughed. He leaned over and kissed her softly on the mouth. "Thanks for this."

"For what?"

"Just this." He kissed her again, and this time he lingered for just a few seconds. When he'd stopped here, there'd been an empty space in the center of his chest. But now he felt whole again. He was still exhausted, but she'd recharged him enough to get through the next couple of hours.

What would he do when she was gone?

ᗯ

Jewel curled on her side and put her arm over her ear to drown out the sound of Penny snoring from the next cot. The girl slept like the dead. Jewel would love to turn off her brain like that. As it was, she was too tired to keep her thoughts from straying to the past, to what happened six months ago in Toledo. To the beginning of her nightmare.

Jenna contemplated the rows of candy. Boxes and boxes lined up on the convenience store shelves. Not the most nutritious food in the convenience store but small, compact, and easily slipped into a pocket. She hadn't eaten since yesterday. Her stomach grumbled as pangs of hunger turned to demands.

Her gaze swept the store. A guy was paying for cigarettes at the counter. The door buzzed as another guy came through it. The clerk's interest was divided between making change and watching a tiny TV on the countertop. No one was paying her any attention.

She angled her body away from the security camera that hung from the ceiling. Her hand swiped three packs of peanut M&M's. She walked up to the register and dug into her pocket. She plunked one bag of candy and a dollar onto the counter. The other two bags nestled in the front pocket of her hoodie. The clerk rang her up, his eyes drifting to the old TV, where a rerun of Friends *played on the six-inch screen.*

She pushed through the glass door out into the parking lot and zipped her hoodie against the cool air. Dawn was only a few hours away. In another few weeks, the temperature wouldn't drop so much when the sun went down, but so far this May, the nights had remained cool. Pausing at the curb, she ripped open the top of the bag and shoved a few pieces of candy into her mouth. Sugar and chocolate burst on her tongue. She ate the rest of the small bag in three handfuls. She'd ration the rest. Where now? She needed a place to hide, to sleep. At night, staying out of sight was easy. But in the daytime, she was too visible. Not that her mom would be looking for her. She was busy with her new boyfriend, Lenny. Her last words had been "You'll be back." Then Lenny had called Jenna an ungrateful little bitch.

The street stretched out in front of her, the surrounding blocks, the entire city, flat as a griddle. Her gaze crossed an empty lot and settled on a strip mall. Laundromat, check cashing, pawnshop, pizza. The smell of fresh pizza wafted toward her, her stomach cramping as if her nose was screaming that the candy in her pocket was inadequate. She needed money, but she'd been turned down for six jobs today. Legitimate employment wasn't an option at fourteen.

Yesterday, she'd slept in a shed behind her neighbor's house, slinking out like a stray cat to feed at night. Maybe she could slip in there again if she was sure the neighbor was still asleep. She couldn't risk being seen. If Lenny spotted her, he'd come after her, and she wasn't going back home until he was gone. Resigned to another night nestled between two rusted bicycles and a stinking bag of potting soil, she stepped off the curb.

Whatever. She wasn't going home. Not while Lenny was there. For all her mom's stranger warnings, she'd brought a creep right into their house. What really hurt was Mom not believing her when she'd told her what he'd done.

Jenna tensed. Her instincts warned her as a tall man coming out of the store focused on her.

"Hey," he called, quickening his steps to catch up.

Since Lenny, she was on alert for unwanted male attention, so she headed away from him.

"I saw what you did," he said to her back.

His words stopped her. Fear whirled inside her. Would he turn her in? The cops would call her mom. She'd end up back at home, with Lenny sneaking into her bedroom while her mom was working the night shift.

"I don't know what you're talking about." She shrugged, setting her gaze on two young men in the rear of the empty lot. A discreet exchange was made, cash for a baggie.

"Hey, I'm not judging." He fell into step beside her. "Do you need a job?"

She hesitated. Her mother's endless warnings about talking to strangers echoed in her head. But Mom had brought home Lenny, so what did she know? "What kind of job?"

"Waitressing."

"You got a restaurant?"

He nodded.

"What kind?" she asked, suspicious. In her world, people didn't do other people favors. Everything had a price.

He shrugged. "Pizza and sandwiches. Nothing fancy."

At the word pizza, *her stomach got excited.*

"I'm only fourteen," she admitted. As she'd learned, jobs required ID, and fake IDs required cash. How could she get one without the other?

"Not a problem," he said. "It's all under the table. What's your name?"

"Jenna."

"Nice to meet you, Jenna, I'm Mick."

She squinted at him. The yellow glow of the streetlight highlighted a lean face. A thin scar bisected his cheek, but he was still good-looking. She guessed he was about twenty-five, with short black hair and a goatee. His jeans and T-shirt were clean, and his broad-shouldered body hadn't regularly missed many meals. He didn't live on the street. A gold chain gleamed from around his neck, just under the tattoo of a skull. There wasn't anything special about him, no warning signs that she should have seen.

But still . . . It seemed too easy. Nothing in Jenna's life was ever easy.

"I don't know."

"Whatever." He lifted a hand and started to turn away. "But a pretty girl like you don't have to be dirty."

Her own body odor hit her nose suddenly, as if she hadn't been able to smell it until he pointed it out. Humiliation spilled into her. The stolen candy weighed heavily in her pocket. Not much of a meal. "Wait."

He glanced back.

"I'll do it." Waitressing was legit, right?

He led her to a shiny town car. Light from the streetlamp reflected off the windshield like a mirror, blinding her to what was inside. She knew she shouldn't get in. The car was way too nice for the neighborhood. But what else was she going to do?

He started the car and shifted into drive. The locks clicked down. Jenna jumped. He drove away from the strip mall. She hunched in the leather seat and stared out the window. He pulled into the drive-through at Carl's Jr. and ordered a burger, fries, and a Coke. A minute later, the Carl's guy passed a bag through the car window. The aroma of fried grease hit Jenna's nose, and her stomach flipped out with a loud gurgle.

Grinning, Mick nodded at the bag. "Eat up."

She ate with the speed of a starving dog.

A few minutes later, he pulled up in front of a door to a cheap chain motel room. Not even the dark of night could conceal the chipped stucco and peeling brown paint.

Her eyes skimmed over the sagging roofline. "Where's the restaurant?"

"Closed now. You can crash with me."

Apprehension tightened around her meal. She set the Coke aside. How many other details did he leave out?

They got out of the car. Jenna turned to run as a flash of panic rushed through her. But his body blocked her escape. "Where do you think you're going?"

Jenna's arms broke out in goose bumps. The apprehension she'd felt in the car grew. She backed away. "I changed my mind. I want to go."

He shook his head. "This is what's gonna happen." He stepped closer, his pretty brown eyes shrinking down to mean, cold marbles. "I own you now. You'll do whatever I say, or I'll hurt you. You try to leave, I'll kill you. You escape? I'll find you, and you'll pay."

Mick's hand shot out. He grabbed a handful of her hair and pulled her into the room. He released his hold, and she stumbled. Locking the door behind them, he crossed his arms. "Your new name is Jewel." He walked to the dresser and picked up a bottle of vodka. "Time to get started." He handed her the bottle. "Drink."

Mick put three blue pills in Jenna's other hand. "These, too."

Jenna put the pills in her mouth. The vodka set her belly on fire. The back of her throat burned. But she did as she was told. Just looking at him, she knew he'd hurt her if she didn't obey.

Minutes later, her vision hazed, and her limbs turned lazy.

"What's your name?" Mick asked.

Terror confused her. "Jenna."

She saw the violence simmering in his eye, but the backhand still shocked her. Pain sliced through her face. She pressed a hand to her stinging cheek. Lenny had handed out worse, but he was older and slower. She'd been prepared for the blows.

"What's your name?" he asked again.

This time, she remembered. "Jewel."

"Good girl." He smiled. "Say my name."

"Mick," she croaked.

He reached out. She flinched, expecting another blow, but he only lifted her chin. "Now it's time for you to earn your keep. You do what you're told, so I don't have to beat you."

Chapter Twenty-Eight

Hannah parked Grant's truck in the driveway and turned off the engine. The windshield wipers stopped, and light rain misted on the glass. In no rush to go inside and be alone, she checked her phone. It was almost four o'clock, and Brody hadn't called. But he'd expected to be tied up all day. Though their meeting had been set for morning, the prosecutor had rescheduled for afternoon at the last minute. Hannah fought the urge to dial Brody's number. Her discussion with the prosecutor had reopened wounds and left her raw.

The text from Grant had only made things worse. He'd messaged her twice this week, and she'd lied outrageously to him both times. But she didn't want him to come home. She didn't want him to get upset, not after he'd made such good progress. She didn't want her family anywhere near Scarlet Falls, but the house felt empty without them.

Since when did she not want to be alone? She spent most of her career either working or alone in a hotel room. Now, returning to that lifestyle held little appeal. She didn't want months to pass without a hug from Carson. She wanted to be here when Faith hit her next milestone. Something within her had changed, shifted, almost as if there was more room inside her. Empty places that needed to be filled, and only one man who could make her whole.

Brody.

The strength of her need for him left her as shaken as the prosecutor's news. Under her instability, a thick layer of anger simmered.

Her cell vibrated. Brody. Finally. Her heartbeat skipped as she answered the call.

"How did it go with the prosecutor?" he asked.

"She's going to let him plead out." The words tumbled out of her mouth with none of her usual control and measure. Her voice tasted bitter in her throat.

"What?"

"The defense attorney intends to haul Grant and Carson through hell, and there's nothing the prosecutor can do to stop him. The charges against Grant and the motion for change of venue were just the openers. He has a big song and dance prepared about his client's psychological state. He's going to drag this out as long as possible." Hannah clenched the steering wheel, her knuckles white with frustration.

"Does she think he'll get the change of venue?"

"No. She's fairly confident in the judge assigned to the case, but she is concerned about the chances of the verdict being overturned on appeal. Frankly, his argument has merit, and she knows it. Publicity on this case has been relentless."

"Much of that news coverage was generated by the defense," Brody said.

"Nobody cares about the source. The only matter under consideration is the possibility of seating an impartial jury. Plus, if Carson is put on the stand, there's no telling what he'll remember. This case could drag out for years. He's six. He should be able to rebuild his life, not be constantly reminded of what he's lost."

"There's enough evidence that Carson shouldn't need to testify. Surely, the court can protect him."

"But the defense is insisting. If Carson doesn't take the stand, that's one more reason for appeal." She swallowed, her throat tasting bitter. "So, she's going to let him plead guilty. She assures me, with murder and the other lesser charges, he'll serve a minimum of twenty-five years before he'll be eligible for parole." But twenty-five years wasn't good enough for Hannah. He should never see daylight again. Lee wouldn't.

"I'm sorry." Brody's voice held more disappointment than shock. "I wish I could tell you bullshit plea deals were uncommon, but they're more common than trials."

"I know, and in reality, the death penalty isn't an option in New York State, so the maximum sentence would be life without parole. The prosecutor thinks twenty-five years is good enough." *And she gets the conviction for her statistics.* "But the assault charge against Grant will go away as part of the deal."

"I know you're disappointed, but a plea will let Grant and Carson get on with their lives."

Disappointed? That didn't even come close. Anger seethed through Hannah's blood. The prosecutor had all but stated that she didn't want to spend the next year working on a case with this many complications and unknowns. An overturned verdict hurt her numbers. A plea satisfied her boss. The case would be closed. Her caseload was enormous, and her resources limited. She wanted to put this case away with no possibility that it would land back on her desk in eighteen months.

But twenty-five years?

Lee's killer could still have part of a life remaining when he was released from prison. Her brother was gone forever. His children were orphans.

"I'm sorry," Brody said. "It's not fair."

"No. But maybe she's right. Maybe it would be best for Carson and Grant to let this go." Hannah's throat tightened. Carson would be thirty-one when the sentence was up. How would he deal with his father's killer being set free?

"I wish I could be there with you, but I have to go into another meeting with the chief and mayor about yesterday's shooting. I don't know when I'll be available again. I'll call you when I'm finished?"

"Please." She wished he were here more than was comfortable. He grounded her. His smooth demeanor offset her turbulence. He could be her ballast if she let him, and the loss of independence that realization represented sent wariness rippling over her skin like goose bumps.

"I will." Brody said good-bye and ended the call.

Hannah got out of the car. She closed her eyes and turned her face to the sky. The wind shifted, carrying the smell of wood smoke and falling leaves to her nose. The cold rain refreshed her skin. She'd dressed for her meeting, but the business suit and makeup felt uncomfortable, wrong, as if she were wearing a costume. Her Prada suede pumps hurt her toes. She couldn't wait to change into jeans and wash her face.

She headed for the front porch. Her body was tired, the beauty of last night with Brody wiped clear by her meeting with the prosecutor. Politics had claimed another victory over justice. This shouldn't happen. People like Lee and Kate shouldn't be murdered. Places like Scarlet Falls shouldn't be tainted by depravity.

The dog barked on the other side of the door. Distracted, she opened her purse to retrieve her key. A movement in the shadow of the house caught her attention. A man stepped into the light and pointed a gun at Hannah's chest.

Cruel, lean face. Goatee. Mean eyes. It was him. The man who had assaulted her in Vegas.

"Remember me?"

Chapter Twenty-Nine

Hannah's body went rigid. Sweat poured from her clammy skin. This man had hurt her before, and this time he was armed. Last time neither of them had been carrying, but today he had the advantage. Just as she'd been unable to carry her gun into New York City, her permit did not allow her to bring a weapon into a federal building. She'd locked her Glock in the safe to meet with the prosecutor. She said a silent prayer of thanks that Grant and the family weren't home.

If he'd been alone, if he hadn't had an accomplice to ram her car, the scenario in the Las Vegas parking lot might not have gone his way. She scanned him from his boots to the backward cap on his head. The saggy jeans and oversize hoodie said city boy.

He gestured toward her with the gun. "Turn around and raise your hands."

Hannah pivoted, the heel of her shoe scraping on the walk. She wasn't dressed for the woods any more than him.

"Move it, bitch." He poked her back with the muzzle.

"Where do you want me to go?"

"My car is behind the garage. We're going to take a ride."

Hannah followed the driveway around the house. On her right, the lawn rolled into the creek and woods beyond. The detached garage sat off the left side, at the edge of the trees that surrounded the property. Her brother used the building for tool storage rather than parking. They walked behind the small building. A Buick sedan sat between the garage and the forest. What could she do?

He pulled a car key from his pocket and pressed the button on the fob with his thumb. The trunk popped open. Stepping to Hannah's side, he pointed the gun at her temple. "Get in the trunk."

So he could incapacitate her, take her to a secluded location, and proceed with the torture-rape-kill scenario she bet was in his mind? She wasn't going to cooperate with that plan.

"From now on, you belong to me." He grinned, confidence and malice filling his dark beady eyes. He motioned toward the trunk with the gun.

Hannah considered her options. He stood three feet from her, too far away to disarm him. She took a step and turned toward the trunk. She glanced over her shoulder. Excitement lit his eyes, and fear gathered behind Hannah's sternum. Getting into that trunk meant certain death. Her gaze flickered to the woods, her best chance for escape.

She shifted her weight as if preparing to climb into the vehicle, then she kicked out behind her. Her foot caught his hand, knocking the gun out of his grip. It landed a few feet away and slid in the grass. He lunged toward the weapon. Leaving her Pradas behind, Hannah sprinted for the woods. After several days of intermittent rain, the ground was slippery under her bare feet. She zigzagged through the trees. Behind her, she heard huffing and crashing as gangsta boy lumbered into the forest like a tank on a Formula One course.

Hannah swung right and doubled back toward the garage, her gray-on-gray ensemble blending into the autumn-bare woods. Slowing, she took care to avoid patches of dried leaves. She paused to take stock and track the sounds of twigs snapping to the man moving a hundred feet away. Ducking behind a group of evergreens, she picked up a short, sturdy branch and waited, hoping the dense greenery was enough to conceal her body. His footsteps came closer and closer. A bead of sweat rolled down Hannah's spine. Her lungs bellowed, and her head spun from the sudden exertion of her sprint. She wasn't in prime condition. Too much work and not enough exercise in her life.

He passed the trees. Hannah lunged. She swung the branch at his head. He ducked, avoiding a direct blow. He lifted the gun in his hand. Before it leveled on Hannah, she dropped the branch and twisted. Both hands came down on the gun, swinging the barrel toward the ground. Applying pressure to his wrist, she turned the weapon toward him, twisting it out of his grip and pointing it at his face.

"You won't shoot me," he said smugly.

"Wanna bet?"

He grabbed for the weapon. Hannah pulled the trigger. *Click.* Empty.

"It ain't loaded. After that scene at the car, I figured you'd try something." He pulled a knife from his pocket and dove at her legs, sweeping both arms toward her knees for a tackle.

Hannah dropped the empty gun and sprawled her legs back. Her hands, arms, and body weight came down on the back of his shoulders. Off balance and surprised by her response, he hit the ground face-first. Still pressing down, Hannah spun on his back. She slid one arm under his chin to encircle his neck and locked him in a choke hold. Squeezing her elbows together, she applied pressure to the sides of his neck and cut off the blood supply to his brain. He flopped on the dirt. Hannah held on. Twenty seconds later, he went limp.

She wiggled out from under him and patted him down. His pockets were full of interesting items. She opened his wallet. His

Nevada driver's license said his name was Mick Arnette. She stuffed his wallet, knife, car key, and cell phone into her pockets. She pulled a few plastic strips from the front pocket of his jeans. "Zip ties. How handy."

She used them to secure his wrists behind his back and bind his ankles together. Then she ran for the garage, visible through the trees. He'd be awake in a few minutes, and it was time to turn the tables on this scumbag. He was going to tell her what he did with Jewel. Was the girl still alive?

As she'd learned from her meeting with the prosecutor, criminals knew the law well enough to use it to their advantage. Once she called the police, Mick would clam up and demand a lawyer.

She opened her brother's garage and scanned the walls of construction tools. She spied a coil of yellow nylon rope. Looping it over her shoulder, she spotted a come-along hand winch on a shelf. She read the label. The cable puller had a four-ton lifting capacity. That ought to do it. A short length of chain was coiled next to the hand winch. Perfect. Taking both, she jogged back to Mick.

Wrapping the chain around a nearby tree, she snapped the hook on one end of the come-along to two thick links. The nylon rope went around Mick's ankles. Hannah looked up and located a sturdy tree limb about twelve feet overhead. A few tosses put the other end of the rope over the branch. She took up the slack in the rope, made a loop, and tied it off. Then she hooked the other end of the hand winch to the loop in the rope. She cranked the handle back and forth, ratcheting Mick's feet off the ground. She worked the hoist until he was hanging upside down with his head about five feet off the ground. The blood rushing to his head would wake him up.

Her father's survival drills had been crazy, but at that moment she was thankful for every brutal second.

He shook his head, his eyelids fluttering.

She smacked his cheek. "Wake up, Mick."

He stirred and blinked at her. His eyes moved in wild arcs, and his body twisted like a worm on a hook. Hatred shone from his eyes, but there was also apprehension. Good.

"You and I need to have a conversation," she said.

"You're going to regret this." He struggled, his body swaying. "Go fuck yourself."

"I hardly think you're in a position to make that sort of suggestion, Mick." Hannah took his knife from her pocket and waved it in front of his nose. "Here's how it works. The person who isn't hanging upside down from a tree gets to ask the questions. You need to start talking."

"I'm not telling you anything. You're going to let me down, and you're going to do what I say." Spite, gleeful and malicious, pinched his face. "If you want to see your friend alive again."

That must mean . . . *She was alive!* Hannah didn't let her relief show on her face. She channeled her contract-negotiating expression—similar to emotional Botox. "Just tell me where she is."

Mick's body went still. "She?"

"The girl."

"What girl?" His face reddened as the blood flowed into his head. "Jewel."

He laughed. "You're hung up on that little whore? She's long gone. I have no idea where she is."

"What did you do with her?" Hannah asked. Then discomfort rode up her spine as she realized the full impact of his statement. "Who were you talking about?"

"Check your e-mail." Glee lit his eyes.

What had he done?

Hannah took her phone from her pocket and opened her e-mail. She had fifty-seven new e-mails. She scanned the list, stopping on a message from theking@hmi.com. Clicking on the attachment, she gasped. Staring back at her was a picture of Chet, bound, gagged with duct tape, and apparently unconscious. She studied the photo. The picture was zoomed in close. Where was he? She couldn't see much of the background. Just grass and weeds under his head. A dark red wall of some sort behind him. He could be anywhere.

"Where is he?" she asked.

"Like I'm going to tell you." He sneered. "My brother is watching him. If I don't call by eight o'clock, he'll kill the old man. He'll enjoy doing it."

An icy ball formed behind Hannah's ribs. She took his phone out of her pocket.

A lock screen appeared. "Pass code?"

"Like I'd give you that." The arrogant bastard actually smirked. "Let me down and untie me. Then I'll tell you."

Right. Not. Hannah debated for a minute. She could call Brody. He'd bring the police. They'd start a formal search for Chet. But would Mick talk to the police? She doubted it. She had a feeling he knew the Miranda warnings by heart.

She waved the knife. "My father was an army ranger. He taught me how to do all sorts of interesting things, like rig snares and hunt game. By the time I was twelve, I could skin and field dress a deer." She reached up and touched his solar plexus with her forefinger. "You make a cut from the deer's sternum to its crotch. That's the tricky part. The cut has to be deep enough to get through the hide and abdominal muscles, but you don't want to puncture the intestines. You need to pull those out intact so their contents don't taint the meat."

His Adam's apple bobbed as he swallowed. The brief shimmer of fear in his eyes gave her hope that he'd tell her where his partner was keeping Chet.

A predatory, egotistic smile split his face. "Nice bluff, counselor. But you aren't like me. You aren't going to cut me. You have morals. You care about doing what's right. And you'd go to prison for it."

A small voice inside her wanted to make him pay. He was the worst example of humanity. He preyed on helpless young girls and old men. He wasn't worth the air he breathed. Once he was arrested, the courts would take over. He'd be one more cog in an overcrowded wheel. He was a plea away from a short sentence.

But she couldn't do it. She'd fight to defend herself or another, but she couldn't hurt a man hanging helpless from a tree, no matter how much the man deserved it. Her father and her brother had fought and sacrificed for freedom and democracy, not vigilante justice. But now she truly understood the anger and frustration that had driven Grant to pound on their brother's killer.

Damn it.

She couldn't let him go, and she couldn't make him talk. That left one option. She had to trust Brody.

Hannah pulled out her own cell and dialed Brody. His voice mail answered. She called the police station. A man answered the call. "Scarlet Falls police. Sergeant Stevens."

"If you call the cops, I'll never tell you," Mick said. "If the old man dies, it'll be your fault."

Hannah ignored him. "I need to talk to Detective McNamara." Hannah stared at the photo of Chet. There must be a clue in the picture that could tell her where Chet was tied up.

"Detective McNamara is unavailable."

"Please, interrupt him." She gave the sergeant her name. "It's an emergency."

"Better hurry," Mick chided. "It's fucking cold out here today. The old dude won't last long. When we grabbed him, he already looked half dead."

Chapter Thirty

"The suspect opened fire first," Brody said for the tenth time. Why was he wasting time recounting the shooting over and over while he'd rather be searching for the killer?

"And you have no idea how seriously he was wounded?" the chief asked.

"No. I saw his body jerk, but he kept running." Brody knew debriefing after a shooting was important, but the chief and mayor were in full butt-covering mode. A killer was on the loose, and they didn't want to assume any blame. Plus, once he was caught, they wanted every *i* and *t* accounted for, in case the criminal sued the township. They always sued the township.

"We have the local ERs on alert in case he seeks treatment." The chief scratched his smooth jaw.

Brody scraped a hand over his own stubble. *He* hadn't taken time to shave.

Stella sat at the other end of the table. As the officer who'd shot the suspect, she'd been put on desk duty. Helping with the search wasn't an option for her.

The mayor slapped both hands on the table. "I think that's enough, Detective."

The chief turned to Stella. "Department policy states that any officer involved in a shooting is automatically placed on desk duty for a minimum of one week. Although I see no indications that this is anything but a justified shooting, I'll be performing a full investigation. You will also be required to see the psychologist. The doctor will have to clear you to return to patrol. You too, Detective McNamara."

She blinked to Brody, and he nodded. He'd follow up with her, as he wished someone had done with him in Boston. Instead, the precinct cops, mostly old-timers, had projected a suck-it-up mentality that he'd felt obligated to emulate. Would his marriage have failed if he'd gotten help then instead of waiting for full-blown post-traumatic stress to develop? It didn't matter, he decided. His wife had left him when the going got tough. Clearly, she'd thought "for better or for worse, sickness or health, and richer or poorer" were multiple-choice options rather than vows. He was better off without her.

A knock sounded on the door.

The chief frowned. "This better be important."

The sergeant opened the door. "I'm sorry, sir." He nodded to Brody. "I have a call for Detective McNamara. She says it's an emergency."

Brody stood. "Excuse me. I'll be right back." He followed the sergeant out into the main room. "Who is it, Sergeant?"

"Hannah Barrett," the sergeant said. "I put the call through to your desk."

Brody hurried to his office, picked up the phone, and pushed the blinking button. "Hannah? What's wrong?"

"I have bad news. There was someone waiting for me when I got home. Let me start with I'm fine . . ."

Brody's limbs turned cold, and his heart stumbled as she gave him a succinct synopsis of her abduction at gunpoint. "You're sure you're all right?"

"Yes. I handled him." Her voice sounded strained. "But his partner has kidnapped Chet. They must have been following me."

"You're at Grant's place?"

"Yes. In the woods behind the garage."

"Is he restrained?"

"Don't worry. He's not going anywhere," she assured him.

"Stay put. We'll be right there." Brody hung up. He returned to the chief's office, summarized Hannah's call, and gave his boss Grant's address. "I'm going there now."

The chief rose to his feet. He motioned for the sergeant. "Get whoever is on patrol out there, and get some backup from the county and state police. They'll have to pull personnel from the manhunt. Brody, do you have any physical evidence other than the haircut the killer gave the second victim to indicate these two incidents might be related?"

"Not yet." Brody ran for the exit. Hannah was in the woods with an armed attacker. Pushing his sedan, he cut the drive out to her brother's place to twelve minutes. He parked near the garage behind a patrol car. Running toward the woods, he yelled, "Hannah?"

"Over here," a male voice answered.

Brody spotted figures in the forest. What the . . . ? Hannah was leaning against a tree, arms crossed, brows knitted. She appeared calm, but Brody could see the turmoil brewing behind her negotiation face. Next to her, a uniformed patrol officer stared at a man strung from a tree by his feet.

"Get me the fuck down from here," the criminal barked.

"You want me to cut the rope?" Hannah pushed off the tree trunk and started toward him.

The criminal craned his head to stare at the ground five feet below his face. His body twisted. "No!"

"Make up your mind." She shrugged, her casual gesture belied by the fury in her eyes.

Brody's gaze swept the scene. Hannah had strung the man up like a side of beef. He and the patrol officer exchanged a look of disbelief—and respect.

His gaze lifted to Hannah. He walked over to her and pressed his forehead to hers. She'd told him she was all right, but until he'd seen her, touched her, his heart had refused to process that fact. "I can't believe you caught him. You're amazing."

She was totally badass, and he was damned glad.

Her eyes were bleak. "Show him the picture, officer."

The patrol cop held out a cell phone. It looked like Hannah's cell phone case. Brody shaded the screen. *Oh, shit.* Chet.

"He won't tell me where he is." Hannah's mouth thinned.

"We'll find him." Brody put an arm around her. More sirens approached. He went over to the patrol cop. "Let's get him down."

The cop grabbed the thug's shoulders. Brody released the gear spool on the winch, and the officer lowered the man to the ground.

The cop handed Brody a wallet. "His name is Mick Arnette. He's from Las Vegas."

"Is this the man who attacked you in Vegas?" Brody asked Hannah.

Hugging her waist, she nodded. Her eyes were bright with moisture. Her control was slipping.

Brody pointed toward the phone the patrol officer was holding. "Where is the man in the picture?"

But Mick claimed his rights before Brody even arrested him. Probably not his first brush with the law.

"I'm not talking unless you let me go. And if you don't, I want a lawyer."

Brody walked over to Hannah.

Her face was drawn and strained. "It's going to drop well below freezing tonight."

"I know. We'll find him."

"Mick said if he doesn't call his brother by eight"—Hannah checked her watch—"that's less than three and a half hours from now, the brother will kill Chet."

Brody took the cell phone from the officer. In the photo, Chet was lying on weeds. There was a wall or something behind him. Was he behind a building? Disappointment filled Brody. There was some writing on the wall in the corner of the picture. Brody expanded the photo, but the image was too blurry to identify the letters.

Chet could be anywhere.

ꞹ

The Scarlet Falls interview room was furnished with one metal table, bolted to the floor, and four chairs. Mick Arnette sat in one chair. A uniformed SFPD officer stood a few feet away.

"OK, Mick." Brody took a seat across the table. "Where is he?"

"I have no idea what you're talking about." Mick leaned back. His handcuffs clanged as he intertwined his fingers. Attached to the ring in the center of the metal table, he didn't have much room to maneuver. His smile was malicious. "I'll talk to Hannah Barrett. No one else."

"That's not going to happen." His relaxed posture sent anger crawling up Brody's throat. He wanted to grab Mick by the hair and slam his face into the table. Never had he been tempted to hurt a suspect. He'd always played by the rules. But today, with Chet's life on the line and the knowledge that this man had hurt Hannah and abducted a teenage girl, Brody had a much better understanding of what had driven Grant to beat the hell out of the man who'd killed his brother. This was personal.

Hannah would talk to this guy. No question. She would never be able to resist helping others.

Brody tossed Mick's phone onto the table. "Why don't you unlock this for me?"

"Why don't you get a warrant? The courts have ruled that I have an expectation of privacy when it comes to the contents of my cell phone."

Great. Another criminal who was an expert on the law.

"The warrant is on its way," Brody said. To expedite the warrant, Stella had driven to the courthouse to personally obtain the judge's signature. A technical expert was on hand to attempt to track the phone's location and usage history the second the warrant was issued. If Mick communicated with his brother by phone, with the number and the records from the carrier, the police might be able to ping the brother's current location.

"Don't expect me to make this easier for you," Mick said.

"Why are you in New York, Mick?"

"I'm not answering any questions from you until I talk to a lawyer."

Brody left the room. He went to the end of the hall and ducked into the conference room. Hannah sat at the long table. She'd already given him her statement, but Brody didn't want her out of his sight, not with Mick's cohort running loose.

Shivering, Hannah had wrapped her hands around her coffee. She'd changed into jeans and a sweater but looked as if she was freezing. She set her cup on the table. "Did you find out where Chet is?"

"No," Brody said. "I'm waiting for a call from the crime scene tech at Chet's house."

"So Mick won't talk?" Her blue eyes went cross-examination sharp. She knew he was holding back. No pulling anything over on her.

Brody hesitated. "He says he'll talk to you."

"I'll do it." She pressed her hands on the table and stood.

Brody shook his head. "No. I don't trust him, and I don't negotiate with criminals."

"But if there's a chance he'll say where he stashed Chet, then it's worth a try." Her jaw was set—as was her mind. "He's restrained, right?"

Brody nodded.

"Then what's the harm?" she reasoned.

I don't want you anywhere near him.

Instead, Brody said, "He gets two minutes. A sheriff's deputy is on his way to pick him up and take him to the jailhouse."

Scarlet Falls's small police station didn't have a holding cell. Brody led the way back to the interrogation room. Mick's gaze focused with intent on Hannah.

"Did you have something to say?"

Malice gleamed in his eyes. "You have no idea how much I want to fuck you."

Rage ignited in Brody's chest. His body was moving forward without any consultation from his brain. Hannah stopped him with an arm across his chest. "Don't. It's exactly what he wants you to do."

Brody eased back. Mick was grinning. Hannah was right. If Brody hit him, he'd have grounds for a lawsuit, and ammunition when it came time for charges to be filed.

"Let's go. He's not talking." Brody opened the door and steered Hannah through the opening.

"I want her to be my lawyer," Mick called after them.

Brody shut the door. His phone vibrated. Vinnie, the crime scene tech, was calling from Chet's house. Brody answered. "What do you have?"

"Not much," Vinnie said. "He broke in through the slider. Chet's phone was on the table, so we can't trace him that way." He paused.

"What is it?" Brody asked.

Vinnie exhaled. "It looked like Chet had been doing some serious drinking last night."

"So he probably didn't put up much of a fight." Brody loosened his tie. Anger, and a hefty dose of fear for Chet, still warmed him. After the turmoil of yesterday, he should have checked on Chet this morning.

"No. They tracked some mud onto the carpet but not enough to analyze or compare the tread."

"Fingerprints?"

"Since they came in through the slider, I expected to find prints on the glass, but there weren't any."

Mick's attitude told Brody he was an experienced criminal. "They probably wore gloves. I want you to compare Arnette's prints with the ones taken from the shooting scene last night."

"OK, and I'll let you know immediately if we find anything else." Vinnie ended the call.

"Nothing?" Hannah shivered, though she was still wearing her jacket.

"No," Brody said.

"See what you can make of this," the middle-aged techie on loan from the county said from behind a bulky laptop. "I can't enhance the image any more."

Brody crossed the room to lean over his shoulder. He pointed to a few blurry white numbers and letters in faded paint above Chet's feet. "What is this?"

Hannah looked over his shoulder. "Those white letters in the rust?" She squinted. "Looks like CR 268 . . . I can't read the last few numbers."

Brody stared at the image. It was a close-up of the red building in the background. The numbers and letters meant nothing to him, but there was something familiar about the image. "I don't know what that means, but I feel like I should."

The county geek said, "I'll run it through whatever databases I can find and send a copy to the state computer forensics analysts. Someone will know what those letters and numbers mean."

"It has to be local, right?" Hannah asked.

"Probably."

"Let me send the picture to Mac. No one knows this country-side better."

"Worth a try." Brody asked the tech to message the pic with just the background, not Chet's face, to the number Hannah provided. "You've heard from him, then?"

"Yes. He texted me this morning."

"Where is he now?" Brody asked. Hannah's youngest brother had a reputation for living off the grid.

Hannah scrolled on her phone. "He'll be here sometime tonight. Hopefully his phone is still charged and he's checking it, but no promises. You know Mac." She lowered her cell. "Now what?"

"I don't know. We keep looking for Chet." Brody paced. "We've called in additional law enforcement from the county and state. Search teams are being organized."

Chief Horner walked into the room. "The state police are setting up a command post at the county administration building. I'll need you there. Also, the mayor scheduled a press conference in two hours. I'd like to have something intelligent to say."

"Yes, sir." Restless, Brody clenched his hands into fists. Prepping the chief for a press release was the last thing Brody wanted to do. He should be out there, looking for Chet. The image of his friend unconscious and gagged twisted his gut every time he looked at it. Chet wasn't in the best health. The sun had been down for an hour, and the temperature outside was dropping.

"Hopefully, the press conference will clear the media from our street." The chief waved at the windows. Outside, media vans lined the street. Using the police station as a backdrop, reporters stood on the sidewalk and spoke into cameras.

Brody waited for the chief to leave. He turned to Hannah. "You can come with me."

"He didn't say that."

"There is no safer place for you to be than a building full of cops. I don't want you to be alone until the guy who kidnapped Chet is apprehended. His brother won't say why he came to New York, but I assume he came for you. Plus, my gut is telling me Mick and his brother killed those two women and shot Lance."

Hannah put a hand on his arm. Her eyes were bleak. "I'm so sorry. This is my fault. I brought this man here. I should have just gone with Mick Arnette. Maybe he would have released Chet."

"I didn't mean it was your fault. Going with him would have been crazy. He would have killed you both." Brody covered her hand with his. "Every available member of law enforcement will be out there looking for Chet. We'll find him."

But would it be too late?

Chapter Thirty-One

Mick sat in the back of the police car. In the front seat, on the other side of the metal barrier that separated him from the cops, sat two sheriff's deputies.

He was fucked. He and Sam hadn't discussed a contingency plan in case one of them was caught. But Mick would never give up on his brother. Sam was around here somewhere, waiting.

The cops turned onto a rural highway. Traffic was light. They approached a bridge. Mick stared out the side window. How was he going to get out of this? That damned blond hadn't done what he'd expected. He'd assumed she'd do as he said to save her friend, but no, the selfish bitch had called the cops.

Didn't she understand she was signing her friend's death warrant?

Not that the old guy was going to survive no matter what she did. Once Sam had an idea in his head . . .

The car approached an overpass. A moving van barreled toward them in the other lane, its high-mounted headlights glaring through the windshield. Just as they hit the end of the bridge, the van swerved toward the police car. With a crash and a groan of metal, the police car slid off the embankment. Mick's body slammed against the seat belt. The deputy grabbed the radio, but the car jerked, and he dropped the receiver.

The car bounced. Mick lost perspective as the world slammed. The vehicle came to a stop. He hung forward, his weight shifted, the seat belt digging into his chest and collarbone. With his hands cuffed behind his back, he hung helpless. The pressure of the strap across his chest forced him to take shallow breaths.

The deputy grabbed the mic on his uniform and called for assistance.

"Shit. You all right, Steve?" the deputy in the passenger seat asked.

"I'm good." The driver unsnapped his seat belt. Turning on the interior light, he glanced in the back. "You alive, Arnette?"

Mick didn't answer. *Fuck that cop. Let him crawl back here and find out.*

A figure appeared next to Mick's head. A man leaned down to look into the window. With the light in the vehicle and the darkness outside, it took Mick a second to realize it was his brother. A long-sleeve jacket covered his tatted arms and the bandage on his bicep where he'd been grazed by the cop's bullet. Combined with a pair of khaki pants, his new look was electronic-store salesman.

"Hey, are you guys OK?" he asked the cops, then pointed a gun through the broken passenger window. Two gunshots echoed in the car as he put a bullet into each cop's head. Mick flinched. Blood splattered the interior. Sam fired two more shots. Making sure the cops were dead, or just for fun?

His brother leaned into the rear compartment, a knife in his hand. He flicked his wrist and cut the seat belt.

Mick fell forward. "I'm glad to see you."

"You didn't think I'd let them take you away?" Sam caught him, his hands gentle.

"Of course not." Mick should have known his brother would come after him.

Sam leaned into the front of the vehicle and searched the cops until he found a handcuff key. The back door wouldn't open, so he released Mick's hands and helped him wriggle out the broken window.

"Did they radio for help?"

"Tried." Mick coughed. "Not sure if they got through."

"Let's get out of here." Sam grabbed his arm, hauled him to his feet, and half carried him up the embankment. The moving van sat on the shoulder of the road. Other than a dented front fender, the vehicle wasn't damaged. Sam shoved Mick into the passenger seat. Rounding the vehicle, he climbed behind the wheel.

Mick looked back. At the bottom of the hill, the cop car was still. From a distance, there was no sign that the two deputies had been shot.

"How's the arm?"

"I've had worse." Sam's wound had been shallow. He accelerated, putting the scene behind them. A mile up the road he turned onto a dirt road. They drove a few hundred yards and turned again. Trees cropped up around the lane. Sam stopped the vehicle behind a half-collapsed, abandoned outbuilding. The Charger was parked behind the building.

Mick rubbed his shoulder. The seat belt had done a number on him. "How did you know where I was?"

"News report." Sam held up a different prepaid smartphone than he'd been using before. "I destroyed the old phone in case the cops got into yours." He rooted in a bag on the bench seat between them and pulled out another phone, which he handed to Mick. "I stole the van and waited down the road. On TV, they showed you being driven away."

Mick shoved the new phone in his pocket. "Did you know that old dude we snatched was a cop?"

Sam nodded.

"What did you do with him?"

"I got him stashed where we spent the night. Nobody's gonna find him." Sam got out of the van.

They'd parked in an isolated spot overnight. It wasn't the first time they'd slept in the car, but it had been damned cold. They'd had to start the car engine every hour.

Mick followed his brother. His whole body hurt.

Sam opened the driver's door of the Charger. He reached in and pulled out a plastic bag. He tossed it to Mick. "Here. Change your clothes. There's a razor in there, too. Your picture was all over the news."

Shivering, Mick stripped off his jeans and T-shirt and tugged on the cheap khakis and blue polo shirt. Appearance aside, he was glad to don the fleece jacket. "I look like an idiot."

"You look like you want to sell me a data plan. Now shut up and shave." Sam tossed him a bottle of water.

Mick used the water and shaving cream to remove his goatee. He nicked himself multiple times in the cold.

Sam squinted at him. "I don't think it's enough."

"Turn on the dome light." Tilting the side mirror out, Mick lathered his head and shaved it bald. The night air froze his bare scalp.

"Better," Sam said. "Do you still want the blond?" His eyes shone as if he was hoping Mick said yes.

"More than ever." Anger surged in Mick's chest. She'd defied him. She'd beaten him. She needed to suffer. He wanted her on her knees and begging. He'd never thought she would best him. How did a woman take him out twice? "She needs to pay."

"All right, but then we're wiping out all the loose ends here and heading south. Imagine how much money we'll make when we don't have to share our take with someone like Mr. K."

"We're going to make a killing."

"Fucking A." Sam grinned. "I have a plan."

"Have to find the woman first. She was with that cop at the police station." Mick rubbed his oddly smooth head in frustration. The cop's body language with the lawyer was all possessive. He'd keep her close.

"I know." Sam grinned. "I GPSed his car."

"You did what?"

Sam shrugged. "Was easy. It was getting dark, and there were so many reporters and cameramen wandering around the parking lot, I just walked right through the crowd and slid it under the fender. Dressed like this"—he gestured toward his torso—"nobody looked at me twice."

He opened an app on his phone. "Look. Here they are." Handing the phone to Mick, Sam hurried to the driver's door. "There's gonna be a press conference over here." He pointed to another point on the map. "I'll bet that's where they're headed. I scoped out a few excellent places along the route for an ambush. Let's go get her."

Mick shivered in the leather seat. Was that a snowflake? Fuck. This. State. "We could just run. Forget about the woman. Forget about the cop. Head somewhere warm."

"Hell, no." Sam's black eyes snapped. "You want the blond, and I want her, too. You promised. I broke you out of jail! You can't go back on your word."

Sam in a rage was way more dangerous than the police. The only way to calm him down was to give him what he wanted.

"You're right. I promised." Mick took the device and got into the passenger seat. He buckled up. The crash had given him new appreciation for seat belts. A small green dot moved on a map. "The GPS was ballsy."

"You think that's ballsy? Wait till you hear the rest of my plan." Sam patted the duffel bag at his side. "Go ahead. Take a look."

Mick unzipped the bag. "Holy fuck. We drove across the country with *that* in the car?"

Sam shrugged. "It's not dangerous until it's detonated."

ω

In the passenger seat of the unmarked car, Hannah rubbed her hand on her denim-clad thigh as Brody ended his call. "That was Detective Douglas in Vegas. Mick Arnette's prints match the one set of prints they found in your rental car. Mick has never been arrested in Nevada, and he isn't in the national fingerprint database either. They're going to check out the address on his license. They'll let me know what they find."

Would they find Jewel?

"Douglas did say that they have a criminal record for Sam Arnette. According to Douglas, Sam is one nasty SOB. He was dishonorably discharged from the army. Douglas doesn't know why. Vegas police arrested him for armed robbery, but the sole witness mysteriously disappeared, so he was never convicted. Douglas is sending me a picture of Sam." His phone buzzed. He swiped the screen with his thumb and handed it to Hannah.

"That's the other man from the attack in Vegas," she said.

Brody nodded. "Makes sense that the brothers would be together."

Police chatter hummed from the radio on the dashboard. Brody's phone buzzed again. He answered it, uttered a few yeses, then signed off with "Call me when you have something."

"The warrant came through for Mick's phone," Brody said. "The geeks are already analyzing his records and trying to track data usage and pings on local towers. Hopefully they'll be able to narrow down the search for Chet." Brody took a deep breath. He looked haggard. The chief had kept him busy for too long. It was almost seven o'clock. Only one hour left until the end of Mick's deadline. Tick tock. "It gets worse."

"Tell me." Her stomach did a slow roll as Brody steered through a turn. She grabbed the armrest. He was pushing the speed.

"The scene of yesterday's shooting? The one where the woman was murdered?"

Hannah's brain shot ahead of his words. "The Arnettes?"

"Their fingerprints were all over the inside of that house. Sam's prints were on the bat used to kill Joleen."

Her hand shot up to cover her mouth. That woman was killed because the Arnette brothers followed Hannah to Scarlet Falls from Las Vegas. Sam had beaten that woman to death with a bat. What would he do to Chet?

"What if we can't find him?" she asked.

"There's no *we*." Brody's tone sharpened. "You're a civilian. Law enforcement will find Chet. Local, county, and state cops are all over this, and the FBI is on alert. Every inch of this county will be combed. There isn't anything else that can be done at this point. Patrol cops are already out searching."

Hannah nodded. "I still feel like it's my fault, and I hate waiting."

"You cannot take the blame for what some psycho criminal does."

She knew Brody was right, but she still felt like she'd brought this danger home. If Grant hadn't taken the family away, who knew what could have happened to them. Instead of Chet, Sam Arnette could have Carson or Ellie or another member of the family in his clutches. The temperature was still dropping. The forecast called for below-freezing temperatures tonight. Snow was a possibility. In the photo, Chet was wearing a thin shirt. No jacket. If he was still alive, he wouldn't last long outside tonight.

A voice call came over the radio. Brody turned up the volume. The dispatcher called off a string of numbers that meant nothing to

Hannah, but the tone was urgent. Hannah caught the words *shooting* and *officers down*.

Brody reached for his phone and speed-dialed a number.

"All units, be on the lookout . . ." Mick Arnette's name and description followed.

Brody ended his call. He curled his fingers around his phone and punched his thigh. "A moving van knocked the sheriff's car off an overpass. Both deputies were shot and killed. Mick Arnette escaped."

He slowed the car and turned right. The rural road was empty, and he punched the accelerator. The car surged forward into the dark.

"He's loose?" Horror crawled up Hannah's throat.

Brody nodded.

"Oh, no." Two women were murdered. Chet was taken, and two police officers were dead. "Now what?"

"Massive manhunt," Brody said. Determination hardened his face. The car approached a wooden bridge over a shallow creek, and he slowed the vehicle.

The bridge exploded in front of them. Wood and dirt plumed into the air as the car hurtled forward into a cloud of smoke.

Chapter Thirty-Two

On instinct, Hannah grabbed for the armrest. Brody yanked the wheel to the side. The car flew down the embankment. The world spun as the vehicle flipped. Momentum and gravity flung her against the seat belt. Something exploded in her face. She had no idea how many times the car rolled before coming to a stop.

She breathed. Fine, acrid dust settled over the car's interior, and the deflated airbag lay across her knees. Her heart banged against her ribs, and her eyes watered, blurring her vision. She wiped a forearm across her face. "Brody?"

In the light of the dashboard, she could see blood from a gash on his temple running over his closed eyes. She touched his shoulder, but he didn't respond.

Bridges didn't blow up by accident. She knew instinctively Mick Arnette was responsible, with his ex-military brother's assistance—and they had explosives. She needed to get Brody out of the car.

Though she suspected adrenaline was blocking her pain—no one walked out of an accident this serious without at least minor injuries—her limbs seemed to be intact and usable. Her fingers were slippery with sweat. She wiped them on her sweater and grabbed for the seat belt release. The button was jammed. A broken piece of rearview mirror on the seat nicked her finger.

Calm down.

But even if she unfastened their seat belts, how would she get Brody out? She couldn't carry him.

They needed help. Her phone. Where was her phone? She couldn't think straight.

"Hurry up," a voice said from outside the car.

Hannah reached for her weapon. Before she could clear the gun from its holster, the door opened.

"Ah, ah, ah." The muzzle of a gun was in her face. Behind it, Mick Arnette was looking into the car. She almost didn't recognize him. He was dressed like a Best Buy clerk, and his head was shaved bald. But the evil glint in his eyes was unmistakable. "Put your hand where I can see it or my brother shoots your boyfriend in the head."

The driver's door opened. Another man stood on Brody's side of the vehicle pointing a gun at his temple. She squinted. In the dashboard light, his features were just visible enough that Hannah could recognize Sam Arnette.

"Get out of the car." He made a small motion with the muzzle of the gun. "Take it slow."

Hannah reached for the seat belt release but it still wouldn't give. Mick pulled a knife from his pocket. "Don't try anything. My brother would like nothing more than to kill the cop."

He took her gun, leaned across her body, and cut her seat belt, then slashed the strap across Brody's chest and took his handgun as well.

Mick backed up. "Let's go, sweetheart."

Hannah swung her feet out of the car. Her fingers closed around the mirror shard. She tucked it up the sleeve of her sweater. Her knees buckled, and her head swam as she tried to stand. Her muscles felt weak and shaky. Her heart pumped triple time.

Mick swirled a finger in the air. "Turn around and put your hands behind your back."

She pivoted, curling her fingers into fists. He bound her wrists with a plastic zip tie. Then he patted her pockets, his hand lingering on her butt. "This ass is mine." He slid his hand between her legs and squeezed hard. Tears poured down Hannah's cheeks.

How would she and Brody get out of this?

Mick's brother hauled Brody out of the car and pulled him over his shoulder fireman style.

"How come I get to carry the man?" the brother complained. "And why can't I just kill him?"

"You're stronger than me," Mick said. "And I want to hold on to him in case we run into trouble and need more leverage."

They climbed the bank to the road. Without her hands to stabilize her climb, Hannah tripped twice on rubbery legs. A moving van was parked on the road next to the demolished bridge. Mick rolled the back door up. The interior was a black void.

Sam heaved Brody into the back. He hoisted himself into the truck, rolled Brody onto his face, and zip-tied his hands behind his back. Another plastic tie went around Brody's ankles.

"Your turn." Mick gestured toward the van.

Hannah climbed up the metal steps into the back.

"Stop," Mick commanded, his gun pointed at Brody's temple. "Get her ankles. Bitch can be tricky."

Sam bound her feet together.

The door slammed down. The van went dark. A metallic click signaled the slide lock closing. A few seconds later, an engine started, and the truck moved. Hannah nearly fell over.

She dropped on her knees beside Brody. A little moonlight came through vents near the roof of the van, just enough for her to see Brody's outline. How badly was he hurt?

ꞷ

"Brody!"

Hannah's voice stirred Brody. What happened? His body felt like someone had beaten every inch of it with a stick. He tried to open his eyes, but they were crusty.

Blinking hard, he forced his eyelids open. Was he blind or was it dark? "Hannah?" His voice sounded hoarse, even to his own ears.

"I'm here." Her lips found his face, and she kissed him on the mouth.

"Is it dark?"

"Yes."

"Thank God." His head pounded. He remembered the bridge blowing, the car rolling . . . His hands were tied behind his back. He tried to move his arms. Pain blasted through his shoulder. "I can't move. Where are we?"

"Back of a moving truck. Mick and Sam Arnette are in the front."

If Brody got his hands on them . . . He stopped himself. That didn't look likely. "Are you injured?"

"No," she said, and a small amount of relief coursed through Brody. Moonlight filtered through small vents in the top of the van. He squeezed his eyelids shut and opened them.

"How badly are you hurt?" she asked.

Brody took stock of his body. "My vision is blurry, my head feels like it's stuffed with C-4, and I'm pretty sure I have a couple of broken ribs. Are you tied up, too?" Brody blinked hard again. Still blurry, but better.

"Yes, but I'm working on that." Hannah was on her butt, her legs stretched out in front of her. Her face was tight with concentration.

"What is that?"

"A piece of rearview mirror."

"Nice." He rolled. Pain slammed through his head and chest. His hands and feet were numb.

"How do you feel?" she asked.

He tested his limbs. Despite the pain and limited movement, everything also seemed to work. "I don't think anything is broken except some ribs. I can move." And if his injuries were more serious, he'd deal with it later.

"Good." She leaned forward, kissed his temple, and pressed her forehead to his for a few seconds. Emotion flooded his throat. He could not deal with these men hurting her. They could kill him, but he couldn't bear the thought of them raping or killing her. His mind went to Joleen Walken's pummeled corpse.

With a shaky breath, she lifted her head. A tear rolled down her face.

"How are you doing with that shard?" he asked.

"It isn't my father's KA-BAR." Her shoulders moved as she worked her hands behind her back. "We should have a plan," she said with conviction.

The corner of Brody's mouth pulled. Hannah would be proactive to the end. She was a fighter. She would never give in, and no matter what happened to their relationship, he could count on her. She would have his back until the bitter end.

She was one of a kind.

"Have I ever told you how much I love and appreciate your stubborn streak?"

Her head tilted. "What?"

"Nothing." He shook his head. "You're right. We need a plan. Tell me everything you saw."

"They're both armed. They had their own guns. Plus, they took ours."

"If that was Sam who ran from the back of Joleen's house, he also has a rifle," Brody remembered.

"Mick has a knife . . ." As Hannah continued to describe their abduction, Brody's hope sank. He and Hannah were still bound. They had one semi-sharp piece of glass. Their kidnappers were skilled and well armed with at least four semiautomatic pistols. How could he and Hannah possibly survive?

Chapter Thirty-Three

Mac stopped at the traffic light in town and speed-dialed Hannah's number. Again. No answer. Again. Where was she? Hannah practically kept her cell phone superglued to her hand, but he'd been calling her for an hour, and she hadn't picked up.

He looked at the photo she'd messaged him. CR 268. What the hell was that? But damn it! There was something familiar about the image. Something from his life a long time ago. The Dark Days, as he called that period of his youth.

He pulled over, a memory nagging at him. Picking up his phone, he opened his messages and stared at the picture.

It popped into his head. He knew where this was taken. He shifted into drive and gunned the gas, trying Hannah's phone again with his thumb. The call went to voice mail. Something had happened to Hannah. He knew it in his soul.

Shit. Shit. Shit.

His sister had needed him, and once again, he'd been unavailable. What the hell? His timing was always crap. He dialed the police station. "I need to speak to Detective Brody McNamara."

"Hold, please." Silence. Then, "Detective McNamara is unavailable."

"I need to speak to someone."

"Hold, please."

Screw this. Mac turned toward the police station. He was still holding when he turned into the lot and parked behind the building, another place in Scarlet Falls filled with bad memories. Nothing good ever happened here. He ended his call and went inside. The place was bustling, and not in a good way.

He went into the reception area and approached the counter. Thick glass separated him from the old cop manning the desk.

"Can I help you?"

"I'm looking for Detective McNamara."

The cop said, "Hold on."

He disappeared. A few minutes later, he came back with another uniformed cop, but this one didn't look like any cop who had ever arrested Mac. She was tall and slim, with black hair coiled in a severe knot at the nape of her neck.

"I'm Officer Dane. Can I help you?" she asked.

"I'm Mac Barrett. I'm looking for Detective McNamara and my sister."

"Can I see some ID?"

Mac pulled out his wallet and passed his driver's license through the gully under the glass.

"What's going on?"

She scrutinized his ID.

Mac ran a hand over his two-month beard. He hadn't shaved or had a real haircut since he left the States, not that he was exactly diligent about those things when he was home. He probably looked as civilized as one of the otters he studied. "I know. I look like a bum. I've been in Brazil, out in the rain forest. I'm a wildlife biologist. My passport is out in my Jeep."

Officer Dane passed his license back. "Come with me, please."

A lock clicked open on a solid door on the other side of the room. Mac went through into the police station. He knew what bad vibes felt like, and the cops in the station were putting them out like radio waves. For all the activity, there were precious few bodies in the station.

"Officer Dane, where are we going, and what the hell is going on?"

She led him to a conference room. Her frown marred her otherwise perfect face. "Have a seat. I'll be right back."

A minute later, a middle-aged man in a fancier uniform came in. He held out a hand. "Mr. Barrett."

At the *Mr. Barrett*, Mac almost looked behind him. He shook the man's hand.

"I'm Police Chief Horner." He gestured to a chair. "Please have a seat."

The chief's somber tone was enough to spin the drive-through burrito in Mac's stomach.

"Just tell me."

"Your sister was with Detective McNamara on their way to the county administration building. They disappeared."

"What do you mean by *disappeared*?"

"Someone blew up a bridge, and we found the vehicle rolled down the embankment. Neither Detective McNamara nor Ms. Barrett were inside." The chief buttoned up. There was more he didn't want to say.

"What else? There's more, isn't there?"

"There was blood in the front seat of the vehicle."

"Shit." Mac jumped to his feet. "Earlier today, my sister sent me a picture and asked me if I knew where it was taken. I think I do."

The chief stood. "Where?"

Mac took out his phone and opened the message. "CR 268. I think *CR* stands for Conrail. This looks like part of the markings on the side of a freight car."

The chief rushed to the door. "The rail yard."

ꟗ

The truck came to a stop. Brody lay still on his side, his ankles pressed tightly together, his hands behind his back. Hannah sat next to him. Their eyes met.

"Are you ready?" he asked.

She nodded.

The door rolled open. Brody's heart slammed against ribs he suspected were broken. Every deep breath he drew felt like a knife slicing him from the inside out. He closed his eyes almost all the way.

"Hello, sweetheart." Mick climbed into the truck. Gun at his thigh, he prodded Brody with the toe of a boot. Brody let his body roll limply.

"Is he dead?" Mick asked.

Hannah sniffed. "I don't think so, but I think he might have some internal injuries. He needs to get to a hospital. Please."

"In a short while, it isn't going to matter much." Mick laughed. He leaned over to grab her arm. "Get up."

Watching through his lashes, Brody wanted to kill him right there and then, but he waited. They had a plan. Hannah wasn't injured. Brody needed to trust her.

Mick bent over. The knife in his hand moved toward Hannah's ankles.

She wobbled, making a show of awkwardly folding her feet under her body. When her boots were planted flat, she launched her body forward, head first. Her forehead struck Mick in the nose. Blood spurted.

"Fucking bitch." He punched her and brought the knife up.

Brody rolled, taking Mick's feet out from under him. Mick went over backward, his knife clattering to the metal floor. He flipped onto his belly and reached in his pocket. His hand came out with a gun. Brody crawled onto his back. Mick leveled the pistol and turned the barrel to aim at Hannah. Brody couldn't move fast enough to disarm him. Instead, he snapped Mick's neck. The body under him went limp.

The sudden movement sent agony rolling through Brody. He panted, unable to take a deep breath.

Hannah rubbed her jaw. With a head-clearing shake, she scooped the gun from the floor and pulled the clip out to check the load. Satisfied, she snapped it back in place.

Light-headed, Brody searched Mick's pockets and cell phone. He pressed a button, and a lock screen displayed. Pass code–protected. No use to them.

Hannah nodded toward the door, no doubt thinking exactly what was on Brody's mind. She whispered, "The brother is out there."

The one who took a bat to Joleen's face.

"We need to get out of here." Brody rolled the dead man into the dark back corner of the truck. Then he peered out the door. Not trusting his vision in the dark, he waved Hannah forward. She nodded the all clear.

A cold wind hit them full force as they climbed down from the trunk. Next to him, Hannah shivered.

Knife in hand, Brody took in their surroundings. Trees in the distance. Large, bulky shapes all around. Where were they? A rectangular structure loomed ahead. There was another behind it. Clouds shifted, and moonlight brightened the landscape. A train.

They were in the rail yard. The same place where Joleen's body had been dumped.

Brody called up a mental image of the area, but the yard comprised multiple acres. They had to move. Sam was out here somewhere, armed, dangerous, and ruthless. Unfortunately, it didn't seem his bullet wound had slowed him down. Footsteps crunched on gravel. Brody pulled Hannah into the shadow of a freight car.

"Mick?" Boots clunked on the metal ladder of the van. "Fuck. No. Mick." An inhuman roar echoed from the moving van. Remorse slid through Brody at the wounded sound.

Sam had found his dead brother.

But Brody would have to process taking another life later. Now, fear for Hannah's life blotted out any other emotional reaction. Sam would be coming for them, and Brody could feel his pain and rage vibrating in the cold night air.

Boots hit the dirt and came toward them. "I'm going to kill you!"

Then Sam went into stealth mode. No more footsteps. No more words. Where was he?

Brody went down on one knee and looked under the freight car. No boots. Hannah turned and faced the other direction. Back to back, they waited. Nothing. Brody pointed ahead. They needed to get out of here.

Hannah inched forward. Brody moved in a crouch, watching the ground under the train, the bent-over position killing his ribs.

The air shifted. Brody sensed more than heard the movement. He turned just as a body dropped on top of him from inside the train.

Chapter Thirty-Four

"Brody!" Hannah lifted the gun. Brody and Sam went down and rolled under the train. She couldn't shoot. She might hit Brody.

She ran ahead a few steps, dropped, and rolled under the next freight car. Turning, she ran back. The bodies had stilled. The figure on top flipped to his side. One arm flopped out into a patch of tall weeds.

Was that Brody or Sam? The grass was too high to see his face. Hannah pointed the gun forward. "Brody?"

"I'm here." Wheezing, he sat up. One hand held his rib cage. "I think he's dead."

Hannah walked closer. She peered over the vegetation. Sam's eyes stared sightlessly at the sky. A knife protruded from his belly.

"Hey, look!" Brody pointed behind her. Red and blue lights swirled in the distance.

Hannah helped him to his feet. Now that the threat was gone, he sagged.

"You need a hospital."

"Need to find Chet," he said.

They limped toward the lights.

ᘓ

Mac rode shotgun in Officer Dane's patrol car. They were flying on the rural straightaway that led to the abandoned rail yard. Lights flickered around them, but the sirens were off. They didn't want to spook the suspects.

She stared straight ahead. "You're really a wildlife biologist?"

"Yes."

"What do you study?"

"Otters."

Her brow lifted. "Otters?"

"Yeah. Otters."

"Interesting." Her tone sounded more puzzled than curious. "How do you know the rail yard so well?"

"I spent considerable time out there as a teenager."

The quick glance she cast in his direction was surprised. "Sex, drugs, or underage drinking?"

"Yes," he said.

The cars pulled through the sagging-open gate. Cops spilled out. With Mac's input, a quick and dirty search plan had already been agreed upon in the conference room of the police station.

"You stay here." Dane pointed at him.

"But I know this place."

"Do I need to handcuff you and put you in the back?"

"No." Mac hung back, leaning on the car and crossing his arms. His memories of handcuffs and the backseats of patrol cars were not pleasant. Nor were the bad decisions that had put him there.

Dane hesitated, glancing back at him. "We'll find her."

Mac nodded. "You'd better."

"Don't you go running off into the dark the minute my back is turned," she warned. "You'll get shot."

Hm. Mac wondered how the cop knew he was going to do just that.

"There they are!" someone shouted.

Two figures limped toward them. Mac ran past the cops. His sister was banged up but on her feet and walking. Relief nearly took him to his knees. He folded her into his chest. "I'm sorry I wasn't here."

"I'm all right, Mac," Hannah said.

He took his first full breath in hours. What if she hadn't been? He would have been too late yet again. He would have put work ahead of his family for the hundredth time. He hadn't been around to help Lee. Hell, he hadn't even known Lee was in trouble, which was totally inexcusable. Lee had saved Mac, and in return, Mac had abandoned him.

He tightened his grip on his sister.

Their childhood had been messed up, but what Mac did with his adult life was his responsibility.

ω

Brody zipped up the winter jacket one of the patrol cops loaned him. Vehicles crowded the yard. Flashlight beams crisscrossed the ground. Every available body had been called in to search for Chet.

Hannah strode next to him. Mac was teamed up with Stella. His knowledge of the yard's layout had proven useful. But two hours into the search of the rail yard, Chet hadn't been found.

"Over here," someone yelled. Brody picked up the pace. A black Dodge Charger was parked behind a rusted engine. A cop shone his light inside the vehicle. "Nothing."

He opened the vehicle door and popped the trunk. Brody surged forward and peered inside. A hand protruded from under a tarp. *No!*

With a silent prayer, he reached down and moved the tarp. *Please let him be alive.* But it wasn't Chet. The face was slender, young, and badly beaten. Shock paralyzed Brody for a second. "It's a woman."

Brody leaned in and pressed two fingers to her throat. A weak pulse tapped against his fingertips. "She's alive."

He tugged off his jacket and draped it over her. Her eyes opened, white-rimmed with fear.

"It's all right. You're safe. We're the police."

A tear ran from her eye.

An ambulance was already on-site, waiting. EMTs rushed in. Brody backed off and returned to the search. Hannah took his hand. "You shouldn't be out here."

"I'm all right."

"You don't look all right. You look terrible." She took his hand. His devotion to his friend only deepened her feelings for him. Brody was the kind of man she'd been waiting for her whole life. However long he wanted to keep searching, she'd be here with him. "But let's keep looking."

"Found him!" A shout floated over the yard.

Brody's breath fogged in front of him as he turned toward the voice.

"He's alive!"

They jogged toward the commotion in front of a freight car. A patrol cop handed Brody up. Chet was on his back, three navy-blue SFPD jackets draped across his body.

"Chet?" Brody knelt.

"He's breathing, Brody," a cop said over his shoulder.

Barely.

Within minutes, the EMTs were in the car, starting an IV, draping Chet with blankets. One of Chet's eyes opened. His fingers made a small motion, gesturing Brody closer.

He leaned over, putting his ear close to his friend's mouth.

"There was an e-mail," Chet rasped. "About Teresa. Follow up. Please. I don't care what she wants. Promise. If I die, you'll find her."

"Done." Brody squeezed his arm and backed away, giving the rescue crew room to work. The EMTs' movements were urgent. Had they found him in time?

Chapter Thirty-Five

Hannah's feet dangled off the edge of the gurney as the neurologist shone a light in her eyes. Concerned about the cumulative effect of concussions, the doctor had run her through the same balance and coordination tests as Royce's neurologist. "Other than minor bruises and abrasions, you seem fine to me."

"Really?" she asked.

The doctor scribbled on his chart. "You passed all the tests."

She'd be able to go back to work. Why didn't that idea fill her with the pleasure she'd expected?

A nurse came in with paperwork. Hannah signed the forms and collected her things.

Brody entered the cubicle. He'd already been poked, prodded, and x-rayed. Despite two cracked ribs and a concussion, he refused admittance. "Well?"

"I'm fine." She hopped down off the table and took his arm. "But you look like you're going to fall down."

"I'm OK," he said, but he allowed her to lead him to the hallway.

"How's Chet?" She moved toward the waiting room.

"Dehydration did a number on his kidneys, and his liver tests don't look good. No shock there. But he's going to recover, at least physically." Brody tugged her down a different corridor. "He's going to start up his search for Teresa again. He found an old e-mail from one of his contacts in a national missing persons organization. Someone who looks like Teresa was spotted in Vegas. Apparently, Vegas is a national trafficking hub. I'm going to put him in touch with Detective Douglas."

"That's something." She tried to sound hopeful.

"For Chet, anything is better than sitting in his house with nothing to do. On a more positive note, Lance is going to make it. They moved him out of intensive care."

Hannah exhaled. She squeezed Brody's hand. "I'm so glad. What about the woman?"

She would never get the sight of that poor girl in the trunk out of her head.

Brody studied their joined hands. "Her name is Marcia Falcon. She's a pharmaceutical rep from Cleveland. She checked into a hotel on the interstate. We think they abducted her from the parking lot of the sports bar next door. The bar gave us the surveillance footage. Marcia was eating there at the same time as the Arnette brothers."

"Oh, no." That poor woman. "Is she going to make it?" Hannah didn't ask if Marcia would be all right. Raped and beaten and kept in the trunk of a car, she would never be *all right* again.

"Yes, physically she should recover. The doctors are stunned that she survived."

"It's amazing what the human body is capable of bearing." Hannah had seen all that her father had endured, and his heart refused to give out.

"I want to go home." Brody steered her toward a rear exit. "I don't want to run into any reporters. I'm not giving anyone a statement or filling out a single form."

"Surely, no one would expect . . ."

He raised a brow. "You'd be surprised."

Outside, a patrol car waited for them. They slid into the back. Brody rested his head against the seat for the ride home. "Do you need to get the dog?"

Hannah shook her head. "Mac picked her up and took her home with him."

"Good," Brody said. "You're still keeping all this from Grant?"

"Yes. Mac and I agreed that none of this would help his posttraumatic stress. We'll tell him in person."

"He's going to be furious when he gets home."

"Yes, he will."

She was still surprised by Mac's response at the rail yard. She'd always thought of Mac as the least emotional of all of them. He'd rather be out in the wilderness than in a room full of people. Maybe she'd been wrong. Grant was reaching out to her for contact, and he said he was doing the same with Mac. Grant shouldn't have to do all the work. Hannah would talk to Mac tomorrow.

The car dropped them at Brody's house. Inside, Danno greeted them with ankle rubs and meows. They went upstairs and shared a hot shower. They were both mottled with bruises and scrapes.

"We are a sad sight." Hannah gingerly blotted a seat belt abrasion across her chest.

"Indeed." Brody tugged her into bed.

She helped him wrap an Ace bandage around his ribs. He settled back on the pillows with a groan of pleasure. He pulled her down beside him.

When his phone buzzed, he lifted it off the nightstand and opened one eye. "It's Douglas."

Hannah stiffened.

Brody sighed and answered the phone. Five minutes later, he ended his call. "The address on Mick's license was bogus, but the Vegas cops found some people in that neighborhood who knew where he really lived. They raided the place today and found five underage girls being kept there by another woman. None appear to be Jewel, though the police are having a hard time identifying any of them. None of the girls will say anything. Three are likely illegals." He paused, and Hannah could tell he was holding something back.

She sat up. "What?"

"They found evidence that someone was being held prisoner in a shed out back. One of the other girls said that was Jewel. Douglas thinks this girl known as Lola is the one who sent you those e-mails. Mick had your purse in the house. Your business card was on the table. Lola won't talk to them, but she asked for you."

"I want to go to Las Vegas," Hannah said. Mac could keep the dog for a couple of days.

"OK."

She lay back down.

"I'll go with you." Brody wrapped his arm around her waist and spooned against her back. "We'll arrange flights in the morning."

"You don't have to go with me."

"Tomorrow morning I'll have a tome of a report to type. But I won't be on active duty until I get medical clearance. According to the ER doc, I'm going to have a few weeks off at minimum." He rested his chin on her shoulder. "And I am not ready to let you out of my sight."

The thought of leaving Brody behind hurt more than any of her injuries. She'd almost lost him tonight. She wanted to spend as much time with him as possible.

She rolled over to face him. Putting a hand on his chest, she said, "I don't want this to end between us. I know we both said we didn't love the idea of a long-distance relationship, but I'm willing to give it a try if you are."

He kissed her. "I'll do anything for you."

ω

Late the next afternoon, Hannah sat in a conference room down the hall from Detective Douglas's office in Las Vegas.

Douglas scanned his report. "We found an arrest record for a weapons charge against Mick Arnette in Ohio. Some of his fingerprints weren't clear, so they hadn't been entered into the national database. After checking the missing persons reports for Ohio, we found a girl we believe is Jewel. Her name is Jenna Young, native of Toledo. Jenna ran away from home about a year ago. Her mother didn't report her missing for several weeks." He put a paper on the table in front of them. A dark-haired teenager smiled sadly at the camera.

Hannah sucked in a quick breath. "That's her."

But she looked different. Her eyes were mournful rather than panicked, and her face was fuller in the picture, as if she had lost weight since.

"Why wasn't she reported missing right away?" Hannah asked.

"Her mother said Jenna had run away before. She thought her daughter would come back on her own." Douglas frowned. "But the Toledo police found out that the mother's boyfriend was a registered sex offender. He'd been convicted of molesting a twelve-year-old girl seven years before. Seems he hooked up with Jenna's mother barely six months after his release from prison."

"So you assume he molested Jenna." The coffee in Hannah's stomach soured. Brody put an arm across the back of her chair and gave her shoulder a supportive squeeze. She couldn't have gotten through this day without him. His solid and quiet support made the most onerous subjects bearable.

"Probably a fair assumption," Douglas said.

"Any ideas on how to find her?" Brody asked.

"We found a computer at the house. Our technicians think the e-mails you were sent originated from that unit. This girl, Lola, claims to have sent them. We recovered a computer. Most of the files have been wiped, but our cyber techs hope to recover deleted files from the hard drive. But we do have the records for Mick's burner phone, and the cyber team followed a data usage trail. We strongly suspect Mick's operation is part of a larger organization."

"So what do you want from Lola?" Hannah asked.

"I'd like her to tell us what she knows. We want to bring down as much of this organization as possible. But she doesn't trust us. Where she comes from, law enforcement is often as corrupt as or in bed with the criminals. With the Mexican cartels, either you do as you're told or they kill you and your entire family."

"I'll do what I can," Hannah offered.

"We know she's afraid of being deported, but if she cooperates with us, we'll help her. Several agencies have been to visit her. She won't talk to them either." Douglas stood. "I'll take you over to the hospital now."

They followed the detective to the hospital in their rental car. Twenty minutes later, Douglas pushed the number on the elevator. Lola was recovering in a room on the fourth floor. "How long will they keep her in the hospital?"

Douglas shook his head. "I don't know. She needs to be detained. It'll take some time to find a safe place to house her and the other girls."

"They're all witnesses." And in danger. Hannah thought of Sam Arnette and the witness who disappeared before his trial. "I'm sure illegal trafficking victims who agree to testify have gone missing in the past."

"Yes." Douglas stopped at the end of the hall and showed his ID to a cop standing guard.

"She doesn't speak much English, ma'am," he said. "But I can translate."

"There's no need." Hannah smiled.

"I'll be right over there." Brody pointed to a U-shaped waiting area. A flat-screen TV hung high on the wall. "Too many people in the room might intimidate her."

"Thanks." She kissed him. Thoughtful man.

She wasn't looking forward to leaving Brody and going to London next week, but she was fit for work. Staying out any longer felt dishonest. She'd called Royce that morning. He hadn't been available, but his secretary said he'd be in the New York office for a few days. Hannah was going to see him as soon as she returned from Las Vegas.

But she'd miss Brody, with his quiet strength and old-fashioned manners. And the kisses . . . Yeah. She'd miss those, too. And maybe even New York. Despite the terrible events of the past week, being in Scarlet Falls felt like home.

She followed Douglas into the room. Lola was sitting up in a bed. Her eyes opened wide when Hannah walked in and greeted her in Spanish. But she wouldn't respond to any of Hannah's questions. The girl's eyes kept shifting to the detective with suspicion.

Hannah turned to the cop. "Would it be possible to give me a few minutes with her alone?"

"I guess it's worth a shot," he said. "I'll be right outside the door."

As soon as the cop left, Hannah pulled a chair to the bedside. "Now it's just you and me," she said in Spanish. "Why did you ask to talk to me?"

"Because you helped Jewel," Lola said in Spanish. "And because I did something bad. I told on her. If it wasn't for me, she might have gotten away." She studied her hands twisting in the sheets. "I was a coward."

Hannah's heart ached. "I'm sure you were scared." What had the Arnette brothers done to this poor girl?

Over the next thirty minutes Lola slowly opened up with her harrowing story and enough details to possibly find more victims. Hannah had also determined that the e-mails hadn't been purposefully cryptic. Lola's English was too limited to express what she'd wanted to say.

Hannah asked her about that night.

"We worked that place often," she said in Spanish. "Men coming out of the club were always looking for sex. That night was a private party. Special arrangements had been made."

Suddenly, Hannah knew. The girls had been hired for Herb's big bash. Initial shock was replaced with fury. How could Herb do this? She liked him. How could she not have seen what he was hiding under his regular-joe charm? Wait. Maybe she was jumping to conclusions. Surely, other private parties had occurred that night. Carnival was huge. But something nagged at Hannah, an image of Herb squeezing his waitress's butt. The girl had been at least thirty years his junior, and there was no question that he treated his female employees like sexual objects. How young was his taste?

She smiled at Lola and told her to hang tight. Out in the hallway, she found Douglas. He rose. "Any luck?"

"Yes. Lola told me about a place she was kept, along with dozens of other girls. A warehouse. It sounds like a processing center of some sort. She might be able to give you enough details to find it."

And maybe Jewel.

Chapter Thirty-Six

If she doesn't stop humming, I won't have to worry about the men with guns. I'm going to kill myself.

Jewel rolled onto her side, pressing one ear into the pillow and covering her other ear with her hand. On the cot next to her, Penny hummed something that sounded like a nursery rhyme, not that Jewel had many warm or fuzzy memories of those.

She was pretty sure her mother had never acted like Penny. She stopped herself from speculating about the girl. She was *not* getting to know her roommate. She glanced toward the closed and locked door. Cellmate.

The muffled sound of boots running came through the door. Jewel sat up.

"What's happening?" Penny asked.

Jewel ignored her. She got up and pressed her ear to the door. Men were running.

"Get the girls," one yelled.

Sweat broke out under Jewel's arms as she backed away from the door. Something was going on. Penny sat up on her cot. Her belly fell between her open thighs. Had it gotten bigger in one day? Her belly button was popping through the T-shirt. Penny cradled it with one hand and pushed off her cot with the other. She waddled to stand next to Jewel.

The door banged open. A man with a rifle passed. "Everybody out. Move it."

Jewel shuffled toward the door. Penny hung behind her. In the hallway, girls paused, eyes wide. A few clung to each other.

"Move it!" a man shouted.

Girls flinched. They shuffled in a pack down the halls. The men herded them into the loading area like livestock. A truck was backed into the cavernous space, the tractor portion extending through the open bay door. A cool breeze blew under the vehicle and chilled Jewel's bare feet. She looked past the truck at the darkness outside. It was night.

The back door of the vehicle gaped open. The engine was still running. Jewel froze. A man pushed past the girls, not looking at them. Instinct stopped her feet.

She could not get into that truck. Her gaze was drawn back to the darkness. She gave her surroundings a furtive scan. The men seemed distracted. One ran by, carrying a gas can in each hand. They were going to burn the warehouse down.

They were cleaning up loose ends.

Jewel watched the first of the girls climb the ladder into the trailer portion of the eighteen-wheeler. There were at least thirty loose ends right there.

She sidled to the edge of the group. Penny grabbed her arm, her grip tight and scared.

Damn it.

A girl fell off the ladder.

The man in charge of loading the girls reached down to haul her to her feet. "Move it." He changed position, moving to the base of the ladder to shove each girl into the truck as she hoisted herself up the ladder. His back was to Jewel.

She slipped along the side of the truck and peeked around the doorframe. No one was outside. She glanced back at the group. Penny was looking for her. There were no other men in sight except the one with his back to her.

No. The massively pregnant girl would slow her down. Jewel took a step through the doorway.

Shit.

She slid back to the group, grabbed Penny by the arm, and tugged. She pulled her through the doorway with her. Outside, she put a finger to her lips. Penny nodded. The moon shone from a clear black sky. Jewel backed into the shadow of the building, frantically scanning for a hiding place or avenue of escape. The warehouse was on a large slab of pavement. A hundred feet away, another building loomed dark in the sky. They'd have to cross a football field of open pavement to get to it. They'd never make it. She glanced at Penny. No way.

Two big SUVs were parked parallel to the warehouse. Beyond them, what appeared to be random construction debris littered the cracked concrete.

She tugged the girl toward a stack of pallets and collection of concrete barriers, the kind used by construction crews, scattered on the blacktop twenty feet or so from the warehouse. They hurried across the ground, gravel and other bits of debris digging into the soles of her feet.

In the center of the barriers, they dropped to the ground, crouching in the shadows.

The cold night air washed over her bare skin. Her feet went numb. Not a bad thing, considering. The truck pulled away and rumbled off into the darkness. A few minutes later, smoke plumed out a broken window.

Jewel held her breath. Next to her, Penny shivered.

A half dozen men ran out of the building and climbed into the SUVs. One paused, his foot on the running board, his eyes scanning the lot around him.

Jewel shrank into the shadow, closed her eyes, and hoped.

ω

"Thank you for coming with me." Hannah opened the car door.

"Like I'd let you come here alone. I've got your back, counselor." Brody shut off the car. He got out of the rental, rounded the front, and opened Hannah's door. His chest tightened as he gazed up at the giant club, Carnival. The surrounding area looked industrial, empty and flat, the nearby businesses closed. "This is where it happened?"

"Yes." Hannah pointed. "Over there, closer to the motel. The lot was full that night. I guess no one goes out clubbing this early in Vegas."

"Are you sure you want to do this?" he asked.

"I'm just going to talk to him."

"Uh-huh." Brody crossed his arms over his chest. It appeared he wasn't buying it for a second.

"You need to wait here." She touched his arm. "He won't talk to me if you're there, giving him your death-ray stare."

"I don't like it. If you're not out in fifteen minutes, I'm coming in after you."

"Twenty." She kissed him.

He frowned. "All right, but not a second more."

At seven in the evening, Carnival was quiet. She stopped at the security desk. The guard recognized her. "Ms. Barrett. Are you here to see Mr. Fletcher?"

"Yes. I don't have an appointment. He told me to drop by if I was in town."

The guard pulled up a screen of approved visitors and scrolled to the Bs. Hannah's name was third from the top. He made a call. "Mr. Fletcher is in his office. He says come right up. You know the way."

"I do. Thank you." Hannah walked down a corridor to a bank of elevators. The car shot smoothly to the twentieth floor. She exited the elevator and went through a huge set of glass doors. After checking in with the cool blond secretary, she waited by a bank of windows that overlooked the city. Other than the Strip, Vegas spread out in an array of randomness, as if the city planners had tossed high-rises, cheesy motels, and empty lots on a game board and built them where they landed.

"Ms. Barrett, Mr. Fletcher will see you now." The secretary opened her boss's door.

"Thank you." Hannah crossed the threshold.

The room was absurdly large. Herb's desk was a mammoth slab of mahogany faced by a semicircle of chairs. In the corner, a conversation area had been formed with a black leather sofa and two matching chairs. An acre of empty space yawned between the workspace and more intimate seating. He might dress like a regular joe, but his office was wall-to-wall swank.

Herb stood as she entered his office. He came out from behind his desk to greet her. "I'm so glad you dropped in." He offered her a hand.

Yeah, that was not going to happen.

Hannah stopped short. Confusion crossed Herb's face. He gestured toward the conversation area. Hannah preceded him, but instead of sitting, she paced in front of the window. The backdrop of Sin City felt appropriate for the conversation they were about to have.

She'd been in Herb's office several times before, but it had never been just the two of them. Alone with him, the cavernous space felt oddly intimate.

"You look like you've recovered. I'm glad to see that. I hope you'll be back to work soon."

"I'm sure I will." Hannah finally took a seat, perching on the edge of the sofa. The thought of her going back to her jet-set career with people like Herb Fletcher gave her indigestion. She felt like she was treading water, working hard and getting nowhere. How did she measure her accomplishments? With dollar signs. She wasn't much different from Herb.

"I'm glad." Herb stopped in front of a chair. He gestured to a wet bar by the window. "Can I get you a drink?"

"No, thank you." Hannah gathered her thoughts.

Herb crossed to the bar. He took a tumbler off the shelf, flipped it over, and set it on the granite top of the bar. He brought his drink back to the chair and eased into the leather. "Something is bothering you, Hannah. What is it?"

She hesitated.

"Please, I'm not one of your smooth-talking, beat-around-the-bush suits." Herb sipped his drink. "If you have something to say, let's hear it."

Right. There was no way to tactfully ease into this conversation. Hannah leaned forward. "The man who assaulted me was involved in a human trafficking ring specializing in underage girls. The night of the party, these girls were working out of the motel behind the club. I also know that someone at that party arranged for a group rate with their pimp." Hannah watched his eyes. No shock. No outrage. "You knew, didn't you?"

Herb waved a hand. "Men have appetites. You saw that during the party. You can take the richest man and reduce him to his basest instincts with the lure of sex with a beautiful woman."

"Not all men," Hannah said, her thoughts flickering to Brody.

He snorted. "Most of the men I know."

"You need to upgrade your social circle," Hannah said. "So, were you in on it? Did you pay to appease your *appetites*?"

Herb looked disgusted. "I like women, probably too much, but I don't fuck children. To be blunt, I like my women stacked, the key word being *women*," he emphasized. "I certainly don't need to use prostitutes. I have a whole club full of gorgeous young women who would be thrilled to have sex with me."

Revulsion curled in Hannah's belly. Herb might not have participated, but he still viewed women as objects to be acquired and used. "If you didn't make the arrangements, then who did?"

"Does it matter?"

"Yes."

"Why? Money can buy anything. It's the way of the world." Herb returned to the wet bar. Setting his glass on the black granite top, he lifted the lid from an ice bucket and used tongs to add a few cubes to his tumbler. Ice cracked as he poured from a bottle of The Macallan. He leaned an elbow on the bar and brought the glass to his lips. He rolled the liquor in his mouth, pleasure lighting his eyes as he appreciated the taste.

His casual stance emanated indifference and arrogance. He thought he was in complete control, that he was above reproach.

"Good scotch?" she asked.

"Very. Distilled in 1939, it was introduced while World War Two was breaking out in Europe. It's one of the earliest additions in The Macallan Fine and Rare series. It's like drinking a piece of history. I paid ten thousand dollars for this one bottle. Do you know why?"

"Because you wanted it," Hannah said. "And as you told me once, you always get what you want."

"Yes. I do." Ego flashed in his eyes. "But in this case, I bought it simply because I could. It reminds me that I've come to a place where I don't have to scrounge for coins in the ashtray of my car to buy food.

"My father was what you would consider *a good man*. If a man took a week off because his wife was ill, my father paid him anyway.

He hired drunks just to give them a second chance. Even though he owned the company, if the crew was a man short, my father would climb on a roof and nail shingles. I have a distinct memory of him taking me along with him to visit one of his workers in the hospital. After he gave the guy's wife some cash to help tide her over, he said to me, 'Herb, we might not be rich with material things, but we are wealthy in our hearts.' What a load of bullshit. He was giving money to other people while our family was living in a two-bedroom shack."

"He sounds like a kind man who had his priorities straight."

"Do you know what all that kindness got him? Nothing. He worked himself into an early grave." Herb gestured with his drink. "After he died, I took that limping, pathetic excuse for a company and built an empire out of it."

"So now you can have anything you want." Hannah's body was stiffer than the chrome sofa frame.

"Exactly." Herb took another sip.

"So if you didn't make the arrangements for teenage prostitutes, who did?" she asked.

He raised a shoulder.

Hannah let out a disgusted breath. "I thought you knew everything that happened in your club."

"Of course I know, but I'm not ratting anyone out." Herb finished his scotch.

"That's some sense of misplaced loyalty, Herb." Hannah rose. "Next time you need a lawyer, don't call me."

"Watch your back, Hannah."

She headed for the door. One hand on the knob, she whirled. "Is that a threat?"

"You have nothing to fear from me. You don't threaten me. But curiosity and integrity can be a dangerous combination, and you should be worried about what's going on in your own house instead of mine."

ω

Brody was walking into the lobby as Hannah came off the elevator. Disappointment was etched on her face.

"Your time was up," he said.

She gave him a tight nod and hurried out of the building. He wrapped an arm around her waist as they crossed the parking lot.

"He says he didn't participate, but he knew. Like that's much better." She swiped an angry tear from under her eye with her forefinger.

"How do you work with people like that?" He pressed the fob and unlocked the car.

Hannah turned, resting her forehead against his chest. "I don't know, and the worst thing is I can't repeat any of our conversation to the police. He's a client of my firm. I'm bound by confidentiality."

"Don't worry. Douglas has Herb Fletcher on his radar."

They drove back to the Venetian and went up to their room. It was glitzy, with a big king-size bed a step down from the seating area. The window had a beautiful view of the city lights, but Brody closed the Roman blinds. He had a feeling Hannah wouldn't want to stare at the glittery landscape of Vegas when they'd spent the day seeing its ugly underbelly.

"I feel filthy." She turned on the shower and stripped off her blouse.

Brody crossed the room. "Hannah."

She was stepping out of her slacks, letting them drop to the carpet. "I don't understand. Why do people have to be cruel? Why do girls get victimized and good family men murdered?"

He pulled her to his chest. Her brother's death last spring had left her scarred.

"Do you know how old Lola is?" She pulled her face away from his body. Anger glittered in her eyes. "Fourteen. She's fourteen years old. The Mexican cartel kidnapped her. They murdered her father right in front of her. What kind of people do that?"

"I don't know." Brody wiped a tear from her cheek. "I love that you can't even understand that concept. I love you."

She burst into tears. Not the response he'd hoped for his first declaration of love.

"I'm sorry. I shouldn't have said that after the day you had."

Hannah cried into his shirt. "I love you, too."

"You don't seem happy about it."

"Obviously, I'm really messed up." She sniffed and lifted her head again. "Make me forget all about today. I need to feel something that isn't tainted. Something pure and clean." She kissed him.

Brody smiled down at her. His hand stroked her face and settled on the column of her neck. He could think of nothing more pure than showing her how much he loved her.

"I'm going to miss you when you're in London." His heart was hers forever, but in a week's time, their bodies would be separated by an ocean.

She kissed him. "I don't want to go."

"Then don't," he said, confused.

"What would I do? I need goals. I need purpose."

"Do whatever you want. You can be a lawyer anywhere, Hannah."

"I worked my whole life for the opportunity that is right in front of me."

"I'll support whatever you choose to do. I would never want you to feel like you were sacrificing something to be with me."

She brushed her fingers across his temple. "Being with you would never be a sacrifice."

Chapter Thirty-Seven

Hannah awoke in Brody's arms. Half the giant bed was empty with her body plastered against his warmth. She lifted her head from his shoulder.

"You're awake." He kissed her. "Good morning."

Her fingers trailed along the muscles of his broad chest. She slid her hand under the covers. He pressed his mouth to hers, tenderly. Regret filled his eyes.

"What is it? Not in the mood?"

"All I have to do is look at you and I'm in the mood. Actually, just thinking about you is enough. But I have some news."

Hannah sat up, pulling the covers over her breasts as the chilly air hit her bare skin. Brody levered up on one elbow. The sheet fell from his torso, revealing his black-and-blue rib cage.

She reached out and touched the skin with a fingertip. "I should have wrapped that for you last night. And we shouldn't have made love. It couldn't have been good for your recovery."

"It was the best thing possible for my recovery." He took her hand. "Douglas called. They found Jewel last night, and she's alive."

Hannah gasped. Shock and joy numbed her. She hadn't expected to ever see the girl again. "When? Where?"

"Lola's information, combined with all the data the trafficking team pulled from Mick's phone records and computer, led them to a warehouse on the outskirts of the city. When the police arrived, the building was on fire, but Jewel and another girl were hiding. Apparently, the traffickers got wind of the raid and cleared the place out during the night. These two girls slipped away in the commotion."

"Oh, my God." Hannah pressed a palm to the center of her chest.

Brody squeezed her other hand. "Douglas said you can see her later today."

"Yes." Hannah read something else in Brody's eyes. He was holding back on her. "What is it?"

He sighed. "About fifty miles away, the police found thirty-six dead girls in a storage container."

"No." Horror wrapped around Hannah.

"I'm sorry." He pulled her close.

Hannah pressed her face to his chest and cried. She had no resolve left. It was done. She'd helped find Jewel. She knew in her brain she hadn't caused the deaths of all those other girls, but her heart was heavy with sadness and guilt.

Ten minutes later, she was empty and spent. Her eyes ached, and her chest hurt. "They were nothing but potential witnesses to those men."

"Probably."

"They'll try to get Jewel and the other girls who survived."

"I'm sure they'll be guarded." Brody stroked her hair. "Douglas and his team are working with the FBI and Border Patrol, plus a host of other agencies who specialize in investigating human trafficking. Homeland Security could get involved. They are taking the girls' safety very seriously. In fact, Douglas said if you want to see Jewel,

I mean Jenna, then you'd better go today. She'll be moved soon to a secure location."

Hannah wiped her eyes. "OK. Give me twenty minutes to get myself together."

Within an hour they were back at the hospital.

Douglas ushered Hannah into the hospital room and stepped out. "The two girls seemed to have bonded, so we're keeping them together. It's important to call her Jenna. She needs to regain her sense of identity. That's one thing traffickers take away early, along with hope and dignity."

A very pregnant teen slept in one bed. Jewel, no, Jenna sat in the bed near the window.

"Hi, Jenna." Hannah approached the bed. "I'm glad you're OK."

A tear rolled down the girl's cheek. "Thank you for everything."

"It wasn't me." Hannah shook her head. "You saved yourself, and it looks like you saved someone else, too. Two someones."

ω

Brody filled a Styrofoam cup with coffee in the waiting area. "What will happen to these girls?"

Detective Douglas popped the tab on a can of Diet Coke. "Jenna has a mother, but I don't know that she'll go back home. The mother's pedophile boyfriend was picked up for violating the terms of his parole, but Mom is unstable and unreliable. Besides, we need Jenna as a witness. We want to keep her safe, and if we hold on to her, she'll get the help she's going to need."

He had the haggard look of a man who saw dozens of dead teenagers the previous day and just couldn't process the sight.

"*Can* you keep her safe?"

"The girls will probably go into safe houses. We've dealt with this before. Witnesses tend to disappear in any case even remotely related to a Mexican cartel."

"This isn't over."

"This will never be over," Douglas said. "But we're a step closer. Mick Arnette and his brother won't be abusing any more girls. We have eyes on Herb Fletcher. We have new witnesses who hold vital information. Mick was in the habit of leaving his computer lying around. He used a password and must have assumed the girls couldn't access it. But Lola said she watched him and learned his password. Jenna did the same. That is one very smart girl. Before she tried to run away from Mick's house, she copied his document files to a cloud account. We have everything. Spreadsheets of income and expenses, client information, and online classified accounts where he advertised the girls. We also have a cell phone that communicated with the parent organization. That's a lot of data to sift through. We're in this for the long haul. On top of all that, we have Sam's girlfriend."

Hannah came down the hall. She wiped her eyes with a tissue.

"Are you all right?" Brody asked her.

"Yes. I gave the girls my card and told them I was available for legal assistance if they need it." She turned to Douglas. "Jenna is worried about a dog that was kept at the house."

Douglas nodded. "There was a pit bull mix chained up out back. He barked a lot but was surprisingly friendly. Poor beast was half-starved."

"What happened to him?" Hannah asked.

Douglas drank from his can. "He was supposed to go to the animal shelter, but one of the guys on the raid team felt bad and took him home. Maybe I can arrange to have the dog visit Jenna. Could help win her trust. Thanks."

"Good-bye, Detective. Let me know if there's anything you need from me." Hannah turned toward Brody.

He steered her to the elevators, and they navigated the hallways to the exit. Outside, the sun washed them with heat. "Going to be cold in New York."

They walked to the car.

"I still can't wait to get home," she said.

But it wasn't really home. Not to her. Brody would miss her when she left. "When will you go back to work?"

"I don't know." She stopped beside the rental car. "Royce is in the Manhattan office. I'll probably take the train down on Monday and talk to him."

"Can't you just call him?"

"No. Face-to-face is better with Royce. On the phone, he issues orders and hangs up on me."

Brody opened her car door. In the back of his mind, he could picture his grandfather doing the same for Gran. They were together for sixty years. Best friends, Gran had said. Brody had always wanted that for himself.

"When will you leave for London?" he asked her.

"I don't know."

"You don't sound too excited."

"I don't know what I want." She turned and splayed her hands on his chest. "You confuse me, and what I feel for you scares the hell out of me. I'm not good at the relationship thing, but I'm working on it."

He kissed her forehead. "I suppose I'll have to give up my wild and crazy dating life and the club scene."

Hannah snorted and got into the car. "In Scarlet Falls? The only clubs in town have greens fees."

He closed the door. Long-distance was better than nothing. But he didn't want her to go to London or anywhere else. He wanted her with him.

Chapter Thirty-Eight

Hannah took a cab from Penn Station to the Manhattan office of Black Associates. She swiped her ID at the security desk and took the elevator up to the twenty-fifth floor. Pushing through the double glass doors, she made a beeline for Royce's office.

Getting off the elevator, she passed two construction workers. The whine of a power tool floated down the hall.

"Miss Barrett. I'm so glad to see you looking well. Mr. Black said you were injured." The secretary pressed a button on her phone. "Let me buzz Mr. Black for you. Go right in."

Royce stood as Hannah went into his office.

"You weren't supposed to come back until the neurologist cleared you." Was that irritation in Royce's eyes?

"I got a second opinion."

He shook his head. "Not good enough."

What was wrong with him? "I don't get it, Royce. Why don't you want me back at work? Obviously, I'm fully recovered."

"No reason. Of course I'm happy to have you back. I simply wanted you to have the very best care." He stood, his posture stiff.

Something felt wrong. Royce was giving off a very strange emotion. He was definitely not happy she was back. Why not?

You should be worried about what's going on in your own house.

Herb hadn't meant *house* as in Scarlet Falls. He'd meant the law firm.

She raised her gaze. Their eyes locked.

Royce's went arctic. "Hannah. What am I going to do with you?"

"You?" Disbelief paralyzed her for a few seconds. "You hired those young girls. You like . . ."

Royce made a face. "Of course not. But some men have a taste for youth."

"The client always gets what the client wants." Hannah turned away. She slid her hand into her pocket and, glancing down, opened the voice memo app on her cell phone.

"Exactly. See, you really do understand." Royce said. "I'll tell you what. I'll make a deal with you. Full partnership. It's what you've been working day and night toward for five years."

Hannah turned back to face him. "If I keep quiet about you hiring underage hookers for a client, you'll make me a full partner?"

"Yes."

"No deal, Royce. I've already given this company my sweat and personal life for five years. I draw the line at my soul."

Royce opened his drawer, and a second later, Hannah was staring into the muzzle of a gun. He came around the desk and stood in front of her. "Then I guess I'll have to ensure your silence in another way."

"Now what, Royce? You can't shoot me in your office."

"I'd rather not, but I can if I must. The walls are well insulated. My secretary has gone to lunch, and the construction on the other side of the building will cover any loud or unusual sounds." Royce cocked his head.

"Have you always kept a gun in your drawer?" she asked. "It's almost impossible to get a carry permit in the city limits."

"Herb called me and gave me a bit of warning."

Bastard.

"Do you really like the Sig?"

"What?" Irritation and confusion lined Royce's forehead.

"I know a lot of people love the feel of the Sig's solid metal frame, but I like the lighter weight of my Glock, especially for concealed carry."

Royce tilted his head. And that moment of distraction was all she needed.

Hannah's hand shot out. In the same smooth movement, she turned her body out of the line of fire. Grabbing the slide bolt on the top of the gun, she redirected the barrel and twisted the gun out of his grip. It was like disarming a kindergartener. "Next time you pull a gun on someone, practice with it so you look half-competent."

She eased the slide back a half inch and checked for a bullet in the chamber. "All this time, you could have helped me find that girl. You paid her pimp to set up one of our clients with underage prostitutes. That's human trafficking, you bastard."

Royce shrugged. "They're just whores."

"They're children! You are as sick and depraved as the men who lust after schoolgirls."

Anger sharpened Royce's eyes. "It's a hard world out there, Hannah."

And she was sick of it. "The client gets what the client wants?"

"That's how it works." Sweat beaded on Royce's forehead. "You can't prove anything."

"Oh, please. If there wasn't a trail of some sort, you wouldn't have pulled this little number on me. It's nearly impossible to keep an activity under the radar in this day and age. Technology has its price." Hannah gestured with the gun. "I do like the feel of this grip."

Suddenly everything was clear. "Sending me to that neurologist, that was all part of it, wasn't it?"

"I wanted you out of the way for a while."

"Why? I was going to London. Isn't that out of the way enough?" Mental head smack. "The girls were for Timothy."

Royce took a step forward.

Anger stirred fresh behind Hannah's ribs. "I wouldn't do that if I were you. I actually know how to use this gun." She reached for her cell phone and dialed 911. "Oh, and I quit."

Two hours later, Hannah sat in a plastic chair in an NYPD chief's office with a cold cup of coffee cradled in her hands. The police had her recording of her conversation with Royce. Her eyes burned with unshed tears, and there was only one person she wanted to talk to. She dialed Brody's number.

ᚹ

Rain misted Hannah's face as she stared at the front door of the nursing home.

"Are you all right?" Brody reached around her and opened the door.

Hannah let out the breath she'd been holding. "I don't know." Her nerves were as frayed as a worn end of rope.

"It'll be OK." Brody put his hand on the small of her back and steered her into the lobby.

Hannah breathed. Her lungs had felt inelastic since the nursing home had called her thirty minutes before to tell her that the Colonel had had difficulty breathing. She'd planned to visit this afternoon but had come immediately instead.

She checked at the reception desk. "How is he?"

The nurse smiled, but her eyes were sad. "His breathing was labored earlier this morning, but he seems a bit better now."

Hannah swallowed and nearly choked. Brody took her hand, his body heat burning hot against her icy skin. She led him to the acute care wing and paused outside her father's room. Through the open doorway, she watched a young male medical tech check the Colonel's vital signs. The young man jotted the readings on a clipboard. Leaving the room, he nodded to them on his way out. Grant was sitting in a chair by the bed. Seeing Hannah and Brody, he joined them in the hall. He and the family had returned home the day before, and he'd been furious when she'd told him everything that had happened while he was away. But his eyes held no anger this morning.

She looked around him into her father's room. "How is he?"

Grant lifted a hand. "Maybe a little better. Hard to say."

"Forgive me yet?" she asked.

"No." Grant gave her a small smile. "But I still love you. I haven't heard from Mac. Do you know where he is?"

Hannah shook her head. "No. I haven't heard from him since I picked up the dog at his place on Saturday night."

Grant's mouth tightened as he stepped aside so she could enter the room.

Hannah let out a smooth breath. Channeling Grant, she left her expectations at the door. *Go with the flow.*

Brody took her wet coat and hung it on the back of a chair by the door. Stepping up to the bedside, she took in her father's continued deterioration. His skin looked tighter, almost translucent. His chest rose with a wheeze and deflated with a shudder. How long could he live like this? His life was nothing but misery. Death would be a kindness for him, but the Colonel would never go gently. It was his nature to scratch and claw for one more breath. His fighting spirit was the one trait dementia couldn't defeat.

His eyelids fluttered and opened. He blinked between her and Brody a few times. Several seconds passed before he focused on her. His lips moved. No words emerged, but his expression changed. Once recognition took hold, his gaze never left her face, as if Brody weren't there. On the bed, the Colonel's fingers curled in a *Come here* gesture. Hannah reached out and took his hand. Brody moved a chair behind her, and she lowered her body onto the seat. Brody's hand on her shoulder grounded her.

The Colonel's eyes closed again. Every breath seemed as if it could be his last. But an hour later, the pattern eased into deep sleep. His hand relaxed and released Hannah's. She let go.

In the hallway, Brody held her coat up. Hannah slipped her arms into the sleeves.

He put an arm around her. "That was rough."

"Yes." She rested her head on his shoulder, grateful for his support.

They passed the nurses' station, and Hannah asked, "You'll call me if he gets any worse?" Her chest constricted with the thought of the Colonel dying alone.

"Of course," the nurse said.

Brody led her out of the building. Hannah lifted her face to the light rain. The mist refreshed her hot skin.

"Do they know how long he has?" Brody asked.

Hannah sniffed. "His body was ready to give up about a year ago."

"But he won't let go."

"He can't," she said simply. "It's not good or bad. It's simply the way it is." When the Colonel was ready, he wouldn't ease into death. He'd march.

Just as she must concede control of her father's condition, it was also time to accept all the good and bad from her childhood and move on. Hardship had molded her into a resilient person. The training drills and lessons from her childhood were crazy, but without them, would she have survived her encounter with Mick Arnette? Probably not.

"I'm probably never going to be a warm or fuzzy person," she said.

Brody raised an eyebrow in confusion. "Where did that come from?"

"I was just thinking about my father and my childhood. Grant has my mother's innate kindness. My father is a hard man, and I'm more like him than I'd like to admit."

"I doubt Carson or Faith would agree." Brody took her hand. "You're so used to putting on a tough act for your job, you've convinced yourself that it's you. But I know it's not. Hard people don't cuddle babies or hug sad little boys. They don't chase pets in the middle of the night to spare a child some distress. They don't fly across the country to help lost teenagers. I've seen the real Hannah Barrett. She's pretty spectacular."

Heat rose into Hannah's face.

"You are strong and dependable and courageous almost to a fault." Brody turned to face her. He lifted her chin with a finger and kissed her. "And you're plenty warm and fuzzy when it matters—and to whom it matters."

Chapter Thirty-Nine

One month later

Brody walked out onto his front porch. Sniffing the smoke-scented December air, he straightened the wreath on his door and walked two blocks to the one-story house just off First Street. Snow had been shoveled from the brick path that led from the sidewalk to the porch. He wiped his feet on the mat and went inside.

Hannah and her brother leaned over a makeshift sawhorse-and-plywood table. Grant pointed to the drawing on the table. "I'll cut the kitchen in half and extend the hallway so clients can access your office directly from the parking area out back."

"That works," Hannah said. She looked up and saw Brody. Her smile lit her eyes. She crossed the room and kissed him.

Brody kissed her back. "Hey there, counselor."

Grant shoved his pencil behind his ear. "Are you two still coming for dinner?"

Hannah shot him a *duh* look she must have learned from Ellie's teenage daughter. "Ellie's grandmother is making macaroni and cheese. Who in their right mind would miss that?"

Grant grinned and grabbed his coat off a chair. "OK, then. I'll see you in an hour." He went out the back door. Hannah flipped the dead bolt.

She waved a hand over a set of plans on the plywood. "What do you think? My office will be here. This is a waiting area. Storage over here."

"What are you going to do with all this space over here?" Brody pointed to the extra rooms on the other side of the house.

"I'm saving that for Grant's office. I've just about talked him into starting his own contracting business. Now I just need to talk Ellie into quitting her job and coming to work for me."

"About time." Brody put a finger under Hannah's chin and turned her to look at him.

"What?"

"Nothing. You look happy."

"I am happy." She kissed him. "Are you ready to go home?"

"Always." Brody took her coat off the hook in the hall and held it for her.

She smiled, turned, and slid her arms in. He settled the coat on her shoulders, a similar memory of his grandparents choking him for a second. Hannah locked up, and they started down the sidewalk. "I can't believe I'm walking home from work. Six weeks ago I thought I'd be spending most of December in Spain."

"So you miss it?" He wondered, always, if she would tire of living in the suburbs. Tire of him.

"Not one bit." She leaned against him. "I don't know what I was looking for, but I found happiness here, with you. Maybe I wasn't looking for something as much as running away. There were a lot of bad memories here."

"Aren't they still here?"

"Yes, but now we're making some good ones to cancel them out."

"I heard from Chet today," Brody said.

"How is he? Has he had any luck?"

Chet was in Las Vegas. Detective Douglas hooked him up with a private organization that searched for missing kids. He was consulting and hoping to find some trace of his daughter. "No luck yet, but he hasn't given up hope. There have been a few leads. He's sober. He's keeping busy, and he seems to have found some purpose helping families find their missing kids." Hope, that's what Chet had found in Vegas.

"That's something."

They walked to the house. Inside, Danno greeted them with a meow, looking over his shoulder and trotting to the kitchen. Hannah handed Brody her coat. "I'm coming."

She followed the cat down the hall. Brody hung their coats on pegs and joined her in the kitchen. She opened the fridge and took out a small piece of leftover chicken. The old cat rubbed on her ankles as she handed him the meat.

"You're going to spoil him." Brody leaned on the wall.

"Yes, I am." Leaning over, Hannah grinned and scratched Danno's head. The old cat purred louder.

Eyeing her long legs and tight butt in her faded jeans, Brody walked up behind her and wrapped his arms around her waist. His lips cruised along her collarbone. "We have an hour."

"Don't you think of anything else?" She laughed, angling her head to give him better access.

He nuzzled the soft skin at the base of her neck. "Once in a while I have other thoughts, but I forget everything when you're in the room."

Just as Hannah had run from her hometown to escape bad memories, Brody had been running away when he left Boston. He'd thought he'd found happiness in Scarlet Falls, but happiness wasn't a place. He could be happy anywhere as long as he was with her.

Acknowledgments

As always, thanks to my agent, Jill Marsal, for her indispensable guidance. Thanks to my editor, JoVon Sotak, and the entire staff of Montlake Romance. An author couldn't ask for a better publisher. Additional thanks to my developmental editor, Shannon Godwin, for helping me balance this book.

I also want to credit the following people for patiently answering my seemingly trivial questions: cousin Cris Villaverde of the Wilmington PD, Dave Thompson of CARSTAR, and computer guru Fran Papillion. Details can make all the difference. Thank you all. Any errors are mine, not theirs.

About the Author

Melinda Leigh abandoned her career in banking to raise her kids and never looked back. She started writing as a hobby and became addicted to creating characters and stories. Since then, she has won numerous writing awards for her paranormal romance and romantic-suspense fiction.

Her debut novel, *She Can Run*, was a number one bestseller in Kindle Romantic Suspense, a 2011 Best Book Finalist (*The Romance Reviews*), and a nominee for the 2012 International Thriller Award for Best First Book. Melinda is a two-time Daphne du Maurier Award finalist. When she isn't writing, Melinda is an avid martial artist: she holds a second-degree black belt in Kenpo karate and teaches women's self-defense. She lives in a messy house with her husband, two teenagers, a couple of dogs, and two rescue cats.

Photo © 2014 Marti Corn Photography